Premodern Korean Literary Prose

Premodern Korean Literary Prose

AN ANTHOLOGY

Edited by Michael J. Pettid, Gregory N. Evon, and Chan E. Park

COLUMBIA UNIVERSITY PRESS

NEW YORK

This book is published with the support of the Literature Translation Institute of Korea (LTI Korea).

Columbia University Press wishes to express its appreciation for assistance given by the Pushkin Fund in the publication of this book.

Columbia University Press
Publishers Since 1893
New York   Chichester, West Sussex
cup.columbia.edu

Copyright © 2018 Columbia University Press
All rights reserved

Library of Congress Cataloging-in-Publication Data
Names: Pettid, Michael J. editor. | Evon, Gregory N. editor. | Park, Chan E. editor.
Title: Premodern Korean literary prose : an anthology / edited by Michael J. Pettid, Gregory N. Evon, and Chan E. Park.
Description: New York : Columbia University Press, 2017. | Includes bibliographical references and index.
Identifiers: LCCN 2017020193 (print) | LCCN 2017031019 (ebook) | ISBN 9780231546010 (electronic) | ISBN 9780231165808 (cloth : alk. paper) | ISBN 9780231165815 (pbk.) | ISBN 9780231546010 (eb)
Subjects: LCSH: Korean prose literature—Translations into English.
Classification: LCC PL984.E8 (ebook) | LCC PL984.E8 P84 2017 (print) | DDC 895.7/1—dc23
LC record available at https://lccn.loc.gov/2017020193

Columbia University Press books are printed
on permanent and durable acid-free paper.
Printed in the United States of America
Cover image: Courtesy of National Folk Museum of Korea

CONTENTS

Acknowledgments xi
Contributor Abbreviations xiii
Conventions for Names, Terms, and Titles xv
Chronology xvii

Editors' Introduction 1

PART I

Pre-Koryŏ and Koryŏ Period Prose 11
   1. *Pre-Koryŏ Prose and Fiction* 13
      1.1. Anonymous, *Tales of the Bizarre* (殊異傳 *Sui-jŏn*),
      Michael Pettid 15

      1.2 "Passion Surrounding the Pagoda" (心火繞塔 Simhwa yo t'ap),
      Michael Pettid 16

      1.3. "Beauties in a Bamboo Tube" (竹筒美女 Chuktong minyŏ),
      Michael Pettid 17

1.4. "An Old Man Becomes a Dog" (老翁化狗 Noong hwa ku),
Michael Pettid   17

2. Koryŏ Period Prose Works   18

2.1. Im Ch'un, "The Tale of Mister Cash" (孔方傳 Kongbang-jŏn),
Sem Vermeersch   20

2.2. Yi Kyubo, "The Tale of Master Malt" (麴先生傳 Kuk Sŏnsaeng-jŏn),
Michael Pettid   25

2.3. Yi Kyubo, "Of Boats and Bribes" (舟賂說 Churoe-sŏl),
Michael Pettid and Marshall R. Pihl   29

2.4. Ch'oe Cha, "Kim Kaein" (金盖仁),
Michael Pettid   30

2.5. Ch'oe Hae, "The Tale of the Hermit of Mount Lion"
(猊山隱者傳 Yesan ŭnja-jŏn),
Michael Pettid   31

2.6. Yi Saek, "The Tale of Mr. Pak" (朴氏傳 Pak-ssi-jŏn),
Michael Pettid   32

PART II

Chosŏn Period Prose   37

3. Early Chosŏn Short Fiction   41

3.1. Kim Sisŭp, "An Account of Drunken Merriment at Floating Jade-Green Pavilion" (醉遊浮碧亭記 Ch'wiyu Pubyŏkchŏng-gi),
Gregory N. Evon   41

4. Chosŏn Long Fiction   66

4.1. Anonymous, *The Tale of Lady Pak* (朴氏傳 Pak-ssi-jŏn),
Jeongsoo Shin and Peter Lee   66

4.2. Anonymous, *A Tale of Two Sisters, Changhwa and Hongnyŏn*
(薔花紅蓮傳 Changhwa Hongnyŏn-jŏn),
Jeongsoo Shin and Peter Lee   100

4.3. Anonymous, *The Pledge at the Banquet of Moon-Gazing Pavilion*
(玩月會盟宴 Wanwŏlhoe maengyŏn, excerpt),
Ksenia Chizhova   123

4.4. Cho Wihan, *The Tale of Ch'oe Ch'ŏk* (崔陟傳 *Ch'oe Ch'ŏk-chŏn*),
Sookja Cho   132

5. *Chosŏn Period "Unofficial" Histories*   162

5.1. Sŏ Kŏjŏng, *Idle Talk and Humorous Stories in a Peaceful Era*
(太平閑話滑稽傳 *T'aep'yŏng hanhwa kolgye-jŏn*)   164

"The Guest Gets a Wife,"
Michael Pettid   164

"The Sage and His Affairs,"
Michael Pettid   165

"The Wailing Ghost,"
Michael Pettid   166

"General Kim Who Was Afraid of Ghosts,"
Michael Pettid   167

5.2. Yu Mongin, *Unofficial Narratives by Ŏu* (於于野談 *Ŏu yadam*),
Michael Pettid   167

"Ghosts of the Sŏnggyun'gwan" (Sŏnggyun'gwan kwisin),
Michael Pettid   168

"Fox Pass" (Yŏu kogae),
Michael Pettid   170

"The Clever Trick of Pak Yŏp to Have an Affair"
(Kkoe rŭl naeŏ sat'onghan Pak Yŏp),
Michael Pettid   171

"The Mother of Kangnamdŏk" (Kangnamdŏk moja),
Hyangsoon Yi   172

"The *Kŏmun'go* of Sim Sugyŏng and a Palace Woman"
(Sim Sugyŏng ŭi kŏmun'go wa kungnyŏ),
Michael Pettid   173

"The Life of Chinbok, a Licentious Woman"
(Ŭmbu Chinbok ŭi ilsaeng),
Hyangsoon Yi   174

"The Starving Thief" (Kumjurin tojŏk),
Michael Pettid   176

"Yi Yesun Who Devoted Herself to Buddhism"
(Pulgyo-e Yi Yesun), Hyangsoon Yi   177

5.3. Anonymous, *Collection of Past and Present Laughs*
(古今笑叢 *Kogŭm soch'ong*)   180

"Falsely Cutting the Narrow Hole" (佯裂孔窄 Yangyŏl kong ch'ak),
Michael Pettid   180

"The Son-in-Law Who Ridiculed His Father-in-Law"
(壻嘲婦翁 Sŏ cho puong),
Michael Pettid   181

"Three Women Examine a Mute" (三女儉啞 Samnyŏ kŏm a),
Michael Pettid   181

"Prerequisite Study for a Virgin" (處女先習 Ch'ŏnyŏ sŏnsŭp),
Michael Pettid   183

"The Five Marvels That Shook the Heart"
(五妙動心 Omyo tongsim),
Michael Pettid   184

6. Late Chosŏn Period: *Autobiography, Social Commentary, and Philosophical Humor*   185

6.1. Pak Chiwŏn, "The Tale of Master Yedŏk"
(穢德先生傳 Yedŏk sŏnsaeng-jŏn),
Charles La Shure   185

6.2. Pak Chiwŏn, "On Names" (名論 Myŏngnon),
Youngmin Kim and Youngyeon Kim   190

6.3. Yi Tŏngmu, "The Book of Ears, Eyes, Mouth, and Heart"
(耳目口心書 Immokkusimsŏ),
Jamie Jungmin Yoo   195

6.4. Lady Yi of Hansan, "The Record of My Hardships"
(苦行錄 Kohaengnok),
Si Nae Park   200

7. Palace Literature   214

7.1. Anonymous, *Diary of the Kyech'uk Year* (계축일기 *Kyech'uk ilgi*, excerpt),
Kil Cha and Michael Pettid   214

PART III

Oral Tradition 233

8. P'ansori, *Narratives in Song, introduced and translated by Chan E. Park* 245

    8.1. *Song of Hŭngbo* (홍보가 *Hŭngbo-ga*, excerpt) 245

    8.2. *Song of Sim Ch'ŏng* (심청가 *Sim Ch'ŏng-ga*, excerpt) 259

    8.3. *Song of Ch'unhyang* (춘향가 *Ch'unhyang-ga*, excerpt) 275

List of Contributors 299

ACKNOWLEDGMENTS

As with any collective work such as this volume, there are many individuals who have given their time and knowledge to help bring this from a seeming good idea to fruition. Certainly to my coeditors I owe an immeasurable debt of gratitude: Gregory N. Evon and Chan E. Park are not only good friends but also experts in their fields and great sounding boards for my various unformed ideas. In particular, Greg has been an immense help in shaping our introduction and the ideas of how best to present this anthology. I certainly look forward to our next endeavor together.

To all the contributors in this volume I am thankful for their dedication to bringing these pieces of literature to life in English. When I initially asked for contributions I had no idea of what I could expect. However, the great variety and range of materials that are now included certainly exceeded my expectations and made this a much richer work. Each of them has great knowledge of the particular works they translated. Without their generous contributions of time and effort, this volume would be woefully thin.

I must also thank my doctoral and masters students at Binghamton University who have devoted time to drafts of some of the works in this volume: Chinshil Lee, Jiseon Kim, Hyejin Kim (now at the University of Hawai`i), and Xijinyan Chen all put a good amount of time and effort in working with these quite difficult materials. The process of working through the materials together enabled better translations, and for that I am greatly indebted.

Gregory N. Evon would like to gratefully acknowledge the support of the Academy of Korean Studies Grant funded by the Korean Government (MOE) (AKS-2011-AAA-2103) as well as Ross King of the University of British Columbia.

I am also thankful for the detailed reviews of this manuscript by the anonymous readers for Columbia University Press. I can state emphatically that in all my years of publishing books I have never received such detailed and helpful comments from outside reviewers. The final work is absolutely better with their keen insight and commentary. I can only hope to pass on such goodwill the next time I am asked to review a manuscript for a peer.

I would be remiss if I did not thank Jennifer Crewe of Columbia University Press for her insight and guidance in seeing this work through to completion. From our initial conversations about such a volume, she has been helpful in bringing our draft to publishable form. Particularly, I am thankful for her unending patience with my relative slowness in completing revisions and the like.

A final word is for my, and Chan E. Park's, late mentor, Professor Marshall R. Pihl, formerly of the University of Hawai`i. Marshall was the one who pushed me to study premodern Korea's literature and culture, and although it has been over twenty years since his untimely passing, I felt this volume was something that could honor his memory and the dedication he had to his field and to his students. I was happy to include in this volume a piece that we had worked on together when I was a graduate student.

We have of course strived to avoid errors and inaccuracies in this work, but nonetheless some might have slipped through the cracks. For this, I take full responsibility. We seek perfection, but it can sometimes be just beyond our grasp.

MP

CONTRIBUTOR ABBREVIATIONS

KC	Kil Cha
KsC	Ksenia Chizhova
SC	Sookja Cho
GNE	Gregory N. Evon
YK and YK	Youngmin Kim and Youngyeon Kim
CDL	Charles La Shure
PL	Peter Lee
CP	Chan E. Park
SP	Si Nae Park
MP	Michael J. Pettid
M Pihl	Marshall R. Pihl
JS	Jeongsoo Shin
SV	Sem Vermeersch
HY	Hyangsoon Yi
JY	Jamie Jungmin Yoo

CONVENTIONS FOR NAMES, TERMS, AND TITLES

We use in this volume the McCune-Reischauer system for romanizing (Sino-)Korean and pinyin for Chinese. Names, terms, and titles that are well known in English are given in their standard English versions but with references to the original texts where deemed necessary. In specific cases, Korean transliterations are indicated as K., Chinese as C., Japanese as J., and Sanskrit as S.

CHRONOLOGY

Three Kingdoms	三國	57 B.C.E.–668 C.E.
Koguryŏ	高句麗	(trad. 37 B.C.E.)–668 C.E.
Paekche	百濟	(trad. 18 B.C.E.)–660 C.E.
Silla	新羅	(trad. 57 B.C.E.)–668 C.E.
Kaya	伽耶	(trad. 42)–562
Greater Silla	大新羅	668–935
Parhae	渤海	698–926
Koryŏ	高麗	918–1392
Chosŏn	朝鮮	1392–1910

Premodern Korean Literary Prose

Editors' Introduction

When the heavens and earth first divided, patterns [文, K. *mun*, C. *wen*] appeared between them. Above the shining sun, moon, and the outstretched stars were the patterns [文] of the heavens, and below the mountains arose and the waters flowed to become the patterns [文] of the earth. The sage drew trigrams to create writing [文], and thus the patterns [文] of the human world spread.[1]

Understanding peoples of the past becomes increasingly complex as we continue to move further away from the particular period in which they lived. We must thus rely upon records, written or otherwise, in our attempts to discover what was important in their lives and how they saw the world. The act of writing in itself has been closely linked to notions of the formation of a civilization and often used as the margin of difference between those so-called civilized people and others. Such a view of writing was commonplace in East Asia and derived from the larger Chinese tradition. As seen in the preceding quote from the preface to Chosŏn Korea's *Anthology of Eastern Literature* (東文選 *Tongmunsŏn*,

---

[1] *Anthology of Eastern Literature* [東文選 *Tongmunsŏn*], 1a.

1478), by the mid to late fifteenth century, it was taken for granted that the very advent of human civilization was connected to literacy, and specifically the use of Chinese writing. In this conception, the patterns of the cosmos, the forces that gave rise to humans, are bonded with the patterns of civilization that allowed human culture to flourish. *Mun* (文) was not conceived simply as writing but rather conveyed a whole array of concepts ranging from literary composition to culture (文明, K. *munmyŏng*, C. *wenming*) and civilization (文化, K. *munhwa*, C. *wenhua*).

In this Confucian way of looking at the world and humanity's place in it, there was an inseparable link between the idea of writing, the recording of events, and society itself. The rise of Confucianism in Korea thus had an immeasurable influence on the prestige given to writing and those who were able to do so.[2] As the importance of Confucianism increased from the late eighth century onward, so too did the quantity and types of writings. This process intensified with the adoption of a civil service examination, based on the Chinese classics, in 958 during the reign of Kwangjong (光宗, r. 949–975). As a consequence, the male elites of the Koryŏ dynasty had an even greater impetus to master Chinese forms of writings.

In much the same manner that Latin served as the written language of European countries such as Italy until the thirteenth century, Koreans spoke their own vernacular while employing Literary Chinese (漢文, K. 한문 *hanmun*) as the dominant means of written expression. While there were adaptations of Chinese to fit the language of the peoples living on the Korean Peninsula—of note are creative systems such as *hyangch'al* (鄉札) and *idu* (吏讀)—the writing style of choice for most literary compositions was that of Literary Chinese. This began to change incrementally after the creation of the Korean alphabetic script *han'gŭl* (한글) in the middle of the fifteenth century, but even then, Literary Chinese remained central to the business of government, historiography, and elite male education. Put in terms of language and genre, as a general rule Korean elite males might aspire to greatness as Literary Chinese poets but not as writers of fiction, and particularly *not* vernacular fiction. Elite cultural values, however, were not all determining, even among the elite.[3]

The purpose of this brief introduction is merely to point to some of the crucial relationships that bond the various selections in this anthology. In order to allow readers better access to these works, we have prefaced them with short

---

[2] For an explanation of this bond in China, see Victor H. Mair, ed., *The Columbia History of Chinese Literature* (New York: Columbia University Press, 2001), 1–4.

[3] For a comprehensive history of Korean literature, see Peter H. Lee, ed., *A History of Korean Literature* (Cambridge: Cambridge University Press, 2003).

introductions to provide context and also to place them and their authors, where known, within the larger sphere of Korean literature.

SELECTION PROCESS FOR THE ANTHOLOGY

The question of representing a literary tradition is vexing. As Harold Bloom described it, "Tradition is not only a handing-down or process of benign transmission; it is also a conflict between past genius and present aspiration."[4] Such conflict is unavoidable, and for each selection in this volume, countless others have been excluded. Let us examine some of the problems in closer detail.

The first canonical work in Korean literary history was the late fifteenth-century *Anthology of Eastern Literature*. It was compiled under royal edict by a team of officials headed by Sŏ Kŏjŏng (徐居正, 1420–1488). Over a long and illustrious career, Sŏ Kŏjŏng made enormous contributions through collecting and anthologizing poetic and literary masterpieces from the Silla kingdom down to the era in which he himself lived. While this work claimed to include all important pieces of literature from the previous ages in Korea, under Sŏ's editorial direction, examples of Buddhist allegories and *hyangga* (鄉歌, native songs), shamanic and Buddhist-inspired poems from Silla, were left out.

The literary elites of Chosŏn looked to China in compiling literary collections, and in the fourteenth and fifteenth centuries there was a great deal of such activity. This culminated with the publication of the *Anthology of Eastern Literature*, which was influenced by *Selections of Refined Literature* (文選 *Wen xuan*) and the *Classic of True Treasures of Literature* (古文眞寶 *Guwen zhenbao*) of China, as well as by late Koryŏ compilations such as the *Mirror of the Literature of the Eastern Country* (東國文鑑 *Tongguk mun'gam*) and *Writings of the Eastern Country* (東人之文 *Tongin chi mun*). It was against this cultural and historical backdrop that the creation of the *Anthology of Eastern Literature* was supported by the Chosŏn government. As Sŏ Kŏjŏng explained in the preface, "His Royal Majesty by nature is fond of learning and every day he attends lectures and enjoys examining the Confucian Classics and Chinese histories. He thought that while [our] writings and literary works cannot be compared to the Six Confucian Classics, the rise and decline of literary vitality can be seen [through writings and literary works]."[5] The creation of the *Anthology of Eastern Literature* was a source of pride for the Chosŏn literati and also a means to

---

[4]Harold Bloom, *The Western Canon: The Books and School of Ages* (New York: Harcourt Brace, 1994), 8–9.
[5]*Anthology of Eastern Literature*, 2b.

measure the achievements of their country vis-à-vis Chinese states. But it was above all else a political statement of the Chosŏn dynasty's right to rule on the Korean Peninsula.

While both the main political factions in fifteenth-century Korea, the Hun'gup'a (勳舊派, Faction of the Meritorious and Conservative) and the Sarimp'a (士林派, Faction of the Confucian Moralists), had different ways of viewing literature, they did understand the relationship between literature and cultivating the Confucian way as being indivisible.[6] Such a view led to a selection from available literary works that matched the overall goals of the government elites, as Sŏ explained in the preface: "I and the other vassals, respectful to this grand commission, collected some literary styles [including those] of lyrics [辭 *sa*], rhapsodies [賦 *pu*], poetry [詩 *si*], and prose [文 *mun*] from the Three Kingdoms to the current dynasty [i.e., Chosŏn]. We selected those in which the expressions and reasons are pure and just, helpful in ruling and educating, and arranged these according to style and organized them into 130 fascicles. The work completed, we presented it [to the king], and he bestowed the title of *Tongmunsŏn*."[7] Such a tradition continued through premodern Korea. Literature deemed helpful or morally correct was promoted by the government and elites. Other literature was shunned and pushed to the side. Thus works such as the novel were the target of much government disdain and hand-wringing, especially in terms of their nefarious effect on the people and their morality.[8] And other works were simply viewed as trite. Thus a strong hierarchy of literature was maintained by the governing elites throughout the Chosŏn period, and certain genres were either altogether ignored or heavily criticized. Although Korean literature in the modern era has largely been liberated from such a hierarchy, it is also clear that the Confucian literary tradition as exemplified by Sŏ's introduction to the *Anthology of Eastern Literature* played a major role in setting the agenda in modern Korea for the study of Korean literature and literary history.

A major concern for the editors in compiling this anthology thus has been one of creating a more inclusive reader for premodern Korean prose. Genres that were largely ignored in the past have been given representation in this volume in order to provide a better picture of what was written and read by Koreans across the social spectrum. We have noted among the works translated into English a dearth of certain genres, particularly narratives that might be classified as

---

[6] Pak Hyŏnsuk, *Chosŏn kŏn'gukki ŭi munhak-ron* [Literary ideology in the age of the formation of Chosŏn] (Seoul: Ihoe munhwasa, 2002), 12–13.

[7] *Anthology of Eastern Literature*, 2b.

[8] For more on this, see Michael J. Pettid, *Unyŏng-jŏn: A Love Affair at the Royal Palace of Chosŏn Korea*, trans. Kil Cha and Michael J. Pettid (Berkeley: Institute of East Asian Studies, 2009), 55–61.

yadam (野談, unofficial histories) and *ilgi* (日記, diaries). Moreover, in terms of content, there has been a general tendency to ignore works that ran counter to prevailing social ideals, especially those that might be labeled as lewd or erotic (肉談, *yuktam*). Likewise, there has been a tendency to focus on the preoccupations of elite men at the expense of women and commoners. Finally, we have included works that owe their roots to oral performative traditions. Although such performance works were not much esteemed in premodern times, they are now deemed important as cultural products that have been handed down through generations of singers and storytellers. Because of the vast changes in historical circumstances, these are all types of works that Sŏ Kŏjŏng could not afford to ignore were he alive today.

ENGLISH LANGUAGE ANTHOLOGIES OF PREMODERN KOREAN LITERATURE

Modern anthologies have typically reflected much of the Chosŏn period mindset over literary value, and many of the same sorts of works are exalted today as they were in the past. To a degree this is fitting. Men such as Ch'oe Ch'iwŏn (崔致遠, b. 857), Yi Kyubo (李奎報, 1168–1241), and Yun Sŏndo (尹善道, 1587–1671), for instance, were key figures in the Korean literary tradition. However, in giving preference to certain genres and the elite men who had mastered those genres, other works have been given insufficient attention. We hope this anthology will be another step forward toward greater inclusion of genres and talents.

One of the main distinctions, especially in terms of what has been published in English, is that between poetry and prose. Poetry was absolutely the preferred and more highly valued genre in premodern Korea by ruling elites. Such a condition has extended to the English language translations, if perhaps to a slightly lesser degree. Verse is copious and deserves proper presentation.[9] But so too does prose, and this is where the chief problem is found in available materials in English. One would also raise a question about an attempt to more accurately represent the *writer* of premodern Korea. Obviously we cannot represent what has not been saved historically. But we can attempt to include the extant writings of women and commoners as well as the works associated with storytellers, singers, and others who have been underrepresented in previous compilations. Indeed, one of the thorniest problems in Korean literary studies has been

---

[9] Among many fine collections, two deserve special mention: Peter H. Lee, *The Columbia Anthology of Traditional Korean Poetry* (New York: Columbia University Press, 2002), and Kevin O'Rourke, *The Book of Korean Poetry: Songs of Shilla and Koryŏ* (Ames: University of Iowa Press, 2006).

the interrelationship of the written and the oral, a point discussed in greater detail in the following. In a similar vein, there is the question of genre, where the edifying work has typically been given primacy over the entertaining piece. Again, framed in terms of Sŏ's preface to the *Anthology of Eastern Literature*, we might note that Sŏ's assumptions about what was worthy of written preservation did not remain wholly coherent throughout the Chosŏn dynasty, as attested by the *p'ansori* narratives included here.

One of the most important factors in making this anthology possible has been the growth of scholarship in Korean literary studies, both within Korea and outside. Seen from that perspective, the enduring contribution of Peter H. Lee's *Anthology of Korean Literature* is all the more remarkable.[10] As the most prominent anthology of premodern Korean literature in English, Lee's *Anthology* has been the gold standard for premodern Korean literature for over thirty years. Our concerns in this present work build on the foundations laid by Lee but are narrower in focusing on prose.

Over the past three and a half decades, Korean literary scholarship has grown with an increasing amount of detailed work in a variety of areas, ranging from the discovery of texts to the publication of scholarly translations to research into specific works and genres. As a consequence, it is possible to see more clearly how pseudobiographies (假傳 *kajŏn*) and commentaries (說 *sŏl*) served as forerunners to the novel (小說 *sosŏl*), which was becoming more prominent by the mid-Chosŏn period. Equally important is the fact that more recent scholarship has forced us to recognize that the literary world of mid to late Chosŏn cannot be adequately represented by focusing on the works of now famous writers, men such as Kim Sisŭp (金時習, 1453–1493), Hŏ Kyun (許筠, 1569–1618), and Kim Manjung (金萬重, 1637–1692). On the contrary, anonymous novels were every bit as important, if not more so. Likewise, there has been much work on the large genre of *yadam*, *yasa*, miscellanies that circulated among both elites and commoners for much of the Chosŏn period and that provide excellent glimpses of life. Finally, Korean scholarship over the past several decades has shown greater attention to the topics of women's writings and the roles of women in the broader context of premodern literature.

CONTENTS OF THE ANTHOLOGY

With an eye to expanding the types and variety of readings available in English on premodern Korean literature, the editors of this work sought out works that

---

[10] Peter H. Lee, *Anthology of Korean Literature: From Early Times to the Nineteenth Century* (Honolulu: University of Hawai`i Press, 1981).

would better represent both the diversity and development of premodern prose. Also, we saw a need to include short introductions for all the contributions to give our readers the context of the piece, who the writer was (if known), and a discussion of the genre in general.

Naturally, we are limited by practical restraints such as length and so on, so meeting all our goals was difficult. One of the first objectives was to demonstrate the development of Korean prose writings, and to that end we wanted to include early prose pieces. We started with pieces from the *Tales of the Bizarre* (殊異傳 *Sui-jŏn*), a work that dates to the late Silla or early Koryŏ period. While the pieces are short, they provide early examples of fiction and display the eclectic worldview of Koreans before the ascendency of Confucianism.

Second, we wanted to include examples of the aforementioned pseudobiographical (假傳 *kajŏn*) and commentarial (說 *sŏl*) styles. These show how fiction developed from Koryŏ to Chosŏn, leading to the early novel. These are followed by an early Chosŏn piece written by Kim Sisŭp before we move to four longer pieces of mid- to late-Chosŏn fiction. Three of these four longer pieces are anonymous, and the other piece is written by a scholar-official. These encompass interests ranging from Daoism to Confucianism to the domestic sphere and thus provide some balance to the typical emphasis on Confucianism in Chosŏn Korea.

Third, to broaden the types of genres represented, we included three groups of *yadam*—one from the early, one from the mid, and one from the late Chosŏn. Here we can see how this genre developed from collections by known writers to the unknown, and how the topics ranged from Buddhism to ghost stories to erotic tales. As with the examples of fiction, through these *yadam* works we can gain better insight into what Koreans read for enjoyment.

In addition, we wanted to include some different types of prose writings that are sometimes overlooked when discussing literature. Thus we added a section on "Autobiography, Social Commentary, and Philosophical Humor." The writings by Pak Chiwŏn and Yi Tŏngmu come out of the elite male milieu, while Lady Yi's autobiographical piece gives voice to concerns that were central to her life. These are followed by an excerpt from *Diary of the Kyech'uk Year* (계축일기 *Kyech'uk ilgi*), presumably written by a palace woman and a representative sample of palace literature. Finally, we end the collection with excerpts from three of the five extant *p'ansori*. These translations are distinguished by the fact that they have been made by Chan E. Park, a transnational singer of *p'ansori* who brings firsthand experience and knowledge of this living art form.

In concluding with these excerpts from the extant *p'ansori*, this collection underscores the complex question of the interrelationship of the written and the oral. Since elements of this question run throughout this collection, some additional comments are needed at this juncture. In its simplest conception, this interrelationship meant that what was written down might be read aloud for others, whereas what was rooted in an oral tradition, in turn, might be written down. Something thus might be transmitted both orally and through writing; *p'ansori* as a genre is the most obvious case in point. In the case of premodern Korea, this interrelationship was complicated by the existence of two distinct forms of literary expression in Literary Chinese and vernacular Korean.

These two types of literacy could interact with each other as made evident in premodern works that were transmitted in both Literary Chinese and vernacular versions. This interaction was also manifested in the use of the Chinese script to write Korean even prior to the invention of the Korean alphabet, but the fact that the Korean alphabet was simple and devised for writing Korean meant that the potential for a tightening of this interrelationship was markedly increased after the middle of the fifteenth century. Even so, literacy remained the exception rather than the rule. Although the question of literacy rates in Literary Chinese and vernacular Korean is extremely complex, there is nothing to indicate that there was anything akin to widespread literacy even in the vernacular during the premodern era. The two principal factors surrounding literacy were class and gender. Elite men were partly defined by their mastery of Literary Chinese. Although some elite women surely knew Literary Chinese, they were most strongly associated with vernacular literacy. The overall result was that in addition to a potential interplay between Literary Chinese and the vernacular, there was also the potential influence of someone reading aloud to others. There are multiple variations of this type of scenario, but several crucial points must be emphasized.

First, even those who were illiterate could listen to others read or narrate a story. Second, those who were illiterate in Literary Chinese but literate in Korean could write down something that had originated in Literary Chinese. Third, something written in Korean could be translated into Literary Chinese or vice versa. Fourth, something originally written in one language and then translated into the other language could, in turn, be translated back. The permutations of these five possibilities were increased by the continuity of manuscript culture. Much of the historical complexity surrounding premodern Korean literature and fiction, in particular, derives from these points and is manifested in the existence of multiple versions of a single work.

There was, however, another factor that was conspicuous in Literary Chinese writings, even those that belonged to the otherwise unrespected genre of fiction, and it served to demarcate the line between literature in Literary Chinese that was meant to be read and vernacular literature that could be read or narrated— that is, read aloud—to others, to put the contrast in an extreme form. This factor was compression. In part, it rested on the well-known concision of Literary Chinese as a language, but this compression was also a consequence of a heightened sense of "literariness" on the part of those who used it. Much of this literariness was reflected through the use of allusions and the incorporation of Literary Chinese poems, which themselves were highly compressed and characteristically employed allusions. Literary Chinese works thus typically assumed that the reader had a broad knowledge of literature in Literary Chinese and therefore could discern what something meant, and quite often these meanings were complex and had to be interpreted in relation to other pieces of literature.

This contrast and its effects can be illustrated through two works of fiction contained in this collection, the Literary Chinese "An Account of Drunken Merriment at Floating Jade-Green Pavilion" by Kim Sisŭp (1435–1493) and the anonymous vernacular *A Tale of Two Sisters, Changhwa and Hongnyŏn*. Kim's "Account" is typically classified as "short fiction," partly because it is one of five stories loosely connected by theme and collected under a single title and partly because in the original it is quite short. When compared with the "long fiction" of *A Tale of Two Sisters*, however, this typology appears odd. This is an effect of compression. The Korean vernacular source text used for the translation of *A Tale of Two Sisters* contained in this collection comprises nearly sixteen tightly packed pages and is roughly twice as long as the Korean translation of Kim's "Account" and roughly three times longer than the Literary Chinese source text. Those relative differences reflect the concision of Literary Chinese. The additional element is "literariness," and that is reflected in the fact that the Korean translation of Kim's "Account" contains well over one hundred annotations, some of which are well in excess of one hundred words. Taken together, the length of the annotations attached to the Korean translation is roughly equal to the length of the Korean translation itself.

This "literariness," however, was a critical feature of such works. It connected the work to a larger body of literature in Literary Chinese, and in that way it implicitly invoked the idea, mentioned previously, that literate expression was fundamental to civilization itself. That Confucian emphasis on the connection between literate expression, civilization, and morality was also manifested through the pivotal use of poems even in fiction. To be civilized was to know how to compose and read poetry against the larger tradition. For that reason, characters might communicate crucial information with each other—and thus, the reader—through the exchange of poems, as exemplified in works such as Kim's "Account."

But as exemplified in *A Tale of Two Sisters*, the Confucian idea that literature was linked to standards of civilized behavior could extend beyond those who commanded a high level of skill in Literary Chinese. Although *A Tale of Two Sisters* was most likely first written down in Literary Chinese, it also circulated in vernacular versions. The vernacular version used for the translation included in this collection begins with the phrase "the story says" (話說 *hwasŏl*). That redundant phrase is omitted in translation, but it is a relatively common convention in premodern vernacular fiction that marks the start of a story and suggests that it is being read aloud. For these reasons, typologies and genres, the interaction of Literary Chinese and the vernacular, and the circulation of literature in written and oral forms remain vexing questions to be pursued by young scholars of premodern Korean literature.

FINAL CONSIDERATIONS

No selection can ever be perfect. We are bound by the same rules as all compilers of such a collection: we are limited by space, time, and our own interests. As Sir Frank Kermode wrote, "Canons, which negate the distinction between knowledge and opinion, which are instruments of survival built to be time-proof, not reason-proof, are of course deconstructable; if people think there should not be such things, they may very well find the means to destroy them. Their defense cannot any longer be undertaken by central institutional power."[11]

Anthologies, no less than canons, are inherently flawed, but they are nonetheless vital to the spread of knowledge. This is especially true in the case of literary studies of premodern Korea, where the number of specialists is extremely limited. It is our hope that this work will help to illuminate the diversity of premodern Korean literature and promote the interest of scholars and students of Korean literature as a whole.

---

[11] Frank Kermode, *Forms of Attention*, quoted in Bloom, *The Western Canon*, 4.

PART I

Pre-Koryŏ and Koryŏ Period Prose

1. Pre-Koryŏ Prose and Fiction

Along with other aspects such as iron culture, the Chinese writing system was adopted in early Korean kingdoms and used for recording history, official correspondence, and inscriptions. As various worldviews such as Buddhism and Confucianism entered the peninsula, the need for formal education in Chinese characters became prominent, and educational institutions, such as the Confucian Academy (太學 T'aehak), established in the Koguryŏ kingdom (高句麗, 37 B.C.E.–668 C.E.) in 372 C.E. for that purpose, were established.[1] Moreover, by the seventh century sons of the Silla (新羅, 57 B.C.E.–935 C.E.) royal family were being sent to China to study, and by the ninth century over two hundred students had been sent to Tang (唐, 618–907).[2] This resulted in a considerable number of individuals able to write in Chinese and certainly aided the spread of literacy on the Korean Peninsula.

---

[1] Ki-baik Lee, *A New History of Korea*, trans. Edward W. Wagner and Edward J. Shultz (Cambridge, Mass.: Harvard University Press, 1984), 72.

[2] Peter H. Lee, ed., *A History of Korean Literature* (Cambridge: Cambridge University Press, 2003), 95.

Also helping spread literacy among the upper status groups was the adaptation of Confucianism among the ruling elites as a means to help in maintaining social order and the administration of the state. For example, Koguryŏ had local educational institutions known as *kyŏngdang* (扃堂) where unmarried youth were taught the Confucian Classics. Indeed, Chinese visitors to Koguryŏ noted the prevalence of educational institutions and the love of books in Koguryŏ, "with a school on every street."[3] A similar situation must have existed in Paekche (百濟, 18 B.C.E.–660 C.E.), where there were teachers of the Chinese Classics who bore the title of *paksa* (博士), and in Silla, where the youth group of the *hwarang* (花郞) was educated in both Confucian and Buddhist texts as a part of their education.[4] Thus we can see that literacy in Literary Chinese had become an important element of education, at least for elites, by this early period in Korean history.

After the fall of Silla's rivals in the mid-seventh century, education in Silla became more formalized with the establishment of the National Academy (國學 Kukhak) in 682.[5] By 788 an examination system had been implemented to help with the selection of government officials. This examination was known as the Reading of Texts in Three Gradations (讀書三品科 Toksŏ Samp'umkwa) and involved reading Chinese texts such as the *Classic of Filial Piety* (孝經 *Xiaojing*), *Analects* (論語 *Lunyu*), *Book of Rites* (禮記 *Liji*), and *Literary Selections* (文選 *Wenxuan*), among other books.[6] This education was decidedly Confucian in character and represents the start of a Confucianism-focused educational system that would remain in place until the beginning of the twentieth century.

It is, however, important to note that Chinese and Korean are quite dissimilar languages, and the adoption of Chinese writing for Koreans was not an easy task. Early on there were modifications of Chinese writing to represent Korean syntax and grammar. One such form was *idu* (吏讀, clerk's script), which used various modifications to reflect Korean particles and grammar; this system of modified writing remained common until the late nineteenth century. *Idu* allowed the recording of "Korean" words such as personal names, place-names, and vernacular poem-songs.[7] Another development was that of *hyangch'al* (鄕札), which used particular Chinese characters only to convey semantic meaning

---

[3] Chŏng Nakch'an et. al., *Han'guk ŭi chŏnt'ong kyoyuk* [Traditional education in Korea] (Kyŏngsan: Yŏngnam taehakkyo ch'ulp'anbu, 2002), 52–53.

[4] Ibid., 46–48.

[5] This was renamed the National Confucian Academy (太學監 T'aehakkam) in the mid-eighth century.

[6] Chŏng Nakch'an et. al., *Han'guk ŭi chŏnt'ong kyoyuk*, 53–54.

[7] Ho-Min Sohn and Peter H. Lee, "Language, Forms, Prosody, and Themes," in Peter H. Lee, *History of Korean Literature*, 27.

while other characters were used to transcribe verbs, particles, and inflections.[8] *Hyangch'al* was used for recording Korean poem-songs exclusively and had died out by the early Koryŏ period.

With the increased emphasis on written culture and education it is natural that literary activities increased and men such as Ch'oe Ch'iwŏn (崔致遠, b. 857) became well known for their writing abilities. Records of the period inform that state-sponsored histories were compiled such as the one-hundred-volume *Extant Records* (留記 *Yugi*) of Koguryŏ or the *Documentary Records* (書記 *Sŏgi*) of Paekche. However, very little of such writing has survived to the present day. Mostly, we have fragments recorded in other, later collections, from which we can imagine how the people of those times viewed their world.

MP

1.1 ANONYMOUS, *TALES OF THE BIZARRE* (殊異傳 *SUI-JŎN*)

This anthology[9] is thought to date from the late Silla kingdom, although it has not survived intact. The authorship of the original anthology has been attributed to Ch'oe Ch'iwŏn, and this work is said to have been supplemented by Pak Illyang (朴寅亮, d. 1096) and others in Koryŏ (高麗, 918–1392). It is not clear if these were a single text or simply three collections of unusual narratives.[10] It is also quite possible that the collection grew as it passed from the late Silla to Koryŏ and is a kind of collectively created text that was added to by various individuals over a period of decades or even centuries.[11]

One aspect of this text that is of great importance relates to the development of fictional works in Korea. These tales are classified as tales of wonder (傳奇, K. *chŏn'gi*, C. *chuanqi*). This form of writing first emerged in seventh-century Tang China and by the tenth century had spread to Japan.[12] Given that authorship is attributed to Ch'oe Ch'iwŏn, who was active in the ninth century, we can see the flow of literary styles outwardly from China. Further we can note the interconnectedness of the East Asian cultures that used similar literary forms in Literary Chinese. In terms of Korea's literary history,

---

[8] Peter H. Lee, *History of Korean Literature*, 68.

[9] Recorded in *The Great Eastern Rhyming Treasure of Assembled Jewels* [大東韻府群玉 *Taedong unbu kunok*].

[10] Cho Suhak, *Chaegusŏng Sui-jŏn* [The reformulated *Sui-jŏn*] (Seoul: Kukhak charyŏwŏn, 2001), 7.

[11] Cho Tongil, *Han'guk munhak t'ongsa* [A complete history of Korean literature] (Seoul: Chisik sanŏpsa, 1992) 1:363–68.

[12] Cho Suhak, *Chaegusŏng Sui-jŏn*, 8–9.

Tales of the Bizarre is highly significant as it demonstrates that fictional forms were being created and circulated by late Silla, which is much more in line with what we can see elsewhere in East Asian literary history.

There are but twelve extant narratives scattered in various historical and literary works, including six recorded in the sixteenth-century *The Great Eastern Rhyming Treasure of Assembled Jewels* (大東韻府群玉 *Taedong unbu kunok*), three of which are translated here. These are the oldest surviving fictional works of Korea, and in them we can note the blend of storytelling with that of prose writing.[13] It seems clear that these are the rudimentary antecedents to the tales of wonder that more fully develop in the early Chosŏn period as full-fledged novels. Thus in this work we can see the first steps of the progression of fictional prose in Korea, most likely in the form of oral narratives being put to paper rather than the creation of new stories by the compilers of the *Tales of the Bizarre*.

While the narratives are simple, we find an interesting worldview that demonstrates a strong belief in the presence of supernatural beings and events in the human world. Moreover, we see a worldview that is yet unfettered by Confucian notions of propriety or focus on the mundane world. Rather, we can note an eclectic blend of indigenous beliefs and introduced worldviews such as Daoism and the interaction of humans and otherworldly beings.

MP

1.2 "PASSION SURROUNDING THE PAGODA" (心火繞塔 SIMHWA YO T'AP)

Chigwi [志鬼] was a slave at the Hwalli post station in Silla.[14] He was deeply in love with Queen Sŏndŏk [善德, r. 632–647] because of her great beauty, so much so that he wept continuously until he could not stand. The queen came to a temple to pray and heard of this and summoned Chigwi. He hurried to the temple and waited under a pagoda for her procession but suddenly fell into a deep sleep. [Arriving,] the queen removed her bracelet and placed it on his chest before returning to the palace. After a while when he awoke, he was so shocked [to see the bracelet] that he fainted for a long spell. Soon a fireball rose out of his chest and swirled around the pagoda a few times: Chigwi had become a fire ghost [火鬼 *hwagwi*].

---

[13] Cho Tongil, *Han'guk munhak t'ongsa*, 1:368.
[14] Post stations (驛) were staffed by a hereditary class of slaves.

The queen ordered a Daoist wizard to make the incantation of "The fire in Chigwi's heart burned his body and transformed him into a fire god. Be gone over the great sea, never to be seen or close [again]!" From that time, it was a custom to put this incantation on doorposts to serve as a talisman against fire.

1.3 "BEAUTIES IN A BAMBOO TUBE"
(竹筒美女 CHUKTONG MINYŎ)

When Kim Yusin [金庾信, 595–673][15] was on the way to the capital from Sŏju [西州], he encountered a strange wayfarer on the road in front of him. Above the wayfarer's head was an abnormal aurora. As the wayfarer was resting under a tree, Yusin pretended to nap. The stranger pulled out a bamboo tube from his jacket, shook it, and then two beauties came out of it. After the stranger sat and talked with the women a while, they returned to the container, and he tucked it into his coat and resumed his journey. Yusin followed him and inquired very gently. Together they traveled to the capital, where on Nam-san [南山] beneath a pine tree they held a feast. Here the two beauties appeared [from the tube] and took part in the feast. The wayfarer [told Yusin], "I live near the West Sea and married a woman from the East Sea. I take my wives when I go to visit my parents." Suddenly, the clouds became thick and he was nowhere to be seen.

1.4 "AN OLD MAN BECOMES A DOG"
(老翁化狗 NOONG HWA KU)

In the time of Silla an old man arrived at the gate of Kim Yusin's residence. Yusin took the old man's hands, went into the house, and prepared a cushion for him [to sit on]. He asked the old man, "Can you still transform yourself as you did in the old days?" The old man then transformed into a tiger, a rooster, even an eagle, and finally a house dog before going out from the house.

---

[15] Kim Yusin was a general of Silla who played an important role in the defeat of its rival states.

2. Koryŏ Period Prose Works

The growth of literary activities in the Koryŏ dynasty (高麗, 918–1392) was in part a consequence of the desire by the ruling class to make a break with the heretofore hereditary-based ruling structures that had dominated Greater Silla (大新羅).[1] The new rulers were largely not of the hereditary ruling class of Silla. Thus they gradually pushed society toward a model based in Confucianism, and one that, at least in theory, would allow a wider group of men with ability to rise in the government structure. Of course this was not an equal society by any means, but compared with the previous period the government bureaucracy was far more inclusive. Since much emphasis was placed on Confucianism and the ability to read and write in Literary Chinese, it is a natural consequence that the number of men who excelled in literary activities would increase. A civil service examination was established in 958 and was open to men of the aristocratic class and petty officials in the provinces. By 992 the Royal Academy (國子監 Kukchagam)

---

[1] Here we use Greater Silla to refer to Silla after the fall of Koguryŏ and Paekche. It has also been referred to as Unified Silla (統一新羅), but such an appellation fails to acknowledge the Parhae (渤海) kingdom occupying the north of the peninsula and much of present-day Manchuria.

had been established in the capital to teach the Confucian classics, mathematics, and calligraphy, among other subjects, and this opened a new avenue to government service. Over the course of Koryŏ there were over six thousand men who passed the prestigious composition examination (製述業), while only around four hundred fifty passed the classics examination (明經業).[2] This reflects the importance placed on being able to compose various types of writing in Literary Chinese.

Education in Confucianism also spread to the royal family, where the first record of Royal Lectures (經筵) being held at the palace is in 1132.[3] Beyond the national level we find that by the early twelfth century the government had established schools in rural areas to help indoctrinate youth into Confucianism.[4] The zeal for education and being able to pass the civil service examination was quite high among the elites of Koryŏ, and this resulted in private educational institutions being established for this purpose. By the middle of the eleventh century the Confucian scholar Ch'oe Ch'ung (崔沖, 984–1068) had established a school (九齋, Nine-Course Academy) for training upper status youth, and this was followed by numerous other such institutions. The push for education was clearly on at this point in Korean history.

However, it was not Confucianism alone that propelled training in Literary Chinese. Buddhism was also of great importance in driving literacy. Monks traveled to China to pursue their studies and were introduced to a wealth of Buddhist scriptures that were brought back to Koryŏ. The zenith of this is the multiple carvings of the Tripitaka Koreana (高麗大藏經 Koryŏ Taejang-gyŏng), the Buddhist canon contained on over eighty-one thousand wooden printing blocks first completed in 1087. It was in this atmosphere that literature written in Literary Chinese began to truly flourish in Koryŏ.

While poetry was held in highest esteem, prose writings were necessary for certain types of information. In particular, writing histories (史 *sa*) was an important means to not only record what had occurred but also to serve as a moral compass and a means of illustrating ethical norms. The earliest surviving history is *The History of the Three Kingdoms* (三國史記 *Samguk sagi*) compiled in 1146 by Kim Pusik (金富軾, 1074–1151). Other early works that demonstrate this fervor for writing include the monk Iryŏn's (日然, 1206–1289) more eclectic history, titled *Memorabilia of the Three Kingdoms* (三國遺事 *Samguk yusa*), and literary miscellanies such as *Notes on Poems and Other Trifles* (白雲小說 *Paegun*

---

[2] Ki-baik Lee, *A New History of Korea*, trans. Edward W. Wagner and Edward J. Shultz (Cambridge, Mass.: Harvard University Press, 1984), 118.

[3] Yi Wŏnho, *Chosŏn sidae kyoyuk ŭi yŏn'gu* [A study of education in the Chosŏn period] (Seoul: Munŭmsa, 2002), 12.

[4] Ki-baik Lee, *New History of Korea*, 120.

sosŏl) of Yi Kyubo (李奎報, 1168–1241) or *Supplementary Jottings in Idleness* (補閑集 *Pohan-jip*) written by Ch'oe Cha (崔慈, 1188–1260).

Histories could be of either an epoch or a biography (傳 *chŏn*) of an individual. Peter H. Lee has explained that biographies could further be divided into official and unofficial biographies. The official biography was generally a part of an official history and compiled by a court-appointed committee. On the other hand, an unofficial biography, which Lee terms "prose portrait," was a much freer form examining an individual by what that person had done in life.[5] Needless to say, the unofficial biographies provide excellent insight into how people lived and a fuller picture of who they were.

Arising from the official and unofficial biographies are the pseudobiographies (假傳 *kajŏn*), and these are where we can see the continued development of fictional prose. The pseudobiographical style was meant to be humorous and oftentimes used personification of an object (for example, liquor, money, a turtle, bamboo, a cane) to demonstrate the writer's ability through clever phrasing and historical precedents and to sometimes give a moral to his readers.[6] This form continued to be important in the subsequent Chosŏn dynasty since it was a fine vehicle for demonstrating excellent writing ability. One should remember that readership of these pieces was extremely limited as very few possessed the intellectual training to understand or even read such works. Still, we can see the beginning of a prose tradition that would continue into the following epoch.

Following are two examples of pseudobiographies and three selections of unofficial biographies. Further, there is one example ("Of Boats and Bribes") of a commentary (說 *sŏl*), a form that served as a place where writers could voice their opinions, reflect on social issues, or give an explanation for some situation.

MP

2.1. IM CH'UN, "THE TALE OF MR. CASH" (孔方傳 KONGBANG-JŎN)

Im Ch'un (林椿) was active around 1200, and though famous for his writing skills, he never passed the civil examination. His family suffered heavily during the military revolt of 1170, and although he escaped with his life, he died in poverty at a young age. His friend Yi Illo (李仁老, 1152–1220) edited a collection of his works, now lost, and included

---

[5] See Peter H. Lee, *A History of Korean Literature* (Cambridge: Cambridge University Press, 2003), 127–29.

[6] Cho Tongil, *Han'guk munhak t'ongsa* [A complete history of Korean literature] (Seoul: Chisik sanŏpsa, 1992), 2:116–23.

some of his poems in his own *Collection to Dispel Leisure* (破閑集 *P'ahan chip*). This story has been preserved in the *Anthology of Eastern Literature* (東文選 *Tongmunsŏn*).[7] In the narrative the copper coin is personified as someone living during the Western Han period; this satirical tale has a sting in its tail, which makes it emphatically clear that the author was opposed to the use of money.

SV

TRANSLATION

The ancestors of Mr. Cash [孔方 Kongbang],[8] aka Stringfellow [貫之 Kwanji], lived hidden in the entrails of Prime Yang Mount and did not mingle in society. In the time of the Yellow Emperor,[9] for the first time they were employed a little. But their character was strong and unbending, not very adaptable to the affairs of the world. The emperor summoned his ministers and craftsmen to look at them. The artisans observed them with trained eyes for some time and said, "They have the quality of the wild mountains; though they cannot be employed in this coarse form, if they were allowed to be transformed by Your Majesty, we will put them through the forge and under the hammer, remove the impurities, and polish them brightly, and then their good quality will appear bit by bit. The royal way lies in using people, measuring their capacities. We wish that Your Majesty will not, because they are just recalcitrant copper, throw them away." Like this they made their appearance into this world.

Later, to avoid turmoil, they went to the charcoal furnaces in the region of rivers and lakes, and made it their home. His father, Fontis,[10] was a minister of Zhou [周, 1111–256 B.C.E.] in charge of the taxes of the states. As a man, Mr. Cash was round on the outside but square inside. He was good at adapting to changing circumstances. He served the Han 漢 as chief minister of the Court of Dependencies [鴻盧卿]. When King Bi of Wu, crafty and presumptuous, usurped power, Mr. Cash made a huge profit for him.[11] At the time of Emperor Wu [武帝,

---

[7] Recorded in the *Anthology of Eastern Literature* [東文選 *Tongmunsŏn*], *kwŏn* 100.

[8] Literally "Square Hole," since the traditional piece of copper cash was round with a square hole, through which a string could be passed to tie several pieces together.

[9] A mythical emperor of China (黃帝 Huangdi).

[10] Quan 泉, meaning "source," was also used in the sense of "coin" or "wealth," since a wellspring is a symbol of unlimited resources.

[11] Liu Bi, king of Wu, cousin of Emperor Wen (r. 180–157 B.C.E.), under whose reign the people were allowed to freely mint coin. Bi added to his already considerable wealth by mining copper and minting coins.

r. 141–87 B.C.E.], the whole realm was laid waste, and the storehouses of the prefectures became depleted.[12] The emperor was worried and entreated Mr. Cash to become duke for making the people prosper [富民侯]. At court he was joined by his follower Mr. Jin, who filled the post of deputy for salt and iron [鹽鐵丞].[13] Mr. Jin addressed him like a brother, not by his name. Mr. Cash was corrupt and unscrupulous by nature. When put in charge of finances, he loved to weigh exactly how much interest was due and thought that this was more convenient for the country than making pottery molds for casting metal.[14] He fought with the people over minute margins of profit, making the prices of commodities fluctuate: the price of grain was devalued and goods became more expensive, causing people to discard the essential activity of farming and pursue the superfluous activity [of trading]. At this point the remonstrance officials frequently sent memorials urging a reconsideration of this policy, but the emperor did not listen.

Mr. Cash was very cunning in serving the powerful and rich; frequenting their homes, he enticed them to procure ranks. Promotion and dismissal from office were in his power; nobles and ministers violated their integrity to serve him. He amassed grains and gathered bribes, hoarded bonds and deeds like mountains, their number was beyond counting. In treating men and receiving persons of note, he did not inquire about their virtue or meanness; as long as they had wealth, he dealt even with market traders—he was what we may call a market trafficker. Sometimes he followed young hoodlums from the streets and played chess or cards. As he was very fond of giving approval [for projects under his jurisdiction], contemporaries said about him, "One word from Mr. Cash carries as much weight as one hundred catties of gold."

When Emperor Yuan of the Han [元帝, r. 48–32 B.C.E.] ascended the throne, Gong Yu [貢禹][15] wrote a memorial: "Mr. Cash has for a long time been in charge of a very important and busy post, yet he has achieved nothing for the

---

[12] In 113 B.C.E. Emperor Wu restored the imperial monopoly on coinage. He also issued a number of fiat currencies in an attempt to finance his ruinous campaigns of foreign conquest. See Richard Von Glahn, *Fountain of Fortune: Money and Monetary Policy in China, 1000–1700* (Berkeley: University of California Press, 1996), 35.

[13] Kong Jin was originally a merchant and producer of iron. When appointed to the Board of Agriculture, he advocated the government's monopolizing the trade of iron and salt. This law was adopted in 120 B.C.E., and he became the first deputy of salt and iron.

[14] I am not sure what is meant here, but it may refer to the use of precious metal simply for its intrinsic value, which, after barter, could be recast for reuse rather than employed continuously as money.

[15] Gong Yu lived in the first century B.C.E. and became a censor under Emperor Yuan. He advised that the money spent on horses, parks, bullfighting, etc., should rather be saved and given to the poor.

crucial farming sector. His followers prosper on [gathering] the income from tolls [on goods], corrupting the country and harming the people. They endanger both the public and the private realms. With lavish bribes they seek to further their affairs in public, thus both causing and profiting from rising criminality, a clear warning for a big change. Please remove him from office as a warning to the greedy and corrupt." Those in government at the time had advanced through a study of agriculture, and since military provisions were insufficient, they wanted to establish a policy to make the borders stable [by paying off enemies]; annoyed by Mr. Cash's actions, they endorsed Gong Yu's words. The emperor then acknowledged Gong Yu's petition, and Mr. Cash was dismissed.

He told his followers, "I recently met with the emperor. To assist in his solitary endeavor of morally transforming and ruling the world, I merely wanted to make the country's resources plentiful and increase the people's wealth. Now for an insignificant misdemeanor, I am cast aside. As for the emperor's employing or dismissing people, there is nothing I can do about it. Fortunately, the rest of my life will not be cut off like a string, nor will it be spent in silence, carelessly cast in a pouch. When life is made impossible for me, I will leave, roaming through different places before returning to the Jiang-Huai area to engage in different activities. I will drop my fishing lines in the brook as I blend [into my native place]. Catching fish and drinking wine, with the Min traders and sea merchants I will float on the wine boats, finding fulfillment in this life. Even the salaries of the Thousand Bells [千鍾 Ch'ŏnjong] or the food of the Five Cauldrons [五鼎 Ojŏng]—how would they suffice to encompass this? However, my skills are ancient and must someday revive."

He Qiao [和嶠][16] of Jin [晉] heard about his customs and was pleased; amassing a property of several tens of thousands, he was incurably in love with him. Therefore Lu Bao [魯褒][17] wrote a treatise to denounce him and his vulgar arrogance. Only Ruan Xuanzi [阮宣子][18] was very transcendent and not interested in material goods. Yet he went carousing with Mr. Cash's followers, and in a wine bar

---

[16] He Qiao (d. 292) was so fastidious that instead of riding, as was customary, in a carriage with his official colleagues, he insisted on having a carriage all to himself. Although enormously rich, he was so mean that Tu Yü declared he had the "money disease."

[17] Lu Bao (third century C.E.) was a poor scholar under the Jin. Shocked by the collapse of public morality and the greed for more wealth that characterized the period 291–300, he composed a satire on the vices of his age known as *Discourse on the Genius of Money* [錢神論 Qianshenlun].

[18] Ruan Xuanzi was a scholar-official of the Jin period. He advocated a fusion of Confucianism and Daoism and demonstrated to contemporaries that ghosts do not exist. He and Wang Yan (courtesy name Yifu) and two others made up the "four friends."

he unceremoniously drank to him. Wang Yifu [王夷甫][19] had never even pronounced the name of Mr. Cash, simply calling him "this filthy stuff." So vulgar did the adherents of Pure Conversation find him.

At the height of the Tang dynasty [唐, 618–907], Liu Yan [劉晏][20] became administrative assistant of the Tax Bureau [度支判官]. Since the needs of the country were not adequately addressed, he requested that Mr. Cash's skills be reused to facilitate the national economy; his words are recorded in the Monograph on Food and Products [食貨志 Shihuo zhi]. At the time, Mr. Cash had been dead for a long time, and his followers had dispersed to the four quarters. Attracted by the material lure, they emerged and were used again. Thus his art flourished again during the Kaiyuan [713–742] and Tianbao [742–756] eras. He was posthumously granted the rank of grand master for court discussion [朝議大夫] and the post of aide at the Court for Palace Revenues [少府丞].

Under the Northern Song dynasty during the reign of Shenzong [1068–1086], Wang Anshi [王安石] was in charge of the country. He invited Lü Huiqing to join him in the administration. He introduced the "Green Sprouts" [青苗法] policy of government loans, and the whole universe was in chaos and need. Su Dongpo [蘇東坡] protested heavily against this and wanted to accuse him but fell into the trap he had set up and was demoted. Because of this the court officials did not dare to speak out. When Sima Guang [司馬光] became senior minister, he advocated its abolition and recommended employing Su.[21] Again the followers of Mr. Cash lost ground and did not crop up again.

Circus [輪],[22] the son of Mr. Cash, was derided for his flimsiness and poverty. He was made commissioner of waterways [水衡令] but was executed for bribery. The historian commented, "One who as a subject harbors two minds to procure

---

[19]Wang Yifu (256–311), famous as a brilliant talker, practiced with great success the laissez-faire policy taught by Laozi. Disgusted with his wife's avarice, he even refused to utter the word "money," and when she strewed cash around his bed so as to block the way, he called out to the servant to take away this "filthy stuff."

[20]Liu Yan, courtesy name Shian, died in 780, after being banished to Korea, where he was allowed to commit suicide. An order was given to confiscate his property, but it was found that his possessions consisted of only a few books. He was fond of urging that there should be no parsimony in great undertakings. His sympathies were entirely with the people, and his best efforts were directed toward shielding the poorer classes from injustice and exaction.

[21]Wang Anshi (1021–1086) proposed a program of sweeping reforms, adopted by Shenzong, ushering in a system of state capitalism. Su Dongpo (1036–1101) and Sima Guang (1019–1086) were his main opponents. Under the influence of the latter the reforms were eventually reversed. Lü Huiqing (1032–1111) remained loyal to Wang's ideology and became its chief proponent after Wang's death.

[22]I have translated yun (輪, "wheel" or "discus") as "Circus" to convey the roundness and also the folly of the character.

great profits, can he be called loyal? In dealing with law and rulers, Mr. Cash showed great resourcefulness. Sealing agreements with a handshake, he perversely enjoyed undeserved favor, increasing his profits and removing obstacles. To repay this preferential treatment, he helped Liu Bi [劉濞] avail himself of power and set up his own party. If he were a loyal official, he would not engage in affairs outside the remit of his office."

After the expiry of Mr. Cash, his followers were reemployed under the Song dynasty [宋, 960–1279]. As a result of their currying favor with the authorities, trapping upright people, even the practice of the most basic principles was obscured. If only Emperor Yuan had heeded Gong Yu's words and eliminated him overnight, how much later trouble would have been averted! But by failing to repress, he let the fraud continue over future generations. How is it possible that those who place greater priority on practical matters when speaking always suffer the fate of not being believed?

SV

2.2. YI KYUBO, "THE TALE OF MASTER MALT" (麴先生傳 KUK SŎNSAENG-JŎN)

Yi Kyubo (李奎報, 1168–1241) is easily counted among the best, if not the best, of the literary talents in Koryŏ. His extensive writings cover a huge range of materials, from discussions of poetry and the classics to folklore and ghosts and even food and liquor. As such, he is a great portal to a better understanding of mid-Koryŏ society and the difficulties and changes that were brought about by the military rebellion of 1170 and the subsequent rule by military officers that saw the persecution of the literati. Yi nonetheless managed to rise in the military-led regime and eventually rose to a position of prominence in the government and was known for his excellent composition of government and diplomatic documents. However, his real accomplishments were in literature, and he was known as a man who enjoyed poetry, playing the kŏmun'go (six-stringed zither), and drink. It is fitting, then, that one of Yi's—a man who loved liquor—most enjoyable prose pieces deals with liquor and its ill effects on society.[23]

MP

---

[23] Recorded in the *Anthology of Eastern Literature*, kwŏn 100.

TRANSLATION

Kuk Sŏng [麴聖, Sage Malt], whose courtesy name was Drunken Haze, was a person of Chuch'ŏn [酒泉, Wine Spring] district. From his youth, he was loved by Xu Mo [徐邈], who bequeathed him his given and courtesy names. His distant ancestors were from the Land of Warm [溫 On] and worked diligently as farmers to become self-sufficient. When Zheng [鄭] invaded Zhou [周], they were forcedly moved, and their descendants thrived in Zheng. His great-grandfather's name has been lost to posterity, but his grandparents moved to Chuch'ŏn, where they established their hometown. Until his father, Ch'a [醝, White Liquor], was appointed as local inspector of grain fields [平原督郵], none held government posts; he married Lady Grain [穀 Kok], the daughter of the chief minister of the national granaries [司農卿], who gave birth to Sŏng.

Even in his youth Sŏng was very magnanimous, and when a guest who came to meet his father met Sŏng, he said, "His heart is overflowing just like roiling waves in vast waters that cannot become turbid or be any clearer. It is not as pleasant to talk with you as it is with your son."

When he grew up, he became friends with Liu Ling [劉伶] from Zhongshan [中山] and Tao Qian [陶潛] from Shenyang [瀋陽].[24] The two friends said that "if a day went by without seeing him, [we] would become miserly louts." Thus whenever the three got together, they would be so happy and forget everything for days, never returning until they were quite drunk.

Although he was selected as the district official charged with storing lees [糟丘椽], he declined. Subsequently, he was recommended by court nobles as retainer for high-grade wine [青州從事][25] and ordered by the king to deliver a royal edict by chariot. Upon seeing him, the king remarked, "He must be Master Malt from Chuch'ŏn district. It has been quite long since I have heard his aromatic name." Prior to this, the grand scribe [太史] had informed the king that the Star of Wine [酒旗星] shone brighter than ever. Given this timing, the king cherished him all the more. He was soon appointed director of the Bureau of Receptions [主客郎中], then promoted to chancellor of the National University [國子祭酒] in addition to minister of ceremonial propriety [禮儀使]. He did everything well and with decorum as the king wished in conducting the feast of the morning court, rites for the royal ancestors, and offering food and liquor during

---

[24] Liu Ling (221–300) and Tao Qian (365–427) were both famous poets in China and also both reputed to have strong affection for liquor.

[25] While both local inspector of grain fields and retainer for high-grade wine are official positions of the time, they were also argots referring to grades of wine. The former is low-grade wine, while the latter is good-quality wine.

ceremonial rites. The king promoted him to spokesman for the ruler [喉舌].²⁶ Treated with great honor, he was allowed to arrive at the palace in a palanquin, and the king addressed him by an honorific title rather than calling him by name. Master Malt was loved by the king so much that the king would burst into laughter simply upon seeing him even when he [the king] was upset. With his delightful and earthy character, Master Malt became closer to the king every day; every day the two became closer. As the king loved him greatly, he always accompanied [Master Malt] to every feast.

His [Master Malt's] sons, Hok [酷, Strong Liquor], P'ok [醃, Untamed Liquor], and Yŏk [醳, Bitter Wine], became impudent because of the king's blind affection for their father. The secretariat director [中書令], Moyŏng [毛穎, Writing Brush], submitted a memorial to the throne urging the impeachment [of Master Malt]:

> A single retainer alone receiving favoritism is widely held an evil. Now Master Malt consumes by small and large measure [斗筲 *tuso*],²⁷ but by chance he came into the royal court and moved up to the Third Rank. He brought a thief deep into the heart of the people and pleasured in injuring them, driving tens of thousands to cry out and suffer pain in their heads and breasts. Given this, he is not a loyal retainer who would heal the country but rather is an enemy who certainly poisons the people. With their father's favor, his three sons infest the people and cause them great torment. Thus Your Majesty should give them the death penalty and keep [them] from the mouths of the masses.

Upon hearing this, Hok committed suicide by drinking poisoned liquor, and Master Malt was stripped of rank and banished as a commoner. Ch'ii-ja [鴟夷子, Leather Pouch], a friend of Master Malt's, also committed suicide, by jumping off a chariot.

Initially, Leather Pouch was loved by the king for his humorous banter and became close friends with Master Malt. Thus he was loved ever more by the king, and whenever the king left or returned to the palace, he accompanied him in his chariot. One day Leather Pouch felt tired and lay down early. Master Malt asked him in jest, "Although your stomach is big, it is hollow; what is inside?" He replied, "It is enough to put hundreds of men like you inside." The two often playfully bantered like this.

---

²⁶This is also a metaphor for excellent liquor that glides smoothly down the throat.
²⁷The meaning here is that his abilities are poor.

After Master Malt had been stripped of office, a band of thieves rose in revolt between the districts of Che [齊] and Kyŏk [鬲].²⁸ The king ordered the revolt put down, but there was no suitable man to do so. Thus Master Malt was appointed marshal [元帥]. He commanded his charges strictly but shared their joys and sorrows as well. They poured water onto Su-sŏng Fortress [愁城, Anxiety Fortress] and took it in a single attack. After enjoying themselves for a long while, they returned, and the king appointed him as lord of Xiangdong [湘東侯].

Two years hence, Master Malt petitioned the king for his resignation:

> Your servant was born to a poor family, and because of my humble birth I was sold here and there. By chance, I met a sage-king, and you took me in with an open heart. You saved me from drowning and embraced me in magnanimity as great as pristine rivers and lakes. However, even when you gave me high positions, I could not help the country prosper. Because of my inability to be temperate, I returned to my hometown and stayed there in comfort; the dew had almost all dried up, but by chance some droplets remained. I dared to rejoice at the brightness of the sun and moon and strained the dregs [from the dewdrops]. It is the nature of things that a bowl full of water will be upset. Now the life of your humble servant, inflicted with burning thirst [痟渴病 *sogal-byŏng*], is in greater peril than a floating bubble. It is my wish that Your Majesty would dismiss me from office and allow me to live out my life in peace.

The king did not allow this, though, and dispatched an emissary to his home with medicines extracted from pine and cassia trees and irises. The master repeatedly declined this, and finally the king granted his request. He thus returned to his home and completed his destined allotment of life.

His young brother Hyŏn [賢, Turbid Liquor] took up office to gain two thousand *sŏk* [石]²⁹ of rice. Hyŏn's sons Ik [酖, Colored Liquor], Tu [酘, Double-Fermented Wine], Ang [醠, Unfiltered Rice Wine], and Ram [醂, Fruit Wine] drank peach-blossom nectar and found enlightenment as Daoist wizards [神仙 *sinsŏn*]. The third cousins of Chu [酎, a type of liquor]³⁰ Mi [醾, Moldy Liquor],

---

²⁸The character for Che is a homophone for 臍, meaning "the navel"; the character for Kyŏk is a homophone for 膈, meaning "diaphragm." Thus the uprising is between the navel and diaphragm.

²⁹A *sŏk* is equivalent to 0.18 cubic meters.

³⁰Chu presents problems regarding an exact translation—in an annotated translation of this narrative the translator does not provide a gloss for this character alone among all the various liquors that are listed. Moreover, the character is not one used nowadays. Thus, I have simply rendered it as "a type of liquor."

and Yŏm [醶, Sour Liquor] were all members of the P'yŏng [萍, Duckweed] family.

An envoy comments, "The Malt family was long a farming family. The master, with his lofty virtue and splendid talent, became the king's heart and stomach [心腹 *simbok*] and deliberated on the affairs of the country. His ability to please the king's mind is merit of great praise. The king's affection toward the master was great, and the public order of the country grew lax. Although calamity was brought upon his sons, he bore no regrets. In his twilight years he resigned his office and departed this world after his allotted time had passed. The *Book of Changes* states, 'Observe the working of things first and then act.' The master came close to this."

2.3. YI KYUBO, "OF BOATS AND BRIBES" (舟賂說 CHUROE-SŎL)

The following piece, also recorded in the *Anthology of Eastern Literature*,[31] reveals how corrupt the author held Koryŏ society to be. While Yi would eventually rise to the highest civil post in the land, he struggled mightily with poverty before finally being awarded a government post.

MP and M. Pihl

TRANSLATION

I was crossing over a river to the south, and there happened to be another boat crossing at that time. The boats were of the same size, had the same number of crewmen, and even the number of passengers and horses aboard was about the same. Then when I looked over again after a bit, the other boat, which was speeding as if in flight, had already reached the other side. The boat I was riding in was irresolute and did not advance. When I realized this, I asked the reason; another passenger replied, "In that boat, they treated the boatmen with liquor and thus the crew is rowing with all their might."

I could not but help feel ashamed and lamented to myself, "If the pace and operation of this small craft depend upon the presence or absence of a bribe, then what of the competition for an official post? Given how little money I have in hand, then no wonder I have been unable to obtain even a lowly post."

I record this as a reference for a future date.

---

[31] Recorded in the *Anthology of Eastern Literature*, *kwŏn* 96.

2.4. CH'OE CHA, "KIM KAEIN" (金盖仁)

This short story is recorded in the middle fascicle of *Supplementary Jottings in Idleness* (補閑集 *Pohan-jip*, 1254),[32] a compilation of tales, biographies, and poetry criticism written by Ch'oe Cha (崔滋, 1188–1260). This work is significant in that it represents the continued development of the importance of recording events in history and movement toward better defining literary activities in Koryŏ. Such writings date to Yi Illo (李仁老, 1152–1220) and Yi Kyubo (李奎報, 1168–1241) and represent the ongoing conversation concerning not only the study of poetics and the writings of the masters (both in China and in Korea) but also the expansion of fictional prose writings. In *Supplementary Jottings in Idleness* the combination of poetry criticism with more profane topics such as love affairs and tales of *kisaeng* (妓生, female entertainers) reveals the diverse pleasures of the literati class of Koryŏ. "Kim Kaein" is a didactic tale, one that helps reinforce notions of reciprocity and repaying favor.

MP

TRANSLATION

Kim Kaein [金盖仁] was from Kŏryŏng-hyŏn [居寧縣]. He had a dog that he loved greatly. One day when he went out, the dog followed behind. Drunken, Kaein had passed out in a field, when a wildfire broke out and approached him. Seeing this, the dog soaked its body in a nearby stream and rolled on the grasses surrounding Kaein to make them wet. The dog extinguished the flames but, its vital energy [氣 *ki*] spent, fell dead. When Kaein sobered up and saw what his dog had done, he was so moved that he composed a song to express his grief, made a grave, and buried the animal. He marked the grave by putting a stick in the ground. As the stick grew into a tree, that spot became known as the Dog's Tree [獒樹 Osu]. There is a poem-song titled "Song of the Dog's Grave" [犬墳曲 Kyŏn pun-gok] that was composed later and reads as follows:

> Although humans feel ashamed of being called an animal,
> They are apt to forget great favor.
> If they would not die for their master in danger,
> How could they compare with a dog?

---

[32] Recorded in *Supplementary Jottings in Idleness* [補閑集 *Pohan-jip*], *kwŏn chung*.

Duke Chinyang [晉陽公][33] ordered a visitor to his home to compose a record of this story and spread it throughout the world. Thus people of the world would know that when they receive favor, they should also return it.

2.5. CH'OE HAE, "THE TALE OF THE HERMIT OF MOUNT LION" (猊山隱者傳 YESAN ŬNJA-JŎN)

This is an autobiographical piece[34] that Ch'oe Hae (崔瀣, 1287–1340) uses to comment on the disdain official society had for one who spoke the truth and did not follow orders and social conventions blindly. The hermit's names in the following are renditions of Ch'oe's own name: when the initial syllable (*ha*) in Hagye and Hach'e is combined with the final vowel (*e*), we have Hae, and when the initial *ch* of Ch'anggoe is combined with the final *oe*, we have Ch'oe. While Ch'oe passed the civil service examination and even served as headmaster (大司成 *taesasŏng*) of the Royal Academy (成均館 Sŏnggyun'gwan), he was not one who could compromise with the political world and retired to a farm, where he put his efforts into scholarship and farming. The following piece aptly demonstrates Ch'oe's mastery of the biographical form (傳, K. *chŏn*, C. *chuan*) as he weaves social criticism and humor into this short work. This same form is later amplified in Chosŏn as full-fledged novels. The narrative is recorded in fascicle 100 of the *Anthology of Eastern Literature*.

MP

TRANSLATION

The hermit's name is Hagye [夏屆] or Hach'e [下逮], and his surname is Ch'anggoe [蒼槐]. His family has been living in the Older Dragon Kingdom [龍伯國 Yongbaek-kuk] for generations.[35] Originally his surname was not two characters, but it changed because the speech of the Eastern Barbarians [夷 I, referring to the peoples on the Korean Peninsula] is slow. Even in his childhood, the hermit understood the providence of heaven. When he started his studies, he did not bind himself to a single field. Rather, once he learned the purpose and direction, he moved on. By doing so, he did not completely finish any study because he intended to broaden his horizons instead of thrusting

---

[33] The reference is to Ch'oe I (崔怡, d. 1249).
[34] Recorded in the *Anthology of Eastern Literature*, *kwŏn* 100.
[35] The Older Dragon Kingdom is a mythical land of giants (巨人國 Kŏin-guk).

himself deep into a single subject. As he grew up, he resolved to raise his social status, but the world did not recognize him. This was owing to his character: he was not good at flattering, he enjoyed liquor, and, after a few cups, he would speak of others' good and evil, and he could not keep what he heard to himself. No wonder there were none who cherished or cared for him. Once, he was about to be appointed to a government post, but he was [ultimately] excluded and thrown out. His friends, who felt pity for him, tried to change his character by giving advice or even sometimes rebuking him, but that only failed. Well into his middle years, he regretted what he had done. Unfortunately, by that time he was already known as a person whom no one would be involved with, and he was no longer wanted by anyone. For his part, it did not change his mind toward the world. He said all along, "Those whom I had friendship with were all good people. Nonetheless, there are many whom I did not recognize. Surely it is difficult to be trusted by people." This was his strength as well as fault.

In his later life, thanks to a Buddhist monk of Lion Valley Temple [師子岬寺 Sajagap-sa],[36] he was able to borrow land to farm. He named the land Sufficiency [取足 Ch'wijok] and styled himself the hermit farmer of Mount Lion [猊山農隱 Yesan Nongŭn], and he put forth his precept:

Your land and your farm,
Bequeathed by the great favor of the Three Jewels,[37]
Whence Sufficiency came,
This should never be forgotten.

While for all his life the hermit had never cared for Buddhism, he was now working as a tenant farmer [for a Buddhist temple]. Thus, in swerving away from his lifelong path, he was deriding himself [with this poem].

2.6. YI SAEK, "THE TALE OF MR. PAK" (朴氏傳 PAK-SSI-JŎN)

Recorded in fascicle 100 of the *Anthology of Eastern Literature*,[38] this short piece by Yi Saek (李穡, 1328–1396) reveals aspects of the lives of the aristocratic families of the late Koryŏ period. The grandson who cannot, or will not, pass the civil service examination

---

[36] The characters 師子 (*saja*) can indicate, in Buddhism, a master and his disciple. However, in this case a homophone of the character 師 (*sa*) is that of 獅 (*sa*), meaning "lion."

[37] The Three Jewels (三寶 Sambo) of Buddhism refer to the pledge to take refuge in the Buddha, the dharma, and the sangha.

[38] Recorded in the *Anthology of Eastern Literature*, *kwŏn* 100.

becomes a wanderer in China. Yi himself was widely traveled, a prominent Confucianist, and a prolific poet and writer, leaving behind some six thousand poems.[39] He is credited with helping spread the reformed Confucianism of Zhu Xi (朱子, 1130–1200) in Koryŏ, but like many of the Confucianists of this period, he was not wholly against Buddhism.[40] While he enjoyed high official positions in his career, he clashed with the groups supporting Yi Sŏnggye (李成桂, the future King T'aejo 太祖, r. 1392–1398, of Chosŏn) and was ousted. His diverse writings reveal many aspects of life in late Koryŏ, such as customs and the realities of life during this time.

MP

TRANSLATION

Based on his literary skills and ethics, Kim Munjŏng [金文正], styled K'waehŏn [快軒], served as a minister during the reigns of Kings Ch'ungyŏl [忠烈, r. 1274–1308], Ch'ungsŏn [忠宣, r. 1308–1313], and Ch'ungsuk [忠肅, r. 1313–1330, 1332–1339]. He had seemingly supernatural powers [蓍龜 sigwi] to solve the difficulties of the country and served as a foundation for the edification of the country.[41]

Within his family, the rules were quite strict. Many of his sons passed the civil service examination. His eldest son died young. His second son, Tunhŏn [鈍軒], and third son, Songdang [松堂], both became state ministers and succeeded the family [tradition]. His son-in-law [surnamed] An held the position of deputy director at the chancellery for state affairs [政堂文學 Chŏngdang Munhak], and [his son-in-law surnamed] Pak was royal secretary [密直代言 Miljik Taeŏn]. They both gained their positions by passing the civil service examination. As [expected of] men of letters, three of An's grandsons passed the civil service examination, as did three of Pak's sons. Soyang [少陽], whose courtesy name was Chunggang [仲剛], was the third son of Pak. Even though he passed the National College Examination [成均試 Sŏnggyun-si],[42] he failed the state civil service examination many times. Thus, I feel pity for him and record his story here.

Chunggang had a lofty character, and he did not care for exegetical studies and usually did not read or study [in preparation] for the civil service

---

[39] Peter H. Lee, *History of Korean Literature*, 125.

[40] Cho, *Han'guk munhak t'ongsa*, 2:226.

[41] In the term *sigwi* (蓍龜), the first character indicates the stalk of a plant used in divinations, and the second refers to a tortoise, also used for divination in ancient China.

[42] This was the preliminary examination held at the National College (國子監 Kukchagam) and also known as the Kukchagam-si (國子監試).

examination. Thus he had little regard for those who had passed the exam. He never failed to arrive at the examination place bringing only a brush, paper, and a lamp, without even a book. He could not pass the examination since he laughed and jabbered while writing and left [the examination place] tossing his exam paper away and without even checking if he had done well or not. Early on he asked himself, "If a great man exists in a gloomy nook, what is the difference [between him] and a frog at the bottom of a well?" With that, he set off to the west and the capital [of Yuan]. He viewed the mountains and rivers, people, palaces, and fortresses and came to have an even greater discernment and more vigorous spirit. This was exactly what he had hoped for. The secretarial censor of the Western Xia dynasty [西夏 Xixia] met and cherished him and had him stay at his home. Although he lavished Chunggang with great hospitality and taught him in his spare time, Chunggang did not care for this. He stayed long in the northern region and became fluent in its language; when he went out and spoke with passers-by, they did not realize he was of the Eastern Country [i.e., Koryŏ]. Quite satisfied with himself, he thought of taking an official office, but he had no mentor. As his relative by marriage was the deputy minister [知事 Zhishi] of the Shannan Surveillance Commission [山南廉訪司 Shannan Lianfangsi], he was employed as an official. He came to Kaesŏng with a report on a victory in a battle, and I had just passed the civil service examination, and we met at an inn and had a great time for a few days. I have never met him since that time.

Ah, there is no means of knowing whether Chunggang is alive or dead. While our envoys travel to Jiankang [建康][43] every year, what is the reason that nobody has heard about him? Perhaps it is because he is far away and has no friends here in Kaesŏng. Or, he might think it embarrassing to meet people from his hometown while hanging around with commoners. Or, perhaps he cannot awaken since he has already passed away. How is it that there is no news of him although there have been many comings and goings for eight or nine years?!

I have not been close with Chunggang since childhood, but I became acquainted with him in Kaesŏng, and also Master Songjŏng [松亭] was an administrant of my examination [座主 chwaju]. How can I neglect his nephew? Thus, whenever I ate, I made certain Chunggang ate his fill, and when I dressed, he had no choice but to wear my clothes as well. Others thought him odd, but I treated him with care and respect. Others thought him dissolute, but I treated him with decorum. So Chunggang did not dare to become acquainted with me carelessly. The descendants of Duke K'waehŏn live well, but Chunggang went to China and has not come back, so posterity would not know him. He would

---

[43] An old name for Nanjing.

be completely lost and there would be nothing to pass down [about his life]. It is this I feel deeply sorry for, so I write this down roughly and wait for people to know him.

If Chunggang achieves great merit in China and is known in history as Pak from Koryŏ whose father and mother were so-and-so, this biography does not need to be passed down. If [he does] not, then this will be a good record for someone who intends to compile a genealogy of the Pak family.

PART II

Chosŏn Period Prose

On one level the dynastic change from Koryŏ to Chosŏn (朝鮮, 1392–1910) dramatically restructured society and the lives of the people, but on another level life in Chosŏn was very much a continuation of what had been in place for centuries. Among the elite, orthodox neo-Confucianism as articulated by the Chinese thinker Zhu Xi (朱子, 1130–1200) became the organizing principle of social, political, and intellectual life, and there was even legislation to reduce what the Confucian elites saw as the harmful influences of Buddhism and shamanism.[1] Despite this, these competing belief systems did not disappear and seem as strong at the end of the dynasty as they had been at the start. It is thus fair to state that the worldviews that guided the lives of the people at large did not change dramatically with the new dynasty but continued as they had for centuries. The emphasis on orthodox Confucianism did, however, affect elite life to a great degree, and in turn it impelled them to try to refashion society.

---

[1] For more on this, see Michael J. Pettid, *Unyŏng-jŏn: A Love Affair at the Royal Palace of Chosŏn Korea*, trans. Kil Cha and Michael J. Pettid (Berkeley: Institute of East Asian Studies, 2009), 7–10.

An already-existing emphasis on scholarship was strengthened in Chosŏn, as was the desire of the male ruling elite to shape life to match their vision of an orthodox Confucian society. The examination systems present in Koryŏ were expanded and enlarged, and the ultimate prize for upper-status males was to succeed in the civil service examination (文科 *mun'kwa*) and enter officialdom. Thus the education system in Chosŏn became the gateway to success for elite males.

At the pinnacle of the education system was the Royal Confucian Academy (成均館 Sŏnggyun'gwan), along with other government institutions such as the Four Schools (四學 Sahak) and the *hyanggyo* (鄉校), rural Confucian schools that were located at shrines devoted to the veneration of Confucius. In these schools, males studied the Confucian Classics, various writing styles in Literary Chinese, poetry, and other items deemed necessary by the current curriculum. There were also private institutions: the village schools (書堂 *sŏdang*), which provided an elementary education to young males, and the private academies (書院 *sŏwŏn*), which were organized around intellectual and factional affiliations and provided a higher-level education. Over the course of the dynasty some 812 examinations were held and over fifteen thousand men passed the civil service examination, with another forty-five thousand having passed the preliminary examination.[2]

Given this emphasis on education, it is no surprise that literary activity blossomed from early Chosŏn onward. For the elites in early Chosŏn the relationship between literature and fostering the Confucian way of life was seen as indivisible.[3] Poetry in particular was a means to conduct Confucian self-reflection and perfection of the self in accord with the principles of nature and the cosmos. At the same time, prose writings were necessary for the compilation of histories, official documents, and other correspondence. In addition, the development of fictional forms continued to grow as the short fictional works of the Koryŏ age transformed into full-fledged novels in Chosŏn.

It was the creation of the Korean script, *han'gŭl* (한글), to write vernacular Korean that truly led to the dramatic expansion of literary creations and the composer class. While upper-status males would predominantly use Literary Chinese for writing until the end of Chosŏn, the creation of the *han'gŭl* script allowed others a means to create their own literature. Thus the writer class expanded to include those of nonelite status and women, and we see a greater diversity in writing and worldviews as a result. While this result was not the aim

---

[2] Chŏng Nakch'an et. al., *Han'guk ŭi chŏnt'ong kyoyuk* [Traditional education in Korea] (Kyŏngsan: Yŏngnam taehakkyo ch'ulp'anbu, 2002), 282–83.

[3] Pak Hyŏnsuk, *Chosŏn kŏn'gukki ŭi munhak-ron* [Literary ideology in the age of the foundation of Chosŏn] (Seoul: Ilchogak, 1997), 12–13.

behind the creation of the vernacular script—which was to enhance Confucian governance—the new script inadvertently empowered a larger number of people to create literature.

We should, however, avoid the inclination to see creations in Literary Chinese and those in the Korean script as being completely separate. As mentioned in the introduction, the two forms interacted in many ways, including translation. It is more accurate to see the relationship as symbiotic, since the two modes of writing "maintained a relationship of mutual influence."[4] Adding to this relationship is the fact that the creators of these works—despite differing social, economic, geographical, and gender backgrounds—were participants in the larger culture of Chosŏn.

However, the creation of fiction was not encouraged by the elite. Indeed, like elsewhere in the world, the ruling elites of Chosŏn had a strong disdain for fictional works. Fictional works allowed for alternative worldviews and situations, spaces that were not necessarily permitted under the norms of a Confucian society. In the pages that follow we can note episodes that have ghostly encounters, women taking the lead in military affairs, and numerous sexual encounters that are beyond the pale of Confucian propriety. Of course, this helps demonstrate the complexity of Chosŏn society as the creators of many of these works were first and foremost Confucianists.

In the following pages we have included various types of writings composed in both Literary Chinese and the vernacular script. We have novels that were transmitted in both Literary Chinese and Korean and that were written by both known and unknown writers, short tales in the genre of "unofficial histories," diaries, and philosophical writings. In terms of gender, social status, historical context, and motivation, these works offer insight into the diversity of literary production in Chosŏn Korea.

MP and GNE

---

[4]Kim Hŭnggyu, "Chosŏn Fiction in Chinese," in *A History of Korean Literature*, ed. Peter H. Lee (Cambridge: Cambridge University Press, 2003), 265.

3. Early Chosŏn Short Fiction

3.1. KIM SISŬP, "AN ACCOUNT OF DRUNKEN MERRIMENT AT FLOATING JADE-GREEN PAVILION" (醉遊浮碧亭記 CH'WIYU PUBYŎKCHŎNG-GI)

This story is one of five extant pieces of short fiction by Kim Sisŭp (金時習, 1435–1493) collected under the title *New Tales of the Golden Turtle (Mountain)* (金鰲新話 *Kŭmo sinhwa*). Composed under the influence of *New Tales (Written While) Trimming the Wick* (剪燈新話 *Jiandeng xinhua*) by the Chinese writer Qu You (瞿佑, 1341–1427, or 1347–1433), Kim's collection was lost in Korea—most likely a consequence of the Japanese invasions of the late sixteenth century—but preserved in Japan in two textual lineages. One of these was the basis for four printings from the mid-seventeenth century to the end of the nineteenth century. Another text was discovered in the Dalian Library (大連圖書館) in China in 1999. It appears to have been donated in the early twentieth century by

---

This work was supported by the Academy of Korean Studies Grant funded by the Korean Government (MOE) (AKS-2011-AAA-2103).

Ōtani Kōzui (大谷光瑞, 1876–1948), a Japanese Buddhist priest, scholar, and explorer who was a collector of Ming and Qing Chinese fiction.[1]

The question of historical settings is significant in Kim's "An Account of Drunken Merriment at Floating Jade-Green Pavilion." As Kang-I Sun Chang has observed, "one of the special attractions of [Qu You's] *New Tales* is the contemporary setting of the narratives, which are [marked by] an overpowering sense of indignation at human suffering."[2] The suffering generated by the turmoil of the dynastic transition from Yuan (1271–1368) to Ming (1368–1644) found a parallel in Chosŏn during the reign of King Sejo (世祖, 1455–1468), who had seized the throne from his nephew, the boy king Tanjong (端宗, 1441–1457, r. 1452–1455). The course of Kim's life was altered by that event. A brilliant student, Kim seemed assured of future success as a Confucian official, but Sejo's usurpation of the throne made a mockery of the principles of Confucian political integrity. Kim instead became a Buddhist monk, thus paradoxically earning fame as a loyal Confucian subject to the deposed Tanjong.

Indeed, an emphasis on Confucian principles is particularly conspicuous in this story. The betrayal surrounding the fall of Old Chosŏn and the founding of Wiman Chosŏn in the second century B.C.E. is central to the story: after becoming a vassal of King Chun of Old Chosŏn, Wiman overthrew the king. In the story, these events are recounted by King Chun's daughter. As Dennis Wuerthner has observed, Kim draws on the founding of Wiman Chosŏn to criticize Sejo's own "obvious lack of legitimacy."[3] In this respect, Kim inserted into the story another significant detail when noting that the events it recounts occurred at the start of the Tianshun era (1457–1464) of the Ming dynasty. That is precisely when Sejo's rule was consolidated. An equally important concern is found in the meeting between the protagonist and King Chun's daughter. It is easy to see this simply as an enjoyable element in making the case against Sejo, but Kim's writings— as well as the writings of his contemporaries—show that there was very real concern over how the living ought to orient themselves toward otherworldly beings.

GNE

---

[1] On the textual history of *Golden Turtle*, see Ch'oe Yongch'ŏl, *Kŭmo sinhwa-ŭi p'anbon* [Woodblock printings of *Kŭmo sinhwa*] (Seoul: Kukhak charyowŏn, 2003), 9–26.

[2] Kang-I Sun Chang, "Literature of the Early Ming to Mid-Ming (1375–1572)," in *The Cambridge History of Chinese Literature*, ed. Kang-I Sun Chang and Stephen Owen (Cambridge: Cambridge University Press, 2010), 8. Available from Cambridge Histories Online, http://dx.doi.org/10.1017/CHOL9780521855594.003, accessed July 30, 2014.

[3] Dennis Wuerthner, "The *Kŭmo sinhwa*—Product of a Cross-Border Diffusion of Knowledge between Ming China and Chosŏn Korea during the Fifteenth Century," *Sungkyun Journal of East Asian Studies* 12, no. 2 (October 2012): 178.

TRANSLATION

P'yŏngyang was the capital of Old Chosŏn [古朝鮮].[4]

After King Wu [武王] of the Zhou [周] dynasty vanquished the state of Shang [商, or 殷 Yin], he called on Kija [箕子]. Kija informed King Wu of the Fundamental Principles of Heaven and Earth and the Nine Laws [洪範九疇, C. Hongfan Jiuchou, K. Hongbŏm Kuju). Therefore, King Wu invested Kija with this land and did not take him as his subject.[5]

The famous scenic spots of P'yŏngyang are Embroidered Silk Mountain [錦繡山 Kŭmsu-san], Phoenix Heights [鳳凰臺 Ponghwang-dae], Fine-Patterned Silk Island [綾羅島 Nŭngna-do], Unicorn Grotto [麒麟窟 Kirin-gul], Morning-Sky Rock [朝天石 Choch'ŏn-sŏk], and Walnut Tree South Knoll [楸南墟 Ch'unam-hŏ], and each is a vestige of antiquity. Everlasting Brightness Temple [永明寺 Yŏngmyŏng-sa] and Floating Jade-Green Pavilion [浮碧亭 Pubyŏkchŏng] are also among those relics.

Yŏngmyŏng-sa is actually King Tongmyŏng's [東明王] Nine-Story Palace [九梯宮 Kuje-gung].[6] It is located some twenty *li* northeast of the castle walls. Looking down on the long river with a level field seen in the distance, the view is endless. Truly it is a place of outstanding scenery.

At sunset, splendid sightseeing boats and merchant vessels anchor at a fishing spot amid a luxuriant willow grove beyond the Gate of Great Unity [大同門 Taedong-mun]. When people stay there for fun, invariably they go upstream and return after visiting Yŏngmyŏng Temple and Pubyŏk Pavilion at their pleasure, having enjoyed themselves to their hearts' content.

---

[4]This translation is based on the original literary Chinese text in Sim Kyŏngho, trans. and ed., *Maewŏldang Kim Sisŭp: Kŭmo sinhwa* [Maewŏldang Kim Sisŭp: New tales of Golden Turtle (Mountain)] (Seoul: Hongik ch'ulp'ansa, 2000), 266–71; hereafter abbreviated SKH. The detailed notes in SKH are often cited in the following, but some questions have been clarified through reference to Yi Kawŏn and Hŏ Kyŏngjin, trans. and ed., *Kŭmo sinhwa: Maewŏldang-jip* [New tales of Golden Turtle (Mountain): Collected writings of Maewŏldang (i.e., Kim Sisŭp)] (Seoul: Hanyang ch'ulp'an, 1995); hereafter abbreviated Yi/Hŏ. In a few instances, it has been necessary to refer to other photoreproductions of premodern texts; these are given a full citation in the first instance, followed by a shortened citation as needed.

[5]These events occurred in the eleventh century B.C.E. and are discussed subsequently in the main text. In general, this presentation suggests that Kim Sisŭp accepted beliefs about early Korean history current during his era. For additional information, see SKH, 152n2, 155n26.

[6]King Tongmyŏng is the putative founder of the state of Koguryŏ (37 B.C.E.–668 C.E.). As SKH, 134, makes explicit in the Korean translation, it seems that the temple was on the site of the palace built by Tongmyŏng.

South of Pubyŏk Pavilion, there are stairways made of trimmed stone. The left side is called Blue Cloud Staircase [靑雲梯 Ch'ŏngun-je], and the right side is called White Cloud Staircase [白雲梯 Paegun-je].[7] Since writings have been carved into the stone and rock posts are erected there, it has become an attraction for people who like such things.

At the start of the Tianshun era,[8] there lived in Songgyŏng [松京] a son from a wealthy family, called Young Master Hong [洪生 Hong Saeng]. He was youthful and handsome, and in addition to possessing good looks, he also wrote well. During the Harvest Moon Festival, he and his companions wanted to have some fun with the ladies at Kisŏng [箕城, i.e., P'yŏngyang], and they moored their boat along the riverside.[9] The noted women from the pleasure quarters of the city all came out and let their desire be known through their winking eyes.

In the city lived Hong's old friend, Young Master Yi, who kindly held a banquet in Hong's honor. When Hong was happy and drunk, he returned to his boat. But it was a chilly night and he was unable to sleep. Suddenly he thought of Zhang Ji's [張繼] poem "Nighttime Mooring by Maple Bridge" [楓橋夜泊] and was overcome by a sense of elegance.[10] So he got aboard a small rowboat, and, with the moon above his head, he rowed upstream. Once his interest was spent, he returned and ended up at the bottom of Floating Jade-Green Pavilion.

He moored the boat in a cluster of reeds, walked up the stairway, leaned against the balustrade, and, gazing about, loudly recited a poem in a clear voice. At that moment, the color of the moon was like the sea, the sheen of the waves like white silk, and as wild geese honked atop the sands by the water's edge, the cranes were startled by the dew of the pines. With great solemnity, it was as if he were ascending to the Palace of the Moon or the Abode of Immortals.

He turned and gazed upon the old capital, and with mist covering the white-painted battlements while waves pounded against the abandoned fortress, he

---

[7]With the exception of Ch'unam-hŏ, the locations and histories of these places are known through other texts. See SKH, 151–53nn1, 4–10, 12–13.

[8]The Tianshun era refers to the reign dates of a Ming Chinese emperor, 1457–1464.

[9]"Have some fun with the ladies" essentially means that they intend to seduce the ladies, and SKH, 135, translates it thus. In the original, this is expressed euphemistically through a quotation from the *Book of Songs* that refers to the seduction of women by men. For additional information, see SKH, 154n19.

[10]Zhang Ji (776–ca. 829) was a Tang poet, and the poem in question has broad relevance here since it depicts sleeplessness and a traveler aboard a boat. See also SKH, 154nn20–21.

was struck by the grief of "barley growing upon the site of Yin's devastation" [麥秀殷墟][11] and thereupon composed six poems:[12]

[1]

It is hard to endure chanting a poem
    while ascending P'ae River Pavilion.
Grief-stricken sobbing, the flowing of the river—
    a gut-wrenching sound.
The ancient capital already conceals
    the might of the dragon and tiger;
But the ruined castle still carries
    the form of the phoenix.
Upon the sandbanks the moon is bright,
    confusing the returning geese;
On the garden grasses the mist settles,
    dotting the fireflies with dew.
The scene is desolate—
    human affairs change.
Within Cold Mountain Temple,
    The bell rings out.

[2]

At the royal palace, the autumn vegetation—
    dreary and dense.
On the winding stone pathway, clouds spread out—
    the path ever more bewildering.

---

[11] Much of the preceding passage beginning from "once his interest was spent" is built on literary allusions (SKH, 154nn22–25). The most important of these is the last and refers to a song that Kija is said to have sung after seeing the destruction of Yin wrought by King Wu of the Zhou dynasty (SKH, 155n26).

[12] For ease of reading, the individual poems have been numbered. In addition, for the sake of consistency and spacing, each line of poetry has been broken into two lines in the translation, with the second portion indented. When the notes refer to "a line," this indicates the original text and appears as two lines in the translation; likewise, when the notes refer to "a couplet," this appears as four lines in the translation.

At the pleasure quarters' old grounds,
    wild pickpurse plants become as one;
And by the parapet with the setting moon,
    night ravens crow.
Fine splendid things
    end up as dust;
And the lonesome deserted castle,
    overgrown with brambles.
Merely the river's waves
    still murmur,
Roiling toward the west,
    where the river meets the sea.

[3]

The water of the P'ae River—
    bluer than indigo.
The vicissitudes of ages long past—
    a bitterness hard to endure.
A well with an ornamented railing, run dry,
    hung with ivy;
A stone dais, moss eaten,
    concealed by tamarisk and camphor trees.
In a strange place with glorious scenery,
    reciting a thousand poems;
Deep emotions for the ancient kingdom,
    getting merry with wine.
With the moon bright, leaning against the parapet,
    unable to sleep.
The night is deep, with fragrant cassias
    drooping down.

[4]

The harvest moon's light
    truly is so lovely,
But one look at the deserted castle—
    utterly disappointed and unhappy.
At the grounds of Kija's shrine,
    the tall trees are old;

On the walls of Tan'gun's sanctuary,
  ivy is climbing up.
The heroes are lonely—
  where are they now?
The grasses and trees are faint—
  "How many years has it been?" I ask.
All that remains—
  a perfect harvest moon from days past.
Clear moonlight, a flowing color
  flashes against my clothes.

[5]

The moon appears over East Mountain,
  and the magpies take flight.
The night is deep, and the cold dew
  piles upon my clothes.
A thousand years' civilization—
  culture and ethics, vanished;
Ten thousand ages' mountains and rivers—
  the castle, no longer real.
The sage-ruler reigns in heaven
  and now will not return;
Idle chatter scatters through the world,
  and in the end, who will help?[13]
Of the golden coach and unicorn-horses,
  there are no tracks.
On the royal carriageway, thick with weeds,
  a monk returns alone.

[6]

The courtyard vegetation, by autumn chill and jade dew,
  is made to wither away.
Blue Cloud Bridge faces
  White Cloud Bridge.[14]

---

[13] "The sage-ruler... help?": The "sage-ruler" refers to King Tongmyŏng; see SKH, 137, 156n37, and Yi/Hŏ, 73n15.

[14] This seems to refer to the two "ladders" or "staircases" mentioned previously.

> The Sui emperor's soldiers followed
>   the crying rapids;
> His son's soul became
>   a sorrowful cicada.[15]
> On the monarch's roadway, mist covers over—
>   the lovely royal carriage halted;
> At the temporary palace, pines have collapsed—
>   the night bell swings.
> Climbing high, I compose a song,
>   but with whom to enjoy it?
> The moon is clear, the breeze is fresh,
>   and my pleasure not yet exhausted.

With his compositions complete, clapping his hands, he stood up, danced, and dawdled there. For each line he chanted, there were several sounds of sobbing. Though without the delights of tapping the side of the boat with the blowing of a bamboo flute for accompaniment, in his inmost heart he felt pangs of sadness sharp enough "to make dance the dragons in hidden grottoes and bring to tears widows in lonesome boats [舞幽壑潛蛟, 泣孤舟之嫠婦]."[16]

By the time he had finished chanting and was about to return, it was already well past midnight. Then suddenly there was a sound of footsteps coming from the west. He thought to himself, "A monk from the temple heard the noise I made and, alarmed, is coming here" and sat down to wait for the monk to arrive. What he saw, instead, was a beautiful woman. Maidservants accompanied her on the left and right, one carrying a jade-handled horsetail whisk and the other carrying a fan of fine silk, and with a solemn manner so proper, her appearance was like some chaste maiden from a noble family.

He descended the staircase and, hiding from her in a recess in the wall, watched what she was doing. The beautiful woman, leaning against the south balustrade, gazing at the moon, and softly chanting a verse, was elegant in deportment and dignified in etiquette. The maidservants brought her a

---

[15] "The Sui emperor's . . . cicada." This couplet refers to the victory of the Koguryŏ armies led by Ŭlchi Mundŏk after Sui (581–618) attacked Koguryŏ in 612. In 604, Yang Di (r. 604–618), then crown prince, killed his father, Wen Di (r. 581–604), and it was during Yang Di's rule that the Sui army was put to rout by Ŭlchi Mundŏk at the Ch'ŏngch'ŏn (or Salsu) River. Kim Sisŭp seems to attribute to the armies of the father, Wen Di, a defeat actually suffered by the armies of his son, Yang Di (see SKH, 137, 156n40, and Yi/Hŏ, 73nn17–18).

[16] This passage draws heavily on the central portion of the famous "Poetic Exposition on Red Cliff" by Su Shi (1037–1101); see SKH, 156n43. In English, see Stephen Owen, ed. and trans., *An Anthology of Chinese Literature: Beginnings to 1911* (New York: Norton, 1996), 292–94.

cloud-embroidered silk cushion, and after composing herself, she sat down and spoke in a bright voice. "In this place there was someone chanting poems. Where is he now? I am not a lovely of the flowers and moon, nor a lotus-stepping beauty.[17] I had hoped to experience this night—with the high heavens stretching into infinity, the sky clear and clouds dispelled, the ice wheel [冰輪][18] in flight and the Milky Way bright, the cassia fruit falling and this magnificent tower so cold—passing cups of wine and chanting poems while leisurely chatting about this charming scene. So what is to be done with this lovely moonlit night?"

Young Master Hong was at once frightened and delighted, and as he hesitated, he let out a small cough. The maidservants came over to look for the source of the sound and said, "Our lady requests your presence." Respectful and cautious, he came forward and bowed and knelt down, sitting on his knees. The lady, however, was not overly courteous to him and merely said, "You too climbed up here." The maidservants quickly shielded her with a short folding screen, and only one half-face looked at the other. Quietly and gently she said, "The poems that you were chanting, what were the words? Say them for me." He recited the poems, one by one, from memory. She smiled faintly and said, "You certainly are a person who can be joined in discussions of poetry."

Thereupon she ordered her maidservants to pour the first round of wine. The dainty morsels of food [served with the wine] were unlike anything of the human world. He tasted them. But they were hard and unyielding, and he could not eat them. The wine also was bitter, and he was unable to drink it.[19] She smiled sweetly and said, "How could a humble scholar know about White Jade Wine [白玉醴 Paegok-rye] and Red Youngling Dragon Jerky [紅虯脯 Honggyu-p'o]?" She then commanded her maidservants, "You are to go quickly to Spirit-Guarded Temple [神護寺 Sinho-sa], ask a monk for a bit of rice, and return." (At the temple there is a *nahan* [羅漢] statue.)[20] The maidservants did as told, leaving for the temple. In a short time, they got the rice and returned. But it was nothing other than rice. And there were no side dishes to serve with it. So again

---

[17]The phrases "a lovely of the flowers and moon" and "lotus-stepping beauty" are drawn from stories of women in the classical Chinese literary tradition (SKH, 157nn45–46). The first embodied the idea that ghosts were able to approach humans whose minds and spirits were deficient.

[18]"Ice wheel" (K. *pingnyun*, C. *binglun*) is an expression for the moon.

[19]"The dainty morsels . . . drink it" is based on Yi/Hŏ, fol. 22, a, lines 9–10, since the punctuation given in SKH, 268, seems somewhat confusing.

[20]*Nahan* (or arhat) is a Buddhist saint or sage. This note is uniformly embedded in smaller print in the various versions of the text. SKH, 157n50, notes that Spirit-Guarded Temple was located not far from P'yŏngyang.

she commanded her maidservants, "You are to go to Wine Crag [酒巖 Chu-am], get some side dishes, and return." (At the bottom of the crag there is a marsh, and a dragon lives there.)[21] Not long thereafter they returned with broiled carp. Young Master Hong ate the food. By the time he was finished eating, she had already followed his poems, thereby matching what was in his mind. She had copied hers down on cassia paper,[22] and she directed the maidservants to place these in front of him. The poems said,

[1]

At East Pavilion tonight,
 the moon shines so bright.
In refined conversation—
 how to handle heart-piercing laments?
The trees' color is hazy—
 a green parasol opened up;
The river's flow glitters—
 a soft silk skirt stretched out.
Time suddenly passes by,
 like flying birds;
Worldly affairs always in tumult,
 like rising waves.
About these heartfelt emotions on this night,
 who can understand?
Several soundings, the bells and gongs,
 come across the misty tangled greenery.

[2]

From the ancient castle's south prospect,
 the P'ae River is vivid:
The water blue, the sands luminous,
 with a flock of honking geese.

---

[21] As just preceding, this note is uniformly embedded in smaller print in the various versions of the text. According to SKH, 157n51, Wine Crag is located not far from P'yŏngyang and is so called because wine is believed to have flowed out of the cracks in the rock.

[22] The term "cassia [tree] paper" (桂箋 kye-jŏn), as SKH, 157n52, notes, seems to refer to some sort of excellent paper, but what it is exactly is not known.

The unicorn chariot has not come,
    and the dragon has already gone;
The phoenix wind has been exhausted,
    and the soil turned to a grave.
In the mountain mist, about to rain,
    composing poems till perfectly complete;
At the rustic temple, with no one about,
    drinking wine till half drunk.
It is so hard to gaze upon
    the copper camel buried in the brambles:[23]
Traces of a thousand years
    turn into floating clouds.

[3]

At the plants' roots—
    the tear-choked, crying cold cicadas.
Atop the high pavilion,
    thoughts grow vague.[24]
Cut rain and ruined clouds—
    grieving over past affairs;
Fallen flowers and flowing waters—
    keenly aware of time.
Waves heighten autumn's signs—
    as the river flows to the sea, its sound so grand;
The tower immersed in the river's center—
    with the moonlight so clear.
This is the spot of remnants of civilization
    from past ages;
And the weed-covered castle and thinning trees
    torment one's own truest heart.

---

[23] The "copper . . . brambles" is a well-known phrase found in the *Jin shu* [Documents of the Jin dynasty (265–420)]. The "copper camel" sat near the royal palace in Luoyang, and one day, someone saw it and uttered the phrase, which foretold the destruction of the capital. For more detail, see SKH, 157–58n54, and Yi/Hŏ, 77n27.

[24] "Thoughts grow vague" seems to emphasize the loss of conjugal love. This is made plain in the following phrase "cut rain and ruined clouds," which is based on "clouds and rain," the commonplace metaphor for sexual intercourse.

[4]

In front of Embroidered Silk Mountain,
  embroidered silk is piled high.[25]
The riverside maples cast shadows over[26]
  the old fortress's remote corners.
Dum-dum . . . from where does this come?—
  sounds of autumn laundering are wearying;
Splish-splash . . . a lone sound—
  as the fisherman's rowboat returns.[27]
An old tree leans on the crag,
  with clutching, climbing ivy;
Broken stone monuments lie across the grass,
  with scattered lichen.
Leaning upon the balustrade, in silence,
  pitying past events.
The glow of the moon, the sound of the waves,
  are but sadness.

[5]

Some small distant stars
  dot the Jade Capital.[28]
The Milky Way is luminous,
  the moon distinct.
Now I know good things
  are all empty things;
And it is difficult to foretell whether
  a future life will match this life.

---

[25] SKH, 141, interprets "embroidered silk is piled high" as referring to piles of autumn leaves.

[26] "Cast shadows" (掩映 ŏmyŏng) is an ambiguous image. Both SKH, 141, and Yi/Hŏ, 78, take this to mean that the maples illuminate the hidden recesses of the old fortress, or city. But this focus on light seems excessive. The maples have lost their leaves, and the light they let through casts shadows.

[27] Each line of this couplet is built on an onomatopoeic device. The sound of pounding on cloth while doing laundry is *chŏngdong* (C. *dingdong*), and here this sound explicitly refers to laundry done in autumn. *Aenae* (C. *ainai*) refers to the sound of rowing a boat.

[28] "Jade Capital" (玉京, K. Okkyŏng, C. Yujing) comes from Daoism and refers to the abode of the Lord of Heaven, or the Creator. See also SKH, 158n57.

With a jug of good wine,
    it is right to drink until merry;
As to the law of wind and dust [風塵三尺],[29]
    pay it no mind.
Heroes, generation after generation,
    become specks of dust,
And in the world idly remains
    their posthumous fame.

[6]

How is this night?—
    This night is about to end:
By the battlement, the wan morning moon
    is at this moment drooping down.[30]
You now think that
    the two worlds are separate,
But having accidentally met me
    instead will wager a thousand days' joy.[31]
At this magnificent tower on the river,
    people will part;
From beautiful trees in front of the stone steps,
    dew starts to drip.
I want to know after this
    where we will chance to meet:
When peaches ripen on Pengqiu,
    and the blue sea dries up.[32]

---

[29] This expression has Buddhist implications. "Dust" (K. *chin*, C. *chen*) refers to the defilements that, as a rule, impede one's attainment of salvation. However, it is ultimately suggested here that one should live for today, valuing the present and the enjoyment therein.

[30] The punctuation used here follows the structure of the original (i.e., question, response, and description and verification), and this translation differs from SKH, 142, and Yi/Hŏ, 79.

[31] "You now . . . days' joy": this couplet is extremely problematic, as evident in the different translations in SKH, 142, and Yi/Hŏ, 79. In turn, this translation is very different.

[32] Pengqiu (蓬丘, K. Ponggu) is another name for Penglai (K. Pongnae), an island in Chinese myth where immortals live and peaches ripen once every three thousand years (see also SKH, 158n61).

54   PART II: CHOSŎN PERIOD PROSE

Young Master Hong received her poems and was happy, but still he was worried that she would leave and therefore wanted to use conversation to make her stay. "May I be so bold as to ask about your surname and family lineage?" he inquired. The beautiful lady sighed and answered, "I am a descendent of the enfeebled king of [the state of] Ŭn [C. Yin] and am a daughter of the Ki [C. Ji] clan. My ancestor was invested with this place, and with respect to etiquette and music [禮樂, K. *yeak*, C. *liyue*] and laws and punishments [典刑, K. *chŏnhyŏng*, C. *dianxing*], he completely followed the teachings of T'ang [湯], and by instructing the people using the eight items [of law], civilization was brilliant for more than a thousand years.[33]

"But one day the fortune of the state began to wane, and circumstances grew difficult, with disaster and catastrophe suddenly coming [upon the state], and my father suffered defeat at the hands of a piece of common trash [匹夫] and lost his throne and country.[34] Wiman seized the moment and stole my father's throne, and the accomplishments of [Old] Chosŏn disintegrated. In poor health and with everything having come to ruin, I was intending nothing more than to guard my chastity and honor and wait for death. But then suddenly there appeared a spiritlike person [神人][35] who comforted me and said, 'I was indeed the founder of this state. After my reign, I entered an island in the sea and became an immortal [仙, K. *sŏn*, C. *xian*], one who does not die, and already [I have lived] for several thousand years. Can you accompany me to the abode of celestial beings [紫府], the residence of immortals [玄都], and take pleasure in joyful activities?'[36] I said, 'Yes.' Finally, hand in hand, he led me off, and upon arriving at where he dwelled, he constructed a separate building for me and had me take the medicine of immortality from the Black Continent [玄洲].[37] I took this medicine for several days. Then suddenly I felt that my body was light and that my spirit [氣, K. *ki*, C. *qi*] was strong. With sounds of cracking and tearing, my bones seemed as if transformed by it.[38] After that, I followed my whims, sauntering to

---

[33] T'ang (C. Tang) was the founder of the Shang dynasty (ca. 1700–1045 B.C.E.), the latter part of which was known also as Yin. In identifying herself as a daughter of the Ki clan, she is referring to Kija. This recapitulates the historical background given at the start of the story.

[34] The "piece of common trash" (匹夫, K. *p'ilbu*, C. *pifu*) is Wiman, founder of the state of Wiman Chosŏn, who is named in the following. The lady's deceased father is King Chun (準王) of Old Chosŏn; he was overthrown by Wiman.

[35] As SKH, 158n65, notes, the "spiritlike person" (K. *sinin*, C. *shenren*) refers to Tan'gun.

[36] The "abode of celestial beings, the residence of immortals" (K. *chabu hyŏndo*, C. *zifu xuandu*) is redundant in the original. The terms are drawn from Daoism. (See SKH, 158nn66–67.)

[37] "Black Continent" (K. *Hyŏnju*, C. *Xuanzhou*) is one of the ten continents where immortals were said to live.

[38] "Transforming the bone" (換骨, K. *hwan kol*, C. *huan gu*) comes from Daoist teachings on the attainment of immortality: one eats certain medicines that transform one's bones, thus

the furthest reaches of heaven and strolling about the entire world—the Realms of Immortals, the Ten Continents, and the Three Islands.[39] There was no place I did not visit, nothing I did not see.

"Then one day, when the autumn sky was clear, the firmament bright, and the moonlight like water, I looked up at the 'toad and cassia tree' [蟾桂][40] and lightheartedly wished to go off far away. Finally, I ascended up to the moon, entered the Storehouse of Expansive Cold and Clear Emptiness [廣寒清虛之府],[41] and had an audience with the Goddess of the Moon [嫦娥, K. Hanga] within the Crystal Palace [水晶宮, K. Sujŏng-gung]. She appealed to my unyielding feminine virtue and literary skill, and said, 'The realm of immortals of the lower world, though said to be a blessed land, is but wind and dust, so how can it compare to the excellence of traipsing about the blue heavens mounted upon a white phoenix, drawing the fine fragrance from the red cassia, wearing the crisp light from the azure sky, merrymaking at your leisure in the Jade Capital, and bathing in the Silver River [i.e., Milky Way]?'[42] Thereupon, she ordered that I serve as the maidservant in charge of the incense table and be in attendance at her side, and such pleasure cannot be described in words.

"But suddenly this evening, I had thoughts of my birthplace, and gazing down upon the ephemera, I looked over my native land. The scenery was the same, but the people were no longer so. The brightly shining moon had concealed the traces of smoke and dust,[43] and the white dew had cleansed the piles of clotted earth and heaped vegetation. So I took my leave, descended from the clear heavens, and gently came down from high above. I paid obeisance to the tombs of my ancestors, and I also wanted to amuse myself once at this riverside pavilion, so as to pacify those feelings of my inmost heart. As luck would have it, I then

---

making one an immortal. "With sounds of cracking and tearing" (磔磔然, K. ch'aekch'aek yŏn, C. zhezhe ran) is an adverbial expression describing that process; see SKH, 143, and Yi/Hŏ, 80. This usage is found in the *New Tales [Written While] Trimming the Wick [Jiandeng xinhua]* by Qu You (1341–1427). See Chŏng Yongsu, trans. and ed., *Chŏndŭng sinhwa kuhae* [Annotated *Jiandeng xinhua*] (Seoul: P'urŭn sasangsa, 2003), 509/76, lines 10–11; for Chŏng's Korean translation and additional comments, see 285.

[39]The "Ten Continents" (K. Sipchu, C. Shizhou) and "Three Islands" (K. Samdo, C. Sandao) refer to places where immortals were said to dwell.

[40]The "toad and cassia tree" is a name for the moon. The basis for this expression is explained in n. 42.

[41]"Storehouse of Expansive Cold and Clear Emptiness" (K. Kwanghan-ch'ŏnghŏ Chi-bu, C. Guanghan-qingxu Zhi-fu) is composed of two elements, Expansive Cold, which in Daoism is a name for a palace of immortals, and Clear Emptiness, which refers to the Moon Palace. As used here, the entire expression seems to refer to the palace in the moon realm. See SKH, 159n74, and the text cited therein; see also Yi/Hŏ, 81n45.

[42]According to legend, there are sweet osmanthus or cassia trees on the moon; see also n. 56.

[43]"Smoke and dust" (煙塵, K. yŏnjin) describes a battlefield. See SKH, 159n81.

met a man of letters, which made me feel both happy and bashful, and suddenly I followed your jadelike compositions and dared to show you my own foolish writings. Yet it is not that I dared to be eloquent, but merely that I wanted thereby to show my own truest feelings."

Young Master Hong bowed twice deeply, lowering his head to the ground, and said, "The lower world is foolish and unenlightened, and its sweet tastes and vegetation alike rot, so how could I imagine that I would be with a lady of the heavenly world who is descended from a king and dare wish to exchange poems with her?"[44] He then looked once over her poems that had been placed before him, and he committed them to memory. Again, he bent forward and prostrated himself and said, "My foolishness, ignorance, and obstacles because of crimes of my previous lives are deep and many, and I was unable to taste all the delicious foods of the immortals.[45] But how lucky it is that I should know a bit about calligraphy and decipher some of the meaning of your splendid songs[46]—it is truly a marvelous thing! The four beauties are hard to possess,[47] so might I request that you once more take this riverside pavilion on an autumn night with a full moon as the topic, match the rhyme forty times,[48] and teach it to me?"

The beautiful woman nodded her head in assent to his request. She moistened her writing brush with ink, and at once whirling it about, with clouds and mist rolling over each other, she quickly wrote out a poem that said,

> The moon white—
> > the riverside pavilion at night;
> A high distant sky—
> > jadelike dewdrops flow.
> The clear moonlight
> > is immersed in the Milky Way;

---

[44] "Sweet tastes" (甘, K. *kam*, C. *gan*): here he seems to comprehend that he could not appreciate the food offered to him by the lady earlier because he is of the "foolish and unenlightened" lower world.

[45] Here again there is a mix of Buddhist and Daoist concepts. The phrase "obstacles because of crimes of my previous lives" (宿障, K. *sukchang*, C. *suzhang*) comes from Buddhism and suggests why he could not appreciate the food eaten by Daoist immortals that the lady had offered him.

[46] "Splendid songs" is, literally, "cloud songs" (雲謠, K. *unyo*, C. *yunyao*). See SKH, 159n83, for the origin of the expression.

[47] This alludes to the famous Chinese poet Xie Lingyun (385–433), who said that a pleasant day, beautiful scenery, a joyful heart, and delightful things are the "four beauties" (四美, K. *sami*, C. *simei*) and that it is difficult to have them all at once. See SKH, 159n84.

[48] "Match the rhyme forty times" (押四十韻, K. *ap sasip un*, C. *ya sishi yun*) refers to the use of rhyming characters at the final position of even-numbered lines. This foreshadows the following poem, which consists of eighty lines with five characters per line.

And heaven's brightness
  obscures the parasol and catalpa trees.
White and clean—
  The Triple Thousand World],⁴⁹
And ever so beautiful—
  this twelve-story tower.
Thin wispy clouds
  without half a speck [of dust];
A lightly blowing wind
  wipes clean this pair of eyes.
Glimmering waves
  follow the flowing waters;
Dim and indistinct—
  seeing off a departing boat.
Ably seen through
  the gaps in a stalk door—
The partially reflected
  reed-flower islet.
Like hearing
  the melody of the "Rainbow Skirts";
As if seeing
  the jade ax's luster.⁵⁰
Oyster pearls
  produce the Cowry Palace;
Rhinoceros halos
  overturn the mundane world.⁵¹

---

⁴⁹"Triple Thousand World" (三千界, K. Samch'ŏn'gye, C. Sanqianjie) refers to the realm of the Buddha. It consists of one billion small worlds.

⁵⁰"Rainbow Skirts" (霓裳, K. yesang, C. nichang) can refer to the clothes worn by immortals. It is also the partial name of the tune "Coats of Feathers, Rainbow Skirts" that is associated with the Tang Chinese emperor Xuanzong (r. 712–756) and his Prized Consort, Lady Yang (see Owen, Anthology, 443, 448, 450, 453). According to legend, the tune was created by Xuanzong after he accompanied a Daoist priest named Gongyuan on a trip to the Moon Palace; Gongyuan is mentioned later in the poem. Similarly, "jade ax" (玉斧, K. okpu, C. yufu) can refer to an ax carried by immortals or spirits.

⁵¹"Cowry Palace" (貝闕, K. P'aegwŏl, C. Beique) is the palace of the Dragon King, which is decorated with purple cowry shells, and "rhinoceros halo" (犀暈, K. sŏhun, C. xiyun) alludes to the "Rhapsody of Dongping" [Dongping fu] by Ruan Ji (210–263) of Wei (220–265), one of the Three Kingdoms of China (220–280) (SKH, 160nn91–92). The passage in "Rhapsody" refers to a merchant who sells hats and goes to Yue (i.e., Vietnam) only to discover that the people there instead "wear rhinoceros horn [head pieces]" (Donald Holzman, *Poetry and Politics: The Life*

Wishing to be with Zhiwei,
 making merry,
And ever following Gongyuan
 on journeys.[52]
The chill of moonbeams
 startles the magpies of Wei;
And the shadowy nights
 make the oxen of Wu gasp for air.[53]
Hazy and vague above the
 green mountain village;
Full and round off in
 a corner of the blue sea.[54]
Being with you—
 a key to open the lock;
Riding upon the excitement—
 a hook to hold up the bamboo blind.[55]
The day Master Li
 put down his wine cup,

---

and Works of Juan Chi A.D. 210–263 [Cambridge: Cambridge University Press, 1976], 43). The origin of the reference is the *Zhuangzi*, which mentions the hat salesman and then abruptly turns to a ruler who forgot about his worldly realm after meeting hermits. See Victor H. Mair, *Wandering on the Way: Early Taoist Tales and Parables of Chuang Tzu* (Honolulu: University of Hawai`i Press, 1998), 7.

[52] As with Gongyuan (公遠), this reference to Zhiwei (知微) is taken from a legend associated with the Tang dynasty (618–907). It is said that Zhiwei practiced the magical arts of Daoism and was able to clear the rain so that he and his friends could view the moon. See SKH, 160n94.

[53] "Startles the magpies of Wei" alludes to a poem by Cao Cao (155–220) titled "Short Song." The relevant passage, translated by Owen, is as follows: "The moon is bright, the stars are few, and magpies come flying south / three times around they circle the tree, where is the branch on which to roost?" According to tradition, Cao Cao, effectively the founder of the Wei (220–265), composed this song before a battle in which his ships were set alight during a battle with Wu (222–280), another of China's Three Kingdoms. For the "Short Song" and other relevant information, see Owen, *Anthology*, 280–81, 291–93; see also SKH, 160n96. Wu was situated in an extremely hot region, and it was said that at night, its oxen would mistake the moon for the sun and pant (SKH, 160n97).

[54] This translation follows SKH, 160–61n98, which cites a poem by Du Fu (712–770) in which a mountain scene is described and *kwak* (郭, C. *guo*), referring to the outer walls of a fortress, is used as a metonym for village. "Hazy and vague" and "full and round" refer to the moon, as made explicit in SKH, 146, and Yi/Hŏ, 84.

[55] SKH, 161n99, cites literary precedents for interpreting "a hook to hold up the bamboo blind" (簾鉤, K. *yŏmgu*, C. *liangou*) in relation to the moon. The dominant idea here is raised in the previous line through the reference to opening a lock; in both cases, something hidden is revealed.

And the autumn Mr. Wu
    cut the cassia tree.⁵⁶
A white folding screen so
    luminously bright and splendid;
A white silk curtain so
    finely decorated and patterned.
A precious mirror—
    polished, from the start hanging down;
An ice wheel—
    rolling on and on, without pause.
Golden waves—
    how tranquil they are;
Silver flows—
    truly so leisurely.⁵⁷
A sword is drawn,
    and the treacherous toad is struck down;
A net is cast,
    and the cunning rabbit is snared.⁵⁸
In heaven's path,
    the new rain ceases;
On the stony lane,
    the thin mist settles.
This banister quells
    a thousand great timber trees;
This staircase overlooks
    a ten-thousand-fathom-deep pond.
On a journey to a far-off place,
    who gets lost?
And at one's old home,
    chances to meet a companion.

---

⁵⁶Master Li is Li Bai (701–762), the great Tang Chinese poet, and this section refers to a line of his poetry describing his putting down his wine cup and questioning the moon. Mr. Wu is the Daoist immortal Wu Gang (吳剛, K. O Kang). According to legend, Mr. Wu committed an offense while studying Daoist magic and was exiled to the moon to cut down a giant cassia tree as punishment. The tree could not, however, be felled. See SKH, 161nn100–101, and Yi/Hŏ, 84nn48–49.

⁵⁷"Precious mirror" (寶鏡, K. pogyŏng, C. baojing), a metaphor for the sun and moon, here refers to the moon; "golden waves" (金波, K. kŭmp'a, C. jinbo) is a term for moonlight; "silver" refers to the Milky Way (literally, Silver River: 銀河, K. Ŭnha, C. Yinhe).

⁵⁸Toad and rabbit can be used to designate the moon. According to legend, a woman stole her husband's elixir of immortality and fled to the moon, where she became a toad. The rabbit was believed to live on the moon and make medicine (SKH, 161nn102–3; see also Yi/Hŏ, 85n51).

Peaches and plums,
　　reciprocally given and received;[59]
While jugs and cups of wine
　　can be offered back and forth.
Good poems compete against
　　the time-marking candle;
Delicious wine remains for
　　the increasing counting sticks.[60]
The brazier burns
　　a black-silver piece;
And the kettle overflows with
　　crab-eye bubbles.[61]
Dragon spit ascends from
　　the sleeping duck;[62]
Excellent wine fills up
　　the knotty cup.[63]
The calling crane
　　on the lone pine is startled;
The chirping cicadas
　　within the four walls are anxious.

---

[59] This reference to peaches and plums designates an exchange of gifts between a man and a woman, following an interpretation of the *Classic of Songs* (詩經, K. *Sigyŏng*, C. *Shijing*) by Zhu Xi (1130–1200). See SKH, 161n104.

[60] The "time-marking candle" (literally, "engraved candle": 刻燭, K. *kakch'ok*, C. *kezhu*) refers to the time it takes for a candle to burn down to a marked spot, used in poetry competitions. Similarly, "counting sticks" (籌, K. *chu*, C. *chou*) refers to an ancient Chinese game of tossing arrows into a vase, and here it is used to count the cups of wine that are drunk. For more detail, see SKH, 161–62nn105–6.

[61] "Black silver" (烏銀, K. *oŭn*, C. *wuyin*) means charcoal, and "crab eyes" (蟹眼, K. *haean*, C. *xieyan*) are the frothy bubbles that appear when something is boiled. Here these are translated literally to show the parallelism of the couplet.

[62] "Dragon spit" (龍涎, K. *yongyŏn*, C. *longxian*) is a type of highly prized incense composed of a waxy substance from the ocean, and it is believed to be secreted by sperm whales; see SKH, 162n109. The "sleeping duck" (睡鴨, K. *suap*, C. *shuiya*) is an ancient type of incense burner that looks like a resting duck, and, according to SKH, 162n110, the smoke comes out of its bill.

[63] As noted in SKH, 162n111, *kyŏngaek* (瓊液, C. *qiongye*) means "excellent wine." As used in Daoism, however, it can also refer to a liquid elixir of immortality. The "knotty cup" (癭甌, K. *yŏnggu*, C. *yingou*) seems to indicate a cup that resembles a knot or lump on a tree. For related literary citations, see SKH, 162n112.

On folding chairs,
  Yin and Yu chatted;[64]
Beside the waters of Jin,
  Xie and Yuan strolled.[65]
Faint and vague—
  the ruined castle remains;
Thick and luxuriant—
  the grass and trees so lush.
The green maples
  sway quietly;
And the yellow reeds
  are cold and crackle.
In the immortals' realm,
  heaven and earth are vast;
But among the dusts,
  the celestial and terrestrial are near.
At the palace of old,
  rice and millet have come into ear;
And by the ancestral shrine in the field,
  catalpa and mulberry trees grow tangled.[66]
Sweet scents linger over
  the collapsed stone monuments;
As to the vicissitudes of existence, I question
  a floating seagull.
The Goddess of the Moon
  is ever sinking and waxing;
While this piled-up earthen lump
  is all but a mayfly.

---

[64] Yu Liang was the younger brother of an empress during the Eastern Jin dynasty (317–420), and Yin Hao was his subordinate. Yu once sat down on a *hosang* (胡床, C. *huchuang*)—a chair that has a backrest and can be folded up—and chatted and composed poems with his subordinates. SKH and Yi/Hŏ see this as indicating the rapport between Young Master Hong and the beautiful lady, despite the difference in their social standings. See SKH, 162–63nn113–15, and Yi/Hŏ, 86n57.

[65] SKH, 163n116, provides an explanation on the identities of Xie and Yuan that differs from Yi/Hŏ, 86n58. Part of the problem might be a misprint or misreading. Both interpretations, however, make the same point: this reference also indicates the warm relationship between Young Master Hong and the lady.

[66] The reference to mulberry and catalpa trees has a specific relevance here. These were planted to make descendants think of their ancestors. That they are tangled and untidy near an ancestral shrine indicates that civilization has been destroyed.

The temporary royal palace
  has become a Buddhist temple;
With former kings
  buried at Tiger Hillock.[67]
Glowworms' and fireflies' lights,
  beyond the curtain and tiny;
And ghostly fires,
  near the forest and dim.[68]
Sadly thinking of the past
  makes for many falling tears;
And grieving for the present
  naturally brings anxiety.
Of Tan'gun remains
  Mount Mongmyŏk;
And of Kija's towns—
  merely Kuru.[69]
In burrows there are
  unicorn hoof marks;
The fields have met with
  Suksin iron arrowheads.[70]
Orchid Fragrance returns to
  the realm of immortals;
The Weaving Girl drives
  a green dragon.[71]

---

[67] "Tiger Hillock" (虎丘, K. Hogu) is a place-name in China. It is said that after the burial of an ancient king, a tiger climbed upon his burial mound. Here it seems to refer to the burial sites of previous Korean kings; see SKH, 163n119, and Yi/Hŏ, 87n60.

[68] "Ghostly fires" (鬼火, K. kwihwa, C. guihuo) is a literal translation. It refers to phosphorescence, and in relation to a burial ground, it can refer to a corpse candle.

[69] Mongmyŏk (木覓) is a mountain located near P'yŏngyang; see SKH, 163n121, and Yi/Hŏ, 87n61. Both SKH (148) and Yi/Hŏ (87) translate Kuru (溝婁) literally as waterway. But Kuru (C. Goulou) is almost certainly a place-name: it is glossed in Sanguo zhi [Records of the Three Kingdoms], by Chen Shou (233–297), as the name of a town in Koguryŏ. This makes sense grammatically—because Kuru is parallel to Mongmyŏk—and in light of the following oblique reference to Koguryŏ.

[70] "Unicorn" refers to the "unicorn-horse" that King Tongmyŏng, the legendary founder of Koguryŏ, is said to have ridden, and Suksin (肅慎) was the name of an area during the era of Old Chosŏn where arrowheads were produced. See SKH, 163nn122–23, and Yi/Hŏ, 87nn62–63.

[71] Orchid Fragrance (蘭香, K. Nanhyang) is the name of a female immortal; for literary references, see SKH, 163n124. The Weaving Girl (織女, K. Chignyŏ) is the star Vega and refers to a Chinese legend that she and her lover, the Cowherd, were doomed to meet only once a year. These references indicate the beautiful lady's imminent departure.

>A learned man halts
>>his beautiful writing brush;
>And an immortal lady stops
>>her lute.[72]
>As the music ends,
>>people are about to scatter;
>The wind dies down,
>>and the oar sounds are soft.

With her writing complete, she set aside her brush, ascended to the heavens, and soared away. No one knows where she went. But just as she was about to leave, she charged her maidservants with conveying to Young Master Hong her orders to tell him that "the emperor's commands are strict, and I am about to mount a white phoenix. But our graceful conversation has not yet concluded, and this saddens my inmost heart."[73]

Not long after that, a whirlwind drove across the ground, blowing down Young Master Hong where he sat and carrying off the beautiful lady's poem. It is also unknown where the poem went. Perhaps this was to keep mysterious tales from circulating throughout the human realm.

Once Young Master Hong came to his senses, he stood up and forlornly thought to himself that it seemed to be a dream and yet was not a dream, that it seemed to be real and yet was not real. He leaned over the balustrade, and, rapt in his longing for her, he committed to memory all that she had said. In recollecting their strange encounter, he still had a sense of deep affection for her. So he then chanted a poem, reminiscing over what had happened while yearning for her:

>The clouds and rain at Sunlight Terrace—
>>in a dream;[74]

---

[72] For additional information on this specific instrument, see SKH, 163–64n125.

[73] "Emperor" is the Jade Emperor, the supreme god in Daoism, who is typically named Okhwang Sangje (玉皇上帝) in Korea and Yuhuang Dadi (玉皇大帝) in China. Both SKH (149) and Yi/Hŏ (88) make this explicit in their translations.

[74] Sunlight Terrace (陽臺, K. Yangdae) and "clouds and rain," a euphemism for sexual intercourse, evoke the introduction to "The Poetic Exposition on Gaotang" [Gaotang fu], traditionally attributed to Song Yu (third century B.C.E.). It describes how a king took a nap and dreamed of being seduced by a beautiful goddess who, upon leaving him, said that in the morning she is the clouds and in the evening, the rain. (For a translation, see Owen, *Anthology*, 189–90.) Sunlight Terrace alludes to Floating Jade-Green Pavilion, as suggested by Yi/Hŏ, 89n65, drawing a parallel between the experiences of the king and Young Master Hong.

> When will I again see
> Yuxiao's bracelet?[75]
> The river's waves,
> though unfeeling things,
> Softly weep and sadly cry out, flowing down
> from the river's bend where we parted.[76]

After reciting this poem, Young Master Hong looked about the four directions: in the mountain temple a bell was ringing; in the riverside village a rooster was crowing; the moon was sinking to the west of the city; and the morning star was twinkling brightly. He heard only the sounds of mice in the courtyard and the chirping of insects about him. Feeling lonely and sad as well as solemn and afraid, he was sorry that it was not possible for him to stay. He returned, boarded his boat, and, feeling dejected and gloomy, arrived at the spot along the riverside from where he had earlier set off. His companions all asked at once, "Where did you lodge last night?" He deceived them, saying, "Last night I grabbed a bamboo pole and, taking advantage of the moonlight, went to the shore at Morning Sky Rock outside the gate of Everlasting Fortune,[77] intending to catch some beautiful fish. But as luck would have it, the night was chilly and the water was cold, and I did not catch a single carp. Is there anything as regrettable as this?" Even his companions did not doubt what he had said.

Afterward, he fell ill with consumption and fatigue while thinking about the beautiful woman, and he was the first to return home.[78] His mind was confused, his speech was rambling, and he tossed and turned in bed. Though much time passed, he still did not recover. One day he was dreaming when he saw a beautiful woman wearing simple makeup.[79] She came and informed him that "my mistress has made a petition to the Supreme Ruler of the Heavens [上皇, K. Sanghwang]. The Supreme Ruler of the Heavens values people of talent,

---

[75] This translation follows SKH, 149, in rendering *hwan* (環) as bracelet. According to a story from the Tang dynasty, Yuxiao (玉簫) became romantically involved with a man who promised to marry her. But while he was away, she worried and starved to death. She was then reborn as his concubine. As SKH, 164n126, suggests, this reference indicates that Hong awaits the beautiful lady's rebirth. Therefore, "Yuxiao's bracelet" might also be a pun for "Yuxiao's return, rebirth" (玉簫還), since the two characters are similar.

[76] The enjambment in the final two lines is also clearly reflected in SKH, 150, and Yi/Hŏ, 89.

[77] SKH, 164n128, and Yi/Hŏ, 89n66, note that "Everlasting Fortune" (長慶, K. Changgyŏng) was the name of a temple in P'yŏngyang.

[78] The implication is that his friends continued to enjoy their visit to P'yŏngyang. SKH, 150, also interprets it thus.

[79] The text in SKH, 271, breaks the graph 妝 into two graphs, 月女. It should read "a beautiful woman wearing simple makeup" (淡妝美人).

and he has put you to work under the direction of the Cowherd.⁸⁰ The Supreme Emperor commands you.⁸¹ Can this be avoided?" Young Master Hong awoke with a start. He ordered his servants to bathe him and change his clothes and to light incense, sweep the ground, and spread out a mat in the courtyard. He lay down for a short time with his chin on his hands, and then he suddenly passed away. It was the fifteenth day of the ninth month. They put his remains on view for several days before burial, yet his complexion did not change. People said that they thought he had chanced to meet an immortal and had abandoned his body to become a spirit.⁸²

GNE

---

⁸⁰The Cowherd (河鼓, K. Hago) is the star Altair and is the counterpart to the star Vega, or the Weaving Girl, mentioned in n. 71. (For additional information, see SKH, 164n129.)

⁸¹ In the original, "Supreme Ruler of the Heavens" is repeated and then followed by "Supreme Emperor" (上帝, K. Sangje). These are all references to the Jade Emperor (see also SKH, 151, and Yi/Hŏ, 90). However, the punctuation in SKH, 271, is confusing. This translation follows the 1884 Japanese annotated version. See Ch'oe, Kŭmo sinhwa-ŭi p'anbon, 277.

⁸²"Abandoned his body to become a spirit" (屍解, K. sihae, C. shijie) comes from Daoism. It refers to the separation of one's physical matter and spirit upon becoming an immortal.

4. Chosŏn Long Fiction

4.1 ANONYMOUS, *THE TALE OF LADY PAK* (朴氏傳 *PAK-SSI-JŎN*)

The Korean Peninsula was devastated twice in mid-Chosŏn (1392–1910): first by Japanese troops from 1592 to 1598 and then again by the Manchus in the late 1620s and 1630s. Because of such suffering, the Korean people were antagonistic toward both their foreign enemies and the ineptness of their own ruling class. These experiences and attitudes coincided with the growing popularity of fiction and are reflected in the three major battle stories from that period: *The Record of the Black Dragon Year* (壬辰錄 *Imjin-nok*), *The Tale of Im Kyŏngŏp* (林慶業傳 *Im Kyŏngŏp-chŏn*), and *The Tale of Lady Pak* (朴氏傳 *Pak-ssi-jŏn*).

Of these, *The Tale of Lady Pak* is arguably the most successful in its literary achievements. It is an anonymous story of a female Daoist immortal who is also a warrior, a magician, and a proper Confucian wife. Although the precise origins of the story are unknown, scholars have concluded that it dates from sometime during the late seventeenth century to the early eighteenth century. Whatever the case, the fact that the story exists

---

This work was supported by the English Translation of 100 Korean Classics program through the Ministry of Education of the Republic of Korea and the Korean Studies Promotion Service of the Academy of Korean Studies (AKS-2010-AAB-2102).

in multiple vernacular Korean manuscript versions—that is to say, handwritten copies—suggests that the story was popular and circulated widely. In addition, no printed version of the work predating the twentieth century has been discovered, nor is there anything to indicate that the work circulated in a Literary Chinese version, whether printed or in manuscript.[1] There was, however, another mode of transmission that would have left no visible trace: oral recitation or storytelling, as those who knew the story or could read recounted it to others in Korean.

Thus to all appearances, the work was transmitted only in Korean, either as a recounted story or through handwritten copies. Among these manuscript copies, scholars consider the one held at Korea University to be the best. At the very end of the manuscript, the copyist dated the work using the Chinese sexagenary cycle, noting that the copy was made in the Blue Sheep Year (乙未). Based on that date and the identifiable events in the story itself, the copy would have been made no earlier than 1655 and no later than 1895. That manuscript version is the basis for this English translation.[2]

The story is set during the reign of King Injo (仁祖, r. 1623–1649) and revolves around Lady Pak, a Daoist immortal, who is reborn in the human, mundane world as the only daughter of Hermit Pak of the Kŭmgang Mountains. In the first half of the story, Lady Pak is shunned by her husband because of her extreme ugliness. But she then metamorphoses into a beauty and proves her true merits in the second half of the story, which recounts her exploits during the Manchu invasions. She foresees the war, makes preparations, and employs various battle strategies to defeat the Manchu generals Long Guda (龍骨大, Tatara Inggŭldai), his brother Long Lüda (龍律大), and their troops. In the end, Lady Pak is honored by the king for saving her people, and her family thus prospers for generations.

The Tale of Lady Pak thus takes Korea as its backdrop as it depicts resistance against the Manchus. In addition, it reflects the factional politics and social turmoil of seventeenth-century Chosŏn through references to a variety of historical figures, including the male protagonist, Yi Sibaek (李時白, 1581–1660), as well as Wŏn Tup'yo (元斗杓, 1593–1664), Im Kyŏngŏp (林慶業, 1594–1646), and Kim Chajŏm (金自點, 1588–1651). Readers can thus gain some insight into how these influential men were critically evaluated by the mass of their fellow Koreans.[3]

By contrast, the female figures in the story—even the bad—are far more energetic and impressive, possessing spiritual-magical powers that underpin their martial exploits: the

---

[1] Cho Hŭiung, *Kojŏn sosŏl ibon mongnok* [Catalogue of different texts of classical novels] (Seoul: Chimmundang, 1999), 164–71.

[2] The manuscript version is reprinted in *Pak-ssi-jŏn, Im changgun-jŏn, Pae Sihwang-jŏn* [The tale of Lady Pak, the tale of General Im, and the tale of Pae Sihwang], ed. Kim Kihyŏn, 140–214 (Seoul: Korea University, Minjok munhwa yŏn'guso, 1995). For an overview of the history of the work as discussed here, see 136–39.

[3] For the scholarship on the story, see Sin Sŏnhŭi, "*Pak-ssi-jŏn* yŏn'gu sa" [A history of the scholarship on *The Tale of Lady Pak*], in *Kososŏl yŏn'gu sa*, ed. U Kwoeje et al., 369–88 [A history of scholarship on the premodern novel] (Seoul: Wŏrin, 2001).

Manchu queen gives her husband, the king, critical advice after observing the movements of the constellations; the female assassin Qi Hongda (奇紅大) comes to kill Lady Pak armed with a flying dagger and a fireball. The main focus of the story, however, is Lady Pak. Her abilities far surpass those of all the men, including her husband, as well as those of all other women.

JS and PL

BIOGRAPHICAL NOTES

Yi Sibaek (李時白, 1581–1660)

Yi Sibaek was the firstborn of three brothers and four sisters in a learned but poor family. He was first appointed lord of Yŏnyang (延陽君, modern Yŏngbyŏn, North P'yŏng'an province) for his role in deposing King Kwanghaegun (光海君, r. 1608–1623) and enthroning King Injo. During the two wars against the Manchus, he successfully carried out many difficult missions and was esteemed by both the court and the people. Later, he served as defense minister and also held many other top positions, including that of chief state councillor (領議政) in 1655.

Im Kyŏngŏp (林慶業, 1594–1646)

Im passed the military service examination in 1618 at the age of twenty-four. As a magistrate, Im protected his city, Ŭiju, from the Manchus in 1636, but he had to abandon the city when the king surrendered the following year. In 1643 and now a general, Im escaped to Shandong and joined the Chinese Ming loyalists, who were fighting the Manchus. Later, he was captured by the Manchu Qing court and sent back to Chosŏn, where he was attacked by his opponents and died as a result of physical abuse administered during his interrogation.

Tatara Inggŭldai (1596–1648)

Tatara Inggŭldai is known as Long Guda (龍骨大) in Chinese and as Yonggoltae in the Korean reading; in the following translation, his name will be given as Long Guda. He was an important diplomat and general in the early Qing court. In the spring of 1636 he visited Korea as a royal envoy and reported back that King Injo would not submit to the Manchu Qing court. The emperor Hong Taiji (洪太極, r. 1626–1643) responded by invading Korea. Injo was captured at Namhan Fortress and forced to kowtow to the Manchu emperor nine times at Samjŏndo.

Kim Chajŏm (金自點, 1588–1651)

Kim Chajŏm belonged to an influential family and therefore was able to obtain official positions without having to pass the civil service examination. He committed critical mistakes while he was in charge of P'yŏng'an province, and in 1636 he ignored warnings about a Manchu attack. As a result, his army was defeated and the country devastated. He was also criticized for his excessive desire for power, marriage alliances with the royal court, and participation in factional politics.

TRANSLATION

During the reign of the last Ming emperor, Chongzhen [崇禎, r. 1627–1644], there lived in the kingdom of Chosŏn a high minister by the name of Yi Tŭkch'un. Having studied deeply since childhood, he excelled in writing and his fame spread throughout the land. He also had a discerning eye for people. He passed the civil service examination while still quite young and rose quickly through the ranks—he was appointed governor of Kyŏngsang province [慶尙監使 *Kyŏngsang kamsa*], enjoyed popularity as the governor of Hamgyŏng province [咸鏡監使 *Hamgyŏng kamsa*], and served as the second state councillor [左議政 *chwaŭijŏng*] in the capital. He then returned home and urged his son Sibaek to devote himself to literary and practical writings. Sibaek soon became well versed in *The Four Books, Three Confucian Classics, The Book of Poetry, The Book of Documents,* and the writings of "the hundred thinkers" [百家, K. *paekka*] of Chinese philosophy, and his schemes and strategies were unrivaled in the capital. Minister Yi proudly loved his son, and all the courtiers praised him. Minister Yi was also a master of the board games *paduk* and *changgi* and excelled at playing the jade flute. When he played his flute in the direction of flowers, the flowers would all fall down. His talent was without equal in the world.

One day, when the minister was sitting alone in the reception hall, a man in a hemp hood and humble outfit came to visit him. The minister looked at him closely. Despite his shabby raiment, his appearance and behavior were those of an exceptional man. The minister quickly rose to greet him politely and, after the man was seated, asked his name.

"I am Hermit Pak from the Kŭmgang Mountains," replied the stranger. "Ever since I first heard of the minister's great virtues, I have wanted to meet you."

The minister sat courteously and expressed his gratitude for the visit.

"Venerable guest, you are an immortal official, and I am a dirty man in this dusty world. The immortal and the mundane clearly differ; your words today are too polite, and they make me feel embarrassed."

The minister ordered assorted drinks and dishes and served them to his guest. Then the hermit spoke.

"I am told that no one can equal you for playing *paduk* and the jade flute. Since I also have some shallow knowledge in these things, I've come here to see."

"I am an ignorant man in this mundane world," the minister said politely. "I admit I know a little about *paduk* and the jade flute, but my abilities surely cannot equal yours. Your compliments today are too kind."

"You are too modest," the hermit replied. "Please show me your talents."

At this the minister weighed the situation in his mind: *I am unrivaled in playing* paduk *and the jade flute. Now when I look at this man, his behavior is unusual, and he also says he knows about them. I will test him somehow or another.* The minister started playing *paduk* with the hermit. After a few opening moves, the minister had to take his time and ponder deeply, while the hermit seemed to move his pieces easily with little thought. It was soon clear that the hermit was extremely talented, far better than the minister. The minister was overwhelmed, and he treated the hermit to more drink and food. He then picked up his jade flute and upon playing it, flowers fell to the ground. The hermit praised him greatly. Then, taking the jade flute himself, the hermit played in the direction of a flowering tree and a gust of wind arose to uproot it. Seeing this, the minister could not control his excitement and expressed his astonishment one hundred times, deeply moved. In this way the two men passed many days together. Finally, the hermit made a request.

"I am told you have one precious son. I would very much like to see him."

The minister thought this strange, but he summoned his son, Sibaek, and introduced him to the hermit. The hermit silently looked at Sibaek for some time.

"Your son is indeed a noble man," he complimented the minister. "He has the head of a phoenix and the face of a dragon. He will become a minister one day without fail." Then he said, "I have come here for no other reason than this: I have one daughter, whose age is sixteen and whose talents are no less than others, but marriage cannot be achieved without heaven's blessing. I have been searching everywhere for a suitable husband, but now I am convinced that no man is equal to your dear son. I ask your permission for their marriage."

The minister thought to himself, *This man's behavior is unusual and many marvelous things have happened. If my son becomes his son-in-law, good things are sure to follow.* He therefore agreed to the hermit's proposal.

"I am an unworthy man in this mundane world. A virtuous man may make plans, but I am afraid my son does not deserve such a one as your daughter."

The hermit smiled.

"After listening to a man of such humble origin as I, you are still generous and considerate. How can I not praise your virtue?" The hermit then read the lines on his palm. "There is one particular day that would be best for you to hold the marriage ceremony. On the day of the marriage procession, I entreat you to become my guest of honor. Do not make the process ostentatious but bring just one servant and come to visit me at the Kŭmgang Mountains."

With that, the hermit bid the minister farewell and left. After parting with the hermit, the minister gathered his family and kinsmen to discuss the marriage, but everyone objected.

"Marriage is a great matter of human relationships," they said. "It is not to be entered into hastily, and in the capital there are many noble households and any number of decent ladies. Why would you go to all the trouble of marrying your son to the daughter of some man you are not familiar with who lives in the mountains? You also know nothing of his pedigree! How could you possibly make such a rash decision?"

"Cancel the marriage," one urged.

"Just do as you intend," advised another.

They continued to talk, but then the minister smiled and said, "Marriage is not achieved by human will. I also see the man. He is different from ordinary men and this is not a chance meeting. This is fate, a decision made in heaven. Moreover, I have already agreed to the marriage, so how can I change my mind? No, I will not waver. Do not discuss it any further."

After arranging the marriage procession, the minister spoke.

"No one knows the hermit's residence, and the journey to the Kŭmgang Mountains is long, so I need to leave in advance."

The minister and his son, Sibaek, prepared to travel. They gave servants bags to carry and set off on their journey. It took them many days to reach the Kŭmgang Mountains, but when they arrived, they did not know where to proceed. They followed an obscure trail over one mountain after another, going deeper and deeper into the wilderness until the trail ended. With the sunlight fading behind a ridge, they were forced to retrace their steps and spend the night at an inn. The next day they found another trail and went farther into the wilderness, through stunning scenery: clouds floating atop a thousand peaks and ridges, a creek murmuring along with a stony path layered by boulders and cliffs. The minister gazed upon the scene and continued on into the wilderness for half a day without seeing a single person. Finally, some woodcutters appeared from the opposite direction. The minister welcomed them and asked, "Do you know where Hermit Pak lives?"

"We are his villagers," one of the woodcutters replied. "But how have you come to this remote area? And why do ask about Hermit Pak?"

The minister was glad and said, "Do not ask my business. Just tell me where he lives."

"We don't know Hermit Pak," said the woodcutter with a smile. "There is a valley where he used to live, but that is only a story old men pass down to their children. We have heard of it only."

Having heard this, the minister was dumbfounded and thought, *Hermit Pak is by no means a man to be distrusted, so he must live somewhere in these mountains. But where?* Mountains were high and valleys were deep. While he was walking hither and thither, the sun sank over a western mountain, tired birds flew back to their nests, monkeys sadly cried, and cuckoos sang, "Better go home," which caused him to be homesick and deeply saddened his heart. The minister and his son had to return to the inn and sleep. The next day they went back to seek the hermit, but how could visitors from the mundane world find the celestial realm? After searching in vain for four or five days, Sibaek said, "Father, from the beginning you listened to an unreliable man's words, and we find ourselves entangled in this mess. Whom are you going to blame? I feel ashamed and worry about being ridiculed."

While agreeing to what his son had said, in another way the minister thought that Hermit Pak was not an imposter at all.

"Tomorrow is the day we scheduled for the ceremony," he replied. "Let us see what the situation is tomorrow, then decide whether to go farther or return home."

The next day they readied themselves and pushed farther into the deep valley, where they encountered a man in a hemp cap and coarse clothes who used a goosefoot stick to push his way through the bush. The minister was glad to see him and soon realized that he was indeed Hermit Pak. He paid his respects to the hermit and said that he had been looking for him for many days.

"Sincere man!" replied the hermit with a smile. "Minister, you have toiled many days."

And he guided them to his place at a leisurely pace. The layered boulders and cliffs of the highest peak of the Kŭmgang Mountains formed screens on right and left, green pines and verdant bamboo grew lush, jade flowers and plants were fully fragrant, and there were phoenixes and peacocks playing. In the middle stood several thatched cottages, in front of the entrance [to the area] were planted willows, and below the willows lay a pond crowded with lotus blossoms. White geese, scattered like spots and specks, appeared to be surprised by the guests from the mundane world. When they arrived at the door, the hermit said to the minister, "My shabby, cramped house has no place to accommodate you, so I entreat you to stay here."

He had them sit on a flat stone in front of the entrance gate.

"It is already dark, so I suggest that we quickly proceed to the ceremony."

The hermit urged the bridegroom to stand in the great ceremonial procession and entered the house, and then he put makeup on his daughter and brought her out. After finishing the great ceremony, the bridegroom was led to a main room, the bride entered a side room, and the guest of honor, the minister, and his servants were seated on the flat stone. The hermit, carrying a bottle in one hand and some vegetables on a small table in the other, came out and said with a smile, "There are no delicacies in these mountains, so this is what I am able to serve. Please do not hold it against me."

The minister bowed and said that he did not mind it at all, but his servants sneered at the hermit. The hermit personally poured the drink and offered a cup to the minister and one cup each to each of the servants. The drink was so strong that they could not drink much and were soon drunk and in a slumber. When they awoke, the night had already passed and the sun perched over an eastern ridge. The visitors, as if awaking from a dream, looked at one another and thought it strange. After a while, the hermit returned with breakfast, which consisted of some vegetables neatly arrayed on big and small tables.

"Yesterday you were so drunk from a cup of pine-flower wine," he said. "Today it may affect your travel, so I am afraid to offer it again."

After they ate the hermit spoke again.

"You have come this long way and it would be wrong for me to make you come back again. Minister, I suggest that you return home today with my daughter."

The hermit let the groom go on foot and the bride ride his horse. Thus they prepared to travel that day. The hermit walked about ten steps away from the gate and bid farewell to the minister, promising to see him again someday.

The minister took the bride and embarked on their journey home. That evening he stopped at an inn and brought the groom and bride into a room. When the bride removed her veil and sat down, he saw that her face and her figure were so unattractive that he felt some anxiety. Her pockmarks were red, rugged like a weathered stone; her lip was cleft all the way to her nose; her eyes popped out like a snail's; her mouth was so enormous that two clenched fists would fit with room to spare; her forehead jutted out like a grasshopper's; her hair was short and shaggy. Her appearance was altogether unbearable to look at. After seeing her only once, the minister and the groom were unable to look at her again, as if they had been scared out of their wits. Their minds were bewildered and their eyes were dim. After barely regaining consciousness, the minister thought, *This woman is so ugly that it would have been better for her to grow old in the inner quarters of her own home rather than getting married off to some other family. But the hermit saw me and agreed to their marriage. This man must know something, and in addition, her appearance is terrible but this is also her lot in life. If I reject her, she will be utterly deserted in this world. It may be that once I regard her with care, she will become our fortune.* After thinking this, he said aloud to Sibaek, "Today I see a bride who will bring my house fortune and you endless bliss. How can I not be glad?"

On the road he made sure the bride was comfortable and that her meals were adequate. When they reached home after many days, family members, relatives, and noble ladies flocked together to see the young woman. The bride came in, removed her veil, and sat down in the main hall. How could one describe her appearance? After seeing her they spat out, sneered, whispered, and scattered like disappearing billows, but with a gleeful face the minister sat in the reception hall and praised the bride's virtuous conduct to the other guests. The minister's wife spoke up.

"The minister has only one child," she said. "You ignored numerous decent ladies in the capital and listened to the absurd claims of someone who lives off in the mountains. We are shamed now and our family is headed for trouble. Please consider sending her back to seek remarriage into another family so that we might look for a more suitable daughter-in-law."

The minister was furious at this.

"No matter how beautiful a bride is," he rebuked his wife, "if she does not behave properly, people will not respect her. There is a saying, 'Consort Yang Guifei [楊貴妃, 713–756] was an absolute beauty but ruined her country.' Today, this bride is our blessing. How can you point only to her appearance and not see her virtue? And if we are uneasy about her, how can we guide our children and our household? Now our house will prosper, so how is it not delightful? I ask you not to mention her appearance again and to care for her well."

But the minister's wife was a closed-minded, ordinary woman, and she could not love her. So the mother-in-law hated the bride. Sibaek also did not visit her chamber at all, so the servants treated her badly. Lady Pak became a lonely wife and harbored sorrow in her heart. Every day she only ate and slept and disregarded everything, and as a result the household hated her all the more. The house brimmed over with reproaches against her, but for fear of the minister, no one dared abuse her to her face. The minister noticed this situation and rebuked the servants firmly to make sure that it would not happen again. He called in Sibaek and rebuked him as well.

"If a broad-minded man seeks only beauty, not knowing virtue," he said, "he will have no fortune and his household will perish. Now, inasmuch as Lady Pak is not pretty, you treat her poorly. If you behave in such a manner, how could you cultivate yourself and make a good family? A long time ago Lady Huang [黃夫人], the wife of Zhuge Liang [諸葛亮], was ugly, but she was virtuous, benevolent, and had unlimited supernatural abilities. Therefore Master Zhuge lived in harmony with his wife, discussing difficult matters. Her name was known through the generations. Lady Pak is the daughter of an immortal and behaves generously, and there is also a saying that a wife must not step down from the main hall if she shares hard times with her husband,[4] so how on earth

---

[4] The reference is to the idea that a wife who faithfully serves her husband and shares difficulties with him cannot be divorced without proper cause.

can you treat such a guiltless, virtuous woman this way? Even with wild animals, if parents are fond of something, their offspring will feel the same. There is no doubt this is the same with human beings. You have treated her badly, which means you also treat me badly."

At this, Sibaek stepped down into the yard and apologized.

"Your disrespectful son has not listened to your orders. I deserve death for such an egregious fault and ask for your forgiveness."

And he left. That night, Sibaek entered Lady Pak's chamber to stay in her inner quarters. But upon seeing her unsightly appearance, he lost all desire to sleep with her and sat in one corner with his back to her. Then he left and slept in another room. After the cock crowed he visited his father's bedroom for the formal morning greeting. The minister, who did not know the real situation and assumed his son had slept in the inner quarters, was delighted. Meanwhile, Sibaek's mother remained disgusted at her daughter-in-law and called her attendant.

"Give her less food," she ordered one of the attendants.

What could Lady Pak do, with everyone hating her no matter how virtuous she was? Unable to stand the situation, she told her attendant, Kyehwa, "Please inform the minister that I have an issue I wish to consult him about."

When Kyehwa delivered the message, the minister followed her at once to Lady Pak's room, whereupon she heaved an anxious sigh and said politely, "This humble woman is unsightly and lacks virtuous conduct and therefore fails to attract the attention of her husband. Therefore please build a side room in the rear garden and let me reside there, out of sight."

The minister, seeing her predicament, sympathized with her. He let out a sigh of anxiety and said, "My son falls short of my wish and does not listen to me. This has happened because I did not discipline him. I will warn him again, so ease your mind and let us see how things will improve."

Lady Pak was moved by his words and yet spoke again.

"The minister's words are most gracious. But the situation is caused by my foolishness, so how can I complain of my husband? I am pained to make this request of you, but I beg you to build a side room for me in the rear garden."

The minister had no choice but to reply, "I will think on this for a while and then make a decision."

After leaving Lady Pak, the minister summoned Sibaek and spoke with great reproach.

"You never listen to me, rejecting your virtuous wife and wanting beauty," he said. "If you do so, how are you going to handle the things that will come your way in life? There is a saying, 'If the country is in turbulence, the ruler misses a benevolent vassal; if the household is in an uproar, the husband misses his benevolent wife.' You are indeed casting away fortune and inviting mishap. If you continue to behave in this manner, Lady Pak will harbor resentment for living alone in an empty room and die of sadness. Then our family will go to ruin, for a dispute over our family's conduct will arise in court and we will be forced to resign from our official positions. Who are you to think about only appearance and reject virtue?"

Sibaek lowered his body as if to await punishment and withdrew, and he thought, *From now on I won't act wrong again.* But whenever he entered Lady Pak's chamber, his mind was spontaneously unwilling and his eyes closed of their own accord. No matter how much he tried, it was hard for him to have conjugal relations with his wife. The minister noticed this situation and lamented, "Now my household shall perish."

He discreetly built a small suite of side rooms and let the attendant, Kyehwa, accompany him to furnish each room. It was an embarrassing scene.

At this time the king sent a secretary to summon the minister as third state chancellor [右議政 Uŭijŏng], so the next day he had to attend the morning assembly. The minister held the royal message in both hands and said to his wife, "Tomorrow I must don court robes and attend the morning assembly."

"I will get many needleworkers and make them for you," replied his wife.

When the minister's wife was about to call many top seamstresses in the capital to make robes, Lady Pak heard of it and ordered Kyehwa, "Bring cloth for court robes."

Kyehwa went straight to inform the minister and his wife of her lady's wish. The minister's wife ignored the news, but the minister was pleased.

"Surely this woman must have a special talent," he observed.

And so he sent cloth for the court robes and first-rate needleworkers to Lady Pak. While Lady Pak worked with her needle by candlelight making the court robes, other top seamstresses there with her found her skills mysterious and were unable to take part. Lady Pak made the court robes overnight, with a phoenix couple embroidered on the front and blue cranes on the back. Her needlework was so fine that it did not appear to have been done by human hands. Everyone who saw it praised it highly. When the attendant, Kyehwa, submitted it to the minister, he was astounded.

"This is handiwork from heaven above, not embroidery done by a human being," he said.

The minister and his wife, nobles and common people alike, and top seamstresses in the capital all declared that they had never seen anything like the robes. All the people saw the court robes and praised Lady Pak.

"No one would have guessed, looking at Lady Pak, that she possessed such talent," said one.

"There is a saying," observed another, "that legal documents are wrapped in a rag sack and a fine chest of drawers is placed in a thatched cottage. It refers to this case." The minister wore the court robes and solemnly prostrated himself in the royal presence. The king peered at him for a while and asked, "Who made your robes?"

The minister lowered his head to the floor and replied, "Your vassal has a daughter-in-law. She made them."

"Then why do you, Minister, allow her to live such a hard life, alone in an empty room?" asked the king.

Hearing this, the minister found his back damp with sweat. Lowering his head still further, he asked, "How has Your Majesty come to know of this situation?"

"The phoenix couple embroidered on the front of your robe—the female loses her mate. And the blue cranes on the back—look hungry among snowy mountains and rivers. How else should I read what I see?"

The minister dared not hide the truth. He lowered his head on the floor and said, "Your vassal's daughter-in-law is hideously ugly, and it causes my unworthy son to lose his desire for the pleasures of the marital chamber. So she has no other choice but to stay in an empty room."

"If a husband and wife share no pleasures of the marital chamber," replied the king, "living alone in an empty room is normal. But why does she suffer from starvation and cold?"

The minister was embarrassed by this.

"I stay in the reception hall and so do not know about the household affairs," he admitted.

"I haven't seen your daughter-in-law's face, but I see her handiwork on your robes, which is beyond human talent. From it, I can see her constancy. I ask you not to neglect her but to treat her well. For the sake of Lady Pak we will confer a three-*mal* stipend [of rice] each day.[5] Make sure you take care of her well."

After bowing to receive the order, the minister returned to his house and called his wife and Sibaek to consider the royal message and the bestowing of the three-*mal* stipend. Then he reprimanded Sibaek.

"From the beginning I have told you not to disregard this virtuous woman. Today the king has delivered a royal message. What kind of man are you to behave in such a wrong way?"

Sibaek, ashamed, lowered his head to the ground and promised to correct his mistakes. Yet the minister quietly admonished him again and asked that Lady Pak be well treated. From that day on the three *mal* of rice conferred by the country was prepared, one *mal* for each meal, three times a day. Lady Pak declined nothing. She ate everything and still it seemed insufficient. What she drank

---

[5] A *mal* is equivalent to about eighteen liters.

and ate was as enormous as the rivers and seas. The household no longer dared to ignore her, and the minister respected her all the more.

Lady Pak asked to speak with the minister again through Kyehwa.

"I have an issue I would like to consult with the minister about."

When the minister promptly came to her room, Lady Pak politely said, "Since our wealth is insufficient, you might want to plan an undertaking."

To this the minister replied, "Wealth and poverty are given by heaven's will. How do you change it by human will?"

"Tomorrow," said Lady Pak, "many Cheju horses will be delivered to Chongno. Among the bound horses is a rowdy, mangy foal. Order your servants to buy it for no more than three hundred *nyang* and to bring it home."

The minister already knew her mysterious ability, so how could he not listen to her? He hastened to the reception hall and called his servants, gave them orders and the money. This greatly puzzled the servants.

"How does our master know Cheju horses will come?" they pondered.

"He also ordered us to buy a rowdy, mangy foal from among them with this three hundred *nyang*, so let's go and see."

They went and looked around, and indeed there were many tied horses, a mangy foal being one of them. The servants asked its price.

"Five *nyang*," said the horse's owner.

One senior servant spoke up.

"Our master bid us buy a small foal and gave us three hundred *nyang*."

At this the horse owner looked up at the sky and burst into laughter.

"What do you mean three hundred for the foal whose price is but five *nyang*?"

He refused to take so much money, and all the people of Chongno also laughed.

"Why do they force money on an owner who doesn't want to receive it?"

It was the servants who felt ashamed of it. Thus they paid only one hundred *nyang*, hid the remaining two hundred, and took the horse to their master. When the minister went to Lady Pak's room and told her that he had purchased the foal, she said, "The horse costs three hundred *nyang* but only one hundred was paid. I therefore ask you to find the remaining money and give it to the horse owner."

The minister was struck dumb by this. He immediately returned to the reception hall and interrogated the servants and confirmed that only one hundred *nyang* had been paid for the foal. He reprimanded the senior servant and ordered him to pay a total of three hundred for the foal.

"Feed the foal well with three *toe*[6] of rice, three *toe* of barley, and three *toe* of sesame seeds for each meal," said Lady Pak.

---

[6] A *toe* is one-tenth of a *mal*, thus 1.8 liters.

Because of his father's words and the king's message, Sibaek didn't want to neglect his wife any longer. He went to her chamber but, finding that he still disliked her face, promptly turned away to avoid her gaze and left. At this time Lady Pak made Kyehwa plant trees in every direction from the side room. In the east was the blue soil, in the south the red soil, in the west the white soil, in the north the black soil, and in the center the yellow soil. She made sure each tree took root and watered them at times as if raising children. And they grew thick and lush. One day the minister asked Kyehwa, "What is your lady doing these days?"

"Lady Pak plants trees," Kyehwa replied, "and this little maid is working hard to make sure that they are watered."

The minister wanted to see this, so he followed Kyehwa and entered the suite at the rear garden. As he had been told, trees had been planted and were growing lushly; they reached out in the four directions wherein dragons and tigers were tangled together and branches and leaves turned into snakes and varied beasts, gazing at one another—a solemn atmosphere, and clouds and fog seemed thick. He stood and observed the scene for a while; between the trees arose wind and clouds, ceaselessly changing. He also looked at the side room and saw a placard hanging above the door, bearing the inscription Hall of Refuge [避禍堂 P'ihwa-dang]. After seeing all this, the minister looked in upon Lady Pak and inquired, "What are those trees? And what's the meaning of 'Hall of Refuge'?"

Lady Pak replied, "Fortune and misfortune, joy and woe alternate in this world. Later, when calamity comes, we may avoid it thanks to those trees, hence 'Hall of Refuge.'"

The minister was alarmed by this and asked if the future held good or bad luck.

"I am embarrassed to say, but I request you to ask no more," replied Lady Pak. "When it happens, you will know it. I cannot divulge the visitation of providence."

The minister was astonished by her mysterious pronouncements and lamented in sorrow.

"Alas, you are indeed a great heroic soul. If you were born a man, you would not have anything to worry about. As the father of a man, I left him spoiled and he disregards such a good person as you. I am already sixty. If I die soon, I fear such a person as you would perish."

Lady Pak cheerfully consoled him.

"My abilities are insufficient and my destiny is checkered, so how can I complain about my husband? If he soon achieves fame and is filial to his parents and loyal to the country, and remarries a decent woman and begets children so that his family would prosper for a thousand generations, then even if my humble life should end, I won't harbor a grudge."

The minister, hearing this, was struck by Lady Pak's good nature and shed tears in sorrow. Then he left and summoned Sibaek and reprimanded him.

"You don't listen to me and mistreat your virtuous wife. Our family is doomed."

Three years passed. The foal purchased on Bell Street had grown into a steed as wild as a Mongol horse. It had the body of a dragon and the head of a tiger, and its gallop was swift like clouds in the autumn sky. Lady Pak said to the minister, "On a certain day of a certain month, an imperial envoy will arrive from China. If you tie up this horse at the Envoy Gate, outside Saemun, the envoy, seeing it, will want to buy it on the spot. When he inquires about the price, ask for thirty thousand *nyang*."[7]

By this time the minister knew Lady Pak's marvelous talents, but he worried that the price was too high.

"This horse is not just a horse," she replied. "It is beyond comparison to any other. Chosŏn covers only several thousand leagues, whereas the great country of China encompasses several tens of thousands of leagues. There is no place to ride this horse other than in China, and so, regardless of the price, he will buy it. Therefore, asking for thirty thousand *nyang* is not too much."

The minister admired Lady Pak's foresight and awaited the day. Finally a tablet was posted announcing a Chinese envoy's visit to Korea, and one hundred officials of the entire court convened to wait for him at the Envoy Gate. The minister ordered his old servant, "Tie up the horse at the Envoy Gate."

When the envoy arrived at the gate, he saw the horse and was so impressed that he asked for its owner. The minister's old servant came in and lowered his head on the ground.

"Do you mean to sell the horse?" the envoy asked.

"I planned on it," replied the servant, "but the proper owner didn't show up, so I was unable to sell it."

"If you intended to sell it," pressed the envoy, "what is the price?"

"Thirty thousand *nyang*."

The envoy was unfazed.

"Seeing this horse," he said, "I would say thirty thousand *nyang* is rather cheap."

---

[7]The Envoy Gate (迎恩門, literally, "Gate for Welcoming Beneficence") was where embassies from China were officially greeted, and Saemun (literally, "New Gate") refers to a large city gate located in the western part of Seoul.

The envoy entered the city and paid the thirty thousand *nyang*. The minister expressed his gratitude to Lady Pak and was moved by her marvelous ability.

At this time, the country being prosperous, the king decreed a civil service examination to find talented men. Lady Pak had a dream at that time in which from the middle of the pond a blue dragon holding a water dropper in its mouth entered her room. At this moment she awoke. She thought it strange and thus went to the pond, where she found a new water dropper. She took it and ordered Kyehwa to request Sibaek to come. But Sibaek scolded Kyehwa, saying, "I am about to go and take the examination. What does this wicked woman want?"

His barking yell was as stern as an autumn frost. When Kyehwa reported it, Lady Pak heaved a sigh and brought out the water dropper.

"Take this to my husband and tell him to use it at the examination hall," she said.

Sibaek received the water dropper and entered the examination hall. He looked at the topic for composition, then tilted the water dropper to the inkstone and ground the ink bar and dashed off a composition and was the first to submit it. After a while the chair of the selection committee announced, "The winner of this examination is Yi Sibaek."

The sound of Sibaek's name echoed throughout the capital. He entered the palace and prostrated himself in the royal presence. The king praised him and bestowed a cup upon him. Then the court put the honorary flower in his hair, set up a canopy in blue and red above his head, arranged flower boys in pairs, and with assorted music, proudly paraded him through the main streets—it was late spring, with flowers in bloom and spectacular scenery. Sibaek had an immaculate face like jade and looked like a celestial officer. Everyone spoke well of him, and the people of the capital jostled each other to see him and praise him.

Alas, Lady Pak was consumed with anxiety, sitting all alone deep in the Hall of Refuge. Her maid, Kyehwa, watched her movements, saddened, and tried to console her.

"Man's destiny—fortune and misfortune, joy and sorrow—are all ordained," said Lady Pak. "Therefore, King Tang [湯王, ca. 1675–1646 B.C.E.] was captured by King Jie [傑王, ca. 1728–1675 B.C.E.] of the Xia dynasty [ca. 2070–ca. 1600 B.C.E.]; King Wen was thrown into Youli prison; and a sage like Confucius [552–479 B.C.E.] labored in the fields of Chen [陳] and Cai [蔡]. So why should a person like me harbor a grudge?"[8]

---

[8] The reference to King Tang and King Jie is backward. King Jie, an infamous tyrant, was overthrown by King Tang. This example, therefore, does not make the point intended by the author.

After hearing this, Kyehwa inwardly prayed for something good to happen to her lady. One day, Lady Pak said to the minister, "Your unworthy daughter-in-law has been married for three years. I haven't heard any news about my family in all that time, so I request to make a short visit there."

"Your request is reasonable," the minister replied, "but the road to the Kŭmgang Mountains is tortuous, rugged, and far away, and traveling with so much to carry for such a trip would be extremely difficult for a woman."

"Packing for travel is unnecessary. I need only two days to make the journey and return."

The minister thought it strange, but Lady Pak's miraculous achievements were difficult for ordinary people to emulate. He therefore allowed her to go and entreated her to return soon. The next day, after the crow of the rooster, Lady Pak took her leave of the minister in his quarters and walked out the door. After only a few steps, her whereabouts were unknown. As she promised, Lady Pak quietly returned the next day and reported her arrival to the minister. When he asked her if things were well at home and how her father was, she replied, "Things are well. And my father said he would come here to visit on a certain day."

The minister was pleased by this. He prepared much drink and food and awaited the arrival of the hermit. When the day came, the minister adjusted his attire and saw that the reception hall was dusted and cleaned. All of a sudden the sound of a jade flute drew nearer and nearer, the glowing clouds shone bright, and the hermit descended from the sky on a white crane and stepped into the hall. The minister greeted him gladly in a courteous manner. While catching up on things, the minister said, "My life is futile. I have only one child, and he has only caused sadness for my virtuous daughter-in-law, and it is all because of my foolishness. I've wronged you in many ways, so how can I describe my shame?"

"My daughter's appearance is vulgar," the hermit replied, "and so is her fate. Such a stormy existence has been entrusted to you, and I am moved by your grace. It is rather I who cannot overcome my shame."

The minister ordered that food and drink be served, and they toasted each other and had a good time with *paduk* and the jade flute. One day, the hermit called for his daughter and said, "The time of your bad luck is now over, so remove your skin."

At this, Lady Pak responded and went into the Hall of Refuge. The minister did not understand this and thought it strange. After a five-day visit, the hermit bid farewell to the minister. The minister was desperate for him to stay, but the hermit would not relent.

"Now that you are leaving, when shall we meet again?" the minister asked.

"Hazy mountains are piled atop one another," said the hermit, "and the Ruo River is far away,[9] so it is not certain we should have another meeting. The circle of human life is ordained by destinies that I cannot control. I wish you one hundred years of blissful life."

Upon hearing this, the minister was overcome with sadness. But Lady Pak, bidding her father farewell, was not sorrowful at all. Soon, as clouds became mysteriously bright, the hermit departed from the hall and soared up toward the void. Afterward, only the sound of the jade flute could be heard. No one knew where he went. That night, after bathing, Lady Pak went into the yard and, looking up at the sky, raised her hands in prayer. Then she went to bed. The next day she got up at first light and, calling for Kyehwa, said, "I shed my skin last night. Therefore go and request the lord to furnish me with a jade chest."

Kyehwa looked at the lady who had cast off her skin. Her jadelike face and moonlike attitude were amazing, and fragrance filled the room. Kyehwa, barely managing to remain calm, kept looking at her. She saw beauty and elegance that even surpassed the famous Xi Shi [西施] and Yang Guifei. Kyehwa went immediately to the minister, her face full of happiness, gasping for breath. The minister, thinking this strange, asked, "What has made you so pleased that you are unable to speak?"

Kyehwa then broke into song:

My mind is gleeful and glad.
Spring color there and the bright moon yonder are dazzling,
Sweetness comes after toil.
This spring color and the moon over there are the ones among hundreds
    of flowers in the spring dream of Luoyang.
Bees and butterflies buzzing and humming over there,
Look around this spring color in clear places of blue mountains and
    green rivers.

The minister, refreshed and moved by what he had heard, rushed to the Hall of Refuge, Kyehwa following behind. He encountered there an ethereal scent and a certain beauty, who pleasantly said, "This unworthy woman shed her skin last night. If you prepare a jade chest, I would like to place my old skin in it and bury it in a propitious place."

The minister, amazed, scrutinized the woman. She was indeed an absolute beauty. Her appearance was brilliant and her manner was elegant like the moon

---

[9] According to legend, the Ruo River is where Daoist immortals were believed to dwell.

goddess Heng'e [姮娥]. The minister was so enchanted that he was left speechless. He ordered that a jade chest be made and sent to her, then went into his house and spoke to his wife and son about what had occurred. Hearing the story, his wife and family rushed to the Hall of Refuge to look upon the woman. Her hair was fine like jade and her face had a delicate blush, and her flowery appearance and moonlike movements were not those of a human being. Who dared not esteem her? When Sibaek heard of this, he also became awestruck. He went to the Hall of Refuge, but, remembering his harsh treatment of Lady Pak, he dared not open the door. During this moment of hesitation, Kyehwa appeared and led him in, humming another song:

> Beautiful, that bright moon is shrouded amid black clouds,
> A bright day turns away the dark, last night of the month,
> The reigning poet Li Bo [李白, 701–762] has no interest in poetry at all,
> Su Shi [蘇軾, 1037–1101] has no way to go boating on the Red Cliff River.
> The celestial void is peaceful and the jade shape is neat,
> Last night's floating clouds are gone,
> The heaven and the earth are bright and vivid, and your mind is also refreshed.
> Great, great, the moon is greatly attractive.
> The bright moon and willows are good for revels.
> My man, enjoy the moon color in the White Jade Tower, that place of beauty.

After hearing this song, Sibaek felt refreshed and encouraged. Yet he still could not enter her inner room but instead peeped in from outside the door. Lady Pak had indeed become an absolute beauty. The inside of the room was bright and fragrant. As he was about to enter, Lady Pak posed with dignity, began to adjust her clothes with her eyes downcast, thus he dared not enter the room but left the reception hall to meet his father.

"Did you meet Lady Pak?" the minister asked.

Sibaek felt so ashamed that he could not reply. He silently sat down, then got up and left, overcome with mortification. He waited for the sun to set. The light of day faded, but he had no thought of eating his evening meal. When he finally entered the Hall of Refuge, Lady Pak lit a candle, and with her face made up, she expressed her dignity and sat there haughtily. Sibaek was about to pass through the door, but he found himself taking a step backward and was unable to enter the room. He could not calm down and thought to himself, *It is not that I cannot go in*. His craving for Lady Pak was uncontrollable, and he hung around outside the door. When he tried to enter, his face turned red, his words became garbled, he could not breathe, and he could barely advance a single step into the room. Finally, after much hesitation, he went in and sat down.

Lady Pak read Sibaek's mind and was amused by his thoughts, but she maintained a stern look as she sat there, unmoving. Sibaek sat with resolution, as if at the risk of his life, and yet his mouth felt heavy, he was speechless, and he stared at Lady Pak intently. Lady Pak sat absolutely still like a statue. Gazing at her in silence, Sibaek was at his wit's end. His throbbing heart abated and yet his timid mind was desperate. No matter how much he pondered, the thought of taking Lady Pak's hand, of talking to her, of sleeping with her seemed more daunting than climbing up to the sky. In this way they spent the night, and after the rooster's cry, Sibaek had no choice but to leave. He departed the reception hall and went to inquire about the minister's morning condition. The minister, not knowing what had transpired overnight, was all smiles.

The next day, Sibaek wandered around near the Hall of Refuge. Unable to enter Lady Pak's room, he thought, *After the sun goes down, I'll go in and admit that I mistreated her and did wrong in the past.* And so he waited. When the sun set, he adjusted his robes and his cap and entered the Hall of Refuge and sat down. He felt a little more in control of himself than on the previous day, but he still found it impossible to say what he intended. Lady Pak sat neatly facing him, dignified— embodying the saying, "A foot of distance feels like a thousand leagues." When a husband mistreats his wife, it is possible for the wife to speak out against it. But for several years of her marriage Lady Pak had been miserable, though she had supernatural abilities to move heaven and earth. So she deliberately acted aloof lest Sibaek should talk to her. Faced with such hardship for many days, even with a liver of iron and a stomach of stone, how could Sibaek stand it? Of course he fell ill. He gave up eating and drinking and soon became haggard—an ailment that, alas, could not be cured even by the legendary physician Bian Que [扁鵲]. The minister became anxious about his son, and the entire family was all in a flutter. But Sibaek dared not confess the situation to anyone. Only Lady Pak knew.

One day, at the onset of dusk, Lady Pak sent Kyehwa to request Sibaek to come. Hearing this, Sibaek rushed to the Hall of Refuge stumbling along the way. Lady Pak, with a prim countenance, softly said, "When a man enters this world, he has honorable obligations. In childhood, he should immerse himself in study and serve his parents with filial respect. When taking a wife, he should guide her wisely so that his family may prosper for ten thousand generations. But my husband has been concerned only with physical beauty and, because of my appalling appearance, did not count me as a person. How then can you hope to adhere to the Five Relationships [五倫, K. Oryun] and sincerely serve your parents? I have given you a hard time because I worry about your heart. Now I am done being indignant and I ask you to listen to me. Henceforth, you must change your approach to self-cultivation and married life."

Sibaek, hearing these polite words, was deeply moved.

"This petty scholar was ignorant and so distressed you. I regret my behavior now but I fear it is too late. You have ceased being angry with me. How could I ask for anything more?"

Lady Pak got up and fetched a quilt and pillow and said, "This is the first time these have been taken out since our wedding."

And with that they spent the night together, and it was incomparably sweet. The news of Lady Pak's transformation was by this time the talk of the capital. Wives of high officials all wanted to see her, and so she sent a letter of invitation to each household. It read, "These are gorgeous days in the third month of spring. For viewing flowers and willows, I cordially invite you to come on a certain day and join me with food and drink at the Blue Tower [青樓, K. Ch'ŏng-ru] at the Pear Garden [梨院, K. Yi-wŏn] in the Nak Mountain forest."

Every lady in the capital accordingly prepared refreshments. Lady Pak did so as well. And on the appointed day, accompanied by her servants, she rode in a floral palanquin to the Blue Tower, where all the other ladies were flocking together. Alighting from her palanquin, Lady Pak, followed by Kyehwa, mounted the tower and exchanged formal greetings with the other ladies, then they all seated themselves on either the east or west side, duchesses and marquises with beautiful faces and in vividly colored clothing, brilliant as a line of nymphs emerging from a jade pond. Amid this host of noblewomen, Lady Pak showed a stately mien and upright appearance with her jadelike face and moonlike manner. As stunning as the other ladies were, no one, neither celestial nor mortal, could match her appearance. The people seated there, looking at her, were stunned into silence. Before long, cups and plates were set out all around. When drink was offered to Lady Pak, she held the cup in her hands and intentionally spilled it on her skirt. She immediately took off the garment and, handing it to her servant, said, "Burn it."

The servant threw the skirt into the fire, and the flames took hold until it seemed only ashes remained. Lady Pak then ordered, "Shake off the ashes and bring the skirt back to me."

When the servant did so, Lady Pak put on the garment again. Its color was even more fascinating and beautiful than before. The ladies in the crowd, seeing all this, were greatly surprised and puzzled and asked about what they had seen.

"This ramie is called Hwahanp'o," Lady Pak explained. "If it is stained, it should not be washed with water but with fire. The silk is woven from the fur of fire rats, which do not exist in this world. It can be found only in the immortal realm."

The ladies asked, "And what kind of silk is your jacket made of?"

"This silk is called Silk of Ice Silkworms [冰蠶緞, K. Pingjamdan],"¹⁰ said Lady Pak. "My father went to the dragon palace to obtain it. If it is immersed in water, it does not get wet. If it is put into the fire, it does not burn. It is not crafted by human hands but is the finest work of a dragon lady."

All the ladies looked at one another in wonder, marveling at the silk. When drink was offered to Lady Pak, she declined it. All the ladies kept pressing her, however, so Lady Pak relented. Accepting the cup, she took a gold phoenix hairpin and drew it across the middle of the wine in the cup, cutting the liquid in two. She then drank half the wine and set the cup down. When the others looked at the cup, they saw that half the wine remained, as if cut by a knife. The ladies all admired Lady Pak's marvelous talents and went on to enjoy a wonderful time all that day and long into the evening as the sunlight danced between the white clouds,¹¹ as fatigued birds headed out to the forest, and the moon rose over the eastern mountain ridge. Finally the gathering broke up and the ladies returned to their homes.

In those days, after returning home from his office, Sibaek would spend time with Lady Pak discussing matters both contemporary and ancient. After a time, he was promoted and made an official of the Academy of Letters [翰林院 Hallimwŏn] and then directly appointed by the king to the post of inspector of P'yŏng'an province. After prostrating himself in the royal presence, while packing in preparation to take his leave, he ordered a carpenter to make a flower palanquin.

"What is the purpose of this palanquin?" Lady Pak inquired.

"The king had unfathomable grace to appoint me the inspector of P'yŏng'an province," said Sibaek. "I plan to take you with me."

To this Lady Pak replied, "Your humble wife has heard it said, 'A man should achieve a great reputation to bring glory to his parents and to show loyalty to his country.' There is also an adage, 'Days for the lord are many, yet days for parents are few.' If I accompany you, who will look after your parents? I will stay here to take care of them. May you arrive at your post safe and manage provincial affairs so as to repay the king's grace with your allegiance."

---

¹⁰Wang Jia (王嘉, d. 390), *Shiyi ji* 拾遺記, 10: "Ice silkworms were seven *ch'i* [寸, one *ch'i* is approximately 3.33 centimeters] in size and black in color. They had horns and scales. After being covered with frosty snow, they spun thread. The thread was about one *cha* [尺, one *cha* is 33.3 centimeters] in length and had five colors. It was woven into beautiful brocade; the thread was not wet even after being soaked, and even after being thrown into fire overnight, it did not catch fire" (有冰蠶長七寸，黑色，有角有鱗，以霜雪覆之，然後作繭，長一尺，其色五綵，織爲文錦，入水而不濡，以之投火，則經宿不燎。).

¹¹The "sunlight danced between the white clouds" is a tentative translation; the full meaning of the original phrase (한걸음 채처 석양이 백말 궁글치고) is unclear.

Sibaek was moved by these words and expressed his gratitude, saying, "How can your words be wrong? You make me feel ashamed for not thinking of it first. Yes, please stay here and support my parents with filial duty, lest I become an undutiful son."

He left to take up his new post that day. Following his arrival in P'yŏngyang, he strove to discover and ease the hardships of the common people and to guide the magistrates' conduct, so that within a year his fame had spread throughout the province. The king heard of this and, thinking highly of Sibaek, summoned him to serve as minister of war. Sibaek read the royal edict, immediately entered the capital, and prostrated himself in the royal presence and promptly undertook ministry affairs. In the eighth month of the Blue Rat Year [1624], when traveling to Nanjing under the royal command, Sibaek took General Im Kyŏngŏp to enter Nanjing. At that moment, a barbarian country to the north experienced the disturbance of Pale Horse Keda [驄馬可達, C. Congmakeda] and requested that the Chinese emperor dispatch troops.[12]

"Appoint the Chosŏn envoy commander in chief of the relief forces and save the northern country," the emperor commanded.

Sibaek and Im Kyŏngŏp shattered Congmakeda's army and saved the barbarian country. Upon their return to China, the emperor showed his pleasure by granting them a large reward of gold, silver, and jewels and appointed them high civilian officials, for which Sibaek and Im Kyŏngŏp were very grateful. Returning to their own country, the king rewarded them further, appointing Sibaek third minister and Im Kyŏngŏp the commander in chief of the capital.

At this time the barbarian country became increasingly belligerent and frequently infiltrated the northern part of the kingdom. The king accordingly appointed Im Kyŏngŏp the governor of Ŭiju, saying, "Protect the people from the barbarian bandits."

---

[12]Pale Horse (驄馬 Congma)—specifically, a white horse with a dark mane and tail—is associated with Chinese government censors because of the type of horse they rode; Keda seems to refer to Shi Keda (時可達, dates unknown), who is named in the *Veritable Records of the Chosŏn Dynasty* [朝鮮王朝實錄 *Chosŏn wangjo sillok*] as a representative of Mao Wenlong (毛文龍, 1576–1629), a Ming Chinese general who was involved in the escalating clashes between Ming China, the Manchus, and the Koreans. In 1624, the year of the Blue Rat named in the story, Shi Keda was criticized for his involvement in seizing food, cattle, and horses from Koreans living in the north. Because there are no Chinese characters in the original text, it is also possible that Kadal (i.e., Keda in the Chinese reading) might be a general term for barbarian (假韃, 靼, i.e., "fake Tartar, Mongolian"). Whatever the case, this section of the story is historically confusing. The critical revolt that occurred in 1624 broke out within Chosŏn Korea and was led by Yi Kwal (李适, 1587–1624), a Korean military official who attempted to overthrow the government. In addition, the following part of the story quickly moves to 1636, thus condensing well over a decade's worth of incidents into a single event in the story.

The barbarian king, meanwhile, was scheming to devour Chosŏn. He inquired of his court officials, "Our generals are no match for the Chosŏn general Im Kyŏngŏp. What should I do?"

His queen was a woman who saw things a thousand leagues ahead when seated, ten thousand leagues when standing. She expressed her opinion to the barbarian king.

"I have observed the secret signs in the sky. They reveal the existence of a divine man in the capital of Chosŏn, so although Im Kyŏngŏp is not there, your plan will be difficult to carry out. If this divine man were killed, Im Kyŏngŏp would no longer be so formidable."

"Then how can we get rid of this divine man?" asked the barbarian king.

"There is no perfect plan," replied the queen. "But the Chosŏn people are known to indulge in beauty, so here is an idea: send a female assassin—someone charming, literate, brave, and skilled with weapons—to kill the divine man."

"Who," asked the king, "would be best qualified to carry this out?"

"A girl named Qi Hongda," said the queen. "She is here in the palace and is made for the role."

The king immediately summoned Qi Hongda, told her what to do, and said, "If you go to Chosŏn and are successful, I will grant you one thousand pieces of gold and ten thousand sacks of grain."

When Qi Hongda was about to depart on her journey, the queen summoned her and gave her a warning.

"If you go to Chosŏn and visit Third Minister Yi Sibaek's house, you will know what to do. Kill the divine man, and on your way home go to Ŭiju and kill Im Kyŏngŏp. May you accomplish what you set out to do. If you fail, a calamity will befall you."

Qi Hongda took her leave, confident in her abilities and sure of success. After traveling for many days, she arrived in the kingdom of Chosŏn.

At this time Lady Pak, seated alone in the Hall of Refuge, observed the secret configurations of the sky and requested to speak to the third minister.

"On a certain month and day," she said, "a beautiful woman will come looking for you. Please send her to the Hall of Refuge."

"What woman do you speak of?" the minister asked.

"When the time comes, you will naturally know her," Lady Pak replied. "The woman will necessarily want to stay in a man's quarters. If she is allowed to stay in the reception hall, you will suffer a disaster. I earnestly request you to take this to heart."

Lady Pak then summoned Kyehwa and said, "You will brew much drink— one-half strong and the other half mild. Any time I am with a certain woman and tell you to bring drink, serve the strong drink to the woman and the mild drink to me. Much food also should be prepared."

One day, when the minister was seated alone in the reception hall, a woman entered and bowed to the ground in the yard. Then she stepped up onto the platform so the minister had a look at her face. He saw that she was an absolute beauty. He thought she was so beautiful that he had to ask, "Who are you?"

"I am a *kisaeng* from the countryside," the woman replied. "I've come to the capital for sightseeing. I have been walking nearby, and I dared to enter this beautiful house."

The minister was attracted by her gorgeous appearance and invited her to come into the hall.

"You said you are from the countryside. Which village? And what is your name?"

"I originally lived in Ch'ŏnma Fortress. After losing my parents when I was young, I drifted about looking for food, then became the servant of a country official. My given name is P'ungmae. I don't know my surname."

"Sit down," the minister said.

He observed her movements. She was by no means an ordinary figure, and she had a stunning face. When he discussed literature, moreover, he saw that she had great literary talent, even more remarkable than his own. Recalling what his wife had requested, he was deeply suspicious of her identity during their long conversation. He therefore said, "Enter the inner quarters and rest comfortably there."

"How dare I stay in the inner quarters of a noble household?" the woman replied. "Let me serve you tonight and bring you drink."

"Tonight I am indisposed. Please go inside." Then he called Kyehwa. "Let this guest rest in the Hall of Refuge."

The woman reluctantly followed Kyehwa to the Hall of Refuge. She paid her respects to Lady Pak and was invited in. Lady Pak had her sit in her room and asked her name. After the woman repeated what she had told the minister, Lady Pak said, "I see from your appearance that you are not a lowborn person. You have traveled far to find our house, yet I fear it has been in vain." She then summoned Kyehwa and said, "A guest has come. Bring some drink and food."

Kyehwa brought an assortment of rare dishes on a jade tray and a large portion of drink.

"My guest must be tired and thirsty from the hardship of travel," said Lady Pak. "Offer her a drink."

Lady Pak and the woman received the same cup in turn, but the wine Lady Pak drank was mild, while what the woman drank was strong. Together, they consumed a great amount of wine, but neither appeared to be affected. Bystanders from all directions and the minister peeped in. Witnessing the amount of drink and food they consumed, each and every one became alarmed. After the drinking bout was over, when the woman conversed with Lady Pak, her words and manner of speech remained excellent, thus her dignity was revealed. The woman thought, *I have seen the amount of drink and food this lady can consume. And when discussing literary matters, I was not her rival; when meeting the minister at the reception hall, he was just talented and handsome; and now I see that this lady is definitely the one who is heroic and divine. Our queen said if I went to the minister's house, I would know whom to kill; it definitely means this lady; I see, I will work on her.*

"I am very fatigued and drunk," she said. "I am embarrassed to ask, but may I lie down for a little while?"

"Lying down after drinking is perfectly understandable," said Lady Pak. "Sleep well."

After being provided with a pillow, the woman lay down. Lady Pak pretended to lie down as well but remained alert to her guest's movements. Presently the woman fell into a deep sleep and then her eyes opened. From them a fireball emerged and rolled around in the room as her breathing echoed throughout the house. Lady Pak got up and opened the assassin's bag. It contained nothing but a dagger on which was carved the phrase, "Flying Swallow Dagger" in vermilion. The dagger came out of the bag and turned into a swallow, which flew about the room to attack Lady Pak. She sprinkled fiery ashes, whereupon the bird could not maintain its form and fell to the floor. Lady Pak took up the dagger and sat on the woman's belly.

"Qi Hongda!" she cried. "Wake up and look at me!"

The sound shocked Qi Hongda awake, and she looked about. She could not move at all with Lady Pak sitting atop her, dagger in hand. Qi Hongda answered in panic, "How do you know my name?"

Lady Pak pointed the dagger at her throat and rebuked her.

"Your barbarian king was in trouble because of Congmakeda's revolt and survived thanks to our minister. But far from paying back his kindness, your king sought to devour our country and then sent such a wicked servant as you to test me. So with this dagger I will kill you first and wreak my fury upon your king."

Roaring thus, Lady Pak looked sharp and stately but cold as autumn frost. Qi Hongda was horrified.

"Lady Pak, you know everything already. How dare I try to deceive you any longer? Indeed, things are as you say. I came here under the royal command, and as his female vassal I could not decline. I entreat you to spare my life."

She pleaded again and again, and Lady Pak cast aside the dagger and got off her belly. Then reprimanding her again, Lady Pak sent her away. Meanwhile, people in the household and the minister saw this scene and were shocked, as if their spirits had flown away and their wits scattered to the winds.

The minister instantly reported this to the royal court. The king, greatly surprised, said, "If it were not for Lady Pak, the country would have faced disaster."

He promptly issued a royal command to the governor of Ŭiju, "Watch out for a suspicious woman." He also graced Lady Pak with the title of Bright Moon Lady [明月夫人 Myŏngwŏl Puin], saying, "In the future, no matter what mishap occurs, you will handle it."

After leaving Lady Pak, Qi Hongda thought to herself, *The scheme is already uncovered. Even if I go to Ŭiju, it would be useless.* She returned to her country right away and reported on her work. The king asked her, "Did you accomplish your task?"

Qi Hongda reported everything from beginning to end and fully explained how she could not succeed. The barbarian king was surprised to hear this, and so he requested the queen to discuss the matter and asked for another good plan.

"These days when I examine the secrets behind the movements of the constellations," said the queen, "I see that Chosŏn has many villainous retainers. They are jealous of worthy men, so do not listen to them. If you quickly mobilize troops and enter the country from the east, instead of from the north, and select a general to block the northern road and stop General Im Kyŏngŏp's troops from passing through, you will certainly succeed."

The barbarian king, greatly pleased, appointed the brothers Long Guda [Inggŭldai] and Long Lüda as commanders in chief and assigned them three hundred thousand crack troops, saying,[13] "Do not march to Ŭiju. Make a detour to the east, but block the path to Ŭiju and cut off their communications."

The queen also summoned the two commanders and said, "If you enter the country from the east and lay siege to the capital, you will catch Im Kyŏngŏp off guard and so achieve your mission. But do not intrude into Third Minister Yi Sibaek's rear garden. If you enter it, you will not only fail in your mission but also lose your life. Burn this into your memories and don't forget it!"

The two generals received the command and led their troops across the Yellow Sea to the east and then headed to the capital without any delay.

At this time, Lady Pak was in the Hall of Refuge observing the secrets behind the movements of the constellations. Requesting a meeting with the minister, she said, "The barbarian enemy has entered our territory. I ask you to urgently report this to the royal presence, so that the king may summon Im Kyŏngŏp to defend the capital, drafting troops to block the enemy's approach."

"If the northern barbarian enemy enters the country," the minister replied, "they will come from the north. Im Kyŏngŏp is the governor of Ŭiju and is in

---

[13] In reality, the Manchu cavalry numbered closer to one hundred thousand. They were concentrated in Shenyang under the direct control of the emperor, Hong Taiji, here referred to as the "barbarian king." Galloping down the peninsula at full speed, they were able to threaten the Korean capital and court within roughly ten days.

charge of defense in the north. Calling him to the capital will leave that whole region undefended."

"The enemy will not come from the north," said Lady Pak. "They will come east, across the Yellow Sea. It is therefore imperative that Governor Im be summoned by royal command."

The minister, shocked by what he had heard, went to the court and reported everything Lady Pak had said. The king was surprised and all the court officials were panicked, and, intending to summon Im Kyŏngŏp, the king spoke with his ministers. The deputy prime minister, Wŏn Tup'yo, submitted his opinion to the king, saying, "The northern barbarians are shrewd by nature. Lady Pak is definitely correct in her assessment. We should do what she says."

Hearing this, Kim Chajŏm flared up.

"The retainers' words are preposterous. The northern enemy has been defeated many times by Im Kyŏngŏp and has been unable to raise an army. And even if they do raise an army, they can only come from the north. So if Im Kyŏngŏp is summoned here and the barbarian enemy captures Ŭiju, we will be unable to stop them and the fate of the country could be decided in a moment. Why do you listen to this wicked woman's advice to pull the army back from the north to protect the east? These are bewitching words. How can you say they are words of wisdom?"

"Lady Pak is a divine person," said the king. "She has a supernatural sense, and there have been many wondrous happenings. I shall do as she says."

But Kim Chajŏm continued to press his case.

"These days—fine and fruitful, peaceful and prosperous—a war won't break out. Lady Pak is an enchantress. How can Your Majesty allow himself to be bewitched by her words and manage the affairs of state like child's play?"

The other court officials all knew that Kim Chajŏm was wrong, but they could not say a word. The king postponed the matter and finished the morning assembly, and the third minister returned home and told Lady Pak the whole story.

"Alas!" lamented Lady Pak, raising her face to the sky. "The barbarian enemy will attack the capital before long, but a treacherous man misleads the ruler and endangers the royal altar! If Im Kyŏngŏp had been ordered to go immediately and lay an ambush in the east and to strike the enemy in strength, the barbarians would not have been hard to wipe out. This hopeless situation is like greeting the enemy with our hands tied. The country is doomed now and I cannot prevent it. Since you already serve the country, even in misery you must remain loyal. Even though completely defeated and killed in the rout, you have that obligation as a vassal of the country. I wish you to leave your honorable name to posterity. Given this urgent situation, if Kim Chajŏm seizes military power, calamity will ensue. I thus entreat you to find a worthy man and place him in charge."

Having heard these words, the third minister could not hide his grief. He looked up at the heavens, sighed, and was overcome with worry. *At the risk of death*, he finally decided, *I will petition the king again.*

He returned to the palace in the tenth month of the Red Rat Year [1636]. Before he reached the royal presence, while still outside the Great East Gate, a gun boomed out, bells and drums sounded, and the earth and sky shook. Barbarian forces had reached the East Gate. They broke through and started massacring people in the capital, causing panic and tumult as the population tried to flee. Countless people were speared and hacked to death by the bandits, until dead bodies were piled up like a mountain. The citizens of the capital looked up at the sky and beat on the ground looking for help. Their cries of anguish shook the heavens and the earth.

The king was totally lost.

"The capital has fallen," he said to the third minister. "Bandits are entering Kuhwa Gate. What shall I do?"

"The situation is urgent," the third minister replied. "You need to evacuate immediately to Namhan Mountain Fortress [南韓山城 Namhan Sansŏng]."

They hastened in a jade sedan chair out the West Gate. Encountering an enemy ambush, the third minister hacked a way through with his sword, risking his own life. He beheaded a barbarian general and managed to get the king safely into the mountain fortress.

Meanwhile, Lady Pak gathered the household and relatives into the Hall of Refuge. The barbarian general Long Guda sent for his younger brother, Long Lüda, and said, "Defend the capital and collect procurements."

Long Guda himself led his troops to lay siege to Namhan Mountain Fortress. Long Lüda took command of the capital and searched for procurements, with the result that the city became as turbulent as boiling water. Numerous runaways were killed. The people sheltering in the Hall of Refuge heard of what was happening and wanted to escape. Lady Pak said, "Every exit from the capital is being guarded by the bandits. And even if you were able to flee, where would you go? If you remain here, you will be safe from disaster, so do not worry."

At this time, when Lüda led over one hundred horsemen in a surprise attack on the minister's house in search of the residents there, he found the place empty. He cautiously entered the rear garden and looked around at all the marvelous trees luxuriantly arranged to the left and right. He thought them strange and took a closer look. In each tree dragons and tigers crouched together, back to back. Every branch was transformed into snakes and beasts, arousing the wind on the ground and clouds in the sky. Death filled the air, and the sounds of drums and bugles could be heard in the distance. In the midst of all this numerous people were sheltered, so Lüda triumphantly rushed in to plunder the Hall of Refuge. Abruptly the sky turned murky, dark clouds gathered, lightning flashed and thunder rumbled, and the trees all about turned into numerous soldiers clad in armor. They surrounded Lüda in a growing mass, branches and leaves turning into eerie banners, spears, and swords like autumn frost, war cries reverberating across the realm. Lüda became terrified and tried to flee, but knife-edged boulders over one thousand *chang* high blocked his way, encircling him in multiple layers. There was nowhere for him to retreat. At this moment, with Lüda afraid and confused and not knowing what to do, Kyehwa emerged from the Hall of Refuge, sword in hand.

"What sort of bandit are you," she demanded, "to enter such an important place as this and hasten your death?"

Lüda placed his hands together and bowed, saying, "I do not know who you are, madam, but I beg you to spare my life."

"I am Lady Pak's maid," Kyehwa replied. "Our mistress, Lady Bright Moon, cast a magic spell and has long been awaiting you. You are an evil bandit. Come, stick out your neck and die by this sword."

Hearing this, Lüda became enraged. He raised his sword and tried to strike her with it, but his hand suddenly became numb and he could not wield the weapon. Helpless, he looked up at the sky and lamented, "Born an ambitious man, I came to this foreign country ten thousand leagues away expecting to accomplish great things. How could I have imagined being killed by the hand of a mere girl?"

"Pitiful! Pathetic!" Kyehwa laughed. "You call yourself a great man of the world yet you can't beat a woman like me. Your cursed king doesn't know the mandate of heaven. He ordered an attack on this country known for its propriety and honor and dispatched a fool such as you. So now your life is mine. Come! Get ready to die by my sword!"

Lüda looked up to heaven and sighed, "This is my destiny."

And with that he killed himself. Kyehwa cut off Lüda's head and hung it outside the gate. Soon the wind stopped blowing and the clouds stopped moving and the sky and the earth became bright and clear.

But the country was doomed. The barbarian horde seized the upper hand and captured the queen, the crown prince, and the royal prince,[14] all because Kim Chajŏm had left the way open for the enemy. It was a deplorable situation. Sadly, for many days they were besieged by the enemy, the situation steadily worsened, and all strength was exhausted. The king thus signed a peace treaty with the bandits. After accepting the peace treaty and while on his way to the capital, Long Guda suddenly heard of the death of his brother, Lüda, and wailed

---

[14] The crown prince was Sohyŏn (昭顯世子, 1612–1645). The prince was Pongnim (鳳林大君, 1619–1659), who later became King Hyojong (孝宗, r. 1649–1659).

for him, saying, "I have already received the peace treaty. Who would dare to do harm to my brother? Today I will take revenge."

He led his troops into the capital and arrived at the Hall of Refuge, where it was reported that Lüda's head was hanging outside the gate. Unable to quell his fury, Long Guda wielded his sword and whipped his horse. When he was about to rush in, one of the commanders looked at the trees and said, "You should swallow your anger. Look at those trees. They are arranged based on the principle of the eight arrays diagram [八陣圖法, K. *p'aljin to-bŏp*] employed by the legendary strategist Zhuge Liang. You should not take the woman of this house lightly."

Long Guda thereupon vented his fury all the more. He took up his sword and shouted, "You say so, yet how can I take revenge for my brother?"

"No matter how furious you are," replied the commander, "if you enter such a strategic spot, you will not only fail to get revenge for your brother but you will die just like him. You therefore need to calm down."

Long Guda thought this to be right, and then commanded his army, "Cut down all the trees!"

A gust of wind suddenly blew; clouds appeared and fog grew thick; the leaves of every tree turned into innumerable soldiers; the sound of gongs and war cries reverberated throughout the realm; dragons and snakes, black birds and white snakes, flocked together in one continuous line, their heads and tails touching, gushing out wind and clouds; banners, spears, and swords glistened like stars; and a divine general, clad in armor, raised a three-*ch'ŏk* sword and chopped off the heads of the barbarian soldiers; cracks of thunder and flashes of lightning seemed to collapse rivers and mountains so that the barbarian soldiers were unable to discern the sky from the ground, and their corpses piled up in great mounds.

Awestruck, Long Guda sounded the gong to withdraw his army. Soon, the sky brightened and the ground became clear. Long Guda became even more enraged. He took up his sword and rushed forward again, and instantly the sky darkened, the land became murky, and the divine soldiers became so numerous again that the barbarians could not advance. Suddenly Kyehwa appeared from a tree to taunt him.

"Long Guda, you fool! Your little brother died at my hands, and now you too want to die?"

"What sort of girl are you to incite my anger?" Long Guda roared. "My younger brother was unlucky and died at your hands, but I have concluded a peace treaty with your country, so now you are all my country's servants and concubines. Hold your tongue now, and receive my sword!"

Kyehwa pretended not to hear him.

"Your brother was killed by my sword, and now you have foolishly placed your own life in my hands."

This made Long Guda even more furious. He cried out to his soldiers, "All of you! Draw your bows! Shoot!"

A blizzard of arrows flew toward Kyehwa, but not a single one touched her. No matter how angry Long Guda was, what could he do? Alarmed by Kyehwa's ability, he summoned the commander in chief of Chosŏn, Kim Chajŏm, and said, "You are now my country's official. How can you disobey my order?"

Kim Chajŏm replied in awe, "I will do what you tell me."

"Collect your army, then!" yelled Long Guda. "Capture Lady Pak and Kyehwa and bring them to me!"

Kim Chajŏm, terrified, fired a gun to muster his army and surrounded the Hall of Refuge. The eight gates suddenly transformed into traps over one hundred *kil* deep. Long Guda witnessed the change and, seeing no way to easily break into the hall, conceived of a plan. He ordered the army to dig a ditch ten leagues, spanning the four directions around the Hall of Refuge, and fill it with gunpowder and explosives. Then he said, "You may have myriad tactics, but how will you deal with this?"

When he commanded that the ditch be set on fire, the gunpowder exploded with such force that it shook the capital for thirty leagues in each direction, flames filled the sky, and one could not count the dead, so great was the number. Lady Pak hung down the jade screen, and, holding a jade celestial fan in her left hand, she fanned a fire that struck the dust-covered barbarians and broke their military formations. Many were burned or stamped to death, while the remaining soldiers fled for their lives. Long Guda could do nothing to stop them.

"I already attained a peace treaty," he said, "but was tested by a small girl and lost a great many soldiers in vain!"

When he withdrew the army to return to his country, he took hostage the queen, the crown prince, the royal prince, and the beauties of the capital. On Lady Pak's command Kyehwa shouted, "Cursed barbarians! Your king is ignorant and thus has attacked the country that saved him, but you cannot take our queen back to your country. If that is what you intend to do, you will not return to your homeland."

To this the barbarian generals replied, "We already have the peace treaty, and the queen is already tied up, so don't even think about rescuing her."

They ridiculed her and some hurled curses at her, so Lady Pak also had Kyehwa shout, "If you insist on acting like that, let me show you what I can do!"

Then two rainbows appeared in the sky; rain poured down across the entire area; a dark wind blew; snowflakes fell; and the ground froze so that the hooves of the enemy's horses became stuck. They could not move even one small step. Only then did the barbarian generals become terrified and realize that any scheme they could conjure up against Lady Pak would surely fail. They had no choice but to remove their helmets, lay down their spears, and kneel before the Hall of Refuge.

"Today we already received the peace treaty," they said, "but we will not carry off your precious queen to our country, so we beg you to spare us."

They implored Lady Pak, silhouetted against the screen, in ten thousand ways, until she said, "I had planned to exterminate your seed, but I have now considered your pleadings and will forgive you. You scoundrels are naturally treacherous and have committed a hideous crime, but I know the time has come for me to send you back alive. Return safely and serve our crown prince and royal prince during the journey. If you fail to do so, I will annihilate all you barbarians. Not a single child will remain!"

The barbarian generals kowtowed and apologized for their faults one hundred times. Then Long Guda said, "I am embarrassed to ask this, but if you return my brother's head, your grace will be equal to Mount Tai."

Lady Pak smiled and replied, "I cannot grant your request. In ancient times Zhao Xiangzi [趙襄子] lacquered the head of Zhi Bo [智伯] and made a liquor cup out of it. By doing so he took revenge for the hardship suffered at Jinyang Fortress [晉陽城]. This story has circulated for countless years. Now we will lacquer your brother's head to wash away the shame we endured at Kanghwa Fortress."

Hearing this Long Guda mourned loudly, but Lady Pak would not relent. After taking their leave, the barbarian generals collected goods and women in the capital and prepared for their journey. The captive women cried to Lady Pak, saying, "Alas, what fortune makes Lady Pak act like this? If we leave now, we do not know whether we will live or die. When shall we look upon the mountains and streams of our country again?"

Hearing their wailing, Lady Pak sent Kyehwa to console them.

"There is a saying," said Kyehwa, "that pleasure peaks and then is replaced by sorrow as well as a saying that the sweat of hardship bears sweet fruit. All these things unfold according to heaven's mandate. Do not grieve too much. If you behave well in the barbarians' country, in three years I will come and bring you back home. So I ask that you take care of the crown prince and the royal prince until then and wait for me to come get you."

It was a miserable sight that followed, as all the ladies set out in tears.[15] The barbarian generals were elated to lead their army on the long journey to Ŭiju. When they drew near the area, a general galloped up, cut down the vanguards,

---

[15] Crown Prince Sohyŏn and Prince Pongnim were taken hostage by the Manchus in 1636. Depending on the source, estimates of the total number of Korean hostages range from several tens of thousands to as high as five hundred thousand.

and stormed a multitude of soldiers. His military prowess was such that they could not turn the tide of the war against him, and they were at a loss. When they hurriedly produced the royal letter of the peace treaty, the general vanished. This man was Im Kyŏngŏp. The barbarian generals recalled what Lady Pak had said, and they were struck by her prediction.

The king, meanwhile, greatly regretted not heeding Lady Pak's advice. He sighed and said, "Alas, if I had listened to her, would I be in this disastrous situation today? If Lady Pak had been born a man, what fear would I have of any barbarian horde? Now Lady Pak is at home alone and yet defeats the barbarians empty-handed. She makes their generals kneel down and revitalizes the spirit of Chosŏn. Such a thing has never occurred from remote antiquity to the current age."

The king, greatly astonished, conferred the title Lady Victorious [折衝夫人 Chŏlch'ung Puin] on Lady Pak, bestowed on her ten thousand pieces of gold, and announced a royal edict that granted positions in government to her descendants to be handed down through the generations for all posterity. A court lady was sent to deliver his letter to Lady Pak. It read, "Alas, this unworthy man was remiss not to recognize Lady Pak's loyalty and thus suffered this calamity. I am to blame. The highest heavens shall behold that Lady Pak's family will prosper generation after generation with children and grandchildren thanks to her loyalty and virtuous conduct." When Lady Pak received the letter, she prostrated herself four times to express her appreciation for the king's grace.

Lady Pak had been unsightly in the beginning because she was afraid that Sibaek might become preoccupied with beauty and thus distracted from his studies. But in the end she bore him eleven children, all of whom grew up and married the sons and daughters of prominent families until her descendants filled the rooms of the home and the family's good fortunes flourished, so that their incomparable happiness bested even that of general Guo Ziyi.[16] Lady Pak and her husband enjoyed their marital life together until their hair turned white and were blessed with robust health to the age of ninety.

It is said that Lady Pak was a woman of virtue who descended to the mundane world as a celestial immortal and took human form in the home of Hermit Pak. Her needlework equaled Su Hui's [蘇蕙, b. 357]; her writings were far superior to Li Bo's [李白]; she knew by heart the victories and defeats throughout all of history as well as the mysterious transformations of the wind and clouds; her military strategies had much in common with the arts of transformation

---

[16] Guo Ziyi (郭子儀, 697–781) is a famous general of Tang China who, among other things, quelled the An Lushan Rebellion (755–763). In subsequent ages, he became known as a deity of riches and glory.

practiced by Sima Zhongda [司馬仲達, 179–251] and Marshal Zhuge Liang; her mysterious powers included transforming herself, which enabled her to temporarily command divine generals; and she created comprehensive and enigmatic battle formations, planting trees so that swords and snakes were in a battle array at the eight gates, and amid gusts of wind and swirling clouds, the dragon and tiger banners unfurled side by side, so that the bandits did not dare draw close. Her extraordinary abilities were truly unfathomable.

The twenty-second day of the first month of the Blue Sheep Year [乙未, copied text].

JS and PL

4.2. ANONYMOUS, *A TALE OF TWO SISTERS, CHANGHWA AND HONGNYŎN* (薔花紅蓮傳 *CHANGHWA HONGNYŎN-JŎN*)

A Tale of Two Sisters, Changhwa and Hongnyŏn, is the story of Changhwa (Rose Flower) and Hongnyŏn (Red Lotus), who lose their mother and then are abused by their stepmother after their father, a local administrator, remarries.[17] It is a classic Korean folktale that also can be described as a ghost story. What makes it particularly interesting is that the core of the story was possibly based on an actual case handled by Chŏn Tonghŭl (全東屹, 1609?–1705) when he was serving as a provincial administrator in Ch'ŏlsan during the reign of King Hyojong (孝宗, r. 1649–1659).[18]

Whatever the truth about the origins of the story, it is clear that Chŏn Tonghŭl's name became strongly linked with the main events recounted in the story because of publication activities undertaken by his descendants over the following centuries. The story was transmitted in both Literary Chinese and vernacular Korean versions as well as through both handwritten manuscripts and printed copies. On balance, it seems that the Korean vernacular versions are based on earlier versions in Literary Chinese.

One of these Literary Chinese versions was completed in 1818 by Park Insu, at the behest of Chŏn Mant'aek, a sixth-generation descendant of Chŏn Tonghŭl's. That

---

[17] This work was supported by the English Translation of 100 Korean Classics program through the Ministry of Education of the Republic of Korea and the Korean Studies Promotion Service of the Academy of Korean Studies (AKS-2010-AAB-2102).

[18] For the background information on the text as discussed here, see the entry on *Changhwa Hongnyŏn-jŏn* in *The Encyclopedia of Korean Culture*, http://encykorea.aks.ac.kr, and Kim Pyŏra, *Changhwa Hongnyŏn-jŏn* (P'aju: Ch'angjak-kwa pip'yŏngsa, 2003).

version was included in *The Veritable Records of Kajae* (嘉齋事實錄 *Kajae sasillok*), a compilation made in 1865 under Chŏn Tonghŭl's pen name, Kajae, by one of his descendants. In 1968, that same version was reprinted in *The Veritable Records of Master Kajae* (嘉齋公實錄 *Kajaegong sillok*), compiled by Chŏn Yonggap. In that same year, Chŏn Yonggap also included a vernacular Korean version in a modernized mixed script style (i.e., inserting Chinese graphs for Sino-Korean words in order to facilitate comprehension) in yet another compilation devoted to Chŏn Tonghŭl. Premodern Korean vernacular versions date back to the latter half of the nineteenth century, and these include handwritten manuscripts and printings made from woodblocks. In the early twentieth century, the story was published numerous times in movable type for a growing commercial market. The translation here is based on a Korean vernacular version reprinted by Chŏn Kyut'ae.[19]

A Tale of Two Sisters recounts the evil machinations of a stepmother who falsely accuses her stepdaughter, Changhwa, of sexual misconduct and then has her drowned in a lake. Hongnyŏn then grows increasingly fearful and finally decides to join her sister by drowning herself in the same lake. Because the two sisters died unjustly—a point repeated insistently throughout the story—they return as ghosts to seek justice. This supernatural element, however, is embedded in a Confucian moral-political context. They do not return to exact personal vengeance on—or even to haunt—those who had harmed them. Instead, they return to seek justice by pleading their case to the Ch'ŏlsan district magistrate. Although they unintentionally frighten several magistrates to death, they finally succeed in their goal of obtaining a legal judgment that clears them of any wrongdoing and exposes their stepmother's wickedness. Their stepmother is then found guilty and sentenced to death, and in order to see that justice is fully carried out, the magistrate retrieves the sisters' corpses from the lake and gives them a proper burial. In doing so, he underscores their innocence and unwarranted suffering, and thus satisfied, they visit him once more in a dream to offer their thanks and to promise to repay his kindness. The magistrate's honesty and good judgment are emphasized in an archetypically Confucian manner: the story assures us that he subsequently rises through the ranks of officialdom.

At this point, the Literary Chinese versions of the story end, whereas the Korean vernacular versions—such as the one translated here—contain a lengthy conclusion that offers insight into the popular beliefs of the vernacular audience. These popular beliefs as reflected in the story are paradoxical. On the one hand, the vernacular versions reject the idea that justice is wholly secured through the punishment of the guilty and the

---

[19]Chŏn Kyut'ae, *Han'guk kojŏn munhak taegye sosŏl-chip* I [韓國古典文學大系 小說集 I, A compendium of Korean classical literature, collected fiction I] (Seoul: Myŏngmundang, 1991): 429–46.

vindication of the innocent. They instead explicitly incorporate the Buddhist idea of karma, or *inyŏn* (因緣), a basic Buddhist belief that individual actions have consequences that influence one's future rebirths. In its popular Korean conception, *inyŏn* encompasses ideas ranging from fate or destiny to good deeds being rewarded while bad deeds are punished (whether in this life or the next) and finally to the possibility of people being connected to each other over lifetimes. In the conclusion, this notion of karma is fully and explicitly developed as the two sisters are reborn to their father and his third wife.

On the other hand, this use of Buddhism ultimately and inadvertently serves to emphasize the centrality of core Confucian tenets in even a popular setting during the Chosŏn dynasty. In essence, the story brings the two sisters back to life so that they can live what was deemed in Confucianism to be an ideal life for an elite woman: filial devotion as a daughter; marriage to a government official; and giving birth to multiple children and, specifically, sons, thus leading to the establishment of sturdy family lines. All these possibilities had been forestalled by the death of the sisters' mother and the scheming of their stepmother. Their rebirth to their father and his third wife thus allows them to live out the lives that they would have lived out were it not for their wicked stepmother.

The story's Confucian emphasis is especially marked in relation to their father. Despite his mistakes of judgment that lead to his daughters' premature deaths, he goes unpunished, is presented as a figure of sympathy, and ultimately prospers. His long life and great worldly success highlight how the father was inviolable in the Chosŏn dynasty's Confucian conception of the relationship between the household and the state: analogous to the king, who was directly responsible for the state and indirectly responsible for the families under his rule, the father was directly responsible for the family. Whatever mistakes the father might make, it was his responsibility to fix them, thus ensuring the integrity of the family and, by extension, the integrity of the state.

The Confucian elements in the Korean vernacular versions are thus significant because they are situated in texts that are far livelier and contain far more fantastic elements than the earlier Literary Chinese versions. Those earlier versions, such as the one written by Pak Insu, were properly more Confucian in their sober presentation. As a consequence, we see how Confucian ideals had become part of the conceptual resources of the story's vernacular audience. The vernacular audience may have demanded that a happy ending be secured through Buddhism, but that happy ending merely served to reinforce Confucian assumptions as to what constituted a proper and happy life. The vernacular aspects of the story are evident in other ways, as well. We can infer that as the story was retold as well as recopied, vernacular narrative techniques became integrated into the text. This aspect is particularly conspicuous in the lengthy description of the wicked stepmother's grotesque physical appearance, something that is strongly evocative of the narrative techniques associated with the marketplace performances of *p'ansori*. Attentive readers will also notice points of implausibility deriving from chronological inconsistencies with respect to characters' ages.[20] There is thus a sense that chronological realities have been slighted in the service of storytelling. Such infelicities, however, remind us that A Tale of Two Sisters is at heart a morality tale recounting how the wicked will be punished and the righteous rewarded.

JS and PL

TRANSLATION

In the time when King Sejong [世宗, r. 1418–1450] ruled the land of Chosŏn to the east of the sea, there lived a man in the Ch'ŏlsan district of P'yŏng'an province. His family name was Pae, and his given name was Muryong. Belonging to a noble family in the countryside, he served as a local administrator and lacked for nothing because he was rich and had a simple and generous temperament. The only thing was that he and his wife had no child to call their own. This caused them much sadness.

One day, his wife, Lady Chang, being tired, lay down to rest. While she dozed, a divine being descended from the heavens and gave her a flower. When she was about to take it, a sudden gust of wind arose and the flower turned into a celestial maiden and entered her bosom. Startled, she rose and realized it was only a dream. She called her husband and told him about the dream, thinking it strange. The administrator said, "Heaven has taken pity on us for our childlessness and is blessing us with a precious child."

They were glad and, indeed, the wife soon started showing signs of pregnancy. After ten months, a strong fragrance filled the house one night, and she gave birth to a beautiful daughter. The baby's appearance and disposition were so extraordinary that they loved her deeply and called her Changhwa, meaning Rose Flower, and they regarded her as if she were a precious jewel. When Changhwa was about two years old, Lady Chang again showed signs of being pregnant. The couple prayed day and night for a son, but she gave birth to another daughter. Though disappointed, they named her Hongnyŏn, meaning Red Lotus. As Changhwa and Hongnyŏn grew, their faces became exceedingly

---

[20] For example, when Changhwa prays just before she dies, she says her mother passed away when she was seven and that her father remarried three years later. Since her step-brother, Changsoe, was born afterward, this would make him about eleven years her junior. Based on other references in the story, Changhwa cannot be anything older than twenty-three, which means that her murderer, Changsoe, is merely a boy of twelve. Such inconsistencies are found throughout the text.

fair, and their temperament and devotion to their parents remarkable. The couple saw how the sisters were growing and loved them most dearly, but they were quite worried about their children's precociousness.

Then misfortune befell the family. Lady Chang suddenly became ill and bedridden. The administrator and Changhwa did all they could day and night, but none of their medicine worked, and her health continued to deteriorate. Restless, Changhwa implored the heavens for her mother's recovery, but Lady Chang felt her death approaching, so taking the hands of her two young daughters, she sadly implored her husband, "Your wife must have been sinful in her previous life because I do not think I have much time left in this world. Dying does not grieve me, but I fear there will be no one to look after our daughters. Though I go to the underworld, I cannot close my eyes and my heart aches as I take leave. What this lonely soul wishes for, since you will remarry after I am dead and it will be natural for your feelings to change, is that you do not forsake your wife's dying wish but, dear husband, think back on the love you had for me and take pity on our two daughters. When they come of age, find them husbands from the same family and match them like a pair of phoenixes. Then, even in the underworld, I will be grateful for your kindness and find a way to repay you."

She then let out a long sigh and breathed no more. Changhwa embraced her sister, looked up to the heavens, and wailed, and the piteous sight was enough to melt even a heart of stone. By and by the funeral day arrived and they buried Lady Chang at the family grave site. Changhwa devoted herself to filial duties by following the morning and evening rituals, and she grieved day and night. Time flowed like a river and the three years of mourning ended, but Changhwa and her sister's grieving for their mother did not subside.

At this time, the administrator was mindful of his wife's dying wish, but he also had to think about continuing the family name and began to look for another wife. He could find no one suitable, so out of necessity he married a woman named Lady Hŏ. To speak of Lady Hŏ's appearance, her cheeks were over a foot long, her eyes were like brass bells, her nose was like a clay pot, her mouth looked like it belonged to a catfish, and her hair looked like pig bristles. She was as tall as a totem pole, with the voice of a wolf and a waist that would take about two people with outstretched arms to wrap around. She had malformed arms and dropsy legs as well as a double harelip, and her mouth would fill ten large bowls if it were sliced up. She was pockmarked like a straw mat full of peas, so much so that it was difficult to look at her directly. And because she was wicked in her heart and delighted in malicious deeds, there was never a moment of peace with her at home.

But Lady Hŏ was of the female sex, after all, and soon started showing signs of pregnancy, and she gave the administrator three sons in a row. He did not know quite what to do about the situation, but he would always think of his deceased wife along with his young daughters. If he did not see them even for a little while, he acted as if months had passed by. And when he returned home, he would go first into his daughters' room, hold their hands, talk to them tearfully, and pity them, saying, "You sisters are deeply cloistered here, missing your mother, and your old father is always sad, too."

Seeing this, Lady Hŏ became enraged with jealousy and thought of ways to get rid of the sisters. When the administrator became aware of this, he summoned her and chided her severely.

"We used to be poor, but because my first wife had great wealth, we now live with plenty. All the food you are eating comes from her wealth, so when you think about our good fortune, it is only proper that you should be grateful. How can you treat those girls so harshly? Do not behave like this again."

He spoke quietly to reason with her. But could a mind such as hers, like that of a wolf or a wild dog, ever know shame? Afterward she turned even more wicked and thought night and day of killing the two sisters. One day the administrator came to the girls' quarters, sat down in their room, and looked at them. They were holding each other's hands, trying to hide their sorrow even as tears dampened their collars. Seeing this, he became overwhelmed with pity and sighed, "This must be from thinking about your dead mother and grieving for her," and he also shed tears and consoled them. "Now that you are all grown, how happy your mother would be if she were here! But fate has been cruel to have brought Lady Hŏ into your lives. With her abuse getting worse, I can guess at your sadness. If something like this happens again, I will make sure to take care of it and give you peace of mind."

Saying this, he left. But Lady Hŏ had secretly been watching this scene through a gap around the window frame, and the heinous woman became all the more enraged. Thinking again of evil schemes, she hit upon an idea and had her son Changsoe catch a large rat. She carefully scalded it, peeled off its skin, rubbed blood all over it, and made it look like an aborted fetus. She then took it into the room where Changhwa was sleeping, put it under her blanket, and came out to wait for her husband. Just then the administrator came in. Lady Hŏ stared at him so gravely, clicking her tongue, that he thought it strange and asked her what was wrong.

"A terrible thing has been happening in this house," she replied. "But I was afraid, my dear husband, that you would accuse me of plotting some harm and I dared not say anything until now. You are their father and always shower them with your affection, but they are completely ignorant and do so many shameful things. Well, I am not their real mother, and so I can only hold my tongue. But today Changhwa didn't get up until late, and I went in thinking she wasn't well. And sure enough, she was lying in bed just having delivered a dead baby. She saw me and was all flustered and confused, and she didn't know what to do with herself. I was in shock, but I kept it quiet, just between her and me. We have been a noble family for many generations. How will we face the world if this ever gets out?"

She seemed most distraught and it astonished the administrator. Taking his wife's hand, he led her into the girls' room and looked under the blanket. Changhwa and her sister were deep in sleep at this time, and Lady Hŏ took the bloodied rat and rambled on hysterically. Ignorant of her wicked scheme, the bungling administrator was greatly startled and asked, "What are we to do about this?"

"This is a grave matter," replied the brutish woman, seeing his consternation. "We could kill her without letting anyone find out about this, but then not knowing the reason, they'll blame me, that I plotted to harm the innocent daughter of your former wife and killed her. But if they found out, I would be so ashamed that I would rather die first to escape such a fate."

She then pretended that she was trying to kill herself. The foolish administrator quickly grabbed her and tearfully begged her to stop.

"I already know of your rare and priceless virtue," he said. "Just show me what to do and I will get rid of her."

Hearing this, the heinous woman was pleased inside. *Now the time has come to carry out my wish*, she thought. On the outside she groaned and said, "I want to die out of shame, but I'll restrain myself, dear husband, since you are so troubled. Our family will come to utter ruin if we do not kill that child. We're in a dire predicament. I beg of you, please deal with this quickly and do not let it come to light."

The administrator thought of his late wife's dying words and was torn inside, but at the same time, he was filled with rage. He discussed with Lady Hŏ a clever way to handle the problem. The heinous woman was delighted and said, "I think the best plan would be to call Changhwa in and trick her. Tell her to visit her mother's brother, but send Changsoe along with her and then have him kill her by pushing her into the lake."

The administrator listened, thought it a good plan, and called Changsoe in and gave him specific instructions. Meanwhile, the two sisters were in a deep sleep after being overcome with sadness thinking about their dead mother, so how could they know anything of their wicked stepmother's plans? Changhwa woke up and found herself in low spirits. She thought it strange and could not fall back to sleep, and so she sat up. It was then that her father called her. Startled, she immediately went out.

"Since your uncle's house is not far from here," he told her, "go visit him for a while."

Because it was such an unexpected command, Changhwa was both shocked and saddened. With tears in her eyes she replied, "Your daughter has never before set foot outside the house or faced any stranger until today. So why, dear father, do you want me to travel a path I do not know on this dark night?"

He grew furious and scolded her, "I told you to take your brother Changsoe with you. Why are you talking back and disobeying your father?"

Hearing this, Changhwa wept loudly. "Even if you were to order me to die, how could I dare disobey you, dear father? But it is late at night and so I speak about the circumstances because of my childish thoughts. Since you command it, I am obliged, but all I ask is that you please let me go when the night has passed."

The administrator, foolish man though he was, began to waver on account of his affection for his daughter. But the heinous Lady Hŏ had heard enough. She barged into the room and yelled at Changhwa, "It's only proper that you obey your father no matter what, so why are you disobeying his command and making excuses?"

Upon seeing this, Changhwa grew all the more sorrowful, but there was nothing she could do, and while weeping, she said, "Since my father commands me so, I have nothing more to ask. I will obey."

She went back to her room and called for Hongnyŏn. Taking her sister by the hand, she said through her tears, "I cannot understand why, but for some reason Father has ordered me to travel to our uncle's house right now, late at night. I dare not disobey and I shall go, but I have misgivings about this trip. I must depart quickly and cannot tell you the whole story, though it troubles me. My only sadness is that we two sisters must now part after depending on each other all these years since our mother passed away, without ever having been apart even for an hour. This sudden event has come upon us, and to think I have to leave you in this lonely, empty room—it breaks my heart and burns me up inside. Even with a piece of paper as vast as the clear blue heavens, I couldn't record all that I am thinking now. But no matter. Farewell! I fear my path will lead to no good end, but if all goes well, I will quickly return. Should you miss me, just be patient and wait. I might as well change my clothes and go."

After she changed her clothes, the two sisters again took each other by the hand and wept, and Changhwa instructed her younger sister, "Be sure to serve our father and stepmother with the utmost care so as to be free of any blame. If you wait for me, I'll go and hurry right back in a few days. I will miss you so in the meanwhile, and words can't express how much my heart aches to leave without you. But don't be sad. Take good care of yourself!"

As she finished, they began to wail loudly, clasping each other's hands, and could not bear to part from each other. How sad! Why was their mother, who had loved them so dearly while alive, unable to look after them in their hour of need? Hongnyŏn felt her blood run cold as she listened to her sister's sudden news of departure, and they held on to each other and wept bitterly. Their pitiful state was beyond words.

Then the brutish woman, who had been listening outside, came in and barked at them like a wild dog, "Why are you making such a big fuss?" She called Changsoe and said, "Take your sister quickly to her uncle's house and come right back."

Then piggish, doglike Changsoe immediately began to thunder, shaking his shoulders and stomping the floor, as if he were under orders from the god of the underworld, hollering at Changhwa, "Come out quickly, Sister! You are disobeying our father and I'm the one getting scolded for no reason. It's not fair and I don't like it!"

Prodded by his fiery words, Changhwa had no choice but to let go of Hongnyŏn, but as she was about to leave, Hongnyŏn grabbed the hem of her dress and cried, "Sister, we have never been apart even for a moment. Why are you suddenly abandoning me and going away?"

When Changhwa saw how Hongnyŏn came out clutching after her, she felt as if her insides were being torn to pieces. But knowing there was nothing else to be done, she comforted her sister, saying, "I'll be away for only a little while, so don't cry and be well."

But overcome by their impending separation, she could not say all that she wanted to, and even the servants could not help but shed tears as they looked on. Hongnyŏn stubbornly reached for her sister's forehead and would not let go. The heinous woman rushed to them at this point and pried Hongnyŏn away from her sister.

"Your older sister is only going to your uncle's house. Why are you acting like a monster!"

Hongnyŏn had no choice but to step back. The heinous woman cast a sly glance at Changsoe, and he began to roughly pester Changhwa again. Reluctantly, she parted from Hongnyŏn, bid farewell to her father, and got on a horse and left, weeping bitterly.

Changsoe led the horse into a ravine and reached an area surrounded by countless mountain peaks, with calm water and a thick forest filled with pine trees. It was a place untouched by humans, where only the moonlight shone brightly and a cuckoo's mournful cries would make one's heart ache. Changhwa looked down and saw that in the midst of the pine forest was a lake spanning about ten *ri*[21] and unfathomably deep. Merely looking at it made her feel dizzy, and the sound of its water saddened her. Then Changsoe grabbed the horse and told Changhwa to get off. Greatly startled, she asked him, "At such a place as this? What are you saying?"

"You know your shameful deeds, Sister," replied Changsoe, pulling her down. "Why do you ask? You're not really going to Uncle's house. Our mother tried to ignore your many immoral acts because she is so kind, but now that your aborted

---

[21] A *ri* (里) is equivalent to 393 meters.

baby has been discovered, she has ordered me to bring you to this lake without others knowing and drown you. Now we are here, so get into the water!"

When Changhwa heard these words, she lost all sense of herself as if struck by lightning on a clear day. She collapsed and cried out, "Oh, you cruel heavens, what is the meaning of this? Why are you letting me be accused of such a senseless lie and thrown into this deep lake to become a hopeless, grieving ghost? Heavens have mercy on me! I have kept myself pure from the day I was born, but today I am unjustly disgraced. Were my sins from my previous life so heavy? Why did our mother forsake this world and leave behind such a sorrowful life as mine? If I have to die like a moth in a flame from the plotting of the wicked, so be it, I am not afraid. But this mortifying falsehood will forever shame me. And what will happen to my poor, lonely sister?"

Thus wailing, she fainted, a sight so pitiful it would bring tears to a heart of stone. But Changsoe, wicked and heartless, stood unmoved and just kept hurrying her into the water.

"It is already late at night in these desolate mountains, and you are going to die no matter what. So why struggle? Just get into the water!"

Regaining her senses, Changhwa calmed herself and pleaded with him.

"Listen to what I vow to you. Although you and I have different mothers, we are of the same flesh and bone as our father. Think of the love we had as siblings. If I die, I return forever to the underworld, so if you will take pity on me and let me stay just for a while, I will go to my uncle's house, bid farewell to my deceased mother at her grave, and ask my uncle to care for my lonely sister and comfort her. I'm not trying to save my life. If I protest, my stepmother will hate me for it, and if I try to save my life, I will be disobeying Father's command. So I will obey. All I ask is that you let me have a little time, and then I will willingly return and seek death."

Although she begged Changsoe desperately, he remained stonehearted and showed not a trace of pity. He finally stopped listening and harassed her insistently to enter the water. Her heart broken, Changhwa raised her eyes to the sky and wailed, "Bright heaven, look upon this injustice! My life has been most unfortunate, my mother passing away when I was seven. My sister and I had only each other to lean on, and our hearts would grieve when we saw the sun setting over the mountains and the moon rising in the east, when we saw flowers blossoming in the backyard or the grass growing between stone steps, our tears falling like rain. Three years later our stepmother came, but her heart was wicked and she only abused us more and more. Our sorrow was almost too much to bear, but we obeyed our father when the sun rose and remembered our dead mother when the sun set. We took each other by the hand and passed the long summer days and lonely autumn nights with many sighs. But now I am caught in the clutches of our stepmother's poisonous trap. I cannot escape and here I am to drown. Oh, heaven and earth, sun, moon, stars, whoever you may be, avenge this hideous wrong being done to me! But look kindly upon my poor sister, Hongnyŏn, and keep her from a life like mine."

Then, turning to Changsoe, she said, "I die now falsely accused, but as poor Hongnyŏn is left all alone, please look kindly upon her and keep her safe. Let her not transgress against our parents. Serve them well, for I wish them to live happily for a hundred years."

With her left hand she held up her long skirt, and with her right she removed her earrings and shoes and laid them by the water's edge. As she stamped her feet and her tears flowed like falling like rain, she looked back at the path she had taken and wailed insanely, "My poor Hongnyŏn! You are left alone in that silent, forsaken room. Whom will you depend on now to live your life? My heart is bitter and torn to pieces because I die and leave you behind!"

With those last words she threw herself, as if flying into the immeasurable expanse of the lake. It was heartrending. Suddenly the waves rose high to the sky, a cold wind blew, the moonlight lost its color, and a large tiger sprang out from the mountain and rebuked Changsoe.

"Your heartless mother has plotted and killed an innocent child. How could heaven ignore such an evil deed?"

Saying this, it rushed at Changsoe and ate both his ears, one arm and one leg, and then it vanished. Changsoe lay on the ground unconscious. The horse that Changhwa had ridden became startled and returned home. The heinous woman who had sent Changsoe had been thinking it most odd that he still had not returned although it was very late, when suddenly the horse Changhwa had ridden came galloping back, neighing. Thinking her son was returning after killing Changhwa, she looked out and saw the horse coming back home covered in sweat, but there was no one else. She was greatly surprised and called the servants. She ordered them to light torches and retrace the path the horse had taken. They did so and came to the place where Changsoe lay. Surprised by the sight, they took a closer look and were astonished to see that he was bleeding and unconscious and had an arm, a leg, and both ears missing. Then, all of a sudden, the air was filled with a strong fragrance and a cold wind chilled them. Thinking this strange, they examined the surrounding area and discovered that the fragrance was coming from the lake.

When the servants brought Changsoe home, his mother was aghast. She immediately gave him medicine and bound his wounds, and eventually he regained consciousness. Greatly relieved, the heinous woman asked what had happened, and Changsoe told her everything. The heinous woman became even more resentful and began to think night and day of ways to murder Hongnyŏn as well. But when the administrator saw what had happened to Changsoe, he realized that Changhwa had died innocent and maligned, and he lamented her and was overcome with grief.

Meanwhile, Hongnyŏn, who had no idea of what was going on in the house, saw all the commotion and, thinking it exceedingly strange, asked her stepmother what was the matter. The woman became filled with hatred and said, "Changsoe was attacked by a tiger while he was traveling with your monstrous sister, and he is terribly hurt."

Hongnyŏn tried to ask another question, but the heinous woman glared at her and roared, "Why do you keep tormenting me with these questions?" and sprang up as if to hit her.

Seeing how coldly her stepmother cut her off, Hongnyŏn felt as if her heart would burst and she could not stop trembling. Back in her room, she wept bitterly, calling for her sister, and suddenly drifted off to sleep. Half awake and half dreaming, she saw Changhwa underwater, riding a yellow dragon and heading toward the North Sea. Hongyŏn rushed to ask questions, but Changhwa ignored her. Crying, Hongyŏn said, "Sister! Why are you pretending not to see me? Where are you going by yourself?"

To this Changhwa replied while weeping, "I am now on a different path. On the order of the Jade Emperor, I am going to the Three Mountains of the Immortals to dig for medicinal plants. The matter is urgent and I cannot stop to converse with you, but do not think that I am being heartless. When the time comes, I will take you with me."

Just as Hongnyŏn was about to speak, the dragon Changhwa was riding suddenly roared and Hongnyŏn realized it had been but a brief dream. It was chilly, but her whole body was soaked with sweat and she felt befuddled. She went to her father and told him of her dream, weeping bitterly.

"What happened today has left me grieving as if I had lost something dear to me, and I fear some evil has befallen my sister while she was traveling."

She wailed frantically. As the administrator listened to his daughter, he could hardly breathe and could not say a word. All he could do was cry. But the heinous woman was there beside him, and her face turned crimson with anger.

"You foolish child! Why are you talking such nonsense and making your father so sad and hurting him so?"

She pushed Hongnyŏn away. Leaving the room and still crying, Hongnyŏn thought, *When I asked about my dream, Father was sad but could not say a word and Lady Hŏ grew angry and abused me*—there must be some reason for all this, and she sought to discover the truth. One day when the heinous woman was out of the house, Hongnyŏn went to Changsoe and gently coaxed him to tell her about her sister's whereabouts. Changsoe dared not deceive her any longer and told her all the details. Hearing for the first time how her sister had died so unjustly, Hongnyŏn fainted from the shock. Regaining her senses at last, she cried out, "Oh, my poor sister! That unfathomably wretched, heinous woman! My gentle sister, so young like a flower just blossoming, wronged with such vile lies, you threw yourself into the waves and became a vengeful ghost for all eternity. How will you satisfy this grudge that is carved into your very bones? How cruel to leave your pitiful younger sister behind, all alone in this desolate room. Where have you gone, never to return? Although you've returned to the underworld, your heart must be crushed from the grief of missing your little sister. Has there ever been such horrible, wretched injustice in the world? Oh, bright heaven help us! I lost my mother at the age of three and depended on you, my sister, all these years, but now I remain alone and I'm being punished for all my sins. I won't face such disgrace as happened to you. I'd rather die and follow you, even as a lonely ghost. We'll play together in the world below!"

She fell silent and felt faint as teardrops covered her face. But no matter how much she wanted to go where her sister had died, she was a maiden from a noble family and thus had no knowledge of the roads beyond the gate of her house, so how was she to find the place? She neither ate nor slept and instead spent her days and nights consumed with grief.

Then one day a bluebird appeared, flying hither and yon among all the flowers in full bloom. Hongnyŏn thought, *I've been grieving day and night because I don't know where my sister died, and now this bluebird, though it may be an insignificant creature, keeps coming and going like this. Perhaps it has come to be my guide.* Thinking this, she became agitated, unable to quiet her sad thoughts. Then the bluebird disappeared, and Hongnyŏn grew exceedingly sad. When morning broke the next day, she waited for the bluebird, but it did not come. Unable to bear her sadness, she cried the whole day. When the sun set, she leaned on the window and thought, *Even if the bluebird does not come, I will now seek the place where my sister died. And since my father will certainly forbid me to go if I tell him, I will explain the circumstances in a letter and then go.* She found paper and a writing brush and wrote a final letter to her father.

"How sad!" she wrote. "Your daughters lost their mother early on and spent many years depending on each other, but suddenly my sister fell victim to someone's wicked plot, and although faultless, she was wrongly accused with a terrible lie and finally became a vengeful ghost. How could I not be aggrieved and bitter? This unworthy daughter has served under the care of her father's home for ten and some years, but today I will follow after my poor older sister. After this, I will never see your face again, nor have any way even to hear your voice. When I think of this, I am blinded by tears and my heart grows numb. But I pray, dear father, that you think not of your unworthy daughter. May you enjoy a long life and perfect health!"

It was now very late at night. Moonlight flooded the garden and a cool breeze chilled the air. Suddenly the bluebird returned and perched on a branch, looking at Hongnyŏn and chirping as if to greet her. She said to it, "Although you are merely an animal, have you come to tell me where my sister is?"

The bluebird seemed to hear her and respond, so Hongnyŏn spoke to it again. "If you are here to let me know, then lead the way and I will follow you."

The bluebird bowed its head as if to answer, and Hongnyŏn said, "Then wait just a moment and we'll go together."

She fastened the letter to a portrait hanging on the wall and left her room, weeping bitterly.

"How pitiful! If I leave this house now, when will I ever see it again?" she said as she followed the bluebird.

Before Hongnyŏn had gone very far, the eastern sky began to glow. She kept going forward amid the countless green mountains filled with tall pines, and the sad cries of swans stirred her emotions. The bluebird paused by the lakeshore, causing Hongnyŏn to look about. From among lustrous clouds, thick above the water, came a sad crying voice, and it called her by name and said, "What sins have you committed that you would so needlessly throw away your precious life in this place? Once you are dead, you cannot live again, poor Hongnyŏn! It is difficult to understand why the world is the way it is, so do not dwell on what has happened and quickly return home and devote yourself to serving your parents. Marry someone who is good and noble, have many sons and daughters, and comfort the spirit of your dead mother."

Hongnyŏn recognized the voice as that of her sister and cried out, "Sister! What sins did you commit in your past life that you would leave me behind to come to this place and be all alone? I can't forsake you and go on living by myself, so I wish for us to wander together as one."

She paused and listened. The sound of weeping continued sadly off somewhere in the void, causing Hongnyŏn to become even more grief-stricken, so that she barely regained some composure just as she was passing out, and, bowing to heaven, she prayed, "I beg and pray, please take away this most wicked slander against my pure and faultless sister, and later in the afterlife, mercifully bring to light Hongnyŏn's most wretched grievance!"

She was weeping loudly and bitterly when she heard the voice calling her name from somewhere off in the void, and she grew ever more sorrowful. She grabbed her long skirt with her right hand, and as if she were flying, she leaped into the water. How sad and pitiful! The sunlight became colorless, and afterward, mournful crying sounds from the thick fog on the water continued day and night, repeating the details of how the innocent sisters had died because of the plotting of their stepmother, so that people far and near would all hear of their story.

The bitterness and resentment with which Changhwa and her sister pleaded their case pierced the depths of the underworld, and they always sought redress for their grievances. But whenever they went to the Ch'ŏlsan district magistrate's office in order to present their bitter grievance to him, the magistrate would drop dead from fright. In this way, anyone who came to Ch'ŏlsan to serve as the district magistrate ended up dying the day after he'd arrived. Soon, no one was willing to take up the position, and the Ch'ŏlsan district naturally fell into disarray. Famine came every year, so that people were on the verge of starvation. Many left their homes, and one of the villages lost all its inhabitants. This state of affairs was reported to the king many times. He became greatly concerned, and there was much discussion at the court.

One day, a man by the name of Chŏng Tongho volunteered to serve as the district magistrate. He was a man of integrity, with a courteous demeanor, and when the king heard, he held an audience with him and gave instructions.

"Strange events have been occurring in Ch'ŏlsan, and one of its villages is said to have been abandoned. The news is very worrisome, but now that you have volunteered, we are glad and commend you for your bravery. But we are also anxious about the situation, so be very careful and serve the people wisely."

Thus the king appointed him magistrate of Ch'ŏlsan. The new magistrate thanked the king and took his leave. Traveling immediately to his new district, he summoned an assistant and said, "I hear that once a magistrate arrives here, he immediately dies. Is this true?"

"It is difficult for me to tell you this," the assistant replied, "but for the past five, six years every magistrate that has come here has had a strange dream at night, between being asleep and awake, that they could not understand. And then they died. We do not know what is behind these deaths."

The magistrate listened and then he gave his orders.

"Turn out the lights tonight but do not sleep, and quietly observe any movement."

The assistant bowed and went out. The governor went to his room, lit a lamp, and began reading *The Book of Changes*. Then, as the night deepened, a cold wind suddenly arose. He began to feel faint and did not know what to do when, out of nowhere, a beautiful woman, wearing a pale-green jacket and a crimson skirt, came into the room and bowed before him. The magistrate pulled himself together and said, "What kind of woman are you to come so late at night? What do you wish to tell me?"

The beautiful woman lowered her head, stood up, and bowed yet again. Then she said, "My name is Hongnyŏn, daughter to Administrator Pae, who lives in this village. The year my older sister, Changhwa, turned seven and I turned three, our mother passed away, and after that we had only our father to depend on. Then he married a second time, a woman fierce and extremely jealous in her disposition, but she somehow managed to bear him three sons in a row. After that, our father was tricked into believing the lies our stepmother told about us, and she treated us worse and worse. Still, we served our stepmother as our mother, but her jealousy and mistreatment of us worsened each day. This was because our mother was from a very wealthy family, with thousands of slaves and farmland that produced over a thousand *sŏk*[22] of rice each year. She had brought with her a cartful of precious treasures. Our stepmother grew jealous that we would take all that wealth for ourselves when we married, and she was determined to give it to her sons instead by killing us. She plotted day and night to harm us and finally came up with an evil plan. She scalded a large rat, pulled out its fur, and smeared it with lots of blood to make it look like an aborted fetus, and she put it under my sister's blanket. After tricking our father and making good on her crime, she made my sister think that she was going to stay at our uncle's house, put her on a horse, and made her leave the house that very night with Changsoe, our stepbrother, with instructions for him to take my sister to a lake and drown her. Once I discovered what had happened, I was overcome with horror and bitterness. Afraid that I would also be caught up in some wicked plot while living my wretched life, I finally drowned myself in the same lake where my sister had drowned. I do not grieve death, but I am all the more bitter because there is no way to be rid of this wicked lie. I want to plead our woeful case, but each and every magistrate has died of fright, and our searing grievance has gone unresolved. But now, by the will of heaven, I have been granted an audience with you, wise magistrate, and I have dared to tell you my woeful tale. Oh, take mercy on this poor girl's grieving spirit and remove this slander against my sister's honor and free us from our everlasting resentment!"

When Hongnyŏn was done speaking, she bid the magistrate farewell as she stood up and left. The magistrate found this strange and thought, *This place has brought this problem on itself and that's why it has fallen into ruin.* The next morning at sunrise he went to his office and began his work as magistrate by calling for his assistant and asking, "Is there an Administrator Pae in this village?"

"Certainly," said the assistant. "Administrator Pae lives here."

"How many children does he have between his first and second wives?"

"His two daughters died some time ago, and he has three sons."

"How did his two daughters die?"

"I do not know for certain as it is someone else's affair but, from what stories I have heard, the older daughter committed some sin and drowned in a lake. Afterward, the younger sister grieved day and night because the two had been so close, and she eventually followed her older sister and drowned in the same lake. The two sisters became vengeful ghosts, and they come sit by the lake

---

[22] A *sŏk* is equal to 0.18 cubic meters.

every day and, while weeping, they say, 'We died because of our stepmother's plotting' and tell their story again and again. It is said that no passerby can stop from crying when hearing their tale."

After hearing this, the magistrate ordered, "Arrest Administrator Pae and his wife and bring them here."

The couple was quickly brought before the magistrate. He said to the administrator, "I hear that you have two daughters from your first wife and three sons from your second. Is this true?"

"Yes, that is so."

"Are they all alive?"

"My two daughters died of sickness. Only my three sons are now living."

"If you tell me truthfully what disease your two daughters died of, your life will be spared, but if you do not, you will be flogged to death."

The administrator's face turned ashen, and he couldn't utter a word. But the heinous woman, startled at hearing this, spoke up.

"Since you ask already knowing the answers, how could we dare deceive you in any way? As already said, my husband had two daughters who came of age, but then the elder daughter became disgraceful in her conduct and became pregnant. Knowing her secret would soon be revealed, I gave her medicine to abort the fetus without even the servants knowing about it. Not knowing the truth, others thought I was plotting against my stepdaughter, so I warned her. I said, 'You deserve to die, but if I killed you, others might think I had plotted against you, so I will forgive you. In the future, do not ever behave this way again, but instead cultivate your mind. If others find out the truth, they will despise our family, and then how will we be able to face anyone?' Knowing how disgraceful her deeds were and ashamed to face her parents, she then went out alone at night and drowned herself in a lake. Her younger sister, Hongnyŏn, then also started behaving like her and ran away at night several years ago, and we have no idea where she could be. Worse still, how could we go searching for a child of a noble family when she has acted so disgracefully and left her home? So we've not seen her."

The magistrate listened to everything and said, "In light of what you've said, you can easily show me if you bring the aborted fetus."

"I was afraid I might face a situation like this," replied the heinous woman, "because I am not of her own flesh and bone. So I carefully hid the fetus and I've brought it with me."

With that she removed something from her bosom. The magistrate saw that it was clearly an aborted fetus and said, "It appears there is no conflict between your words and the facts. But because the deaths occurred a long time ago and there are no clear indications as to what all this means, I will think on the matter again before making a decision. You may return home until morning."

The magistrate then released them. That night, Hongnyŏn's sister appeared before the magistrate, and she bowed to him and said, "We unexpectedly met such a wise magistrate and had hoped to be freed from the false accusations against us. How could we have suspected that you would be fooled by the cunning tricks of the heinous woman?"

As she sadly wept, she continued, "Dear magistrate, as bright as the sun and the moon, please be deeply upset by this matter. They say even Emperor Shun of ancient China was abused by his stepmother, and so too our searing grievance is known even among all the little children, but now you have been taken in by what this heinous woman has said. Since you do not see the truth, how could we not be heartbroken? We pray that you call her again and tell her to produce the aborted fetus. If you cut open its stomach and have a look, there will certainly be something there to help you judge. Please take pity on us and bring us the light of the law. But we also implore you to forgive our father completely, because, owing to his kind but simple nature, he was deceived by the cunning schemes of that heinous woman and couldn't tell black from white."

Done speaking, Hongynŏn's sister rose and bowed to the magistrate, and then she left, soaring off through the air riding a blue crane. After hearing this, it was finally clear, and the magistrate became even more furious upon realizing that he himself had been tricked by the heinous woman. He waited until daybreak, and then as the sun rose, he went to his office and began working. The administrator and his wife were promptly arrested, and without asking anything else, he ordered them to immediately produce the aborted fetus. Upon examining it closely, he clearly saw that it was not an aborted fetus. His voice was as cold as ice when he commanded his assistants to cut open its stomach. Responding to his order, the assistants fetched a knife and cut open the stomach, and it was filled with rat excrement. Seeing this, the many clerks and servants of the magistrate's office all realized the heinous woman's scheme, and as each and every one spat in disgust and rebuked her, they wept out of pity for the innocent deaths of Hongnyŏn and her sister. Infuriated by the sight, the magistrate had large cangues locked around the necks of the couple, and, raising his voice, he thundered, "You deceitful bitch! You have committed a most wicked crime, but you impudently deceive with elaborate words. I released you before of my own accord, and now, what other fabrications will you concoct to excuse yourself? You make light of the kingdom's laws, commit atrocities, and have killed an innocent child of the first wife. Now speak truthfully of your deeds or suffer the most severe punishment!"

When the administrator saw what was happening, he deeply regretted the tragic death of his innocent child and wept.

"The punishment for my crimes of stupidity is in your hands, My Lord. Even if I were the most foolish peasant, how could I not know what is right and wrong?

My former wife, Lady Chang, was most wise and virtuous, but sadly, she passed away, leaving behind two daughters. We managed, depending on and comforting each other as father and daughters, but because I had to continue the family line, I found another wife. She gave me three sons, and I was delighted. But then one day I entered the women's quarters, and this heinous woman flew into a rage and said, 'Husband, you've always thought Changhwa is the most precious thing in the world. But her behavior has been most unfortunate, and now she has had an abortion. Go in and look!' She lifted my daughter's blanket and in shock I saw that thing with my dim eyes, and I was convinced that it was an aborted fetus. Because of my stupidity, I just didn't realize what was going on, and what's more, I was deceived by this wicked plan, forgetting my first wife's dying words. Since it is clear that I have committed an unforgivable crime, I would not refuse having to die ten thousand times for what I have done."

As soon as he finished speaking, he started sobbing, but the magistrate told him to be quiet. The magistrate then had the heinous woman laid on the rack and began interrogating her. Unable to withstand the flogging, the heinous woman spoke.

"My family had been powerful and influential for many generations, but it became feeble and its wealth squandered, so when the administrator asked, I agreed to become his second wife. He had two daughters from his former wife, and as their bearing was exquisite, I raised them as my own. But once they reached maturity, their behavior gradually became wicked. I would tell them a hundred things, but all fell on deaf ears. They were often insincere, which made me resentful, but I only admonished them and reasoned with them from time to time in order to teach them how to behave properly. But one day I happened to overhear their secret conversation, and as I had always feared, they were talking about such scandalous matters that I was shocked and angry. But I knew that if I told their father, he would think I was plotting against them. So out of necessity, I tricked him. I caught a rat, smeared blood on it, and then put it under Changhwa's blanket and told him that she had had a miscarriage. Then I gave instructions to my son Changsoe to lure Changhwa to a lake and drown her. Afterward, her sister, Hongnyŏn, became fearful that she would also come to harm and fled in the middle of the night. I will wait for any punishment the law dictates, but I pray that my son Changsoe be spared because he has already been punished by heaven and become a cripple."

Then Changsoe and his two brothers all spoke at once, "We have nothing else to say, but ask only that you let us die in place of our old parents!"

After listening to what the administrator's wife and Changsoe and the others had to say, the magistrate realized what the heinous woman had done, and at the same time, he felt great pity for the tragic deaths of Changhwa and her sister. He said, "This criminal is so different from others that I cannot make a decision on my own."

He reported the incident to the provincial office, and the governor was greatly startled and said, "There has never been an incident like this!" With this in mind, the governor promptly relayed the report to the royal court, and when the king read it, he felt pity for the two sisters and gave his decree.

"This heinous woman's crime is unimaginably wicked, and she shall die by dismemberment[23] as a warning to all posterity. Her son Changsoe shall die by strangulation. Erect a stele for Changhwa and her sister and inscribe an epitaph on it to redress the injustices they suffered and pacify their spirits, and let their father go free."

The governor received the king's command and immediately forwarded it to the Ch'ŏlsan district magistrate's office, where the magistrate immediately carried out the order. He had the heinous woman dismembered and hung her head up high for all to see, and he had her son Changsoe strangled to death. Then he made the administrator kneel in the courtyard and admonished him.

"No matter how gullible you may be, how could you fail to see through that heinous woman's lies and kill your innocent child? Although your crime deserves to be punished, Hongnyŏn and her sister wish it otherwise, and the king has also decreed it thus, and so you have been given a special pardon."

The administrator expressed his gratitude for the king's beneficence and went away with his two remaining sons. After this, the magistrate personally led the clerks and servants from his office to the lake where the two sisters had died. They drained the lake and saw that the bodies of the two sisters were lying down, as if asleep on a jade bench. Their faces were unchanged, and they looked as if they were alive. The magistrate was amazed to see this. He had the bodies placed in inner and outer coffins, buried them on a splendid mountain, and erected a headstone three feet high in front of the graves. On the headstone he had engraved, "In eternal remembrance of Changhwa and Hongnyŏn, daughters of Pae Muryong, from East of the Sea [Haedong—i.e., Korea], in the kingdom of Chosŏn, P'yŏng'an province, Ch'ŏlsan district." Once the funeral was completed, the magistrate returned to his office and went to work administering state affairs. Then one day, when he was exhausted and dozing with his head resting against his pillow, Changhwa and her sister suddenly entered. They bowed and expressed their gratitude.

---

[23]The punishment in question was *nŭngji ch'ŏch'am* (陵[凌]遲處斬). It is well known in relation to Chinese history and is typically known as "death by slicing," "death by a thousand cuts," and other variations. Although the punishment was not administered in exactly the same way at all times and in all places, it entailed execution and dismemberment. In the context of this story, it seems that the punishment is to be administered strictly, with the woman to be executed by dismemberment.

"Dear magistrate, whose brilliance is like the sun and the moon, since our meeting you have relieved us of our most bitter grievance, gathered our bones for burial, and pardoned our father. Your kindness soars above Mount Tai and is deeper than the Yellow Sea, and so even though we are in the dark netherworld, we will repay your kindness. You will soon see your fortunes rise in public office. Please wait and see."

The sisters vanished into thin air, and the magistrate was startled awake. Thinking that it was but a fleeting dream, he recorded its details and afterward looked for portents. Sure enough, beginning that month he received one promotion after another until he was made the chief naval commander for the southern half of the kingdom.

Although the heinous woman had been torn to pieces as dictated by the laws of the state and the two daughters' vengeful spirits had thus been comforted, Administrator Pae, on the contrary, had no joy in his heart and merely grieved day and night over his two daughters' innocent deaths. It seemed as though he could see them and hear their voices, and he nearly went mad, praying constantly that he could once again be their father in this world and relieve them of any lingering resentment. On top of that, there was no one to feed him and no one upon whom he could pour out his affections, and so inevitably he looked for a wife. He eventually married the daughter of a local man, Yun Kwangho. She was an eighteen-year-old girl of extraordinary appearance and talent, with a gentle temperament and the qualities of a lady. The administrator was delighted, and their marital relationship was exceptional from the start.

One day, the administrator was in the outer quarters, tossing and turning, unable to sleep, deep in thought over his two daughters. Suddenly, Changhwa and her sister clearly entered the room, beautifully dressed. They bowed to him and said, "Because of our unfortunate lot, we lost our mother at an early age, and because of the sins of our past lives, we met with a heartless stepmother. Eventually, we were falsely accused and parted with you, dear father. Overcome with bitterness, we took our grievances to the Jade Emperor, and he wept and said, 'Your situation is pitiful, but that is your lot. Whom could you blame? However, since your karmic connection with your father back in the world has not run its full course, return to the world to resume your relationship with him and resolve your grievances together.' He then dismissed us, but we do not know what it all means."

The administrator was just about to take hold of them and welcome them back home when he was startled awake by the crowing of a rooster. He felt as if he had lost something, and in the lingering presence of their image and scent, he struggled to get control of himself. Meanwhile, his new wife, Lady Yun, also had a dream, and in it a celestial maiden descended to earth riding a cloud and gave her two lotus flowers.

"These are Changhwa and Hongnyŏn," said the maiden. "Because they died unjustly accused, the Jade Emperor has taken pity on them and is blessing you with children. Value them and raise them well, and you will be richly rewarded."

The maiden vanished, and the first thing Lady Yun realized was that the flowers remained in her hand and the room was filled with their fragrance. She thought this exceedingly strange and called for the administrator. She told him of her dream, and then asked, "Who are Changhwa and Hongnyŏn?"

The administrator listened and looked at the flowers. They were swaying gently in the wind, as if they were greeting him. He felt as if he was seeing his two daughters again, and after weeping and telling his wife all that had happened, he said, "My first wife had a dream like that in the past, and today you also had such a dream. This must be a sign that two daughters will be born to you."

They rejoiced together, put the flowers in a jade vase, and placed it in a chest. They loved looking at the flowers from time to time, and their sadness naturally vanished. Lady Yun started showing signs of pregnancy from that month, and as the tenth month drew near, the fullness of her belly was well known and it was clear that she was carrying twins. When she was at full term, she lay down in bed physically exhausted and at long last safely delivered twin girls. The administrator, who had been waiting outside, hurried in to comfort his wife and saw the babies. Their appearance and disposition were without parallel in beauty, like carved jade or gathered flowers, as if they were those lotus flowers in the jade vase. Overjoyed, the administrator and his wife looked back at the flowers in the jade vase and saw that they had already vanished. They thought this most strange and said that the flowers had surely turned into the girls. They named the twins Changhwa and Hongnyŏn and raised them as if they were precious jewels.

Months and years rushed past, and at the age of four or five, their physical appearance was extraordinary and they served their father and mother with filial devotion. When they matured and turned fifteen, they were full of virtue, and, moreover, their talents were outstanding, and so the love that the administrator and his wife felt for them was without equal. The couple sent old women matchmakers far and wide to find worthy husbands for the sisters, but in the end, no suitable matches could be found and they were greatly worried. Around that time, there was a man named Yi Yŏnho in P'yŏngyang. Although extremely wealthy, he had been sad because he had had no children. But then in old age, he fathered twin sons after a spirit appeared to him in a dream. Their names were Yunp'il and Yunsŏk, and they were now sixteen years old. They were so splendid in appearance and such outstanding scholars that all those living in the province with daughters coveted them and sent old women matchmakers to try to arrange marriages with them. Their parents were also extremely concerned about choosing suitable daughters-in-law, so when they heard that the twin daughters of Administrator Pae were so extraordinary, they were intent on arranging marriages with them. The two families consulted each other, immediately agreed that their children should marry, and chose an auspicious date. The day for the weddings was to be in autumn, sometime in the middle of the ninth month.

At that time, all was at peace throughout the realm and the country had reason to celebrate, and so the government administered a state examination to recruit court officials. Yunp'il and Yunsŏk took the examination overseen by the king and tied for first place. The king admired their scholarly talents and immediately appointed them to the Office of Royal Decrees as Hallim Academicians.[24] The brothers, now called the Hallim brothers, expressed their gratitude and then asked for a temporary leave of absence. The king granted their request, and they immediately returned home, where their father held a celebration for family and friends. The local officials all sent musicians, mats, and cushions for the party, and the governor and the deputy magistrate called on the new arrivals and praised them as they all drank together. The family's glory and renown were truly exceptional.

In no time, the wedding day was upon them, and the Hallim brothers solemnly arrived at the home of the brides as music played. At the conclusion of the marriage rites, they returned home with their brides, and the two daughters-in-law were presented to their father-in-law and mother-in-law. Their beautiful demeanor was like lustrous beads on a pair of scissors or two uncut gems, and so the bridegrooms' parents were immeasurably happy. The newly married sisters honored their father-in-law and mother-in-law with filial devotion and were obedient to their husbands. Changhwa gave birth to two sons and one daughter. Her elder son became a civil official, eventually serving on the State Council, while her younger son became a military official and went on to become a general.[25] Hongnyŏn also had two sons. Her elder son became an official in the southern region, while her younger son became a learned scholar who lived in seclusion among the mountains and forests, where he took the wind and the moon as his friends and delighted in his zither and books.

---

[24]The name Hallim is from Hanlin (翰林), the name of a prestigious scholarly-administrative office in China. During the Chosŏn dynasty, the appellation Hallim academician was used for those employed in the position of third diarist (檢閱 kŏmyŏl) in the Office of Royal Decrees (藝文館 Yemun'gwan).

[25]The text refers to the elder son's position on the State Council (議政府 Ŭijŏngbu) in a general and complex fashion, without specifying the position by name. This ambiguity underscores the prestige and importance of the State Council. Because it handled the most important matters of state, to attain any position in its ranks was a mark of great accomplishment.

And so it came to pass that when Administrator Pae turned ninety, the king specially appointed him to the State Council as the Fourth State Councillor [左贊成 Chwach'ansŏng] in the kingdom. He concluded the remaining years of his life in that position, and then his wife, Lady Yun, also passed away. Changhwa and her sister grieved for them. After the parents of the Hallim brothers also died, the two then lived together under one roof with all their children and grandchildren. Changhwa and her sister alike died at the age of seventy-three, and the Hallim brothers died at the age of seventy-five. Their children and grandchildren brought forth many more sons and daughters, and their descendants flourished in happiness and prosperity.

JS and PL

4.3. ANONYMOUS, *THE PLEDGE AT THE BANQUET OF MOON-GAZING PAVILION* (玩月會盟宴 *WANWŎLHOE MAENGYŎN*)

The longest novel in Korea's traditional canon, *The Pledge at the Banquet of Moon-Gazing Pavilion* comprises one hundred eighty manuscript chapters that constitute twelve volumes in modern print.[26] The four extant manuscripts of *The Pledge* attest to the relative popularity of this text, its massive size notwithstanding. *The Pledge* is also the only traditional novel that is connected to the name of a female author: Madame Yi of Chŏnju (1694–1743) is mentioned as the author of *The Pledge* in a nineteenth-century miscellany, but the matter of her authorship remains subject to dispute.[27] A text unique in many ways, *The Pledge* is also the epitome of the tradition of the lineage novel (家門小說 *kamun sosŏl*), which flourished in Korea from the late seventeenth until the early twentieth

---

[26] Kim Chinse, ed., *Wanwŏlhoe maengyŏn* [The pledge at the banquet of Moon-Gazing Pavilion], 12 vols. (Seoul: Seoul National University Press, 1987–1994). All the excerpts cited in the following come from this edition.

[27] The name of Madame Yi of Chŏnju is mentioned by Cho Chaesam (1808–1866) in his encyclopedic miscellany *The Journal of Songnam* [松南雜識 *Songnam chapchi*], but the lack of other evidence to support this claim leaves Madame Yi's authorship a matter of dispute. Several scholars, however, assert that as a member of a cultured family and a person of elevated status, Madame Yi indeed possessed sufficient education and time to compose such a lengthy and sophisticated novel as *The Pledge*. See Chŏng Pyŏng-sŏl, *Wanwŏlhoe maengyŏn yŏn'gu* [Study of *The Pledge at the Banquet of Moon-Gazing Pavilion*] (Seoul: T'aehaksa, 1998), 172–223, and Han Kilyŏn, "*Paekkye yangmun sŏnhaengnok* ŭi chakka wa kŭ chubyŏn: Chŏnju Yissi kamun yŏsŏng ŭi taehasosŏl ch'angjak kanŭngsŏng ŭl chungsimŭro" [The author and the social context of *Paekkye yangmun sŏnhaengnok*: Women of the Yi of the Chŏnju family as potential authors of romans-fleuves], *Kojŏn munhak yŏn'gu* 27 (2005): 329–61.

century. The exact number of lineage novels is hard to ascertain, but Hong Hŭibok (洪羲福, 1794–1859), a court translator and an avid reader of fiction, wrote that about forty texts of lineage novels were known to him, and his testimony can be taken as a rough guide.[28]

Fiction was generally frowned upon in traditional Korea for fear of its ability to lead readers astray from their productive occupations, but lineage novels were considered worthy of an elite audience, and they were read mostly by elite-status women. Several factors contributed to the lineage novel's prestige. First, the educational value of these texts firmly inscribed the lineage novel in the canon of elite women's literature. The lineage novel shares its moral paradigm with Confucian classics and histories. Tracing out the lives of ever-new descendants of established civil lineages, lineage novels unfold in the manner of family trees and thus embody the idea of social stability and continuity of the familial tradition of moral rectitude and civil service. Written in vernacular Korean,[29] lineage novels contain intertextual allusions to the Confucian Classics, histories, and Chinese novels, such as *Romance of the Three Kingdoms* (三國演義, K. *Samguk yŏnŭi*, C. *Sanguo yanyi*) or *Journey to the West* (西遊記, K. *Sŏyugi*, C. *Xiyouji*). Lineage novels also describe in great detail the key life-cycle rituals performed in the home, and they thus impart both practical and literary knowledge. Second, circulating mostly in manuscript form, lineage novels were specimens of fine vernacular Korean calligraphy and thus objects of aesthetic value. Manuscripts of lineage novels were treasured and transmitted through generations in the families who took pride in their cultured status.[30] Not mere aesthetic objects, these manuscripts were also mementos of the deceased scribes and hence artifacts imbued with sentimental value.

At the same time these long and unruly novels can be taken as sophisticated studies of emotional excess: its sources, its contradictions, and, ultimately, ways of reinscribing feelings into the structures of order. Unlike the normative Literary Chinese canon, which lays out the paradigm for governance and moral cultivation, lineage novels combine

---

[28] Hong Hŭibok, "*Cheil kiŏn sŏ*" [Preface to *Cheil kiŏn*], in *Cheil kiŏn* [Flowers in the mirror], ed. Pak Chaeyŏn and Chŏng Kyubok (Seoul: Kukhak charyowŏn, 2001), 22.

[29] In premodern Korea vernacular Korean script, promulgated in 1443, existed alongside the unspoken but written Literary Chinese, the language of the public sphere used in historical, legal, and men's philosophical writing.

[30] The Kyujanggak manuscript of *The Remarkable Reunion of Jade Mandarin Ducks* [玉鴛再合奇緣 *Ogwŏn chaehapkiyŏn*] contains numerous marginal notes praising the calligraphy of grandmothers, mothers, and mothers-in-law, which illustrates the longevity of this manuscript and its intergenerational reading audience. See Sim Kyŏngho, "Naksŏnjaebon sosŏrŭi sŏnhaengbone kwanhan ilgoch'al: Onyang Chŏngssi p'ilsabon *Ogwŏn chaehapkiyŏn*kwa Naksŏnjaebon *Ogwŏn chunghoeyŏn*ŭi kwan'gyerŭl chungsimŭro" [Study of the manuscripts of Naksŏnjae novels: The relationship between *Ogwŏn chaehapkiyŏn* copied by Madame Chŏng of Onyang and Naksŏnjae manuscript of *Ogwŏn chunghoeyŏn*], *Chŏngsin munhwa yŏn'gu* 38 (1990): 169–88.

normative discourse with inquiries into the innermost dimension of human experience—private passions. To borrow Mikhail Bakhtin's term, *The Pledge* is a product of "dialogic imagination"—of a way to conceive of the world not in terms of hierarchy dominated by an exhaustive ideological viewpoint but as a polyphonic confluence of voices, each validated in its own right.[31] *The Pledge* is centered on an illustrious family of civil officials—the Chŏngs. The vignette of the family banquet, referenced in the novel's title and translated in the first excerpt, embodies the stability of the Confucian institutions of family and lineage. The scene opens and closes the novel, but the extensive one hundred eighty chapters of *The Pledge* show how fulfillment of this idealized vision comes with trial. Beautiful and brilliant, So Kyowan, or Madame So, whose violent passions upset the harmony of the Chŏng family, is the protagonist of *The Pledge*.

Madame So marries Chŏng Cham to take the place of his deceased wife, Madame Yang. Having no son of their own, Madame Yang and Chŏng Cham have already adopted an heir, Chŏng Insŏng, and this settles the problem of patrilineal succession.[32] Madame So, however, soon bears her own children, twin brothers Injung and In'ung, but with Insŏng having already been designated as the family heir, Madame So's son Injung is denied the succession privilege a priori. Madame So does all to murder Insŏng, his wife, Yi Chayŏm, and their newborn son to clear the way for Injung. The scenes of Madame So's violence often border on the grotesque, but she is certainly far more complex than the figure of an evil stepmother that appears in numerous traditional Korean tales. As striking as her violent outbreaks is Madame So's thoughtful pondering on her inner being: she cannot help but admire Insŏng for his virtue and lament her son Injung's readiness to assist her schemes, and she is also quite sober in her assessment of Chŏng Cham's unprovoked suspicion of her, which, she claims, leaves her no other way of acting. The excerpts translated here provide multiple perspectives on the figure of Madame So, highlighting the complexity and drama of her station and illustrating the dialogic imagination of *The Pledge* at the height of its sophistication. While Insŏng's unwavering devotion to his stepmother appeases Madame So toward the end of the novel, the

---

[31] Mikhail Bakhtin, *The Dialogic Imagination*, ed. Michael Holquist, trans. Caryl Emerson (Austin: University of Texas Press, 2008), 259–366.

[32] Chosŏn Korea effected a patrilineal structure of succession, in which the eldest son of the primary wife would inherit ritual privileges and the family's property. Elite men in traditional Korea could have several secondary wives, but only one primary wife, whose children would be eligible for inheritance. In a case where the primary wife died and the widower remarried the daughter of a *yangban* family, she would then become the new primary wife. In the case when the primary wife failed to produce a descendant, an heir was adopted, often from the husband's extended family. Children born of secondary wives, so-called secondary sons, were denied social privilege and were barred from taking the prestigious civil service examination and thus access to the ranks of the government bureaucracy. See Martina Deuchler, *The Confucian Transformation of Korea: A Study of Society and Ideology* (Cambridge, Mass.: Harvard University Asia Center, 1992), 89–129, 203–31.

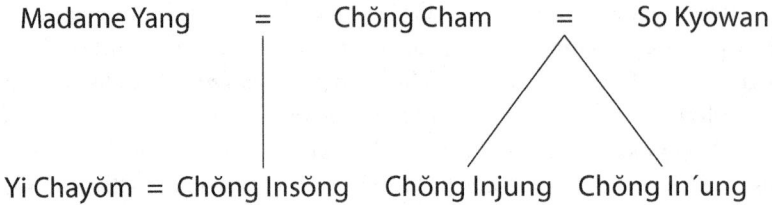

massive span of The Pledge monumentalizes the discourse of feelings that needs to be acknowledged within the Confucian moral paradigm.

KsC

TRANSLATION

The birthday banquet of the patriarch, Chŏng Han, the father of Chŏng Cham, opens the novel as an ideal vision of family harmony that will haunt the narrative of turmoil and trial that ensues. The banquet is a showcase of the family's prosperity, in which the Chŏngs' wealth is matched by the emperor's trust and favor.[33] *The banquet also embodies the perfectly fulfilled ritual ordering of human bonds. During this celebration, marriages are pledged between the young children of the Chŏngs and those of close kin and friends, and the ritual adoption of Chŏng Insŏng as Chŏng Cham's heir also takes place. The triumph of ritualized emotion over blood ties, which Chŏng Cham and Madame Yang effect in this scene, dramatizes the subsequent confrontation of Insŏng and Madame So.*

On this day, the upper seats are arranged according to the royal decree, and the lower banquet is set up by the two Chŏng brothers, offering prayers for the patriarch's longevity. Imperial relatives are present, and luminous clouds and auspicious energy permeate the place, while wine fumes cloud the minds. Precious gems are in abundance just like seashore pebbles, and beautifully made-up faces are everywhere, like common sand. There are maidens, tender and pure, and ladies, gentle and delicate. This truly is the congregation of honor, elegance, virtue, and sagacity. Bright jewels dangle over mistlike robes, and cloudlike fans waver softly. The matriarch's dignified look is complimented by her daughters-in-law—with Madame Yang's wisdom, Madame Sang's cordiality, and the

---

[33] The overwhelming majority of premodern Korean novels are set in China, and *The Pledge* is no exception, having the reign of the Ming emperor Yingzong (英宗, r. 1427–1464) as its historical background.

uprightness of Madame Hwa. All the guests' eyes are riveted upon them. Next enters the patriarch. All the women retreat[34] and the guests rise from their seats in greeting. After everyone is seated again, Insŏng is brought in to pay his respects. Insŏng and Chŏng Cham then proceed to perform the father-son rite . . . Chŏng Cham and Madame Yang receive Insŏng's bows with such a look that one cannot easily guess if they are his birth parents or adopted parents. The couple's love for Insŏng is so warm, and their affection for him so overwhelming, that it can hardly be eclipsed even by his birth parents' feelings. There is hardly a feeling that can surpass this profound affection that fills preordained human bonds. Chŏng Cham's bright eyes beam with the gentleness of a spring breeze, and his scarlet lips fail to conceal the dazzling whiteness of his teeth. The tormented expression of Madame Yang, furrowed with years of exacting illness, gives way with a slight tremor; her face glows anew with peaceful warmth that inundates from her eyes and reaches heaven itself. The two faces, like jades shining with morning glory, turn toward each other, issuing the fragrance of a plum tree covered with snow. Like a lotus flower that rises on its emerald stalk above the stillness of an autumn pond, smiles ascend the two faces, tender as apricot flowers [I, 1:50].[35]

The seamless harmony that governs the relationship of Insŏng and his adopted parents, Chŏng Cham and Madame Yang, is broken after the death of Madame Yang and Cham's remarriage to Madame So to fill the place of his deceased wife. Madame So refuses to recognize Insŏng's status in the Chŏng family, and she uses all her means to kill him and his wife to secure the succession privilege for her own son Injung. A scene of grotesque violence, this passage depicts Madame So's fierce attack upon her daughter-in-law and the wife of Chŏng Insŏng, Yi Chayŏm. Having forged a letter in which Yi Chayŏm allegedly exposes Madame So's vices, Madame So uses it as a pretext for her attack.

---

[34] In traditional Korea, distinction was the major principle that regulated relations between men and women. After reaching a certain age, boys and girls were brought up separately, expected to function in distinct spheres: women were consigned to the domestic or inner space, while men's activity belonged to the outer, or public space. Women and men, unless married or related by blood, were not to be seen in the same space, and living quarters were divided into inner and outer. A semipublic occasion, a banquet also required that women be seated separately from men.

[35] In the in-text citation, the Roman numeral refers to volume number in the printed version, followed by the number of the manuscript chapter, which is also reflected in the printed edition, and, after the colon, by page number in the printed version.

Madame So folded the letter and threw it onto the table. Her clear eyes blazed coldly upon Chayŏm, as though hurling a thousand arrows upon the girl. Venomous fire flashed in her gaze when Madame So opened her lips: "In your letter, you say that in my inhuman cruelty I am worse than any villain. Indeed, how could I ever measure up to your wisdom and virtue?! What do I care if people call me a harpy—I will take your heart out to see what is truly on your mind."

With these words, Madame So came closer to Yi Chayŏm, who lay still on her bed. She straddled the girl, bringing into disarray her cloudlike layered coiffure. No matter how hard Madame So tried, the silk of Chayŏm's hair would slip away from her hands, and she ended up grasping only air. Then Madame So grabbed a golden pin and started lashing Yi Chayŏm's shoulders. Annoyed that a few layers of clothing still covered the girl's body, Madame So took a knife and cut the back seams of Chayŏm's colorful robes, until only a single gauze blouse was left over Chayŏm's skin. Then Madame So slashed Chayŏm again. With every strike crimson blood welled forth, staining white cloth with bright red flowers. Prostrate on her bed, Chayŏm did not breathe and did not move at all, so who could know if she was dead or alive?

Succumbing to her frenzy, Madame So could not stop, and in a short while the girl's blouse turned crimson, with not a single patch of white. Chayŏm herself lost her senses in a swoon. Facing such a sight, even one's mortal enemy could hardly forbear pity, but hatred permeated Madame So's very bones, and she could not restrain herself. First banging Chayŏm's head against a wall, she pulled the body to herself, rolled Chayŏm's sleeves up to reveal jade hands, and plunged her teeth into Chayŏm's hand. The beautiful head was bruised and blood flowed; jade flesh tore off and was like shreds of meat in the teeth of Madame So. Madame So quickly reached for the knife and was about to cut Chayŏm's legs when a little maid stormed into the room and, risking death, grasped Madame So's knife and, clinging to her, prevented Madame So from going further [V, 68:217].

In the novel, Madame So appears to be a victim of dramatic inner conflict, which is revealed in this powerful confession she offers to her son In'ung. In'ung suspects that his mother and brother have conspired to kill Yi Chayŏm and Chŏng Insŏng's firstborn son. In'ung pleads with Madame So to reform her ways, and while Madame So admits to In'ung's accusations, she also uses this chance to speak of her inner turmoil. Strikingly objective, eloquent, and sincere, Madame So's testimony provides a compelling perspective on her relationship with Insŏng.

In plentiful words you say that no one could match Injung and me in their atrocities, wondering how people like us could be tolerated by heaven and earth. If people hear you say that it was so fortunate for a newborn child, tied and thrown outside in a violent storm, to survive, they will either think this is empty talk or imagine some crafty spell-casting monster at work. It would be best not to speak of this at all, but you cannot stop, as if the affairs of the world were all given to your care. It is absurd and futile to go around with cries like "Unbelievable!" and "Unnatural!" and so I did not want to listen to you from the beginning.

Preoccupied with Insŏng's family, you seem to be sick with suspicion of your mother and elder brother [Injung]. Yes, that terrible plan of harming the child was indeed devised by your mother and brother. How strange and amazing it was for that child to survive! Now that you know everything, your mother and your brother—your own kin—appear to be no match for Insŏng's righteousness, and you know no measure in your idle words. But now that you, in your long speech, admonish me to reform my ways, let me also open my heart and find some comfort.

A while ago, in the *chŏngmyo* year,[36] your mother entered the Chŏng family. Although I lacked the virtue that other people possess, I was properly instructed by my parents and followed wifely ways with no fault, so while I cannot call myself a wise woman and a worthy person, I could be accused of no glaring misconduct. Suppose one is accused of a fault or some inhuman trait that one does not possess—what comes of it? Your father, since the very first day, considered our marriage a misfortune and ceaselessly suspected me, worrying that some trouble might be caused to Insŏng. Although I am not bright by nature, how could I not know his heart? Could I not be disturbed? Could I not be furious? Numerous virtues and great wisdom—even if I possessed them—would never be acknowledged or approved by my husband. So I decided that indeed I would live up to his suspicions and spare no effort in tormenting his beloved son. Once I had made up my mind, there was no way to turn back. Insŏng is truly outstanding, and in vain would I wish that Injung were his match, but Injung, too, is his father's son, even if his father's coldheartedness does not befit this fundamental human bond.[37] And now, when Insŏng has a son of his own, your father is so overjoyed that he gives all his love to Insŏng's family. When I see this, my grief and regret know no measure, so indeed I do not wish any good

---

[36] Traditional Korea used the sexagenarian-cycle calendar, in which each year was designated by two Chinese characters, which made sixty combinations and were repeated after the completion of each sixty-year cycle. Thus there were *chŏngmyo* years every sixty years, such as in 1675, 1735, and 1795.

[37] In the Confucian society of traditional Korea human relationships were defined through the Three Bonds (三綱, K. Samgang, C. Sangang) and Five Cardinal Relationships (五倫, K. Oryun, C. Wulun), which encompassed the totality of human interaction in society. The nature of the five hierarchized bonds is first described by Mencius as follows: "love [親, K. ch'in, C. qin] between father and son, duty [義, K. ŭi, C. yi] between ruler and subject, distinction [別, K. pyŏl, C. bie] between husband and wife, precedence [序, K. sŏ, C. xu] of the old over the young, and faith [信, K. sin, C. xin] between friends." See *Mencius*, trans. D. C. Lau (New York: Penguin Books, 1970), 102.

to Insŏng and his wife. But while my hatred is a matter of a moment, I know with all my heart that Insŏng and his wife are very filial and virtuous, and I admire them for it, so one might indeed find it strange that I can commit all these atrocities and turn into a monster.

Confucius teaches that people do what is right, and Mencius considers human nature to be wise. Even without your encouragement, I do hold goodness and benevolence in highest esteem and do not delight in cruelty and violence. How could I encourage Injung to violate cardinal human relations? Unfortunately, you and Injung are of very different natures, contrary to what I hoped for. Although I lament this deeply, I also cannot easily denounce my own son in front of others. I kept it quiet for a long time, but little by little Injung's behavior will become known, so do you really think I will not be able to restrain my love and continue to remain indifferent to his ways? Rest assured of my intentions and do not worry yourself over this matter too much. Indeed, Injung himself is not of lowly nature, and he will not end up as an outlaw [IV, 54:258–59].

Not only her own words but also the opinions of external observers characterize Madame So as a person of outstanding qualities, and her situation—as extremely complex. The following passage gives a glimpse of Madame So's character from the perspective of her parents, Lord So and Madame Chu. In this scene, Madame Chu has had early intimations that her daughter's passionate and powerful nature is ill fitted for the position in which Madame So finds herself upon marrying Chŏng Cham.

Lord So and Madame Chu had no worries over their other children, but Kyowan, Madame Chŏng,[38] was their late child and youngest daughter. All parents love their youngest children the most. Madame Chŏng, moreover, was of an outstanding and unique nature, so how could her parents help loving and admiring her, their tender affection itself being preordained by the heavenly bond between parents and children. Lord So, however, possessed exceptional wisdom, and his astuteness surpassed that of others. He did not rejoice in his daughter's extraordinary qualities and was concerned over finding her a fit husband. When Chŏng Cham sought marriage after the death of his first wife, Lord So had many concerns when sending his daughter over.

Madame Chu harbored her laments. The great love she felt for her youngest girl prevented Madame Chu from feeling joy even after finding a high-ranking

---

[38] In traditional Korea, women retained their natal last name after marriage, and Madame So is usually referred to by her natal last name as well. In rare instances, however, she is called by her husband's last name, Madame Chŏng, as in the given excerpt.

son-in-law and seeing her daughter move into her own house and give birth to twins. Although her daughter now enjoyed honor and riches, received the honorary title as wife of an esteemed minister, and was of noblest rank, Madame Chu saw this as a great responsibility, a hindrance to easeful life. In his utmost loyalty to the state, Chŏng Cham pledged to forget about his family and fame, turning away from all matters of private importance. Facing such a prospect, Madame So sighed without stop, and Madame Chu could foresee her daughter's lifelong anxiety and the longing she would feel when hearing the cry of wild geese or seeing swallows return in the spring. Madame Chu did not find any joy in her daughter's glory and nobility, and she could not help thinking that the easeful life of her first and second daughters was so much better than the outstanding nobility and riches of her youngest girl.

Marriage matches are not made according to human will. Madame Chu knew well of her husband's plan, although she never mentioned it to him. While she never liked this arrangement, Madame Chu only harbored her regret. In this vast, vast world, should they search long enough, would they not find an excellent son-in-law? Should they really send their daughter, still too young, to become a second wife? Moreover, Madame Chu knew that this child's temper prevailed over her virtue, and that her rage could never be tempered by her will: she prides herself in her abilities and is not eager to obey, and her virtue and benevolence fall very far from the sage teachings. What will happen if Madame So fails to continue the virtuous conduct of the deceased person and instead turns against [Madame Yang's] child? Is it not wrong to instigate your own daughter to commit an offense and produce calamity out of nothing? [VII, 91:29–30].

The Pledge ends with a scene of original harmony regained. Marriages pledged at the novel's beginning are celebrated, and Madame So is also transformed under the unwavering moral influence of Insŏng, who retains his equanimity toward his stepmother throughout all the trials she prepares for him. The novel's last words return to the figure of Madame So and monumentalize the discourse of emotion. Identifying Madame So's story as central, The Pledge *articulates its main narrative focus: the trying process of incorporating violent passions into the structure of Confucian order.*

Even if the wise deeds of Chŏng Insŏng and his great filiality permeated the entire realm, without the moral transformation of Madame So and Chŏng Injung, this story would not be possible and the people of the world would know nothing about it. Now that Madame So and Chŏng Injung have been transformed, the life story of Chŏng Insŏng has been recorded in great detail, but without the atrocities of his stepmother and stepbrother, the story of [Insŏng's] suffering in the spirit of filiality and brotherly love would not be the same; without the transformation of Madame So and Chŏng Injung, this story would not take shape. In human affairs, the old times and the present differ greatly, but it is pathetic that good and evil still continue to revolve [XII, 180:313].

KsC

4.4. CHO WIHAN, *THE TALE OF CH'OE CH'ŎK* (崔陟傳 *CH'OE CH'ŎK-CHŎN*)

The Tale of Ch'oe Ch'ŏk, also known as *Records of a Fortuitous Encounter* (奇遇錄 *Kiurok*), was composed in Literary Chinese by Cho Wihan (趙緯韓, 1567–1649) in 1621 during the reign of King Kwanghae (光海君, r. 1608–1623). Cho Wihan, whose pen name was Hyŏn'gok (玄谷) or Soong (素翁), hailed from Seoul and passed the civil service examination at age forty-two. He experienced the Japanese and Manchurian invasions and, seeking refuge from the Japanese forces, lived for a while in Namwŏn (南原), a major backdrop for this tale. The story is often understood as based on Cho Wihan's war experiences and overseas travels.

The tale centers around the reunion of Ch'oe Ch'ŏk's family members—the marriage, separation, and reuniting of the male protagonist, Ch'oe Ch'ŏk, and his wife, Ogyŏng, serving as the overriding theme of the story. Ch'oe Ch'ŏk, a native of Namwŏn, falls in love with Ogyŏng, who comes from Seoul to avoid the chaos triggered by the war. He and Ogyŏng finally marry, but the outbreak of the war causes them to endure long-term separation and hardships. However, they finally reunite and restore their family thanks to their strong will and the guidance of the Sixteen-Foot-High Buddha[39] of Manbok Temple in Namwŏn. The tale also depicts how Ch'oe comes to meet his son, Mongsŏk, in the northern part of China while he is held as a captive by the barbarian army. Similarly, we see how Ch'oe's Chinese daughter-in-law, Hongtao (K. Hongdo) unexpectedly meets her father in Korea, who was considered dead after serving in the Ming army helping Chosŏn defeat the Japanese forces.

Apart from the theme of family unity, the tale also shows the history of premodern Korean fiction. For example, it highlights the romance of Ch'oe Ch'ŏk and Ogyŏng, whose love forms the basis of their marriage but is challenged by the ensuing war and their forced travels. Yet the image of Ogyŏng as a passionate lover who pursues Ch'oe and as a capable life partner who plans to sail back from China to Korea distinguishes this tale from previous Korean romances in which women are largely passive in seeking romance and marriage partners and are confined to typically female, domestic spaces.

---

[39] This is the so-called Korean foot (尺), equal to 11.9 inches.

In addition, in portraying increased mobility between land and people, the tale illustrates what Koreans imagine life to be in foreign spaces during wartime. Ch'oe's family members find shelter with the help of kind foreigners, including a Chinese general and a Japanese merchant, demonstrating that Koreans were connected with foreign places and people through shared ethical values such as benevolence, compassion, loyalty, trust, and filial piety. Such aspects of the tale not only cast a positive light on engaging with foreign peoples and lands but also signal an expansion of discursive space in Korean fiction, brought about by an increased awareness of others during seventeenth-century Korea.

Because of its depictions of the devastation of war, scholars have often categorized the tale as belonging to the war literature of the seventeenth century, similar to *The Tale of Caitiff Kang* (姜虜傳 *Kangno-jŏn*) by Kwŏn Ch'ik (權侙, 1599–1667) and *The Tale of Kim Yŏngch'ŏl* (金英哲傳 *Kim Yŏngch'ŏl-jŏn*) by Hong Set'ae (洪世泰, 1653–1725). However, this tale is also notable for its emphasis on the humanity and shared ethical values among interconnected East Asian countries, values evoked by the turmoil of forced mobility and unexpected encounters with people of different cultures.

A similar tale, titled "Hongdo," is found in Yu Mongin's (柳夢寅, 1559–1623) *Unofficial Histories by Ŏu* (於于野談 *Ŏuyadam*), but the relationship between the two needs further research. The different manuscripts of the story here show little difference in plot; they include editions from Seoul National University, Korea University, and Tenri University in Japan. This translation is based on Pak Hŭibyŏng's recent collated edition included in *Han'guk hanmun sosŏl kyohap kuhae* (A critical edition of selected Korean fiction in Chinese, 2005).

SC

TRANSLATION

In Namwŏn, there lived a boy named Ch'oe Ch'ŏk. His courtesy name was Paeksŭng [伯昇]. He lost his mother when he was very young and lived with his father, Ch'oe Suk [崔淑], at the eastern side of Manbok Temple [萬福寺], located outside the West Gate. From a young age, Ch'oe Ch'ŏk was broad-minded, ambitious, and fond of making friends. He valued keeping his promise, and he was not confined to minor principles and manners.

One day, his father admonished him, "Since you don't study hard and wander around purposelessly, what kind of a man do you think you will become later in your life? It is frustrating and deeply concerns me that you only go out hunting at a time when every town in the country has been recruiting young soldiers ever since the war broke out. You should devote yourself to books and study hard for the civil service examination. You might not get first place, but at least you would not be dragged onto the battlefield. Chŏng sangsa [上舍, licentiate],[40] who lives in the south of the city, is an old friend of mine. He has studied devotedly and mastered literary composition. He is the very person to teach a novice like you, so go and learn from him."

With his books clasped under his arm, Ch'oe Ch'ŏk immediately went to see Chŏng sangsa and asked for instruction. He studied hard day and night. A few months later, his writing skill had improved so dramatically that he produced writings as if a dam had burst. The villagers were all impressed by his talents. Whenever he studied at Chŏng sangsa's house, a seventeen- or eighteen-year-old girl came by the window and listened to his voice while hiding herself from him. Her eyebrows were like a painting, and her hair was as dark as lacquer.

One day, Chŏng sangsa was yet to finish his meal in the house and Ch'oe Ch'ŏk was alone reciting poems. All of a sudden, a slip of paper flew in through the crack by the window and fell into the room. Ch'oe picked it up to take a look. On it was written the last line of the poem "Fruit Dropping from the Plum Tree,"[41] which describes the longing of an unwed girl seeking a soul mate.

The poem caused his heart to flutter and his soul to take wing. Unable to calm down, he thought about sneaking into her room and embracing her in the darkness. But he immediately repented the imprudent thought, reminding himself of the story of Kim T'aehyŏn,[42] who rejected his teacher's daughter when she revealed her feelings for him. As he pondered, he found himself in a battle between morality and desire.

When Chŏng sangsa came into the room, Ch'oe Ch'ŏk quickly hid the slip of paper in his sleeve. As he was leaving the room after the lesson, a maid dressed in blue followed him, telling him, "I need to speak to you."

Ch'oe Ch'ŏk, who was already captivated after reading the poem, felt intrigued but also a little strange at the maid's words. Nodding his head, he gestured at the maid to follow him to his home. When they arrived, Ch'oe started

---

[40] Sangsa refers to a Confucian scholar who either passes the classics licentiate (生員 saengwŏn) or literary licentiate (進士 chinsa) examinations.

[41] "Fruit Dropping from the Plum Tree" (摽有梅, C. Biaoyoumei, K. P'yoyumae) is included in "Odes of Zhao and the South" [召南 Shaonan] in the section titled "Airs of the States" [國風 Guofeng] of The Book of Songs [詩經 Shijing]. Based on James Legge's translation, the last line reads as follows: "Dropt are the fruits from the plum-tree / In my shallow basket I have collected them. / Would the gentlemen who seek me / [Only] speak about it 摽有梅. 頃筐墍之. 求我庶士. 迨其謂之."

[42] Kim T'aehyŏn (金台鉉, 1261–1330) was a scholar-official during the Koryŏ period. When he was young, he studied with a teacher (a senior scholar) whose daughter was a young widow. One day, she sent a secret poem revealing her love for him through a crack in a window. After this, Kim stopped going to his teacher's house. This story is seen in many records, such as A Miscellany of the Eastern Country [海東雜錄 Haedong chaprok].

asking her questions. The maid answered, "I'm Ch'unsaeng [春生], a maidservant of Maiden Yi's. She sent me to obtain a reply poem from you."

Unsure about what the maid had said, Ch'oe asked her, "You are a maid from the Chŏng family; why do you call the maiden of the Chŏng family 'Maiden Yi'?"

The maid answered, "Maiden Yi's family used to live in Ch'ŏngp'a town outside the South Gate of Seoul. Her father, Yi Kyŏngsin [李景新], passed away at an early age. Since then, Lady Sim, Maiden Yi' mother, has lived alone with Maiden Yi. Maiden Yi's name is Ogyŏng [玉英]. She is the one who cast the poem through the window. Last year, we came to Hoejin in Naju from Kwangha by boat to take shelter from the unrest triggered by the war. This fall, we finally moved from Hoejin to here. The master of the house, Chŏng *sangsa*, is a relative of Lady Sim's and is taking good care of us. He is looking for a husband for her, but he has yet to find a suitable candidate."

Ch'oe asked, "Raised by a single parent, how could Maiden Yi learn to read and write? Was she born literate?"

She answered, "Maiden Yi had a brother, Tŭgyŏng [得英]. He was well versed in literary composition. He died, unwed, at the age of nineteen. Maiden Yi learned a little bit over his shoulder when her brother was studying at home, so she knows only enough to write her name."

Ch'oe then treated the maid to food and drink, took out a small piece of paper, and wrote a reply, as follows: "I was enthralled by the message I received this morning. Having met a blue bird bringing a happy message, how could I not be joyful? I was lonely, as the phoenix without a partner that used to cry over its appearance reflected in a mirror,[43] and I was yearning for a lover, but it was difficult to summon a real person from that depicted in a painting.[44] I know how to bring about love[45] and how to steal fragrant incense,[46] but I found it difficult to know more of you, just as I could not fathom how distant Mount Penglai and how deep the Ruo River were when I wanted to reach them.[47] While

---

[43] This refers to a story that a phoenix that had lost its mate cried over its own image reflected in a mirror.

[44] This refers to an anecdotal story of Emperor Wu (156–87 B.C.E.) of the Han dynasty (206 B.C.E.–220 C.E.). Emperor Wu drew an image of his beloved, the late Lady Li, and actually summoned her using the magic power of a Daoist master.

[45] This phrase recalls the story of Sima Xiangru (司馬相如), who seduced the young widow Zhuo Wenjun (卓文君) using his musical prowess.

[46] This phrase refers to the event of a daughter of Jia Chong's (賈充, 217–282) who stole some precious incense her father had received from the emperor and gave it to her lover Han Shou (韓壽). This story is often used as a metaphor for having a secret love affair.

[47] Mount Penglai (蓬萊, K. Pongnae), also known as Penglai Island (蓬島), is a fabled abode of the Chinese Eight Immortals. The Ruo River (弱水, K. Yaksu) is a transcendental region known for its difficulty to cross.

pondering what to do, my face became sallow and bloated and my neck gaunt. Today, beyond my expectations, the rain of Yangtai has come, allowing for a dream of meeting the goddess,[48] and a letter from the Western Queen Mother has suddenly arrived.[49] If our two families can make a good marriage, as the Jin and Qin states during the Spring and Autumn period established their marriages for generations, and become united with silken threads by the Old Man Under the Moon,[50] then my wishes for the threefold lives[51] would be fulfilled. So please don't abandon the promise of being together even after death. While writing is not enough to fully express words, how can I expect words to fully express my meaning? Here I present my sincere letter in reply to you."

Ogyŏng was happy to receive his letter. The next day, she wrote another letter and had Ch'unsaeng deliver it to Ch'oe Ch'ŏk. The letter read as follows:

> I was born and raised in Seoul and learned only a little about the chaste and gentle conduct expected of women. Unfortunately, I lost my father when I was young. Since the war broke out, I alone have taken care of my widowed mother, having no siblings. We wandered about in the southern part of the country for some time and finally came to rely on our relatives. The time for marriage has come, but I am not yet married. Since bandits are rampant everywhere in the midst of this war, I am always worried whether I can keep my body unharmed and safe from brutal and ferocious men. For this reason, my old mother is distressed and worries about me very much. However, what makes me really worry is I need to find a good, dependable husband, just as a vine needs a tree to rely on. As a woman's happiness and misfortune all depend on a husband, how can I wish to marry a man and put my life in his hands if he is not a good person? I have observed you from a short distance and found that your words are gentle, your conduct decent, and your face full of trustworthiness. If I want to find an honorable man, how could it be

---

[48] The rain of Yangtai (陽臺之雨, K. *Yangdae chi u*) alludes to a famous sexual encounter between the King of Chu (楚王) and a goddess of Mount Wu (巫山, K. Musan). The goddess told the king that she was a cloud in the morning and rain in the evening and also that she could be found on the Yangtai (Sun Terrace) of Mount Wu. "Clouds and rain" has become a euphemism for lovemaking.

[49] The Western Queen Mother (西王母, K. Sŏwang Mo) is a goddess living in the Kunlun Mountains (崑崙, K. Kollyun). She is in charge of longevity and other material blessings. Here the reference is to Ogyŏng.

[50] The Old Man Under the Moon (月下老人, K. Wŏlha Noin) is the one who determines marriage partners. He appears during the night and randomly unites couples using his threads representing a different man and woman. Once he has joined two different threads, no one can change marriage partners.

[51] "Threefold lives" means one's former, present, and future life.

someone other than you? I would rather be a concubine of yours than the wife of an inferior man. However, looking back on my humble disposition and misfortune, I'm afraid my wish may not come true. I sent the poem to you yesterday not out of lewdness but to know of your intentions. Though I lack knowledge, I am not of low origins. How could there be an illicit sexual relation? I promise to remain honest and chaste and to respect you with all my might should we marry upon receiving permission from our parents. By throwing a poem [through the window], I have already disgraced myself by committing the scandalous act of being my own matchmaker. I then made the added mistake of exchanging letters with you, which has made me lose the virtue of being composed, serene, and pure. Now that we know each other's hearts, we must be careful that our letters not escape our hands. From now on, please be sure to communicate through a matchmaker. I entreat you to be careful so that I am free from any accusations of being a loose woman who plays with any man.

Pleased with the letter, Ch'oe went to his father and said, "I have heard that there is a widow staying at Chŏng *sangsa*'s home. She has a beautiful young daughter. Could you please send a marriage proposal on my behalf to Chŏng *sangsa* so that I don't lose her to someone with faster feet?"

His father said, "They are originally from a noble family in Seoul. Since they now live in a place away from home, relying on a relative, wouldn't they want to get a son-in-law from a wealthy family? They would definitely not accept our proposal because our family is poor and from the lower class."

Ch'oe kept beseeching him to send a proposal, saying, "Would you please just go and talk to him about this marriage? The result will depend on heaven's will."

The next day, Ch'oe's father went to Chŏng *sangsa* and spoke about the marriage of his son. Ch'ŏng *sangsa* replied, "It is true that I have a younger female cousin staying with us, fleeing the turmoil in Seoul. She has a daughter of good appearance and conduct. I have been looking for a good husband for her who can support her household. Your son is a very gifted and handsome man, so I think he would make a wonderful husband. However, your poor family background somewhat worries me. Let us talk again after I have had a conversation with my cousin."

Ch'oe's father returned and told Ch'oe about his conversation with Ch'ŏng *sangsa*. Ch'oe agonized and was anxious for days, waiting for the decision.

Ch'ŏng *sangsa* discussed the matter with Lady Sim. She frowned and said, "Because my family has wandered for a long time and has nothing to rely on, I want my only daughter to marry into a wealthy family. No matter how smart and wise he is, I do not want to give my daughter to the son of a poor family."

That night, Ogyŏng went to her mother because she wanted to say something to her, but she could not open her mouth. Her mother said, "If you have something on your mind, please tell me everything without holding back."

Ogyŏng, blushing, hesitated for a moment but at last took courage and began to speak:

"I understand that you are looking for a son-in-law from a rich family for my sake. Indeed, it would be wonderful were I to marry the wise son of a wealthy family. However, even with a lot of money, if the man is not wise, he will not be able to maintain the wealth of his family. If I have someone without a conscience as my husband, how can I eat even if there is rice in the house?

"I have secretly observed a man called Ch'oe who studies at Uncle's home every day. He seems to be loyal, virtuous, sincere, and trustworthy, far different from a scoundrel. I would die with no regrets if I married that man. Further, to live a poor life is common for a scholar. I don't want an unrighteous but affluent life. So please let me marry him. I know it is not proper for an unmarried girl like me to say this, but I dare to speak out because marriage is a matter of grave concern. If I say nothing, marry an inferior man, and ruin my entire life, what good would that be? It would be like trying to make a cracked pot hold water again or restore dyed thread to its original color. Crying or regretting is of no use once it's done.

"Furthermore, my situation is different from that of others. I have no strict father at home, and there are bandits near our area. In such a chaotic and perilous situation, whom else can we rely on if not a trustworthy man? For this reason, I will not avoid imploring you regarding my own marriage and desire to select my own husband, just as Lady Yan and Lady Xu did.[52] I can't confine myself to the inner chambers, merely waiting to see what others say about my marriage, because that might put me in danger."

Left with no choice in the matter, Ogyŏng's mother told Chŏng *sangsa* the next day, "I thought long about the marriage proposal last night. Mr. Ch'oe seems a great scholar, although his family is poor. One's status and wealth are contingent on heaven's will and therefore beyond human capacity. It would be wise to have Ogyŏng marry someone with whom we are already acquainted rather than choosing a total stranger."

Chŏng *sangsa* said, "Since you insist, I will bring about this marriage. Mr. Ch'oe is indeed poor, but he has a disposition like jade. Even if we searched in

---

[52] Both Lady Yan and Lady Xu seem to refer to women who chose their own marriage partners. However, the reference to Lady Yan is unclear. Lady Yan appears as Lady Du (杜) in a different edition. Lady Xu (徐) was the younger sister of Xu Wufan (徐吾犯). She selected her own husband, Kongsun Chu (公孫楚); see "The First Year of Zhaogong" (昭公), in the *Zuo Commentary on the Spring and Autumn Annals* [春秋左傳 *Chunqiu Zuo zhuan*].

the capital for a man with such a rare capacity, we wouldn't find one. When the time is right, he will become a very successful man."

Chŏng *sangsa* immediately sent a matchmaker and formalized the engagement. It was decided to hold the marriage ceremony on the fifteenth day of the ninth month. Thrilled, Ch'oe could scarcely count down the days to the wedding.

Before long, the former administrator Pyŏn Sajŏng[53] raised a righteous army in Namwŏn to march to the Yŏngnam region. Having heard that Ch'oe was good at horse riding and archery, he brought him into his army.

On the battlefield, Ch'oe was gripped with anxiety and eventually became sick. As the wedding day came nearer, he submitted a petition requesting a leave of absence for a few days. However, the commander of the army was furious about his petition and said, "How dare you ask for wedding leave at an urgent moment like this? Our king has fled [the palace] to the countryside. As subjects of the king, we scarcely have time to sleep even on a pile of swords and with spears as a pillow. Moreover, you are still young for marriage. Thus it won't be too late for you to wed after all the enemies are defeated," and he denied Ch'oe permission to leave.

Meanwhile, Ogyŏng became anxious since Ch'oe didn't return for their wedding. The promised wedding day passed without Ogyŏng knowing Ch'oe's whereabouts. Day after day, in despair, she was unable to eat or sleep.

In the neighboring village, there lived the Yang family. They were very wealthy. Having heard that Ogyŏng was wise and that her fiancé Ch'oe Ch'ŏk had not come back from battle, they proposed a marriage, taking advantage of the situation. They secretly sent money and goods to Chŏng *sangsa*'s wife and continually urged her to mediate a marriage. Chŏng *sangsa*'s wife finally said to Lady Sim, "Ch'oe Ch'ŏk is destitute, constantly worrying about his daily meals. He even has difficulty supporting his father and borrows money from others. Given that, how can he feed and take good care of his entire family without problem? Furthermore, since he has not yet returned, who knows whether he has died in battle? On the other hand, everybody knows of the Yang family's abundant wealth, and their son is as good as Ch'oe Ch'ŏk."

Chŏng *sangsa* and his wife continued to speak highly of the Yang family son, and eventually Lady Sim was swayed. She settled on marrying off her daughter to the Yang family and chose an auspicious day in the tenth month for the wedding.

---

[53] Pyŏn Sajŏng (邊士貞, 1529–1596) was a junior administrator, ninth rank (參奉 *ch'ambong*). As a general of a righteous army during the Japanese invasions, he fought many battles, including at the Siege of Chinju from 1592 to 1593.

Ogyŏng found out about their plan and appealed to her mother that night: "Mr. Ch'oe has not returned because he is detained by the order of the commander of the righteous army, not because he is neglecting the marriage promise. If we break the engagement without waiting for word from him, we will be committing a serious wrong. If you persist against my will, I swear that even until death I will have no other mind. Oh, my mother and heaven, why do you not understand me?"[54]

Lady Sim said, "Why are you so stubborn like this? You ought to follow your parents' words! My daughter, you don't know anything!"

Lady Sim went to her bed and fell asleep. In her dream that night, she suddenly heard choking sounds. Awake, she ran her fingers over the spot where her daughter had been sleeping and found that she was gone. In a panic, she went out to look for her daughter. Underneath the window, Ogyŏng was lying facedown, having apparently strangled herself with a towel. Her body was already ice-cold. The sound of her breathing grew weaker and weaker and eventually stopped. Lady Sim, screaming, hurried to untie the towel and then roused Ch'unsaeng with a kick and ordered her to fetch a lamp. Holding Ogyŏng's body in her arms and in deep grief, Lady Sim hurried to pour a few drops of water into Ogyŏng's mouth. After a while, Ogyŏng revived. Thrown into an uproar, the Chŏng family came to aid in her further recovery. After that, no one ever mentioned the marriage proposal from the Yang family again.

Ch'oe Ch'ŏk's father wrote a letter to his son informing him of what had happened. At this time, Ch'oe was lying in bed ill. The news shocked him greatly, worsening his illness. The commander of the righteous army heard of the event and ordered Ch'oe to return home.

Several days after his return, Ch'oe recovered fully from his illness. On the first auspicious day of the eleventh month, the wedding ceremony was held at Chŏng *sangsa*'s house. The two beautiful young people were united, and there is no need to mention how happy they were.

Ch'oe Ch'ŏk brought his wife, Ogyŏng, and his mother-in-law, Lady Sim, to his home. When they walked through the gate, all the servants were pleased. As they ascended to the hall, all the relatives congratulated them. Their house was filled with joy, and praise flowed through the neighborhood.

Ogyŏng lifted her lapels when carrying a small table.[55] She also fetched water and pounded rice in a mortar by herself. She showed respect to her father-in-law

---

[54] The passage beginning "I swear..." is the last two lines of each stanza of the song "The Cypress Boat" [柏舟, C. Bozhou, K. Paekchu] included in the "Odes of Yong" [鄘風] in the *Book of Songs*.

[55] The original text (Pak Hŭibyŏng's edition) has 攝衽抱機, but it should be corrected to 攝衽抱机, meaning "carrying a small table lifting one's lapels." This expression refers to one's

and served her husband with sincerity. She treated her elders with respect and those younger with kindness and proper manners. Word about Ogyŏng spread widely, and people concluded that even the virtuous wives of Liang Hong and Bao Xuan could not be better than Ogyŏng.[56]

Everything went well with Ch'oe after marrying Ogyŏng. Their wealth increased and they enjoyed an affluent life. The only thing that caused them worry was that they were yet to have a child who could carry on the family line. So the couple went to Manbok Temple on the first day of each month and prayed to have a son.

On the first day of the first month of the following year, the year of Kabo [甲午, 1594], they also went to the temple and prayed. On that night, the Sixteen-Foot-High Golden Buddha[57] of the temple appeared in Ogyŏng's dream and said, "I am the Buddha of Manbok Temple. I am so touched by your sincere devotion that I am going to grant you a gifted boy. There will be an unusual birthmark on this child."

Ogyŏng soon became pregnant and gave birth to a son just as foretold. There was a red birthmark as big as a baby's hand on his backside. She named him Mongsŏk, which means, "Dreaming of Buddha."

Ch'oe played the flute very well. He often played at night when the moon was bright and in the early morning when the flowers were in full blossom.

It was on a bright night in late spring. A rustling breeze blew, and the white moon shone brightly. A petal, flying in the wind, touched Ch'oe's clothes, and its subtle scents lingered in his nose. Ch'oe ladled some wine from the jar, filled his cup, and drank deeply. Then he leaned against his desk and started playing the tune of "Sannong."[58] The beautiful tones of the flute echoed.

---

respectful behavior. Its reference is found in the "Biographies of Lu Zhonglian and Zou Yang" [魯仲連鄒陽列傳] in vol. 83 of the *Records of the Grand Historian* [史記 *Shiji*].

[56] Liang Hong's (梁鴻, K. Yang Hong, fl. first century C.E.) wife, Meng Guang (孟光, K. Maeng Kwang), is known for her subservience toward her husband. Whenever she served meals, she knelt and held a lacquer tray raised to the level of her eyebrows in order to show her respect for her husband. Bao Xuan's (鮑宣, K. P'o Sŏn, d. 3 C.E.) wife, known as Shaojun (少君, K. Sogun), respected her poor husband and served him to his heart's desire. Both wives helped their husbands succeed with their respect and selfless support.

[57] Buddha is said to have been sixteen feet tall (one *zhang* and six *chi*). Many temples, including Manbok Temple, have a Buddha statue of that size, called Changyukpul (丈六佛). The particular Buddha of this story is made of gold, so it is sometimes called the Sixteen-Foot-High Golden Buddha.

[58] "Sannong" (三弄) can be translated as "playing three times," but it often refers to "Three Variations of Plum Blossoms" [梅花三弄 Meihua sannong]. "Meihua sannong" is one of the most famous Chinese musical pieces, whose origin dates to the Eastern Jin dynasty (317–420). It is said to have been favored by Chinese scholars for its representations of purity, peace, and integrity.

Ogyŏng fell into deep thought and said, "I have always felt uncomfortable with women reciting poems, but in this atmosphere, I cannot contain myself." Then she began to recite a seven-syllable quatrain, which reads as follows:

Prince Jin plays the flute[59] as the moon draws near.
The blue sky is like an ocean and cold dew falls.
Let us fly together with the blue phoenix;
We will not lose our way on Mount Penglai covered with haze and glow.

Ch'oe listened to Ogyŏng's recitation in surprise, for he had been unaware of her ability to compose fine poetry. Greatly impressed and inspired by her poem, he wrote a quatrain in reply.

The distant Jade Terrace reddens with early morning cloud;[60]
A flute is played and the melody has not reached its end.
The reverberating sounds of the music fill the air as the mountain moon sets.
The shadows of the garden flowers are swayed by a fragrant breeze.

When Ch'oe finished reciting his poem, Ogyŏng was delighted. However, the happy moment was soon followed by sadness. Overwhelmed with emotion and her eyes full of tears, she said, "There are many misfortunes in this world, and bad things tend to happen among the good things. People say that there is no fixed rule in one's separation and union. Because of this, I can't help but fall into sad thoughts."

Ch'oe wiped her tears with his sleeves and consoled her, saying, "Bending and stretching, full and empty are the basic principle of the Heavenly Way. One's having good or bad fortune is all part of human affairs.[61] Even if besieged by misfortunes, we should try to have peaceful minds according to our luck and not fall into the arms of sorrow. The ancients taught us not to be worried or

---

[59] Prince Jin refers to Wangzi Jin (王子晉), heir to King Ling (靈王, r. 571–545 B.C.E.) of the Eastern Zhou (東周, 771–256 B.C.E.). He is also known as Wangzi Qiao (王子喬, K. Wangja Kyo). He was a child prodigy, who later became a Daoist immortal residing on Mount Song (嵩山).

[60] Jade Terrace (瑤臺, C. Yaotai), along with Mount Penglai, is also said to be the abode of legendary immortals and fairies.

[61] The original text has four characters, 吉凶悔吝 (kilhyung hoerin), which are borrowed directly from the Book of Changes [周易]. While the phrase can be interpreted variously, one common reading is "good and bad fortune are the result of the two attitudes: one deeply introspecting oneself [悔]," which leads to good fortune, and the other "not allowing for reflection on one's conduct because of closed-mindedness [吝]," which is the cause of bad fortune. In the text, it seems to generally mean the alternation of good and bad fortune in life.

doleful. They also said, 'Say only beneficial things, not harmful things.' Indeed, we do not need to ruin our happy moments or corrupt our happy feelings because of our worries and anguish."

From that moment on, the couple's love became deeper and deeper within them. They called each other "true friends,"[62] and they were never apart even for one day.

It was the eighth month of the Chŏngyu year [丁酉 1597] when the Japanese army forced its way into Namwŏn city and took the fortress. The people of Namwŏn scattered and fled the city. Ch'oe Ch'ŏk's family also fled deep into Yŏn'gok [燕谷] Valley of Mount Chiri [智異山]. Ch'oe told Ogyŏng to dress like a man so no one would notice her as being a woman among the crowd.

Several days passed after they had taken refuge on the mountain. The food they had brought while fleeing was exhausted, and everyone in the family was suffering from hunger. Ch'oe and a few vigorous young men managed to descend the mountain to procure some food and to scout the movements of the Japanese forces. When they reached Kurye [求禮], they saw a group of enemy soldiers coming their way. They quickly hid themselves in a crack between some boulders and waited for them to pass by.

That same day, the enemy troops penetrated into Yŏn'gok Valley, attacking and capturing all the refugees. With all the roads blocked by the enemy, Ch'oe couldn't return to Yŏn'gok.

The enemy soldiers left Yŏn'gok after three days, and Ch'oe was able to return. The place was strewn with corpses, and blood trickled and pooled on the ground. A faint groaning could be heard from the forest. Ch'oe approached and saw a number of elders who were moaning because of their wounds. One of them recognized Ch'oe and spoke to him in tears, "The enemy was here for three days. They looted and slaughtered people indiscriminately. They dragged all the young people to the Sŏm River [蟾江], where they stopped and built a camp. If you want to find your family members, go to the riverside and ask around."

Ch'oe cried out, collapsed to the ground, vomited blood, and hurried to the Sŏm River. On his way, he heard the faint sound of groaning coming from one among the scattered dead bodies. It was unclear whether the person was dead or alive. He tried to determine who the person was but couldn't since the entire face was covered with blood. He then looked over the person's clothes, and they

---

[62] "True friends," *zhiyin* (知音, K. *chiŭm*), means, literally, "understanding music." The origin of this expression goes back to the story of the musician Boya (伯牙) and his friend Zhong Ziqi (鐘子期). Boya was a *qin* player and Zhong Ziqi was a good listener. When Zhong Ziqi died, Boya destroyed his instrument, believing there was none to understand his music. The term "understanding music" thus came to mean a true friend.

appeared like those worn by Ch'unsaeng. So he shouted out, "Are you not Ch'unsaeng?"

Ch'unsaeng barely opened her eyes and looked at him. She spoke in a weak voice, "Oh, master! Master! Our family members were all captured by the enemy. I was struck by a blade and fell down since I couldn't run fast while carrying young Master Mongsŏk on my back. I almost died but came to after several hours. I don't know what happened to the young master." After uttering these words, she breathed her last and died. Stricken with sorrow, Ch'oe beat his chest and kicked the ground before collapsing and finally passing out.

After a time, he recovered but had no idea what to do. He soon regained his composure and headed for the Sŏm River. By the riverbank, he saw groups of wounded older people sitting together and sobbing. Ch'oe approached them and asked what had happened. One of them answered, "We were dragged here from Yŏn'gok Valley. When we arrived at the Japanese ships, they put the young on their ships and struck the older ones with their blades and abandoned us here."

Ch'oe wept ceaselessly and decided to commit suicide since he had no strength to face living in the world alone. However, those nearby stopped him. Ch'oe plodded around the riverbank but had nowhere to go. Ch'oe decided to walk back to his hometown, which took him three days and nights. There he found only wrecked walls and broken tiles scattered in the town. His house had been burned down, and some of it was still smoldering. Piles of human remains were everywhere, such that he could not find open ground to step on.

Ch'oe was resting by Kŭm Bridge [金橋]. He was exhausted from traveling without eating for days and had no strength left to even stand up.

Suddenly, a general from Ming China emerged from the city with about a dozen cavalrymen to wash their horses under the bridge. Ch'oe could speak some Chinese from having given wine to Ming soldiers when he served in the righteous army. He explained to the Ming general what had happened to him and his entire family and asked to go to China with the general so that he could live there. The general, taking a pity on him and sympathizing with him, said, "I'm Regiment Commander [千摠 Qianzong] Yu Youwen [余有文] under the leadership of Regional Commander [摠兵] Wu Zongbing. My home is in Yaoxing [姚興] prefecture, Zhejiang [浙江], and though poor, there is no shortage for basic living. In a lifetime, there is nothing more valuable than meeting with someone who knows one's true self. Regardless of whether the land is close or distant, to enjoy time to one's own content would be enough. Why do we bother remaining in one small corner and leading a needy life?"

Then the Ming general gave a horse to Ch'oe to ride and brought him to his camp. Ch'oe was very handsome, meticulous, and considerate. He was also good at archery and horse riding as well as writing. For this reason, General Yu was fond of him, sharing a table when eating, and sharing a blanket when sleeping.

After a short while, Regional Commander Wu withdrew his army and returned to China. Regiment Commander Yu brought Ch'oe to Yaoxing, China, as a replacement for a soldier who had died in battle, and they lived together.

This is what happened when Ch'oe Ch'ŏk's family was captured and dragged to the Sŏm River. The Japanese army, thinking that Ch'oe's father and mother-in-law were too old and sick, didn't put a heavy guard on them. Ch'oe's father and mother-in-law escaped when no one was on watch, and they hid themselves in the reeds. When the enemy left, they came out of hiding. They wandered from place to place, begging for food on the street, which eventually led them to Yŏn'gok Temple. There they heard a baby crying. Lady Sim said to Ch'oe Suk, "I don't know whose baby it is, but it sounds like the crying of our grandson."

Ch'oe Suk opened the door in a hurry and looked inside the temple. It was indeed their grandson, Mongsŏk. Ch'oe Suk held the crying baby in his arms and patted him for a while. Then he asked the monks, "Where did you find this baby?"

A monk called Hyejŏng [慧正] answered, "I heard the baby crying from among a pile of corpses. I decided to bring him here out of pity and hoped for his parents to show up. Now that my wish has become reality, how can it not be the will of heaven?"

Reunited with his grandson, Ch'oe Suk decided to return home. He and Lady Sim took turns carrying the baby on their back along the way. When they arrived, they gathered all the servants who used to work for them and started running the household.

Meanwhile, Ogyŏng had been captured by an old Japanese soldier called Tonu [頓于]. Being a devout Buddhist, he was against killing. As a former a merchant with expertise in sailing, he had been conscripted into the army as a captain by Konishi Yukinaga.[63] Tonu liked Ogyŏng for her astuteness and hoped she would stay with him. So he gave her good clothes and food to make her feel comfortable. In fact, Ogyŏng tried to commit suicide a number of times by jumping into water, but she was caught by Tonu.

One night, the Sixteen-Foot-High Golden Buddha appeared in a dream and said to her, "I'm the Buddha from Manbok Temple. You should not die because good things will come later." Ogyŏng woke and thought deeply about the dream. She told herself that what the Buddha had said could happen, so she forced herself to eat to survive.

---

[63] Konishi Yukinaga (小西行長, 1558–1600) was a daimyo under Toyotomi Hideyoshi (豊臣秀吉, 1536–98). During the Japanese invasions, he marched on P'yŏngyang at the vanguard of the Japanese army but soon withdrew upon the death of Toyotomi.

Tonu's home was located in Nagoya. There were an old wife and young daughter in his family. He let Ogyŏng stay in the house but forbade her to go inside the inner quarters because [owing to her still being dressed in men's clothing] he thought Ogyŏng was a man. Ogyŏng deceived Tonu and said, "I was born as a small weakling who was frequently ill. Back in my homeland, I was never selected to do man's work. I could do nothing other than sewing and cooking."

Hearing this, Tonu had sympathy for her. He named her Sau [沙于], and whenever he went on sea trips for trading, he assigned Ogyŏng the job of navigation officer, and they traveled to the Fujian [福建] and Zhejiang areas of China together.

Around this time, Ch'oe was staying in Yaoxing with Yu Youwen, who had sworn brotherhood with him. Yu Youwen presented his idea of marrying his sister to Ch'oe, but Ch'oe firmly refused, saying, "Separated during the chaos, I don't even know whether my old parents and feeble wife are alive or dead, so I can't host a memorial service for them. Given that, how can I acquire a new wife and live a comfortable life?" Yu Youwen knew Ch'oe's words to be righteous, and he no longer talked about the marriage.

That winter, Yu Youwen died as a result of an illness. Unable to find someone to depend on, he began to wander along the Yangzi [陽子江] and Huai [淮水] Rivers and visited famous historic sites. He sightsaw in Longmen[64] and toured the mausoleum of Emperor Yu.[65] He reached the Yuan and Xiang Rivers,[66] crossed Dongting Lake,[67] and climbed Yueyang Tower[68] and Gusu Terrace.[69]

He recited songs in the mountains and by the rivers and danced amid the clouds in the sky. He came to desire the life of a hermit, leaving everything behind. He heard that Daoist Master Haichan [海蟾] Wang Yong [王用], who retired to a hermitage on Mount Qingcheng [青城山], created pills of immortality made of gold and could ascend to heaven in the daytime. So he decided to go to the Shu area[70] where Mount Qingcheng was located to get training from the master.

---

[64] The place-name Longmen (龍門) is found in many provinces. However, here it seems to refer to the Grand Historian Sima Qian's (ca. 145–86 B.C.E.) birthplace, near present-day Hancheng, Shaanxi province.

[65] The tomb of Emperor Yu (禹穴) is located on Mount Kuaiji in Shaoxing, Zhejiang province.

[66] Both the Yuan River (沅水) and the Xiang River (湘水) flow into Dongting Lake (洞庭湖).

[67] Dongting Lake is located in Hunan province, China.

[68] Yueyang Tower (岳陽樓) is located in Yueyang, Hunan province, overlooking Dongting Lake.

[69] Gusu Terrace (姑蘇臺) is in Suzhou, Jiangsu province.

[70] The Shu (蜀) area is in present-day Sichuan province.

At that time, a man called Song You,[71] whose pseudonym was Hechuan [鶴川], lived in a house in Yongjin Gate [湧金門] in Hangzhou [杭州]. He was well versed in the classics and histories but had no interest in seeking fame. He made his living writing books. He enjoyed helping others and was loyal to his friends. He regarded Ch'oe as a true friend. When Song You learned that Ch'oe was about to leave for Shu, he brought some wine to share with him.

They exchanged cups of wine until they were quite drunk. Song spoke to Ch'oe, calling him by his courtesy name.

"Paeksŭng! Who, in a moment like this, would not want to attain longevity and immortality? However, there was never such a thing in the past or present. Moreover, why do you even bother to take medicines and endure hunger, given that you have only a limited life? What's the point of volunteering to undergo such hardship and becoming a neighbor of mountain ghosts? Please join me on a ship sailing the trade routes between the Wu and Yue areas.[72] We will sell silk and tea! Don't you think spending the rest of our lives doing that will also be considered the work of an enlightened person?" Ch'oe was persuaded by Song's remarks and followed him.

It was spring in the year of Kyŏngja [庚子, 1600]. Ch'oe, following Song, joined merchant sailors from the same town to trade in the Annam area.[73] When they arrived at a harbor in Annam, they saw about ten Japanese ships at anchor. They stayed there for more than ten days.

On the second day of the fourth month, there were no clouds in the sky, and the color of the sea looked like beautiful silk. The waves calmed as the wind dissipated. Silence reigned over the shadowless sea. People onboard fell into a deep sleep, and from time to time the cries of a seagull could be heard. There also was sorrowful chanting from a Japanese ship.

Ch'oe leaned against the window of the ship alone and thought about his situation. To forget all he had been through, he took a flute from his shirt and started playing a sad tune in order to release his deep sorrow.

This flute sound made the sky sadden, and the clouds and the mist looked melancholy. Those sleeping inside the ship were awakened by the sound, and they all showed gloomy faces. As the sound of the flute spread, the chanting from the Japanese ship also stopped.

A few minutes later, the sound of a seven-syllable quatrain in the language of Chosŏn could be heard: "Prince Jin plays the flute as the moon draws near./The blue sky is like an ocean and cold dew falls./Let us fly together with the blue

---

[71] Song You (宋佑) appears as Zhu You (朱祐) in other editions.
[72] Wu (吳) and Yue (越) are the present-day areas of Jiangsu and Zhejiang.
[73] Annam (安南) refers to Vietnam.

phoenix;/We will not lose our way on Mount Penglai covered with haze and glow." At the conclusion of the poem, there sounded a deep sigh. When he heard this, Ch'oe was startled. He dropped his flute unconsciously and stood as stiff as a dead person.

Song asked, "What's wrong with you? What's wrong with you?" He asked two times, but there was no answer from Ch'oe. Song asked a third time; Ch'oe tried to say something, but he was choked with emotion and began to weep instead.

After a while, he calmed himself down, and said, "That poem was written by my wife. I know it as my wife's, but no one else could recognize it. The voice reciting it is also similar to my wife's voice. I wonder if my wife is onboard that ship or not . . . but no . . . no . . . it could not be her . . ."

Then Ch'oe explained about what had happened to his family during the attack by the Japanese army. People inside the ship were surprised at the story and thought it extraordinary.

Among them was a person named Du Hong [杜洪]. He was young, brave, and chivalrous. The moment he heard Ch'oe's story, he, out of his high spirits, hit on the sides of the oars. Then he jumped up and said, "I will go to the ship and snoop around."

Song You detained him and said, "I'm afraid that attempting anything during the night bears the risk of your getting hurt. We'd better look into this in a calm and careful way tomorrow morning." Everyone agreed with him. Unable to sleep at all, Ch'oe stayed up and awaited the break of dawn.

At last the sun rose in the east. Ch'oe could wait no longer. He went down the hill and approached the Japanese ship. Ch'oe asked in the language of Chosŏn, "The person who recited a poem last night must be a person from Chosŏn. I, too, am from Chosŏn. I would be delighted like the wanderer of Yue if I could meet a person from my homeland in a distant place such as this.[74]

The previous night, Ogyŏng had heard the sound of the flute, and she knew that it was a melody from Chosŏn that she had learned long ago. Therefore, she recited her poem to test whether her husband was on the ship from which the sound of the flute had come.

When she heard that someone from Chosŏn was looking for her, she was perplexed and didn't know what to do. She rushed to disembark, tripping and tumbling a couple of times in the process.

---

[74]The story of the wanderer of Yue is seen in "Xu Wu gui" [徐無鬼], in chapter 24 of the *Book of Zhuang zi* [莊子 *Zhuang zi*]. The wanderer, having left his state, found happiness when encountering anyone from his own state whom he had previously met or known in the Yue area. As time went by, he was even glad when he saw anyone who appeared to be a native from his own state.

The two immediately recognized each other, shouted, hugged, and rolled in the sand. Being overwhelmed, they couldn't say a word. When their tears were exhausted, they wept tears of blood instead, obscuring their vision.

Sailors from both countries gathered in a line like a long, circular fence to see the sight. They first speculated that the two Chosŏn people were relatives or friends. But when they learned that they were actually husband and wife, they looked at each other and said, "How strangely odd this is! This must be thanks to the help from heaven and ghosts. This kind of thing never happened in the past."

When Ch'oe asked about their family members' whereabouts, Ogyŏng said, "We escaped from the mountain to the river. Father-in-law and my mother were safe until then. It grew dark and we were separated while we rushed to board a boat."

They wept bitterly again, looking at each other. Those looking at them also shed tears. Song You asked Tonu whether he could buy the freedom of Ogyŏng for three taels of white gold. The Japanese man became angry and said, "We have been together for the past four years. I loved his [her] decent and sincere behavior and treated him [her] as my own sibling while sharing food and bed. I have never been away from her, but I never noticed that she is a woman. Having observed this with my own eyes, I came to think that this is a matter to impress all the ghosts in the world. Though I'm an unwise man, I'm not a callous person. I can't receive money in return."

Then he took out ten taels of silver and gave them to Ogyŏng, saying, "After having lived together for four years, now we are about to part. I'm so saddened by this and can't suppress my sorrow. However, to be reunited with your long-lost husband on a remote sea after having gone through so many hardships is an unprecedented thing. If I selfishly care only about my own wish, heaven will punish me. Good-bye, Sau! I hope you take good care of yourself!"

Ogyŏng bowed deeply to Tonu and said, "Thanks to your protection, I have survived and finally been reunited with my husband. Your grace is already remarkable, and now that you give me money, I don't know how to repay my debt to you."

Ch'oe also thanked the old man over and over. He brought Ogyŏng to his boat, holding her hand. People from neighboring boats all came for several days to celebrate their reunion. Some of them presented gold, silver, and silk as gifts. Ch'oe gratefully received the gifts and showed his sincere gratitude to the people. Song You, after returning to his home, provided the couple with a clean room so that they could live comfortably.

Ch'oe again found happiness after finding his wife. However, living in a foreign land with no relatives nearby made him constantly think about his old father and baby son, and the thought made him bitter. His anxiety and broken heart continued day and night. He prayed fervently and wished that one day he could return to his home country.

One year passed. Ogyŏng gave birth to another son. On the night she delivered her baby, the Sixteen-Foot-High Buddha appeared again in a dream. So she looked over her newborn baby and found a red birthmark on his back. The couple named their new son Mongsŏn [夢仙], as if their first son, Mongsŏk, had been reborn.

When Mongsŏn reached adulthood, the Ch'oe couple wanted to find him a wise wife.

Among their neighbors, there was a girl from the Chen family. Her name was Hongtao [紅桃, K. Hongdo]. Her father, Chen Weiqing [陳偉慶, K. Chin Wigyŏng], following Regional Commander Liu Zongbing, had gone to Chosŏn before she had turned one hundred days old and had never returned. Hongtao's mother passed away before Hongtao was fully grown. She grew up under the guardianship of her maternal aunt, deeply regretting that she couldn't remember the face of her father, who she thought had passed away in a distant land. Her only wish was to visit the country at least once where her father had died and to hold a ritual invoking her father's spirit.[75] She engraved her wish in her heart. However, as a woman, she didn't know how to find a way to fulfill her wish.

At that time, word was going around that a Chosŏn man, Mongsŏn, was looking for a wife. Upon hearing the news, she explained to her aunt her wish to marry him, saying, "I'd like to become a daughter-in-law of the Ch'oe family so that I can go to the Eastern Country [Chosŏn]."

Her aunt also knew very well Hongtao's intention and immediately went to Ch'oe to discuss the matter. The Ch'oe's couple said, "How extraordinary she is to hold such a goal!" They accepted Hongtao as their daughter-in-law.

In the next year, the year of Kimi [己未, 1619], Nurhači[76] brought soldiers and attacked Liaoyang.[77] Liaoyang soon fell under Nurhači's control, and many generals and soldiers were killed. The Ming emperor was furious about the incident and summoned all the soldiers in the country to defeat Nurhači's army. A native of Suzhou [蘇州], Wu Shiying [吳世英], fought in this war as company

---

[75] This ritual is Zhaohun (招魂, K. Ch'ohon), one of the funerary rites. In this ritual, a relative of the deceased takes a coat worn by the deceased and goes to the roof of the house. Then the person calls out the name of the deceased while waving the coat. This is an attempt to bring the spirit back to the body, the present world. After this, the person takes the coat and covers the deceased's body with it.

[76] Nurhači (努爾哈赤, 1559–1626) is the founder of the Qing dynasty.

[77] Liaoyang (遼陽) is located in Liaoning (遼寧) province.

commander [百摠 Baizong] under Brigade Commander Qiao.[78] He had heard about the talent and bravery of Ch'oe from Yu Youwen at an earlier time, so he wanted to bring him to his camp by appointing him as a document clerk [書記 shuji]. When Ch'oe was about to leave, Ogyŏng, with her eyes full of tears, grabbed his hand and bid him farewell, saying, "Because of my sad fate I had to endure all kinds of troubles and sufferings in my early life. However, through divine help, I was able to survive them all, and finally we reunited. Our broken karmic affinity as husband and wife has become connected again, as if a broken string on a zither were reconnected and a broken mirror put back together. Luckily, we have produced a son who will hold ancestral rites for us. Our time of sharing life and happiness together is already more than twenty years. Looking back on these past days, I have no regrets even if I were to die now. I always wanted to return your favor by dying before you. Today, contrary to my expectation, in my late years, I am about to be separated from you just like the *sam* and *sang* stars.[79] From here to Liaoyang is tens of thousands of leagues away, and I imagine it will be very difficult for you to come back alive. How can I expect to see you again in the future? I'd rather commit suicide at this time of parting so that I can rid you of your feeling of longing for me and me of my suffering days and nights. I hope my beloved husband will be safe by all means. I must leave you forever now! I must leave you forever now!"

Upon finishing her words, Ogyŏng took her dagger from her breast and tried to slash her throat. Ch'oe, however, quickly snatched the dagger from her hand and said, "Do you think such a barbarian army can be a match for this great country? Now the army of the emperor goes to the front. They will defeat the enemy easily, like a big mountain squashing an egg. Serving in the army will make it difficult for me to come and go for quite some time, but don't be so foolish as to create unnecessary worries and anxieties. Let's have a cup of wine in celebration of the time I return victoriously. Moreover, our son Mongsŏn is an adult now. You can count on him. Please eat well and don't cause the one leaving to worry about you." Eventually, he packed and left.

Ch'oe's army arrived in Liaoyang and then passed over hundreds of leagues of barbarian land to finally meet up with Chosŏn soldiers. Together, they set up a camp in the area of Niumaozhai [牛毛寨]. However, because of the Ming

---

[78] Brigade Commander Qiao (遊擊喬 Youji Qiao) is the military official Qiao Yiqi (喬一琦, 1571–1619), who, under the command of Liu Ting (劉綎, 1560–1619), fought against the Latter Jin army. He committed suicide when his army was defeated.

[79] In this constellation, the two stars Sam (參, C. Shen, Orion) and Sang (商, C. Shang, Antares), never appear at the same time. For this reason, they became a common symbol of a separated couple.

general's underestimation of the Latter Jin[80] enemy, the whole army met a devastating defeat. NurhačI ruthlessly killed all the Ming soldiers but did not kill the Chosŏn soldiers, treating them with both threats and conciliation.

Brigade Commander Qiao led his remaining ten soldiers or so to the Chosŏn camp and asked for uniforms of Chosŏn soldiers. Supreme Commander [元帥, K. Wŏnsu] Kang Hongnip of Chosŏn wanted to help them survive by giving the uniforms, but Chief Administrative Officer [從事官, K. Chongsagwan] Yi Minhwan, after taking away the uniforms, captured the Ming soldiers and sent them to the enemy.[81] He did so in fear of Nurhači's possible retaliation if he offered help to the Ming soldiers.

Since he was originally a person of Chosŏn, Ch'oe survived alone by sneaking into the Chosŏn camp during the confusion. However, as Kang Hongnip surrendered to the Latter Jin, Ch'oe was also taken captive along with the Chosŏn soldiers.

At this time, among the Chosŏn soldiers under the command of Supreme Commander Kang was Mongsŏk. He had been drafted from Namwŏn as a low-ranking military officer [武學]. Nurhači divided the surrendered Chosŏn soldiers into different prisons. Ch'oe and Mongsŏk were placed in the same prison. However, although they were father and son, they did not recognize each other.

Noticing that Ch'oe spoke the Chosŏn language poorly, Mongsŏk speculated that Ch'oe was a Ming soldier pretending to be a Chosŏn man to save his life. Out of suspicion, Mongsŏk asked Ch'oe where he lived. Ch'oe, suspecting Mongsŏk to be a spy from the Latter Jin army, answered ambiguously and inconsistently, saying variously that he came from Chŏlla province or Ch'ungch'ŏng province. Because of this, Mongsŏk became more even suspicious of him, but there was no way for him to discover who Ch'oe was.

While spending several days together, the two men became closer. They developed a sort of sympathy between them, and they came to trust each other. Ch'oe told Mongsŏk everything about what had happened to him. Mongsŏk's face changed color a couple of times while listening to his words, and his heart was pounding hard. He couldn't believe it, and he even become suspicious of the story he was listening to. Then he asked Ch'oe in detail about the son he said he had lost, especially about his personal traits like his age and physique. Ch'oe answered, "It was in the tenth month of the year of Kabo [1594] that he was born,

---

[80] The Latter Jin (後金) was founded by Nurhači in 1616. Its capital was at Shenyang (瀋陽), and it adopted the new name of Qing in 1636.

[81] Kang Hongnip (姜弘立, 1560–1627) was dispatched by King Kwanghae-gun to aid the Ming's attack on Nurhači's army. Kang's troops joined the Ming army led by Liu Ting, but in 1619, Liu Ting's army was defeated, and Kang's troops surrendered to Nurhači. Yi Minhwan (李民寏, 1573–1649) recorded details of this event.

and he died in the eighth month of the year of Chŏngyu [1597]. He had a red birthmark on his back as big as the palm of a small child."

After hearing this, Mongsŏk was shocked and momentarily fainted. He then took his shirt off and showed his back to Ch'oe and said, "I'm your son."

Ch'oe finally came to realize that Mongsŏk was his son. They asked each other about their parents' safety, then hugged and cried. Their crying continued for days.

There was an old barbarian soldier who frequently came to the prison camp to guard the captives. He seemed to understand the words of Ch'oe and his son, and he showed deep pity for them. One day, when all the other soldiers were out, the old soldier secretly came to Ch'oe's cell and took a seat. Then he asked in the Chosŏn language, "Your crying seemed very unusual. Something must have happened. What happened? I'd like to hear about it"

Ch'oe hesitated and couldn't tell the truth because he wasn't sure what would happen if he told the true story. The old barbarian soldier said, "Don't be afraid of me. I'm originally a member of the local indigenous soldiers of Sakchu.[82] I couldn't stand the tyranny of the local magistrate, so I fled with all my family members. I have settled in the land of the barbarians for more than ten years. The barbarians are honest and there is no tyranny among their governors. Our lives are as short as the morning dew. What is the point of living in hardship in one's own hometown? Nurhači gave me eighty elite soldiers to prevent Chosŏn captives from escaping. But now listening to your talk, I can't help but think what happened to you is a very unusual thing. I will probably be punished by Nurhači, but how can I not release you two?" The next day, the old barbarian brought a bag of food and gave it to them. He ordered his son to show them a side road to make sure that they escaped successfully.

In this way, Ch'oe finally returned to his homeland with his son after some twenty years. He couldn't wait to see his father, so he hurried to the south at twice his normal pace. On his way, he developed an abscess on his back but pressed on without attempting to cure it. When he got to Ŭnjin,[83] however, his condition worsened and he couldn't move anymore. He couldn't help but stay at an inn, but his illness became far worse. His breathing was rough, and he looked as if he was about to die. Mongsŏk didn't know what to do. He searched everywhere for treatment using acupuncture or medicine but could find none. At that time, a Chinese man, who kept a low profile, traveled to Kyŏngsang from Chŏlla province. On his way, he saw Ch'oe and said in surprise, "His condition is very serious and he looks as if he couldn't have survived had I found him after today."

---

[82] Sakchu (朔州) is located in P'yŏng'anbuk-to.
[83] Ŭnjin (恩津) is in Nonsan, Ch'ungch'ŏngnam-do.

The Chinese man took an acupuncture needle out of his bag and pierced the abscess and squeezed the pus out. Ch'oe then showed significant improvement. After two days of walking with a staff, he was able to return to his home. Ch'oe's unexpected entrance surprised the whole family. They were all as happy as if a dead person had been resurrected. Father and son hugged each other and cried until the sun set. They couldn't discern whether it was a dream or reality.

The years following the loss of her daughter had been a misery for Lady Sim. She lived day to day, relying only on Mongsŏk. However, after he had joined the army, she received no news of him. Thinking that he may have been killed on the battlefield, she was heartbroken and bedridden for months.

When she heard the news that Mongsŏk and his father had come back alive and that Ogyŏng was also alive, she screamed out and didn't know what to do. It was hard to tell whether she was sad or happy.

Grateful to the Chinese man for his treatment of his father, Mongsŏk brought the man to his home to repay his good deed. Mongsŏk asked the Chinese man, "You said you were from Ming China. Then where do you live? What is your name?"

The Chinese man answered, "My surname is Chen, and first name is Weiqing. My hometown is in Yongjin Gate, of Hangzhou. I came down here to Chosŏn in the twenty-fifth year of the Wanli [萬曆, 1597] reign under the leadership of Provincial Military Commander Liu.[84] I was stationed in Sunch'ŏn [順天]. One day, I was out to spy on the enemy, but I violated our commander's orders, for which I was to be punished. So I ran away in the middle of the night and ended up here."

Ch'oe was surprised to hear this and said, "Do you have a family there? Your parents, wife, or kids?"

Chen Weiqing said, "I have my wife there. We had a baby girl just several months before I went into the army."

Ch'oe asked him, "What is the name of your daughter?"

"I named her Hongtao [Red Peach] because a neighbor brought us a peach on the day she was born," said Chen.

Ch'oe rushed to grasp his hand and said, "This is a very strange karmic affinity. When I was in Hangzhou, I lived next to your home. Your wife, I heard, passed away because of an illness in the ninth month of the Sinhae [辛亥, 1611] year. Your daughter, Hongtao, who was left alone, was raised by Wu Fenglin [吳鳳林], husband of her aunt, and I married her off to my son when she was grown. I have never imagined that I could meet my in-law today."

---

[84] Provincial Military Commander Liu (劉提督 Liu Tidu) is Liu Ting (劉綎).

Chen was also very surprised to hear this astounding revelation. At the same time, he grieved over his sorry fate. Then he said, "Ah . . . I stayed in Taegu at the house of a person whose surname was Pak. There I happened to learn the skill of acupuncture from an old woman, and now I take that as my profession. Now having heard your words, I feel I'm already back at my home. I'd like to rent a room and live together with you."

Mongsŏk stood up and said, "You are a most gracious person who saved my father. Furthermore, my mother and my brother live on your daughter's support. Now that we have become one family, there isn't any problem in your staying with us." And he welcomed Chen into their house.

After hearing the news that his mother was still alive, Mongsŏk thought about how he could go to Ming and bring his mother back, but he couldn't think of a good plan and thus shed tears.

Meanwhile, Ogyŏng in Hangzhou heard the news that all the Ming soldiers had been killed. Believing that Ch'oe had died on the battlefield, she cried day and night. She decided to kill herself and didn't take any water and food. One day, the Sixteen-Foot-High Buddha appeared to her in a dream. After gently touching her head, he said, "Do not give up your life. There surely will be good news."

Ogyŏng woke up from her dream and said to Mongsŏn, "When I was dragged off by the Japanese enemy, I wanted to commit suicide by jumping into the sea. But the Sixteen-Foot-High Buddha of Manbok Temple appeared in my dream and stopped me, saying, 'You shouldn't give up. There will surely be a happy moment later.' After that, four years passed, and I met your father again at an Annam harbor. Today, when I tried to kill myself, I had the same dream, which might tell us that your father is still alive. If he lives, I will be alive even after death."

Mongsŏn cried and said, "I have recently heard that Nurhači killed all the Chinese soldiers but spared the lives of the Chosŏn soldiers. My father was originally a Chosŏn man—he will surely be alive. How can the appearance of the Sixteen-Foot-High Buddha of the temple be a false sign? Mother, please forget about the idea of committing suicide and wait for my father's return."

Ogyŏng changed her mind, and said, "It would take only four or five days to get to the border of Chosŏn from the base of Nurhači. Therefore, if Ch'oe was able to escape, then he must have gone to his homeland. It seems impossible for him to walk over ten thousand leagues to get back to us. So, I will go to our home country and look for your father. If he has already passed, I will go to the Ch'angju[85] area to conduct a ritual for consoling his soul. Then I will bury him

---

[85] Ch'angju (昌州) refers to the northern area of P'yŏnganbuk-to.

in our family graveyard so that his soul can be free from wandering, suffering from hunger in the desert. That is my duty! A bird from the Yue area builds its nest in the direction of the south, and a horse from the Hu area will neigh toward the north.[86] As the day of my death nears, my longing for my hometown grows stronger and more desperate. Separated during the war, I still don't know the whereabouts of my father-in-law, widowed mother, and infant son. A few days ago, I heard rumors from Japanese merchants that some of the Chosŏn people held captive by Japanese soldiers were sent back to Chosŏn. If what they said is true, why couldn't it be one of our missing family members among them? If your father and grandfather have died abroad, who will be able to take care of our ancestral graves? Maybe some of our relatives have survived the war. If we happen to find some of them, that will be good enough. Your job is to borrow a ship and prepare food. By waterways, the distance from here to Chosŏn is only two or three thousand leagues. If we get a favorable wind with heaven's help, we will arrive at the shore within ten days. My plan is set."

Mongsŏn, in tears, implored, "Mother, why do you say such a thing? It would be great if we could successfully reach our country. But how can we cross such a long and dangerous sea by only a small boat? There will be unpredictable dangers such as furious waves and wind and *kyo* dragons[87] and alligators about us. Further, there will be pirates and patrol ships all over the sea blocking our path. What good would it bring to my dead father if you and I ended up being food for fish? I am not bright, but I must speak against your plan because of the great danger."

Hongtao, who was sitting next to him, spoke out, "Please do not go against your mother's will. Her plan is based on her careful thinking, so at this moment it is pointless to worry about any external difficulties that we may encounter. One can reside in a normal place, but it does not guarantee safety from flood, fire, and the looting of bandits."

Ogyŏng added, "While it is true that the waterways are unpredictable, I have gained much experience at sea while held captive in Japan. I made a merchant ship my home and frequently made passage to the Fujian and Guangdong areas in spring and the Ryukyu Islands in autumn. I learned how to survive in furious waves as high as a mountain and to predict the tides using the constellations, so

---

[86] Yue (越), as mentioned, represents present-day Zhejiang province in southern China. Hu (胡) refers to steppe nomads in the western and northern lands. In Korean literature, Hu often refers to northern nomadic people or their northern land. Both Yue and Hu are often used to represent south and north, respectively.

[87] The *kyo* dragon (蛟龍, C. *jiaolong*) is a legendary water dragon capable of controlling rain and floods.

I will manage the high tides and strong winds and deal with other difficulties in sailing. We will prevail over any obstacle in our path."

Ogyŏng took prompt action to make both Japanese and Chosŏn clothes and taught her son and daughter-in-law the languages of the two countries. She instructed her son Mongsŏn, "A sea voyage depends on the mast and oars, so make them strong. We also must have a compass. I will pick a good day to put the boat in the water, so act accordingly with my plan until then."

Mongsŏn listened to his mother in silence and raised no objection to her before leaving the scene. Alone with his wife, he scolded her, "Do you think my deceased father will come back alive if my mother does not look after her own well-being and invent ten thousand dangerous plans to get herself killed? This plan will put her into a grave, and you go along with her plan? How can you be so thoughtless?"

Hongtao answered, "Mother has put sincere efforts into making this important plan, so there is no longer any need to raise an argument. We cannot stop her now, and stopping her now will only make her regret it later, so it is better to follow her words. How can I speak about what I have in mind? My father died on the battlefield when I was but a few months old. The remains of my father must be tumbling about in a field, and his soul must be tangled with weeds. Knowing that as a daughter, how can I raise my head and walk among other people and call myself a human being? Recently, I heard some rumors that there are remnants of defeated Ming troops wandering in Chosŏn. It is conceivable that my father is among them. I hope you can comply with your mother's wish so that we can all go to Chosŏn. If I can at least console my deceased father's lonely soul that wanders about the battlefield, I can die on that day with no regrets." And she wept deeply.

Mongsŏn came to realize that he couldn't change their minds, so he packed their things and put the boat in the sea the first day of the second month of the Kyŏngsin year [庚申, 1620].

Ogyŏng said to Mongsŏn, "Since Chosŏn is located to the southeast, we must wait for the wind from the northwest. Pay heed to what I instruct while firmly holding the oars."

Ogyŏng tied a feather to the end of the flagpole and placed a compass at the bow of the ship. Then she meticulously checked the inside of the boat. Everything needed was in place.

They set out soon and, a school of swellfish appeared swimming in the sea. When the feather on the pole indicated the northwestern wind, they gathered their strength to set sail, bringing the boat to full speed. They sailed through the day and night, even though a thunderbolt fell upon the waves and a stroke of lightning hit the ocean. They arrived at Dengzhou [登州] and Laizhou [萊州]

and passed by Qingzhou [青州] and Qizhou [齊州] after a short while.[88] Islands were floating on the vast ocean, but they soon disappeared in the blink of an eye.

One day, they encountered a Ming patrol ship. An officer of the ship questioned, "Where are you coming from and going to?"

Ogyŏng answered in Chinese, "We are coming from Hangzhou. We are going to Shandong to sell tea."

Then the Ming patrol ship simply left. The next day, a Japanese ship approached. Ogyŏng quickly switched her clothing to Japanese garb before the ship could draw near. A Japanese seaman asked, "Where are you coming from?"

Ogyŏng answered in Japanese, "We actually went out to fish and ended up drifting and losing our boat after struggling against the severe wind and waves. We are now heading back in a borrowed boat from Hangzhou."

The Japanese man said, "You've been through much. This route deviates from the one to Japan. Head further south." Then the ship left.

That night, fierce gales rose from the south, causing waves high enough to reach the sky. Heavy clouds and fog in all directions prevented seeing even a short distance. With the mast and sail broken into pieces by the winds, they didn't know where to go. Mongsŏn and Hongtao were shivering from fear and fell down struck with seasickness. Ogyŏng remained calm and prayed to heaven, chanting the name of the Buddha.

As the night deepened, the weather settled. They anchored their wrecked boat off a small island and went ashore to repair it. Several days later, over the horizon, they saw a ship approaching little by little. Ogyŏng asked Mongsŏn to hide the tools and other belongings in a cave between the rocks.

After a while, the mysterious ship arrived and its seamen came ashore shouting raucously. From their clothes and utterances, they didn't seem like either Korean or Japanese. They seemed instead more like Chinese. They started to beat Ogyŏng's family with a white club and demanded their valuables.

Ogyŏng implored them in Chinese, "We are Chinese. We were out fishing but were adrift at sea and finally landed on this island. We don't have anything of value."

Ogyŏng cried and begged for her life. They didn't kill her but took the boat by tying it to their ship.

After this ordeal, Ogyŏng said to Mongsŏn, "They must be pirates. I have heard there are pirates who rob people coming and going between China and Chosŏn, but they never kill anyone. They must be those pirates. I carelessly started this voyage without considering the problems you raised about the plan. As a result, we have undergone many ordeals and heaven must not be on our

---

[88]These four places are all located in Shandong (山東) province, China.

side. With our boat now gone, what should we do? We cannot fly across the endless sea ahead of us. Neither can we make a wooden raft or sail on bamboo leaves. What is left for us is to die. I have lived enough, but how pitiful you two are to die here because of me."

Ogyŏng wailed loudly with her arms around her son and daughter-in-law. The weeping sound was so desperate as to make the hills tremble. Her infinite pain was transmitted and accumulated in multiple layers of sea waves so much so that it seemed as though the god of the sea shrank from her mourning and the mountain goblins frowned and moaned.

Walking toward the edge of a cliff, Ogyŏng was about to jump into the sea, but Mongsŏn and Hongtao stopped her. Ogyŏng turned to her son and said, "Why did you stop me? Do you have a better plan? We have in the bag barely enough food for three days. Before starving to death, I'd rather die now!"

Mongsŏn said, "It won't be too late to die after our food is exhausted. If we can get some help before that, there is no use repenting later."

Mongsŏn and his wife escorted her back down the hill. They all slept huddled in a crevice in the rocks. The dawn came. Ogyŏng said to her son and daughter-in-law, "It happened to me while I was so weary and taking a short nap: the Sixteen-Foot-High Buddha of Manbok Temple appeared again and said the same thing as before. This is a very unusual thing."

The three gathered, chanted the name of the Buddha, and prayed, "Buddha of Great Compassion, please save of us, please save us!"

Two days passed. They saw a ship in the distance beyond the horizon. Mongsŏn said in dismay to Ogyŏng, "I can't discern the ship's origin. I have never seen such a ship. I am worried."

Ogyŏng saw the ship and exclaimed in joy, "We are saved now! It is a ship of Chosŏn!"

Ogyŏng put on Chosŏn garb quickly and asked Mongsŏn to go up the cliff and wave a cloth. The ship approached the island and lowered its sail. One seaman came to them and asked, "Who are you? Why do you live on this lonely island?"

Ogyŏng answered in the language of Chosŏn. "We are originally gentry people from Seoul. On our way to Naju, a severe storm came upon us and capsized our boat, drowning everyone else on board. Luckily, we were able to grab broken poles on the water and drifted to the island."

The people on the ship took pity on them. They anchored at the island and took the family onboard. They said, "This is a trade ship of T'ongjesa [統制使, regional navy commander]. We are not allowed to deviate from our route since we must conduct our duty on schedule."

In the fourth month of the Kyŏngsin year [1620], the ship arrived at Sunch'ŏn, Chosŏn, and the family went ashore.

Ogyŏng led her son and daughter-in-law and, taking a shortcut, finally arrived in Namwŏn after five or six days. She presumed all her family members had died, but she wanted to see the place where her old house used to be. She looked for Manbok Temple to find her old house. When she reached Kŭm Bridge, she could see the old castle walls, and the whole village looked the same as before.

She looked at her son, pointed with her finger, and said in a sobbing voice, "That house is your father's old home. I'm not sure who lives there now. Let's go and see. We can stay there one night and think about what to do next."

They finally arrived at the gate of their old house. Outside the gate, Ogyŏng saw a man who resembled Ch'oe Ch'ŏk hosting guests sitting in the shade of a willow tree. As she came closer, Ogyŏng soon realized that he was her husband. Soon she, along with her son, broke into tears. Then Ch'oe also saw his wife and son standing before him. He shouted, "I can't believe it. Mongsŏk's mother is here. Is she a heavenly being or a human? Can this be real or is it a dream?"

Mongsŏk heard the shout and rushed out barefoot to meet his long-lost family. The happy reunion of mother and son needs no description. In excitement, they practically lurched into the room together. Lady Sim, who was ill, fainted out of shock and almost perished when she heard her daughter had returned. Ogyŏng carefully held Lady Sim to her chest and revived her. Soon vitality returned to Lady Sim. Meanwhile, Ch'oe Ch'ŏk apprised Chen Weiqing as to who everyone was and said, "Your daughter is also here!" Ch'oe asked Hongtao to explain to her father all that had happened since he had left for the war when she was still an infant.

All family members hugged their children and cried. Their crying could be heard everywhere. Curious villagers started to gather around the house and listen to the family's story. They thought it was rather strange at first, but when they had finished listening, they were all deeply touched, prompting them to spread the story door to door.

Ogyŏng said to her husband, "All thanks to the secret act of benefaction of the Sixteen-Foot-High Buddha we are reunited today. I have heard that the golden Buddha statue is surrounded by ruins, so that people have no place to pray and offer Buddhist rites. The spirit residing in heaven did not let us die in vain but saved us. We must be thankful and repay the favor."

They prepared sacrificial food and went to the temple ruins. They washed their bodies and offered their Buddhist worship with full sincerity.

Ch'oe and Ogyŏng lived happily ever after in their old home on the west side of Namwŏn, respecting their parents and taking care of their sons and daughters-in-law.

Alas, father and son, husband and wife, father-in-law and mother-in-law, and [the two] brothers were separated in the world for almost thirty years. Having been to the bandits' lair and in the jaws of death, they were reunited in the end and lived happy lives. How can this be the work of a human being? It must be that an ordinary man and woman moved heaven and earth with sincerity and brought forth this outcome. Heaven also couldn't defy a woman's devotion since it is undeniable. It must be that heaven and earth were moved by the devotion of an ordinary man and woman and brought forth this outcome. When an ordinary woman has such devotion, heaven also does not defy it. Indeed, a woman's devotion like this cannot remain hidden!

When I stayed at Chup'o[89] in Namwŏn for a short time, Ch'oe Ch'ŏk visited me from time to time. He told me this story and asked me to record everything so that it would never be lost. I couldn't decline his request, so I wrote the main parts of it.

Recorded by Soong Cho Wihan on the intercalary second month of the Sinyu year [辛酉, 1621], the first reign year of Ch'ŏn'gye.[90]

SC

---

[89] Chup'o (周浦) is an area in Namwŏn. Cho Wihan lived there after his retirement.

[90] Ch'ŏngye (天啓, C. Tianqi, 1621–1627) refers to the reign years of the sixteenth emperor Xi (喜) of Ming.

5. Chosŏn Period "Unofficial" Histories

"Unofficial histories" constitute a most interesting genre of the Chosŏn period, one that adds significant depth to accounts of how people lived, what they thought, and where they found entertainment. Nonetheless, it has been largely overlooked because of the eclectic nature of the narratives, especially the dividing line between fiction and nonfiction. Indeed, many of these works are recorded as factual accounts, and given the common presence of supernatural elements, this has caused the narratives to be dismissed as simply "tales heard" or, in current parlance, urban legends. Yet that is a disservice to the genre and the recorders of these works.

In the many extant literary miscellany (文集 *munjip*) or unofficial history (野談/野史 *yadam/yasa*) collections are elements of culture in Chosŏn that are simply not found elsewhere. We find the syncretic worldviews that guided the lives of the people, the belief in the interaction between the human and sacred worlds, humor and conflict in domestic life, and also the encounters that were no doubt commonplace in everyday life. Thus, by reading narratives in this genre we can appreciate the multifaceted lives of the people in Chosŏn, not simply the Confucian-dominated society that has been given perhaps too much hegemony in other genres. We can find a world of ghosts, biting satire, and sex, a world that certainly is more interesting to glimpse and one more plausible than a staid, uptight Confucian one.

The genre itself is highly important in that it helps provide a fuller picture of life and culture in Chosŏn. It lacks the self-editing that many writers incorporated into their works in order to hone a didactic edge for their creations. In the genre of the novel (小說 *sosŏl*) we often find the reoccurring theme of *kwŏn sŏn ching ak* (勸善懲惡), or "reward of goodness and punishment of evil." This leads to the greater portion of novels in the Chosŏn period having more or less happy endings that tend to reaffirm the in-place social systems. Also prominent is the validation of the Confucian ruling structures, which demonstrates to readers that virtues such as those of the Three Bonds[1] are in fact ones that function in a positive manner in the lives of the people.

Yet as we can imagine, life was not such for many people at various times in Chosŏn. As Chosŏn was a highly hierarchical society that strongly privileged the upper-status elites, the lives of those of lower social statuses were inevitably filled with hardships such as poverty, enslavement, and the like. These unofficial histories reveal this part of Chosŏn and show that the lives of the people could be quite difficult. So more than simply being stories that were written to pass the time or share a laugh, the unofficial histories open new windows through which to appreciate the nuances and complex relationships in Chosŏn. We can see in these narratives that life was not really so different then from nowadays: people had hardships, successes, loves, and odd events that took place in their lives.

While it is not possible to provide translations of all the unofficial histories of the Chosŏn, we have tried to demonstrate the evolution of the genre in the following pieces. To that end we have selected works from three collections: *Idle Talk and Humorous Stories in a Peaceful Era* (太平閑話滑稽傳 *T'aep'yŏng hanhwa kolgye-jŏn*) of the late fifteenth century, *Unofficial Narratives by Ŏu* (於于野談 *Ŏu yadam*) of the early seventeenth century, and *Collection of Past and Present Laughs* (古今笑叢 *Kogŭm soch'ong*) of the nineteenth century.

MP

---

[1] The Three Bonds (三綱 *Samgang*) are those of loyalty, filial piety, and distinction between husband and wife.

5.1 SŎ KŎJŎNG, *IDLE TALK AND HUMOROUS STORIES IN A PEACEFUL ERA* (太平閑話滑稽傳 *T'AEP'YŎNG HANHWA KOLGYE-JŎN*)

Following are four pieces from Sŏ Kŏjŏng's (徐居正, 1420–1488) *Idle Talk and Humorous Stories in a Peaceful Era*. This is an impressive collection, written in Literary Chinese, that contains a wide variety of narratives that discuss famous personages, legends, historical events, and amusing anecdotes. Sŏ explains in the preface to this work that it was meant to help people forget the worries of the world and provide them relaxation and humor. While it was a collection intended for enjoyment, it is also an extremely valuable source for the oral stories that were circulating in late fifteenth-century Korea. It also shows the double life that many scholar-officials must have led: Sŏ was the leading literary man of his day and the chief compiler of the aforementioned *Anthology of Eastern Literature*, yet his tastes also included the sometimes bawdy narratives of this collection.

The pieces are not titled in the original work; titles have been added here for ease of reference.[2]

MP

TRANSLATION

"THE GUEST GETS A WIFE"

There was a local functionary [衙前 *ajŏn*] with the surname of Chu who was handsome and had a good physique. While on his way to his hometown to visit his parents, he happened to stay the night at a home where the owner was about to hold a wedding ceremony for his daughter. Thus Chu, hoping to be treated to drinks, changed his clothes and waited at the main gate. When the wedding party was held at the owner's house, Chu was able to come in and sit among the guests.

As the night wore on the guests went off to their homes; the groom, who had had many cups, went outside to piss between stacks of grain bags, but fell and did not get up. Sitting alone at the table, Chu was mistaken for the bridegroom

---

[2] All translations from this work are from Sŏ Kŏjŏng, *T'aep'yŏng hanhwa kolgye-jŏn* [太平閑話滑稽傳, Idle talk and humorous stories in a peaceful era], ed. Pak Kyŏngsin (Seoul: Kukhak charyowŏn, 1998).

by the servants of the house, and one holding a candle pulled back the curtains and another charged with decorum [禮 ye; for the wedding rite] bowed to him and ushered him [into the bridal chamber]. Chu entered the chamber and the bride followed him. Chu enjoyed the night with the bride.

At daybreak the groom had sobered up and attempted to go into the house. However, the gate was securely locked and there were no sounds of people around. He pounded on the gate and shouted, "I am the bridegroom!"

Those who heard him yelled back, "The bridegroom has already completed the beautiful ceremony. How dare you act like a crazy jerk [奴 no]!"

The groom, vexed, went out and informed his relatives who had accompanied him [to the wedding ceremony].

"Someone has wronged me! Someone has wronged me!"

Then the whole house was in an uproar, and it turned out that the man outside was the bridegroom. Bewildered, the elderly house owner asked Chu, "Who are you?"

Chu replied, "I am the guest that stayed here yesterday."

The old man replied, "Why are you causing such problems with my family?"

Chu answered, "I was escorted in by the one charged with the ceremony."

With no other choice, the old man was about to throw Chu out and let the bridegroom enter. Then Chu, attired in his official cap and gown, made a deep bow to the old man at the stone step, saying, "I wish to say one thing before I leave. As far as I know, it is propriety that once a woman sleeps with a man, till the end she does not go to another. If she loses her fidelity, a virtuous man would be chagrined to call her his wife and neighbors would feel shame to call her name. As parents, do you wish to preserve her chastity [節 chŏl]? Or do you want to keep her deficiency [虧 hyu]? Esteemed master, if your daughter comes with me, she will be faithful; if she goes with [the other], she will be flawed. Now, you are not able to control your temper, but while she is with me, her fidelity is intact, but if she is with another, she is flawed: is that really the best course? I [have no wife and] can become your son-in-law. Please reconsider."

The old man clucked his tongue for a bit and said, "What can I do since a thief has already outsmarted us?"

Then he decided to accept him as his son-in-law, and Chu later led the family and his generation to thrive greatly.

"THE SAGE AND HIS AFFAIRS"

There was a man called Student Sŏng [成生] who committed adultery with the daughter of his wife's wet nurse.

His wife was furious, saying, "Although there is distinction of noble and base [貴賤 kwi ch'ŏn], the nanny's daughter is as my own sister! How can you violate morality like this?"

Sŏng replied, "When the great sage Shun [舜] took the two daughters of Yao [堯] for his wives, there was no objection and it was not against the customs of posterity. How much less [is an affair with] the daughter of a lowly nanny?"

Enraged, his wife asked, "Do you think you are Shun?"

Sŏng retorted, "What sort of person was Shun and what sort of person am I?"

So whenever the couple quarreled, she mockingly called him Shun.

One night when they were sleeping a thief entered their house and stole a purse and lock box. His wife said, "You always call yourself Shun, so why could you not catch the thief?" This was because the word *xun* [巡], indicating a watchman, was pronounced similarly to Shun, the great sage.

"THE WAILING GHOST"

In P'ungyang [豊壤] there was a servant of a noble family who had a prosperous house in his hometown. The servant had a daughter by the name of Chongga [從佳]. She was only sixteen years old, but so beautiful and virtuous that she seldom left her home. A young student by the name of An Ryun [安掄] stayed nearby. He had heard talk of the young girl's striking beauty and talent and tried by every means to get close to her but failed. Consequently he dyed his body yellow with the fruit of a pagoda tree and feigned illness as if he were about to die. His mother had an old woman tell the girl's parents, "Master An is critically ill because of your daughter and may die in the morning or evening. Thus, if he dies, it will be a curse on your daughter."

Because of this the girl's mother urged her to accept him, and the two shared a deep and intimate love.

The noble family was so furious that they took the girl away, worked her very hard, and even locked her up in a remote building. As there was no way for her to share her love with An, she felt miserable and worried deeply. Her disheveled hair was like stalks of mugwort and her face was covered with thick dirt. In a fit of anger, the noble family married her off to a strong and fierce man with a bushy beard. She swore off her life, hanging herself. An was deeply grieved and heartbroken. He kept wailing and could not fall asleep even while lying down.

One night, after midnight, the moon was bright in the sky and all was silent. Sitting alone and lost in reflection, An heard the sound of dragging shoes, and it seemed as if a woman were standing before him. Although looking intently, he could not see [her] but just heard the sound of wailing in the empty air. This continued for days on end before finally ceasing. Whenever An thought of her, he could not forget her. So, whenever drinking, he held back his tears and lamented bitterly. Years later, he also died.

"GENERAL KIM WHO WAS AFRAID OF GHOSTS"

A general with the surname of Kim was by nature wild and fierce, but he was also fearful of ghosts. When the ancestor rites for his father were held at Chunghŭng Temple [中興寺], there were a few mischievous young students who stayed at the temple doing their reading. On the evening of the rites, the monks prepared a sleeping place for the spirit in an outer room. The bed was surrounded by paper curtains, and a grand offering table with confections, noodles, rice cakes, and so on was arranged to the front.

One student hid behind the curtains with his hands and forearms painted black. When the general prostrated himself in front of the spirit tablet [靈座 yŏngjwa] while wailing and offered a cup of liquor, the student with his painted hand reached out from behind the curtain and grasped the cup while saying in a ghostly voice, "You are a filial son."

The general was greatly frightened and shook off the hand and extended his fist, saying, "If this is a ghost, I am overcome by it even if it is my father!"

He then went to his quarters with an ashen face and feeling so frightened that he could not speak. After the monks also scattered, the crowd of crazed young students gathered before the spirit tablet and ate up everything on the offering table.

5.2. YU MONGIN, *UNOFFICIAL NARRATIVES BY ŎU* (於于野談 *ŎU YADAM*)

This collection follows in the tradition of the preceding collection by Sŏ Kŏjŏng. The emphasis was on the actualities of society and stories that were in circulation. The work does have a didactic edge, as seen in Yu Mongin's (柳夢寅, 1559–1623) inclusion of commentary at the end of some of the pieces. While this genre was criticized, at least publicly, by Confucian scholars at the time, the popularity is undeniable. Moreover, the contents of this work, written in Literary Chinese, reveal much about how people lived, their wishes, and many other historical circumstances that would not have been recorded in the government-sponsored works of the day.

The titles here, too, have been added to the translation, in this case by the editors of the works listed in the note.[3]

MP

TRANSLATION

"GHOSTS OF THE SŎNGGYUN'GWAN"
(SŎNGGYUN'GWAN KWISIN)

Early in the [Chosŏn] dynasty, the Sŏnggyun'gwan [成均館, Royal Confucian Academy] had East and West Dormitories [東西齋].[4] Each dorm had dozens of rooms that had wooden sliding walls and no heated floors. It felt so chilly that scholars living there tried to stay warm by lying close together with many layers of blankets under them on the floor. In the Chinsa Room[5] of the West Dormitory [西齋], a young student with a beautiful countenance always read the *Classic of Encountering Sorrow*.[6] Two *chinsa* fought over him, each pulling on one of his legs since they wanted to sleep next to him; however, he died after his legs were torn off. Since that time, on dark and rainy nights the sound of reciting, "As a descendant of Emperor Gaoyang's [帝高陽之苗裔]"[7] was sometimes heard in the Chinsa Room. This continued for several years, and most students who stayed in this room were hagridden with terrible nightmares.

Later, King Yŏnsan-gun [燕山君, r. 1494–1506] roamed the streets [seeking pleasure] and happened to be caught after curfew. At that time he figured out that if he said himself to be Yi *chinsa* [李進士], even the police who captured thieves would not punish him. Believing that titles such as *saengwŏn*[8] and

---

[3]Yu Mongin, *Ŏu yadam* [於于野談, Unofficial narratives by Ŏu], ed. Yi Wŏryŏng and Ch'ae Kwisŏn (Seoul: Han'guk munhwasa, 1996); Yu Mongin, *Ŏu yadam*, trans. Sin Ikch'ŏl, Yi Hyŏngdae, Cho Yunghŭi, and No Yŏngmi (Seoul: Tolpegae, 2006). Translations of the individual pieces are designated as either 1996 for the former work or 2006 for the latter.

[4]This translation is from the 1996 edition listed in n. 3.

[5]*Chinsa* (進士, literary licentiate) is the title given a person who has passed the preliminary literary licentiate examination (進士科) that was taken before the government service examination (科擧 *kwagŏ*).

[6]The *Classic of Encountering Sorrow* [離騷經 *Lisao jing*] is a lengthy poem attributed to the Warring States period (475–221 B.C.E.) aristocrat Qu Yuan (屈原).

[7]This is the first line of the *Classic of Encountering Sorrow*.

[8]*Saengwŏn* (生員, classics licentiate) is the title given a person who has passed the preliminary classics licentiate examination (生員試) that was taken before the government service examination.

chinsa could intimidate even people in power, he thus made those people carry his palanquin every time he went out.

Sometime later the dining hall at the Sŏnggyun'gwan was demolished and in its place Hogwŏn East and West Dormitories [虎圈東西齋] were built. Here, many *kisaeng*⁹ gathered and stayed. There was one *kisaeng* who stayed in the Chinsa Room and died in an evil and odd manner. Since that time, the scholars staying there had dreams, inevitably frightening nightmares, where a beautiful woman appeared.

On the fifteenth day of the sixth month in 1578 [萬曆戊寅], a Sŏnggyun'gwan official treated the students with *soju* and roasted dog meat.¹⁰ At that time there was a certain *saengwŏn* named Chang Ŏnjin from the Honam region.¹¹ He stayed in the Chinsa Room, and on that day he was exhorted by his friends to drink copious amounts of *soju* and died as a result. On the same day of the next year the Sŏnggyun'gwan official again prepared *soju* and roasted dog meat for the scholars. The night before, *chinsa* Yi Ch'ŏlgwang [李哲光] slept in the Chinsa Room, and a scholar whom he did not know appeared in his dream saying, "I am *saengwŏn* Chang Ŏnjin. Tomorrow you will be treated by an official with liquor and meat. Please allow me to taste some as well."

After waking, Ch'ŏlgwang thought the dream odd and asked of the others who had slept in the same room, "Is there a person by the name of Chang Ŏnjin here?"

Someone answered, "Yes."

Ch'ŏlgwang asked, "Will the officials treat the scholars with liquor and meat?"

They all replied, "Yes."

[Yi] continued, "Is Chang Ŏnjin alive?"

They all replied, "Last year he drank too much *soju* and died."

Ch'ŏlgwang was greatly surprised and told the group about his dream. That morning he attended the feast. He set aside an extra bowl with dog meat and another with *soju*. He put the bowls in the middle of the table and sat kneeling with his hands clasped, never touching his own meat or *soju*. The others elbowed one another and laughed, saying, "Student Chang offers you a cup of liquor; how can one remain a *saengwŏn* for ten thousand years on this earth?

---

⁹*Kisaeng* (妓生) refers to female entertainers.

¹⁰The fifteenth of the six month is *yudu* (流頭), a popular holiday in Chosŏn where people would picnic and wash their hair in streams. It is also the advent of the hottest season in Korea, and this was marked by eating dog meat as a means of giving the body the energy it needed to endure the difficult season. *Soju* (燒酒) is a distilled liquor of varying, but oftentimes high, alcoholic content.

¹¹Honam (湖南) is the southwestern part of the Korean Peninsula.

Student Yi offers you [Chang] some meat; how can one remain a *chinsa* for ten thousand years on this earth?"

MP

"FOX PASS" (YŎU KOGAE)

Kwach'ŏn [果川] lies south of the Han River and north of Ch'ŏnggye [青溪].[12] The main road winds behind the government office residence [官舍 *kwansa*] of Kwach'ŏn; this road is called Fox Pass [狐峴].

Long ago, a wayfarer passed by on this road. Looking around, he saw a small thatched-roof house from which the sound of pounding emanated. The wayfarer peeked inside the house and saw an old gray-haired man sitting on a cowhide while carving a wooden ox's head. The wayfarer looked on and asked, "What's the ox's head for?"

[The old man answered,] "It has a purpose."

Before long, the old man finished the ox's head and handed it to the wayfarer, saying, "Put this on."

He also handed the wayfarer the cowhide and said, "Try it on."

Thinking this a joke, the wayfarer took off his headgear and put on the ox's head. Then [after removing his clothing] he put the cowhide on. The old man said, "Take it off."

The wayfarer tried to take off the articles but could not; he was simply a large ox. The old man tied him up in a stall, and the next day he went to the marketplace riding on the ox. Since it was the peak season when there was much farmwork, the wayfarer-ox would fetch a high price.

The wayfarer-ox shouted loudly at the marketplace, "I am a man, not a cow!"

Although he told the whole story of what he had experienced, those who came out to buy and sell things could not understand what he said. Someone said, "Did this ox leave a calf at home, or does it have a bezoar in its stomach? Why is it so loud like this?"

The old man sold the wayfarer-ox at the high price of fifty bolts [端 *tan*] of hemp cloth and instructed the buyer, "Do not go to a daikon radish field with this cow; it will die as soon as it eats daikon radish."

The buyer rode the ox to his home. The wayfarer-ox carried heavy loads for long distances and plowed fields. He was exhausted and gasped for breath, but on any such occasion, he was whipped, and he could not bear the pain. In

---

[12] The translation is from the 1996 edition listed in n. 3.

anger he complained, but his owner could not understand. The wayfarer-ox lamented to himself that he, a human—the greatest creation of the cosmos— had lost his form and been transformed into an animal. He wanted to die but he could not.

The barn of that house was near the gate, and a boy servant entered with a basket full of washed daikon radishes. The wayfarer-ox thought about the old man's saying that he [the ox] would die if he ate daikon radishes, so he struck the basket with his mouth and knocked the radishes to the ground and ate them quickly. As soon as he ate the radishes, the ox's head fell off him as did the cowhide. He was completely naked. When the master of the house asked in surprise, the wayfarer told him the whole story and then set off for Fox Pass again. There, the thatched-roof house had disappeared, but a few bolts of hemp cloth were left. This is how the pass became known as Fox Pass.

A man of virtue [君子] said, "Although this is close to a groundless story, it is enough to enlighten people about the ways of the world as they are. In difficulties many people lose their way and fall into wicked places. They sell themselves to those who are cunning and they end up being exploited like oxen. Even if they wish to explain their hastiness with thousands and thousands of words, it is certain that people will not believe them. Alas, how deplorable this is!"

MP

"THE CLEVER TRICK OF PAK YŎP TO HAVE AN AFFAIR" (KKOE RŬL NAEŎ SAT'ONGHAN PAK YŎP)

When Pak Yŏp,[13] the future magistrate [府尹] of Ŭiju [義州], was young, he experienced the wars and became a drifter, wandering here and there.[14] During this time, he happened to arrive at a house where he saw the beautiful form of the owner's wife, and the two exchanged glances. A bit later the owner, a young and handsome man, came around, and Yŏp knew things would not go as he had hoped.

After the night had passed and the day was about to break, Yŏp went into the cowshed and untied an ox from its tether and opened the gate. He then stabbed the ox in its rump with an awl, causing the ox to run away through the [open]

---

[13] The translation is from the 1996 edition listed in n. 3. Pak Yŏp (朴燁) may refer to a near contemporary of Yu Mongin who lived from 1570 to 1623 and was a scholar-official.

[14] The "wars" (亂離 nalli) indicate the Japanese invasions of 1592–1598.

gate. Yŏp pounded [the door] and shouted. The house owner asked, "What is this noise?"

Yŏp informed him, "The ox pushed the gate [open] and ran off."

The owner hurriedly dressed and chased after the ox. The ox, already frightened after being stabbed with the awl, ran further away when it saw the man chasing after it. With this scheme, Yŏp was able to share an unforgettable love with the owner's wife.

Well after daybreak, the owner returned in dew-soaked clothes, leading the ox.

MP

"THE MOTHER OF KANGNAMDŎK" (KANGNAMDŎK MOJA)

The mother of Kangnamdŏk [江南德] was the wife of Hwang Pong, a boatman of the West River.[15] Hwang had a home in Chamdu and made a living by selling seafood. In the Early Wanli period [1573–1619], he went out to sea. But he met a typhoon and could not return home. His wife put on mourning garb and held his funeral. After three years of mourning, she lived as a widow for many years. One day, a man who had just returned from China delivered Hwang's letter to her. Written in the letter was the following: "Drifting in the sea, I reached a certain place in China. There I became a pieceworker for private houses."

Reading the letter, Hwang's wife broke into tears and lamented, "From the beginning, I thought that my husband was buried in the belly of a fish, but now I am hearing that he has saved his life and is living in China. Even though I may collapse in the street and die while begging with a gourd dipper, I am determined to go search for him."

Villagers tried to dissuade her, saying, "There are barriers between our country and China that prohibit a border crossing, so a person who speaks a different language and wears different dress does not dare to cross them. In addition, there is a prescribed punishment for those who violate this ban. If you make a long journey alone now for ten thousand *li*, you are bound to fail to reach China, ending up as a skull by the roadside."

But the wife did not listen to the villagers, shook out her sleeves, and departed. She crossed the Amnok River surreptitiously, walking straight into the land of China. With her clothes in tatters, her hair unkempt, her face covered in dirt, and barefoot, she begged for food in the street. About a year later, she

---

[15] The translation is from the 2006 edition listed in n. 3.

reached the South of the River mentioned in her husband's letter and was finally reunited with him in a remote province on the seashore. At last, they set forth on their return to Chosŏn. On their way back home, she became pregnant. When they arrived at their old home, she gave birth to a girl. The baby girl was named Kangnamdŏk [Virtue of the South of the River], so the villagers called the wife the mother of Kangnamdŏk instead of using the name of her natal hometown. People considered her an eccentric that would appear only in a book.

In my opinion, there are clearly marked borders between Chosŏn and China that distinguish the inside and the outside. Thus, both countries were strict in banning comings and goings before war became utterly chaotic. As a mere woman, the mother of Kangnamdŏk dared to enter China by herself and return home as if she had visited a neighboring village and eventually found her husband in such a vast and boundless land. There had been no such incident like this under heaven. It can duly be said that her strong and courageous fidelity firmly established the Three Bonds throughout time, both past and present.[16]

Since the war broke out in the year of Imjin, those Chosŏn men who were swept into the Chinese army and killed in battle were listed on the roll of honor. Those who were carried in bags and crossed the border gate into China are countless. However, I have never heard of even one person who privately crossed the border into China and then escaped back to Chosŏn. Is there anyone who does not have parents and a spouse? Everyone, however, loves his body. No one would risk his life by entering a land of ten thousand deaths and then try to escape. A person like the mother of Kangnamdŏk can surely be said to be the most unusual of the unusual. The mother of Kangnamdŏk died in the spring this year, and she was eighty years old.

This was recorded in the summer of the first year of Tianqi's reign [1621].

HY

"THE *KŎMUN'GO* OF SIM SUGYŎNG AND A PALACE WOMAN" (SIM SUGYŎNG ŬI KŎMUN'GO WA KUNGNYŎ)

Prime Minister [相國] Sim Sugyŏng [沈守慶, 1516–1599] from a young age had great mien, comportment, and musical talent.[17] From a young age he

---

[16] This is an interesting statement by the writer, since women were generally expected only to be dutiful wives in terms of the Three Bonds.

[17] A *kŏmun'go* is a six-stringed zither that is plucked with a short bamboo stick. The translation is from the 1996 edition listed in n. 3.

temporarily stayed at the outer annex of Prince Ch'ŏngwŏn [清原君]. One autumn evening when the moon was high in the sky he played his *kŏmun'go* at a pavilion by a lotus pond. A beautiful young palace woman approached and bowed to him. The [future] prime minister greeted her and allowed her to have a seat in the pavilion.

The palace woman said, "I, all alone in this palace, have greatly admired you in my heart seeing your dignified manner. Now I have dared to come forth and greet you to hear the elegant and beautiful melody of your *kŏmun'go*. I hope to again hear your playing."

The [future] prime minister played a few more songs before leaving with his *kŏmun'go*. Afterward he never again visited that pavilion. The woman, with a lovesick heart, was driven to great despair and eventually died from illness.

MP

"THE LIFE OF CHINBOK, A LICENTIOUS WOMAN" (ŬMBU CHINBOK ŬI ILSAENG)

Chinbok [珍福] was born to the concubine of a minister, but I will not reveal who her father is because Chinbok is notorious for lewdness.[18] The minister, seeing his concubine lovingly cuddling her daughter, took pity on the mother, so he asked both female and male shamans about the girl's fortune. One of them said, "Although her parents love her, it is not a good idea for them to raise her. It would be better to let her be adopted as someone else's daughter and raised in a different home."

In those days, there was an old woman living in Chikcho-ri [織組里] in Seoul. She was wealthy but had no children. She visited the minister's concubine on holidays, always treating her kindly with the first seasonal harvests. The concubine told the old woman everything that the shamans had said about her daughter and expressed her desire to find shelter for her daughter in the old woman's home. The old woman willingly agreed to her proposal, saying that she would adopt the girl as her stepdaughter and pass down her family business to the girl. The concubine could not have been happier to hear this, so she made a firm promise and gave her daughter away to the old woman. Reaching the age of sixteen, youthful Chinbok boasted a beautiful face and a graceful figure, and the old woman loved her as if she had been her biological daughter.

The old woman had many relatives, all of whom hoped that the rich but childless woman would adopt their children. However, they all became angry

---

[18] The translation is from the 2006 edition listed in n. 3.

because she did not adopt a boy from her own family but a girl with a different surname, in her pursuit of power.[19] They tried every possible way to devise a scheme to break the old woman's plan. Since no sweet talk could persuade her to approve their requests, they decided to incite Chinbok in such a way that the old woman would hate her. One day, one of the woman's relatives with a fluent tongue told Chinbok quietly, "The other day, a young scholar working as a recorder [注書 chusŏ] in the Office of Royal Secretariat [承政院 Sŭngjŏng'wŏn] was passing by your house and happened to see you standing against the gate. He could not help stopping and asking in hesitance, 'Whose daughter is that girl in this house? She is truly a rare beauty. I would love to have her as my concubine even if it were to cost me a fortune. If permitted, I will set a date quickly and welcome her by sending a horse and an old servant.' But Great Aunt by nature covets wealth, so she is planning to marry you off to a son of a merchant without checking whether the bridegroom is a good man or not. You are originally a daughter of a minister, and how can you become the wife of a merchant? Since you are now old enough to marry, you must hurry to come up with a plan for yourself."

As she was listening to him, the girl felt so ashamed that she could not say a thing. But the glib man called on her for several days, trying to lure her secretly, and she began to vacillate in spite of herself. Moreover, deep down Chinbok envied her mother, who enjoyed wealth as the concubine of a scholar. At last, Chinbok believed the words of the glib man. Shortly thereafter, a horse and a servant from the scribe arrived and waited for her in front of the gate. Chinbok put on new makeup, changed into beautiful clothes, sneaked out at night, and nimbly mounted the horse.

She passed several bends of a winding road, galloping in all directions, and finally reached a place where she found tall gates wide open. As soon as she got off the horse in front of a board fence, the glib man led her inside the gates. She passed a big garden to discover a tall house with a large pond. Blue lotus flowers bloomed along the red rail of the pond, but the place was empty with no sign of a man. The inside of the house was covered with a folding screen and curtains. The glib man led her and sat her inside the folding screen. Shortly thereafter, a man with a long, shaggy beard appeared in hemp clothes and barefoot. He embraced her and had his way with her as he pleased. He soon ran away, abandoning her, but not even one servant was to be found there. She called the glib man but to no avail. There was no way of knowing where he had disappeared.

Chinbok was born and raised deep within the women's quarters [of a scholar family's home] as a well-cared-for girl, and she had never left the inner court in

---

[19] Even though Chinbok was born of a concubine, her father was a powerful minister. Thus the adoption would be a bond with his family.

her life. How could she know the long road with thousands of forks that she passed across Seoul? Even though she wanted to ask someone, no one was there to ask, and even though she tried to return home, she had no idea of the way back. Thus, she was wandering the streets in tears.

As the sky began to brighten, she asked a person in the neighborhood, "Whose house is this?"

"It is the Office of the Inspector General [司憲府 Sahŏnbu]."

She asked if there was a man with a long beard in the office. The answer was that he was the Ink Man in the Office of the Inspector General. When she finally made her way back home, it was already midday. Appalled, the old woman said, "I have nothing to say for myself to the family of the noble master."

As the minister's family heard about this incident, they decided to disown Chinbok as their daughter and expel her. They gave her completely to the old woman, letting the girl do whatever she wanted to do. Realizing that her parents would no longer accept her because she had already lost her chastity, Chinbok abandoned her body, turning into a lascivious woman. As a result, she could not find a companion for the rest of her life, leading a debased and impoverished life until she died.

Chinbok had a younger sister, who married a military general. This sister was permitted to attend parties at the minister's house whenever they held them for a wedding or for honored guests. However, they excluded Chinbok, who thus could not participate in the banquets. Not only that but she was not even allowed to sit on the wooden veranda and be close to the other women.

Alas! Chinbok was once a loose woman who certainly deserved lifelong shame and disgrace because of that one mental mistake. And yet how can we not fear man's jealousy and wickedness that can throw someone's life into such an immeasurable quagmire?

HY

"THE STARVING THIEF" (KUMJURIN TOJŎK)

In the present year, a scholar who lived in Seoul traveled hundreds of leagues to buy rice since the price had become very expensive at the markets of Seoul.[20] He was traveling back with a load of rice when he reached a pass in the mountains. At that time a man wearing a long sword stepped in front of his horse and bowed to him.

---

[20]The translation is from the 1996 edition listed in n. 3.

The scholar asked, "Who are you?"

He answered, "I am a wayfarer."

The scholar queried, "Why does a wayfarer bow to me?"

He replied, "My group wants some rice since we have had nothing to eat and are starving."

Because the scholar could not respond at once, his servant replied, "You can have half the rice."

The man replied, "We have so many mouths to feed that half the load will not do—give us the full load."

As the scholar nodded his head and gave all the rice to the man, the man spoke again, "The rice is too heavy to carry. If you lend me your horse, I will return it later after I am done."

At the end of the mountain path, he returned the horse, saying, "I am sincerely grateful to you for giving us the rice. Please allow me to escort you, sir."

After some distance they arrived at the bottom of the valley, where a group of people wielding clubs and weapons blocked the path. The man who had escorted the scholar said, "The general ordered me to escort this scholar since he gave us a load of rice."

Thus through all these troubles, the scholar returned safely.

After a bad harvest the common people [良民 *yangmin*] suffered from starvation and came together to form brigands. They only robbed and did not hurt others. One day thereafter, an itinerant peddler [行商 *haengsang*] ran into a thief on the street and chased after him. Unlike the peddler who could eat his fill, the thief, weak from hunger, fell to the ground, and this gave the peddler a chance to prevail [over the thief]. The thieves were soon scattered bit by bit and became all the more pitiful.

MP

"YI YESUN WHO DEVOTED HERSELF TO BUDDHISM" (PULGYO-E YI YESUN)

Ogyŏ Yi Kwi [玉汝 李貴, 1557–1663] was a friend from my youthful days.[21] As magistrate (府使 *pusa*) of Sukch'ŏn, he rose to *kasŏn taebu* [嘉善大夫] of junior second rank. He had a daughter named Yesun, and her husband was Kim Chagyŏm, who was a grandson of Kim Ŏngyŏng's and a son of Magistrate Kim T'ak's.

---

[21] The translation is from the 2006 edition listed in n. 3.

Kim Chagyŏm was deeply absorbed in Buddhism, which he practiced together with his friend O Ŏn'gwan, the son of a concubine. In terms of residence and food, Kim made no distinction between male and female. He even slept in the same room with women and children. Later when he was taken ill and lay on his deathbed, he asked O to take care of his wife. He then composed a verse.

> I arrived nowhere when I came.
> Going away is like the clear autumn moon.
> Coming is not coming in reality.
> Going is not going in reality.
> True appearance of things delights my nature.
> Only this should be followed as the true way.

On finishing this verse, Kim passed away.

After Kim's death, O visited Yesun's house frequently as if it were his relative's. He brought her many books on Buddhism. Soon Yesun declared that she had gained an ability to see into other people's minds. Her body emitted a mysterious fragrance, and mystical lights filled her room. Some people called her a living Buddha.

One day Yesun wrote a letter, placed it in a box, and left her father to follow O to Mount Tŏgyu [德裕山] in Anŭm [安陰]. There she shaved her head and became a Buddhist nun. Yesun and O cut bamboo trees, built a hut with them, and lived therein. People in town venerated them, so they gathered rice and donated it to them. However, when their manservant was caught stealing by the police, the local government arrested Yesun and O and incarcerated them. As this incident was reported to the provincial governor, their case came to be known to the court.

O changed his name to Hwang, and Yesun changed hers to Yŏng'il, which was the name of O's deceased wife. They were transferred to Seoul. This happened when a treason case was being investigated there; therefore, the court was suspicious of their activities and interrogated them at the palace compound. O died during the interrogation, and Yesun was imprisoned. She composed a quatrain and gave it to her brother. The poem read,

> Now my monastic robe is soiled with yellow dust.
> Why does the Blue Mountain not allow me in?
> The world may confine my body.
> But even the special police force cannot stop my wandering spirit [遠遊].

Her confession in the police record is roughly as follows: "I learned how to read and write when I was six or seven years old. At that age, I was already indifferent to worldly delights. I married at age fifteen, but I was not interested in the affairs between a man and a woman. I set my mind only on the ultimate Way. After practicing diligently for eight or nine years, I seemed to have achieved something."

She also said, "In my view, Śākyamuni became the world-presiding Buddha ten years after he gave up his country as a crown prince and left his castle to practice as an ascetic in the snow-covered mountains. Mañjuśrī [文殊, K. Munsu], who in a previous life had been female, engaged in the Way without looking after his body and finally attained perfect enlightenment. As a queen, Lady Wŏnang made a long journey in search of the Dharma. But when she realized that she could not reach it by herself, she lived an ascetic life even by selling herself. She was Avalokiteśvara's [觀音, K. Kwanŭm] previous form. Besides Lady Wŏnang, a countless number of people pursued ascetic lives in history. During the Tang dynasty, Buddhism did not thrive greatly, but innumerable ladies from prominent families became nuns. However, there are many cases in which we do not know how they died. Although the past and the present times are different, would their will be any different?"

Yesun continued. "There are three religions in the world: Confucianism, Daoism, and Buddhism. By cultivating the virtues of one's own and others, Confucianism helps king and subject and father and son realize the Five Relationships. Confucianism also helps all beings be peaceful in their proper positions and thereby benefits even insects and plants. This is what makes Confucianism stand out. Daoism is capable of training body and spirit with water and fire so that they may transcend the material realm. By doing so, Daoism prevents sickness and pain from approaching us and aging and death from invading us. However, it cannot help us escape the kalpas of the cycle of reincarnation. Therefore, its help is limited to the glory of longevity. Buddhist teaching is like the white moon in the sky; it helps one suddenly realize one's innate Buddha-nature and thereby purify one's original nature by itself. Bad habits are eliminated spontaneously, and delusions are cleared up spontaneously as well. Gradually this spreads throughout and [one] becomes free. As miraculous changes occur without any obstructions, the thread of reincarnation comes to an end, and so hell is destroyed forever. A bad karma from the past turns into dispersing clouds and scattered rain. As one crosses over to the shore of enlightenment, together with one's embittered friends from the last kalpa, one becomes all the stronger for an infinite period. If this is true of even a tiny bit of dust, there is no way of fully explaining the rest in words.

"I was born in the body of a woman, so even though I wanted to learn Confucianism, there was no way for me to realize its ultimate teaching by serving a king properly and conferring a benefit on people. The Daoist Way is one of appropriating the principle of harmony and playfully manipulating it on a large scale. Thus I studied Buddhism, and so, when I had barely grasped a little bit, I tried to return the kindness of the rural Buddhist community by not losing that understanding throughout my life. Now I have fallen into disgrace and have very little time until death. However, the disintegration of one's bodily form is merely like taking off one's shoes, and the law of life and death is not different from the way morning comes when night passes. It is all the more so, as I am going to die without committing a sin. Dying is, on the contrary, living. Therefore, I have no lingering regrets."

HY

5.3. ANONYMOUS, COLLECTION OF PAST AND PRESENT LAUGHS (古今笑叢 KOGŬM SOCH'ONG)

This anonymous work dates from the late Chosŏn period and is written in a mixed script of *han'gŭl* grammatical particles and sentence endings and Chinese characters. This demonstrates the broadening of readership to those outside simply male elites to commoners of both sexes. The compiler of this work drew material from earlier Literary Chinese collections and supplemented them with other narratives in circulation at the time. The work has been categorized as being a collection of lewd or erotic tales, but that seems too judgmental. Rather, it reflects the social realities of the late Chosŏn, when there was a keen need for entertainment that might have matched life experiences or hidden desires. With the weakening of Confucian values in literature, carnality could come more to the fore, as we see in the following pieces from this collection.

The titles in the following are those from the original work.[22]

MP

TRANSLATION

"FALSELY CUTTING THE NARROW HOLE" (佯裂孔窄 YANGYŎL KONG CH'AK)

On his wedding night a groom suspected that his new bride had already had experience [with a man]. He was determined to have her tell the truth. While

---

[22]Translations are from *Kogŭm soch'ong* [古今笑叢, Collection of past and present laughs] (Seoul: Minsog'wŏn, 1953).

stroking her vulva with his hand, he said, "Your hole seems too small—I should cut it to make it larger, and then I will be able to put my thing in you." He took out his dagger and pretended to ready himself to cut her. The panicked bride snatched away the dagger, saying urgently, "In yonder village, the youngest son of Deputy Magistrate Kim has never had to cut [me]. Maybe it is because he is said to be good at inserting without having to cut."

MP

"THE SON-IN-LAW WHO RIDICULED HIS FATHER-IN-LAW" (壻嘲婦翁 SŎ CHO PUONG)

A father-in-law and his son-in-law happened to sleep in adjoining rooms. One night while the father-in-law and his wife were having sex, they reached a great climax. The man said, "It is as though both my ears had been deafened." His wife replied, "I feel as if my limbs had melted away."

When they were finished, the wife told her husband, "Our son-in-law might have heard our talk. We should warn him not to speak of this." The man smiled and said, "We should do that."

The next morning the father-in-law called on his son-in-law and admonished him, "Beware of gibberish coming from vulgar people." The son-in-law replied, "I am not like that. When I hear of others' faults, I feel as if both my ears were deafened and my limbs were melting away."

The father-in-law smacked his lips, not knowing what to say.

MP

"THREE WOMEN EXAMINE A MUTE" (三女儉啞 SAMNYŎ KŎM A)

In Sinjang [新昌] there lived three unmarried women. Because their parents died and the family was poor, they were not able to marry. All had passed twenty years of age and the best age for marriage.

One spring day the three were enjoying the fragrance of flowers in the garden.

The youngest mumbled, "It is said that there is a pleasure of men and women. What could that be?"

The second sister replied, "I too have wondered about that."

The eldest said, "Let's ask the maidservant, since she is fond of her husband."

The women asked of this pleasure to the maidservant, who replied while smiling, "How can I speak of that plainly?"

The three women pressed her, and she answered, "Between a man's legs is a meat club that looks like a pine mushroom. It is as long as two fists and called a *ch'ŏl* [凸, protuberance]. The marvelousness [of this] cannot be fathomed. It comes into being and comes into being and changes and changes. Thus I have never left it alone for even a day."

The three women together urged, "Tell us more about it."

The maidservant continued, "The man's *ch'ŏl* is put into the woman's *yo* [凹, hollow], and being combined, the pleasure that I feel then is indescribable."

The three sisters queried, "How is that pleasure?"

The maidservant replied, "When the *ch'ŏl* is put into the *yo*, it rubs as it moves up and down. As the movement becomes faster, I feel the bones of my limbs melting away. I cannot tell if I am alive or not alive, dead or not dead."

Fascinated, the sisters said, "You should stop now since we are feeling befuddled." But after that, the three sisters schemed about how to see the male [part]. "If we were to see a mute beggar, we could see a male *ch'ŏl*."

At that time a young man happened to pass by the wall of their home and heard what the three women had been talking about and thought that he would trick them. He returned to their house in ragged clothes and holding a gourd to beg for food with his mouth shut tightly as if he were a mute. The three women saw this with delight. They took him to a small room, took off his pants, and exposed his *ch'ŏl*.

The eldest handled the *ch'ŏl* and exclaimed, "It's leather!"

The second grasped it and said, "It is a mass of meat."

The youngest took hold and said, "It is bone!"

This change was because of [the youth's] becoming gradually stimulated. The girls sat around and played with it, holding it and letting it go. Suddenly the *ch'ŏl* jerked up and down. The three women delightedly exclaimed, "This thing is going crazy!"

The youth then grasped the hands of the three women, sat up, and said, "Originally it is not crazy, but you three have made it so. Once it is crazy, though, it should go into your *yo* to calm it."

The three women turned pale and trembled. The youth told them, "If I speak a word of this, your house will be disgraced." The girls could not avoid this and submitted. Eventually he had sex with each of them. He did not stop in his indulgence until after a full day and night had passed and the dawn had broken. When he rose to leave the room, he could not take even a step. The three women helped him to his feet and sent him on his way.

MP

"PREREQUISITE STUDY FOR A VIRGIN"
(處女先習 CH'ŎNYŎ SŎNSŬP)

There was a young girl who was pretty but had an indecent disposition. When she turned fourteen or fifteen, her parents selected a distant auspicious day on which to have her married off. One evening she stopped by a neighbor's to ask about something. However, a youth in the house had a lusty desire for her.

He said to her, "It is only a few days before your wedding and you have not practiced yet; when you meet your husband, what will you do? You will be embarrassed."

With a terrified look, she asked, "Stop speaking annoying words and teach me."

He replied, "Not a problem, just follow me."

He led her to a detached hut to have sex, saying, "There are six pleasures [六喜 yukhŭi] a woman should have in order to give pleasure [助歡 chohwan]. Whether a woman is happy or not originates in this."

The girl asked, "What are these six pleasures?"

The youth recited, "First is to be narrow [窄 ch'ak], second to be warm [溫 on], third is teeth [齒 ch'i],[23] fourth is move one's body [搖本 yobon], fifth is to make pleasurable noises [甘唱 kamch'ang], and sixth to finish quickly [速畢 sokp'il]. These are what is meant by the six pleasures for a man. What you are lacking is body movements and pleasurable noises."

She replied, "I am too young to know those, so please teach me."

He said, "These things cannot be taught by words but only by practice. We should practice."

Until her wedding day, she learned all the six pleasures that women should master [with the youth].

On her wedding night the new bridegroom was about to take her, and she started using her body-movement techniques and making pleasurable noises. The bridegroom knew at once that she had been with another man. "Who is the man you had illicit sex with?"

The woman shed false tears and did not answer.

In a rage he said, "Given how you moved your body and made pleasurable sounds, you are certainly familiar with men. You are not a virgin!"

He then kicked her and went out of the room; the family expelled her.

Her mother admonished her, and the girl responded, "Master Kim [the youth] in the house over there told me that I had to learn beforehand."

---

[23] This usage of teeth, ch'i, seems related to the verb to chew (ssipta) and the verb for copulating (ssip hada). The noun ssip can also indicate the vulva or copulation.

Her mother scolded her, "You are a fool! Master Kim is not your bridegroom! How could you use what you learned from him?"

She responded, "When I was reaching orgasm, I thought it was Master Kim. I could not remember that it was my new bridegroom."

When people hear this story they cover their mouths with their hands.

MP

"THE FIVE MARVELS THAT SHOOK THE HEART"
(五妙動心 OMYO TONGSIM)

Yi Hangbok met Namgung Tu when he was young. At that time, Namgung was already eighty years old or so. But he looked forty at most.

Hangbok asked, "Sir, although you are about eighty years old, your stamina is like that of a young man: what is the secret for that? I would like to learn."

He replied, "My secret is so easy. I have only abstained from sex with women."

Hangbok asked, "As a man loves sex with women, how can he abstain from it? If he stays away from sex, what is the good even if he lives for a thousand years?"

Tu replied with a smile, "What you are saying is not right."

Hangbok said playfully, "A man would be attracted to a girl with any of these: a blooming face like a flower, slender body, virtuous character like an orchid, singing in a crystal clear voice and dancing mesmerizingly like a snow flurry blocking a cloud, charming words and accents like rolling beads, the scent of her rouge and powder touching one's nose and mind, and playing the coquette on the silk blanket at night like a beautiful flower. Furthermore, if she has the five marvels in her appearance, character, voice, scents, and charm, how can even a man of an iron heart like Song Jing[24] keep from being moved?"

Tu responded, "How could you know that these five marvels are not those of the messenger [差使 ch'asa] sent by King Yŏmna?"[25]

Hangbok said with a smile, "There should be a woman even in the palace of the king of the underworld, shouldn't there?"

Tu just smiled without saying a word.

MP

---

[24] Song Jing (宋憬) was a famous subject during the reign of King Xuanzong during the Tang dynasty and a man of great integrity and righteousness.

[25] The retainer of the king of the underworld or the one sent by a district magistrate to apprehend a criminal.

6. Late Chosŏn Period

Autobiography, Social Commentary, and Philosophical Humor

6.1. PAK CHIWŎN, "THE TALE OF MASTER YEDŎK" (穢德先生傳 YEDŎK SŎNSAENG-JŎN)

Pak Chiwŏn (朴趾源, 1737–1805) occupies a special place in the history of Korean literature. Though born into a distinguished eighteenth-century family, he eschewed the traditional path to success; it was not until he was married at the age of fifteen that he began his studies in earnest, and he never passed the civil service examination. His son later wrote that he would submit his examination papers unfinished or covered in strange drawings. His unconventionality was also evident in his writing as he sought to breathe new life into Korean literature written in Literary Chinese. Unlike many authors of the time, who placed great value on polishing their words and following the precedents of old, Pak Chiwŏn cultivated a simple style that depicted his subjects unvarnished. His stylistic innovations were considered so radical that King Chŏngjo (定租, r. 1776–1800) initiated reforms to steer literary style back toward time-honored conventions. These reforms were a considerable setback to the development of Korean literature, but Pak Chiwŏn's works remain as a testament to his philosophy and ideas.

Pak Chiwŏn courted controversy in the content of his works as well. He did not hesitate to lampoon long-cherished institutions and traditions, turning these ideas upside down in an attempt to reform not only literature but also society as a whole. "The Tale of Master Yedŏk" is a fine example of this. The simple structure of a dialogue between teacher and disciple will be familiar and accessible to most readers. The question posed by the disciple is also simple enough: with whom should one make friends, and how should those friends be made? The teacher answers this question, but he also takes the opportunity to make a statement on social values. Ŏm Haengsu, the "Master Yedŏk" of the title, is a worker who makes his living collecting manure. Although he would seem to be the lowliest of individuals and unworthy of being the friend of a noble scholar, the teacher points out that it is because of the manure he collects that the farmlands of Seoul can thrive. In other words, it is what one achieves, not one's birth or status, that matters. With suitable references to classical sources and historical figures, the teacher shows that those who quietly contribute to society with no pretenses to greatness are in fact the noblest of all—a lesson that is as applicable today as when it was first written.

CDL

TRANSLATION

Sŏn'gyulcha[1] had a friend called Master Yedŏk.[2] This friend lived to the east of Chongbon Pagoda[3] and made a living cleaning up the feces in the village. The people of the village all called him Ŏm Haengsu, "Haengsu" being a term for an old laborer and "Ŏm" being his last name.

Chamok[4] asked Sŏn'gyulcha: "I once heard you talk about friends, and you said, 'A friend is like a wife with whom one does not live, and a brother with whom one does not share blood.'[5] Friends are indeed this important, are they not? Many are the learned and noble men who have desired to sit at your feet, but you have received none of them. And yet, though this Ŏm Haengsu is the

---

[1] Translation from *Writings of Yŏnam Pak Chiwŏn* [燕岩集 *Yŏnamchip*], kwŏn 8, "Outsider Tales of Panggyŏnggak" [放璚閣外傳 *Panggyŏnggak oejŏn*]. Sŏn'gyulcha (蟬橘子) is one of the pen names of Yi Tŏngmu (李德懋, 1741–1793), a Practical Learning (實學 Sirhak) scholar and friend of Pak Chiwŏn's. The term translates literally as "he of the cicadas and tangerines," and it is said that he took this pen name because his study was as small and cramped as a cicada skin or a tangerine peel.

[2] The two characters that make up this appellation are *ye* (穢), meaning "filth," and *tŏk* (德), meaning "virtue." Together, they are generally interpreted in Korean to mean "filthy virtue" (i.e., improper conduct), but given the context, this phrase might also be interpreted here as "the virtue of filth" or "virtue in filth."

[3] Chongbon Pagoda (宗本塔) is another name for Wŏn'gaksa Pagoda (圓覺寺塔), a ten-story stone pagoda built in 1467 that can still be seen in T'apkol Park in Seoul.

[4] Chamok (子牧) is a pen name of Yi Chŏnggu (李鼎九, 1756–1783), a disciple of Yi Tŏngmu's.

[5] This quotation is from a poem by Yi Tŏngmu included in *Collection That Embraces the World* [幷世集 *Pyŏngse-jip*], an anthology of contemporary poets published by Yun Kwangsim.

most lowly of laborers in the village, lives in the filthiest of places, and does the most disgraceful work, you heap praise on him for his virtue, calling him 'Master,' and seek him as your friend. As your disciple, I find this utterly shameful and no longer wish to study beneath you."

Sŏn'gyulcha laughed and said, "Sit down. I will tell you about friends. There is an old saying, 'A doctor cannot cure his own illness, and a shaman cannot perform her own ritual.' Everyone believes that there is something they do well, but if others fail to recognize this, they instead feign interest in hearing about their faults. Constant praise is akin to flattery and is thus dull, while speaking only of flaws is akin to carping and is thus heartless. Therefore, when someone does not do something well, if you do not mention it directly but only hint at or allude to it, no matter how sternly you may rebuke him, he will not grow angry. This is because you have not touched on what makes him uncomfortable. And if you should happen upon something he does well and subtly mention this, like one who is able to determine the genuine article from among many imitations, his heart will be filled with gratitude, as if you had scratched an itch. There is a proper way even to scratch an itch. When scratching someone's back, one should not go near the armpits, and when rubbing someone's chest, one should avoid the neck. If someone's words, though they be empty, sound beautiful, you will be overjoyed and say that this person truly knows you. Is this the proper way to make friends?"

Chamok covered his ears and hastily backed away, saying, "You would teach me the ways of the libertines in the street or lowly servants!"

Sŏn'gyulcha said, "I see that it is not the former that you find shameful but the latter.[6] All libertines make friends based on profit and win companions by flattering them to their faces. So no matter how close you might be, there is no one who will not become distant if you seek his help thrice, and no matter how deep-rooted the grudge, there is no one who will not become amiable if you profit him thrice. Thus it will be difficult to maintain a relationship based on profit, and a relationship based on flattery will not last long. An outstanding relationship does not need to be face-to-face, and a good friend does not need to be that close. One need only form relationships based on the heart and seek friends based on virtue. This is the moral way of forming relationships. A friend from ages past is not too remote, and even ten thousand leagues[7] is not too great a distance for two to abide together.

---

[6] Here, "the former" refers to lowly friends such as Ŏm Haengsu, while "the latter" refers to the superficial friendships described in the previous paragraph. Thus Sŏn'gyulcha is saying that it is not *with whom* one makes friends that troubles Chamok but *how* those friends are made.

[7] The text refers to *li* (里), a unit of distance equal to roughly 393 meters, although here it is used with the figure "ten thousand" not to denote a specific distance but to convey the idea of someone at great remove.

"Take this Ŏm Haengsu. He has never asked for any recognition from me, yet I have always been eager to praise him. He takes his time when eating, he is timorous when he walks, he slumbers deeply when he is tired, and he cackles when he laughs. He lives like a fool. He built a hut out of mud and covered it with straw, and in the wall he made a hole, so when he enters, he crouches down like a shrimp, and when he sleeps, he curls up like a dog. Yet he rises with cheer in the morning, takes up his straw basket, and goes into town to clean the privies. When the rain and frost come in the ninth month and thin ice forms in the tenth month, whether it be the human waste left in privies, the horse manure in the stables, the cow manure in the barn, the chicken droppings beneath the roosts, dog dung, goose droppings, pig manure, rabbit droppings, or sparrow droppings, he gathers them all as gently as if they were gems. Though he keeps all the profit for himself, his righteousness is not sullied, and though he seeks to acquire much, no one calls him unfair. He spits on his hands and wields his spade, and he bends his back to his work like a bird pecking at feed. No matter how beautiful a written passage may be, he pays it no heed, and no matter how joyful a tune may be, he shows no interest. Though all may desire riches and honor, simply wanting something does not mean one will attain it, so he covets not these things. Thus praising him would not add to his honor, nor would slandering him add to his shame.

"All the finest fields—such as the radish fields of Wangsimni, the turnip fields of Salgoji, the eggplant, cucumber, watermelon, and squash fields of Sŏkkyo, the red pepper, garlic, chive, green onion, and shallot fields of Yŏnhŭigung, the water-parsley fields of Ch'ŏngp'a, and the taro fields of It'aein[8]—rely on Mr. Ŏm's manure to fertilize their soil and ensure plentiful harvests. For this they pay him six thousand *chŏn*[9] per year, and yet he eats one bowl of rice in the morning and is invigorated for the day, and it is not until evening that he eats another bowl of rice. People have urged him to eat meat, but he replies, 'Once you swallow them, both vegetables and meat alike fill the stomach, so what does it matter how they taste?' People have urged him to wear new clothes, but he replies, 'I am not

---

[8] All these neighborhoods are located in Seoul, or Hanyang (漢陽), as it was known at the time. The neighborhoods of Wangsimni and Ch'ŏngp'a still exist today with the same names, while Salgoji refers to the area of Ttuksŏm (Island) in Yongsan district; Sŏkkyo refers to the neighborhood of Sŏkkwan in Sŏngbuk district; Yŏnhŭigung was a royal villa located in what is now the neighborhood of Yŏnhŭi in Sŏdaemun district; and It'aein refers to the neighborhood of It'aewŏn in Yongsan district.

[9] This is a considerable yearly salary for a humble laborer. To put this amount into perspective, a bushel of rice in Seoul in 1768 cost 20 *chŏn*. In eighteenth-century Korea, a strong horse cost 400 *chŏn*, a decent-sized (ten *kan*) thatched-roof house would have cost around 1,000 *chŏn*, and a tiled-roof house of the same size would have cost around 2,000 *chŏn*.

used to clothes with wide sleeves, and if I were to wear new clothes, I would not be able to carry the night soil.' It is only on the morning of New Year's Day that he puts on his finest clothes and visits all his neighbors to perform his New Year's bows. But when he returns, he changes back into his old clothes, takes up his straw basket, and goes back into the village. Someone like Ŏm Haengsu could be called a great man who hides his virtue beneath filth.

"It has been said, 'If by nature he is rich and of high status, he acts in accordance with riches and high status, and if by nature he is poor and of low status, he acts in accordance with poverty and low status.'[10] 'Nature' here means that a man's station is predetermined. It is said in the *Book of Poetry* [詩經 *Shijing*], 'We toil from dawn to dusk, as truly no two fates are the same.'[11] 'Fate' here refers to a man's lot in life. All people, when they are brought into being by the heavens, have fixed lots in life. Thus one's fate is one's nature, so how can anyone hold a grudge? When people eat pickled shrimp, eggs come to mind, and when they wear clothes made of kudzu fibers, they long for ramie clothes. Thus the world is thrown into chaos, the common people rise up in anger, and farmlands are laid waste. How could the followers of Chen Sheng, Wu Guang, and Xiang Ji[12] have been at ease with hoes and mallets[13] in their hands? This is what the *Book of Changes* [易經 *Yijing*] refers to when it says, 'If a bearer of burdens nonetheless rides in a carriage, he will attract thieves.'[14] Even though you are given a large stipend, if it is not given justly, then it is not clean, and if you should amass a great fortune with no effort, your name will reek. Thus people put brilliant beads into the mouths of the dead to show that they were clean.[15]

"This Ŏm Haengsu makes his living by carrying feces on his back, so it could be said that he is exceedingly unclean, but the way in which he makes his living

---

[10]This quotation is from the *Doctrine of the Mean* [中庸 *Zhong yong*] and can be found in the fourteenth section, according to the divisions made by Zhu Xi in the twelfth century. The passage as a whole discusses how the "superior man" (君子, C. *junzi*, K. *kunja*) always acts in accordance with his situation or station.

[11]This quotation is from the poem "Little Stars" [小星 *Xiao xing*], found in the section titled "Odes of Shao and the South" [召南 *Shao nan*].

[12]All three of these figures were Chinese military leaders who rebelled against the Qin dynasty in 209 B.C.E.

[13]Along with the hoe, the mallet mentioned here is also a farming implement; after the soil was broken by a plow or hoe, the mallet was used to break down the clods of earth so that the dirt could be spread over newly planted seeds.

[14]This quotation is from the commentary on the third line of the fortieth hexagram, 解 (*xie*), a character that is variously interpreted as "loosing," "deliverance," or "solution."

[15]This is a practice known as *fanhan* (飯含) in Chinese (K. *panham*); before the body is shrouded the day after death, the chief mourner uses a willow spoon to place grains of rice and beads in the mouth of the deceased.

is exceedingly fragrant. The way he conducts himself may be exceedingly filthy, but the way he upholds righteousness is worthy of praise. Based on this, it is obvious how he would act even if he were given a large stipend.

"Judging by this, we can see that even among the clean there is that which is not clean, and even among the filthy there is that which is not filthy. When I struggle to bear the hardships of life, I cannot help but think of those who are less fortunate than I, and when I think of Ŏm Haengsu, there is nothing I cannot bear. Thus he who wishes not to sneak in through the side gate[16] cannot but think of Ŏm Haengsu. And if one dwells on these thoughts long enough, one may even attain sagehood.

"If one lives in poverty as a scholar, it is shameful to allow this to show on one's face, and if one has achieved one's purpose in life, it is shameful to allow this to show in the way one carries oneself; there are few who would not be mortified when compared with Ŏm Haengsu. I have taken Ŏm Haengsu as my teacher—how could I dare call him my friend? Thus I do not dare call him by the name of Ŏm Haengsu, but instead call him Master Yedŏk."

CDL

6.2. PAK CHIWŎN, "ON NAMES"
(名論 MYŎNGNON)

Following is another piece by Pak Chiwŏn. Pak Chiwŏn, pen name Yŏnam (燕巖), was a literatus in eighteenth-century Chosŏn Korea, a special time in East Asian history.[17] The establishment of the Qing dynasty (淸, 1616–1911) was having profound repercussions with regard to state identities in the region. In particular, for the vast majority of Korean intellectuals who had both cultural and political allegiances to the Ming dynasty (明, 1368–1644), the Qing's replacement of the Ming represented neither dynastic change nor simple power realignments in the East Asian international political structure. Instead, there was the radical transformation of their worldview itself, in that a barbarian had conquered the very center of the civilized world. In responding to this cultural predicament, the Noron (老論, Old Doctrine), the mainstream political faction at the time, espoused a "little China" (小中華 sojunghwa) ideology. Sojunghwa held that the Chosŏn embodied the authentic culture of China—especially Confucianism—while other countries had failed to do so in the face of the Qing barbarian domination of the center of the

---

[16] That is, a thief; the phrase is used here to indicate one without honor.

[17] This project was made possible through the support of a grant from the Templeton Religion Trust. The opinions expressed herein are those of the author(s) and do not necessarily reflect the views of the Templeton Religion Trust.

civilized world. Pak Chiwŏn also found himself in such a cultural environment since his family belonged to the Noron faction.

However, Pak Chiwŏn had the chance to travel to Qing China in 1780 as an unofficial member of a Chosŏn embassy, which was led by Pak Myŏngwŏn (朴明源, 1725–1790). The official purpose of the travel was to commemorate the Qianlong emperor's seventieth birthday. Pak Chiwŏn's experience of Qing China in 1780 gave a sensational color to his life, setting him apart from most of his contemporaries. In particular, his exposure to international culture and Western learning in Qing China at that time contributed to the development of the intellectual movement known as Northern Studies (北學 Pukhak). Northern Studies represented a new departure from the prevailing Zhu Xi version of neo-Confucianism and the "little China" ideology.

Pak Chiwŏn's stories written during this trip were collected in his *Diary of a Journey to the Imperial Summer Palace at Rehe* (熱河日記 *Yŏrha ilgi*). These stories stand out today for the ways that they challenged conventions of established literary genres and are thus hailed as major works in the history of Korean literature. Accordingly, much has been written about the artistic achievements of the *Diary*. However, there has been very little literature through which the reader outside the specialist realm of Korean belles lettres can attempt to assess Pak Chiwŏn's contribution to Korean intellectual history more broadly. "Myŏngnon" is an essay that demonstrates Pak's talent as an intellectual with a keen eye for social criticism.

It is not clear when Pak wrote this philosophical essay. It was included in the so-called Peacock House manuscript (孔雀館文稿 Kongjakkwan Mun'go), which was edited when Pak Chiwŏn served as a local magistrate. The casual reader might mistake "On Names" for one of the conventional essays on names, which has been the topic of intellectual discourse since the *Analects*. However, the essay is anything but that.

It reveals an exemplary self-consciousness about the symbolic dimension of human experience and the human capacity to make and entertain symbolic forms. Pak's thought-provoking essay begins with a seemingly Daoist statement: "The world is an empty vessel." Consider first its striking contrast with a passage of *Reflections on Things at Hand* (近思錄 *Jinsilu*), which was widely circulated as a primer of neo-Confucianism in East Asia: "As there are things, there are their specific principles." As it implies that the world is devoid of any inherent values, it deconstructs the theoretical foundation on which the neo-Confucian political vision is built. Despite his apparent departure from neo-Confucianism, Pak does not deny the importance of moral norms as a means to hold the world together. Pak's unique contribution lies in that he approaches moral norms from an extramoral perspective and puts moral norms on a new theoretical foundation. What constitutes the theoretical foundation is names, by which Pak means a wide range of symbols that impart significance to an otherwise neutral reality. Seen in this way, the salient feature of human beings becomes neither the propensity to maximize one's material interests, perhaps seen best in capitalist economics, nor the aspiration to realize one's moral nature, as is defined in neo-Confucianism. Above all, human beings desire to seek, generate, and consume meaning in their lives. The most important area of life for ordering the world is symbolism.

YK and YK

TRANSLATION

The world is an empty vessel.[18] What sustains the vessel? It is names. What brings about names? It is desire. What nourishes the desire? It is the sense of shame. The myriad things are easy to scatter, and so there is no way to connect them. It is names that bind them. The Five Cardinal Relations[19] are easily destroyed, in which case no one can be on intimate terms. It is names that bind them. Only then can the huge vessel be full and complete, so that there is no need to worry about its tilting to one side, overturning, collapsing, or being dislocated.

As there are too many people who do good deeds, it is impossible to give all of them government positions. Instead, one may encourage a morally superior man [君子, C. junzi, K. kunja] to do good deeds by names. As there are too many people who do bad deeds, it is impossible to punish all of them. Instead, one may make a morally inferior man [小人, C. xiaoren, K. soin] feel guilty by names. Suppose that a piece of beautiful jade is cast when it is dark.[20] Under such a circumstance, everyone would be tense with worry and thus draw one's sword. Why? They all know that this is a name without a cause and thus cannot be happy to get the jade. How much more true is this of the world as an empty vessel. Suppose that since a king has passed away, a silk court dress is placed on the throne according to the court ritual. Under such a circumstance, everyone would adjust the collar of one's clothes and walk with short steps when passing before the throne. Why? They all know that there are names that cannot be disregarded. How much more true is this of the situation in which there is a real object of royalty and filial piety one should feel compassion for.

This is the reason the hegemons did not dare to usurp the throne even when they expanded their control over the empty vessel as the Zhou state was gradually declining in power. They minded the empty name. Deer and horse are

---

[18] The translation is from Pak Chiwŏn, *The Collected Works of Yŏnam* [燕巖集 Yŏnamjip], 17 vols. (Seoul: National Library of Korea, 1932), kwŏn 3.

[19] The Five Cardinal Relations (五倫 Oryun) are those between ruler and subject, father and son, husband and wife, elder and junior, and friend and friend.

[20] On the story of beautiful jade, see chapter 83 of *The Grand Scribe's Records* [史記 Shiji] and chapter 39 of *Selections of Refined Literature* [文選 Wenxuan].

somewhat similar in appearance. Once the distinction between them is blurred, people commit regicide.[21] Alas! Despite the fact that the distinction between deer and horse is not a matter of world crisis, people cannot get along in the world without such a distinction. How much more true is this of the distinction between good and bad and that between honor and disgrace.

Nothing is more terrible than being free from desire. The sage-kings were worried that people's discipline would grow slack and thus would—far from progressing—retrogress more and more. Thus, they stimulated the sense of sight through patrician ceremonial robes, the sense of hearing through various musical instruments, the body through seals and carriages for high officials, the spirit through paying high tribute to one's good deeds, erecting memorial tablets, and singing hymns of praise.

The goal here is to rouse people into activity, to harden their will, and to have them feel a surge of enthusiasm for their work without falling into a dejected state. However, if people only have the audacity to move on without any idea of retreat, the biggest problem with the world will be that people are quite unruffled without a sense of shame. Therefore, the kings of past times wanted to cultivate noble character by placing rolls of silk with round pieces of jade on their robes and the virtue of modesty by encouraging and enlightening.

"Awe and military might cannot bend" people if people become men of principle.[22] Those who are above the rank of a great officer cannot be controlled by punishments if they cultivate a sense of honor.[23] Even when corporal punishment such as cutting off the nose and tattooing the face and banishment is employed, one should express sorrow and commiseration. It makes people control themselves and not indulge themselves of their own accord.

People are supposed to wish for wealth and fame above all. However, when they wish for something other than wealth and fame, they can decline even noble titles and stipends. People are supposed to be ashamed of being punished.

---

[21] On the story of the distinction between horse and deer, see chapter 6 of *The Grand Scribe's Records*: "On the *chi-hai* 己亥 day in the eighth month, Chao Kao decided to rebel. He was afraid that Ch'in's vassals would not listen to him, thus he first made a test: He presented a deer to the Second Emperor, calling it a horse. The Second Emperor laughed and said: 'You must be wrong to call a deer a horse!' He asked his attendants. Some of them kept silent, some said a horse to comply with Chao Kao, and some said a deer. Chao Kao thus plotted to implicate, in terms of the law, those who said a deer. Afterward, all Ch'in's vassals held Chao Kao in awe" (Ssu-ma Ch'ien, *The Grand Scribe's Records, Volume 1: The Basic Annals of Pre-Han China*, ed. William H. Nienhauser Jr. [Bloomington: Indiana University Press, 1994], 1:161).

[22] Brian W. Van Norden, *Mengzi: With Selections from Traditional Commentaries* (Indianapolis: Hackett, 2008), chapter 6.

[23] James Legge, *The Sacred Books of China: The Texts of Confucianism; Part III, The Li Ki* (Oxford: Clarendon Press. 1885): 90.

However, when they are ashamed of something other than punishment, they are willing to tread upon even the naked blade of a sword.[24] What makes such things possible? It is names, isn't it? That being so, rewards and punishments are ways of governing that will eventually be unworkable; boosting names is a way of governing, which will be workable under all circumstances.

Why? There are some people who do not expect rewards while doing good deeds. For they think that even governmental positions do not outweigh their doing good deeds. There are some people who do not fear punishments while doing bad deeds, for they think that even the infliction of physical injury on them would not prevent them from doing bad deeds. In these cases, one should make them feel spiritual elevation without relying on rewards and make them feel shame without relying on punishments. When they are motivated in that way, nothing can stop them.

It was said: the connotations of righteousness are impartial and great; those of names are partisan and selfish. This theory would make all the people in the world play the hypocrite. As for those who dislike names, they do so on an individual level. Although they dislike names, they would not sink into the league of most corrupt. As for those who like names, even they would humble themselves if they were overpraised and overrated. Being on such an edge, they could not enjoy such reputation. We don't have to worry that this would make all the people in the world play the hypocrite. If, hypothetically speaking, everyone is a morally superior man [*junzi*], we don't have to care about names. If people have the urge to practice with concerted effort,[25] one can induce moral conduct and make them feel ashamed of immoral conduct by utilizing this urge. If people are so indifferent to the point that they do not care about names, the methods by which the former kings exercised leadership over people and ordered the world would not work, and loyalty, filial piety, humanity, and righteousness would be hollowed out. How then do leadership and ordering become operative on their own?

YK and YK

---

[24] Andrew Plaks, ed. and trans, *"Ta Hsüeh" and "Chung Yung" ("The Highest Order of Cultivation" and "On the Practice of the Mean")* (London: Penguin Classics, 2004), chapter 9.

[25] Ibid., chapter 20.

6.3. YI TŎNGMU, "THE BOOK OF EARS, EYES, MOUTH, AND HEART" (耳目口心書 IMOKKUSIMSŎ)

How should one write? In writing a literary work, how does the author express his or her own individuality? What would be the most important prerequisite of literature: canonic rules or raw talent? In "The Book of Ears, Eyes, Mouth, and Heart," miscellaneous notes on reading and writing, Yi Tŏngmu (李德懋, 1741–1793) addresses these issues in terms of the reception of late-Ming literature of China, particularly the Late Seven Masters (後七子, C. Houqizi) and the Gong'an (公安, K. Kong'an) schools.

The Late Seven Masters versus the Gong'an: Traditionally, the Late Seven Masters include Li Panlong (李攀龍, 1514–1570), Wang Shizhen (王世貞, 1526–1590), Xie Zhen (謝榛, 1495–1575), Xu Zhongxing (徐中行, 1517–1578), Zong Chen (宗臣, 1525–1560), Liang Youyu (梁有譽, 1522–1566), and Wu Guolun (吳國倫, 1524–1593). The literary thought of this group is often characterized by the term *pokko* (復古, C. *fugu*), which means "restoring antiquity." These writers argued that only the prose of the Qin and Han (秦漢) and the poetry of the High Tang (盛唐, Shengtang) should form the canon for proper writing.

Beginning around 1590 and into the 1650s, the Gong'an school appeared in the literary history of China as a reaction to orthodox tradition and formalism, which had been proposed by the Late Seven Masters. The early years of the seventeenth century saw a trend in emphasizing the natural self, individual creativity, and intense emotion in literature and the arts. Its philosophical underpinnings were articulated in most detail by Li Zhi (李贄, 1527–1602). Li Zhi influenced the three Yuan brothers of Gong'an—Yuan Zongdao (袁宗道, 1560–1600), Yuan Hongdao (袁宏道, 1568–1610), and Yuan Zhongdao (袁中道, 1570–1623). The influential Gong'an school of writing obviously owes much to Li Zhi for its antiarchaist theoretical tenets, including the rejection of the authority of the past, the shunning of imitation, the insistence that each writer express individual "native sensibilities," and the promotion of fiction and drama as important, legitimate forms of literature.

Transmission to Chosŏn: How did late-Ming literature fit the needs and desires of Chosŏn Korea, a different time and society? How did late-Ming literary ideas take on new meanings with the reading practices of people from different historical contexts? Unlike in Chinese literary history, the transmission of these two literary schools to Chosŏn did not follow an exact chronological sequence, although the introduction of the Late Seven Masters occurred slightly earlier than that of the Gong'an group.

Initial contact with late-Ming literature was made through Chinese envoys, who were visiting Chosŏn in the mid-sixteenth century. According to *Wŏlchŏngmallok* (月汀漫錄), a collection of essays written by Yun Kŭnsu (尹根壽, 1537–1616), in 1521, Tang Gao (唐皋), a Ming emissary, informed that Li Mengyang was the most renowned writer in China of the day, but this name was still unknown in Chosŏn.²⁶ Later, in 1572, Li Mengyang's collected works, *Kongtongji* (崆峒集), were purchased in Beijing by *yŏnhaeng* emissaries of Chosŏn.

As for the introduction of the Gong'an group, it was initially introduced to Chosŏn around 1606. Hŏ Kyun (許筠, 1569–1618) obtained a book by Yuan Hongdao from a Chinese emissary who was visiting Chosŏn. Later, in 1614, Hŏ went to China and obtained more than four thousand volumes at the Liulichang market. After he returned to Seoul, he made his own anthology of late-Ming writings, including Gong'an literature, titled *Hanjŏngnok* (閒情錄).

Introduced in the early seventeenth century, Gong'an literature attracted readers in Chosŏn and gained popularity more than a century later. The beginning years of the eighteenth century witnessed a few critics and neo-Confucian scholars, such as Kim Ch'anghyŏp (金昌協, 1651–1708), who critically reviewed the negative influence of the Late Seven Masters in Chosŏn. In order to denounce the excessive formalism of the archaism of the Late Seven Masters, they drew on major theoretical tenets of Gong'an. As neo-Confucian scholars, they expressed disapproval of the Gong'an group for their Buddhist inclinations and use of vernacular (*baihua* 白話) expressions; however, their criticism is also evidence of the critical attention that Gong'an writers were beginning to gain in Chosŏn in the early eighteenth century.

By the late eighteenth century, around the time when Yi Tŏngmu wrote "Imokkusimsŏ," the archaist position of the Late Seven Masters existed only as a negative literary model to be overcome, whereas the Gong'an literature continued to gain popularity. The literature of the Late Seven Masters was harshly blamed for its slavish imitation and excessive formalism. Those who advocated Gong'an literature argued that literature should be a developing phenomenon and that each age had a distinctive character and style; therefore, imitation makes writers lose their individual character of expression, and one should not be bound by the rules and conventions of accepted literary forms.

"The Book of Ears, Eyes, Mouth, and Heart"²⁷: In "Imokkusimsŏ," written from 1765 to 1767, Yi Tŏngmu opposed the literary archaism and orthodox tradition of the late Ming. He believed it imposed "excessive restrictions," because imitation stifled creativity and inspiration by suppressing the "transcendent talents" and "unfettered spirits" of writers. This position is often found in writings from the late eighteenth century. Similar to claims by the Yuan brothers in the Ming, those who advocated for the Gong'an in the late Chosŏn argued that "literature is a developing phenomenon, and ages all have their own distinctive characteristics and style. Imitation makes writers lose touch with their individual character of expression. Therefore, individuals should not be

---

²⁶ Kang Myŏnggwan, *Konganp'a wa Chosŏn hugi hanmunhak* [공안파와 조선후기 한문학, The Gong'an school and late Chosŏn literature] (Seoul: Somyŏng, 2007), 8.

²⁷Translation from *The Complete Collection of Yi Tŏngmu* [青莊館全書 *Ch'ŏngjanggwan chŏnsŏ*] (Seoul: Minjok munhwa ch'ujinhoe, 2000), *kwŏn* 48.

bound by the rules and conventions of accepted literary forms." Emphasis on the formal imitation of the *fugu* practice was harshly criticized as slavish formalism. Many literati in the late eighteenth century used the Gong'an literature as a theoretical methodology to criticize the literary practices of their predecessors and also as a foundational logic to develop their own new literary styles and notions.

Although Yi Tŏngmu agreed with the antiarchaist theoretical tenets of Gong'an literary thought, he was concerned lest Yuan Hongdao become another iconic figure to emulate. For Yi, writing should above all reflect individual genuineness and embrace a variety of styles; individuals should not mindlessly follow someone else's style—even if it was someone who had proposed novel ideas such as Yuan Hongdao. Yi added that "everyone should have his own way of mysterious understanding and profound enlightenment; therefore, it depends on how much each person can recover this ability and interpret the old rules individually" (且古人軌轍, 不可拘束, 亦不可專然拋棄也. 自有妙解透悟法, 在人人各自善得之如何耳).

JY

TRANSLATION

[1] Someone posed a question: Suppose that Li Panlong showed up here along with Wang Shizhen on his left and Zhang Jiayin on his right, accompanied by a group of people such as Xie Zhen and Xu Zhongxing,[28] and then argued, "When we write prose, we ought to imitate the *Commentary of Zuo* [左傳 *Zuozhuan*], *Scripts from the Warring States* [國策 *Guoce*], *Annals* [史記 *Shiji*], and *Book of Han* [漢書 *Hanshu*].[29] Anything written later than the period of Han Yu and Liu Zongyuan[30] is not worth discussing. For poetry, we should take as models for imitation the works written during the years of Jian'an, Huangchu, Kaiyuan, and Tianbao,[31] and anything written after the period of Yuan Zhen

---

[28] Those mentioned here are the aforementioned Late Seven Masters. Yi Tŏngmu lists here Zhang Jiayin (張佳胤, 1527–1588) as one of those who advocated the idea of *fugu*.

[29] The books listed here are model works of *guwen* for writing prose.

[30] Han Yu (韓愈, 768–824) and Liu Zongyuan (柳宗元, 773–819) are the central literary and intellectual figures of the Middle Tang (中唐 Zhongtang). They represent the consolidation and self-conscious theorization of prose writing. Literary histories often state that they founded the "*guwen* movement." Later, in the late Ming, the Seven Masters promoted the position of Han Yu and Liu Zongyuan and considered them to be model writers for the practice of *fugu*.

[31] Jian'an (建安), Huangchu (黃初), Kaiyuan (開元), and Tianbao (天寶) refer to the reign periods of the Chinese emperors Xiandi of Han (漢獻帝), Wendi of Wei (魏文帝), and Xianzong of Tang (唐玄宗), respectively. The Seven Masters recognize only poetry written before the High Tang as part of the proper literary canon.

and Bai Juyi[32] should not be considered. There might be people who dare not follow this principle and even propose another, but I would tell them that [in that case] all their work is not considering true literature." How would you respond to that?

[1-1] I would say, I answered, that this is an excessive restriction. If you pursue those principles with your excellent talent, then you could achieve a desirable result. Among all literati in the world, you might be able to find someone who has exceptional talent as good as yours and who is also skilled [in imitating the models of other writers]. If you have such a person follow the writing regulations, then he could produce a certain work at a certain level of quality. However, suppose that there is a group of people who have sublime and transcendent talent or eccentric and unfettered spirits. How would it be possible to force them to lower their heads and agree to follow what you do, so that they willingly follow the fashion of the times? Even if they follow your suggestions and devote themselves to imitating the works of others, the results would not be as good as what they could create [by following their own proclivities]. Those people might have the technical skills of You Meng who emulated Sun Shuao almost perfectly;[33] even in this case, however, their writing would be more naturally genuine and less artificial. By contrast, [imitating] the writing style of someone like you would [produce something that is] more artificial and less genuine.

[1-2] Literature is a creation [造化, K. *chohwa*]. How could it be possible to regulate the creative process and make every literary work conform to a certain canonical model? In practice, everyone conceives his own [idea of what constitutes] complete literature. What one harbors in one's heart is as unique as one's distinctive face. If all literary works are required to be the same, then isn't [art] just like a woodblock or an answer sheet for an exam? By the same token, how could I insist that you abandon all the rules that people of former times abided by? This does not mean that you should be fettered by the rules and not able to express yourself. The rules were completed amid the absence of rules. Therefore, how can I say that you should throw them away? You might be able to

---

[32] Bai Juyi (白居易, 772–846) and Yuan Zhen (元稹, 779–831) of the Middle Tang were active in the same period as Han Yu and Liu Zongyuan. Their literary circle was famous for founding a poetry genre, new *yuefu* (新樂府). They theorized that the primary motivation for writing the *Shijing* [詩經, Classic of poetry] and the Han *yuefu* (漢樂府) was to present a vivid image of the social ills of the times to the ruler in order to persuade him to effect reform. The Late Seven Masters concur with their view that the *Shijing* and Han *yuefu* should be recognized as part of the canon of great poetry, and the *fugu* sentiment of the new *yuefu* movement represented proper literary practice.

[33] The anecdote of You Meng (優孟) and Sun Shuao (孫叔敖) appears in the "Story of Huaji" [滑稽] of the *Shiji* [史記]. You Meng was an actor of the Chu (楚, 704–202 B.C.E.). He disguised himself as Sun Shuao after Sun died in order to console Sun's son.

arrogantly look down on the world within the four oceans and expound your grandiose discourse. But I am afraid that the current fashion of imitating others might prove no better than banal expressions and also harm your vigorous energy. However, this universe embraces everything thoroughly. Therefore, your talent of imitating the people of former times should not be left out. Fortunately, I had a chance to read your writing collection and thought that your work is extraordinary.

[2] Suppose Yuan Hongdao, the man continued, showed up with Xu Wei on his left and Jiang Yingke on this right, bunched together with a circle of people including Zeng Keqian and Tao Wangling,[34] and then asked, "How could there be a fixed rule for writing? Why should the principles be the teachings of the people of former times, and why should the words be [restricted to] the sayings of the wise people from the past? We should free ourselves from all restraints and make good play, then the gate will be unlocked and heaven will be open to us. If someone just stitches together the words of the people of former times, how could that be called a masterpiece of literature?" What would you say to this?

[2-1] I would certainly say, I answered, that this is another restraint. If you [pursue those principles] with your excellent talent, then you could [achieve a desirable result]. Among all the literati in the world, you might be able to find someone who has exceptional talent, as good as yours, who could resist worldly conventions and teach this idea and who could produce work of a similar quality. However, among the talented people in the world, there are not only those who have unrestrained spirits; there are also those who pursue decorous and dignified styles, or plain and easy styles. In spite of the diversity, if each one promotes his individual position and establishes a new and eccentric style, then I am afraid lest it would harm the original nature and become aloof above the high and vast realm. Wouldn't it have a negative impact on the original principle? In promoting the literature of many writers, how could there be one single proper law? Wouldn't that be just another restraint? If we care only for how unique or perfect individual works are, then there might be some works worth considering. There is an endless variety, such as rising and falling, granting and depriving, direct admonishing and hidden satire, following the stream or countering it. We should not allow stylistic variety to harm the original genuineness of nature; we need only eradicate stale and rotten banality. And the rules and model works of the people of former times should be neither [used as] a restraint nor abandoned entirely. Everyone should have his own way of mysterious understanding and profound enlightenment; therefore, it depends on how much each person

---

[34]These men are of the Gong'an school.

can recover this ability and interpret the old rules individually. If you get upset whenever you think all writers in the world do not follow your way and then consider it a great fault, then I am afraid lest the act of writing would harm the Way in the end, and the deceiving words and illusive discourses could be so many and unruly that they could not be rectified. How sad it would be. However, this universe is all-inclusive with everything totally. Therefore, your talent of creating new expressions should not be omitted. Fortunately, I had a chance to read your writing collection and think that your work is extraordinary.

[3] Which side are you going to take?, he asked.

[3-1] I would accept, I answered, both positions first and then remove the extreme points of each. However, people like Fang Xiaoru,³⁵ Wang Yangming,³⁶ Tang Shunzhi,³⁷ and Gui Youguang³⁸ formed separate schools. How could they be willing to obey and be limited by the rules of the two sides? In general, the grandiose style of the Li Panlong group cannot be surpassed by Yuan Hongdao and his followers; and the insight and enlightenment of the Yuan Hongdao group cannot be reached by Li Panlong and his followers. They have opposing orientations and each has its own weakness. Despite those faults, however, both of them are outstanding talents in history. Throughout our Silla and Koryŏ, we have not had anyone who could match them. Alas.

JY

6.4. LADY YI OF HANSAN, "THE RECORD OF MY HARDSHIPS" (苦行錄 KOHAENGNOK)

"The Record of My Hardships" (1719)³⁹ is an autobiographical narrative by Lady Yi of Hansan (韓山李氏, 1659–1727) composed not long after her sixtieth birthday. Of *yangban*

---

³⁵ Fang Xiaoru (方孝孺, 1357–1402) was a prose writer of the early Ming. He was called the master of right learning (正學先生) because he defied stylistic embellishment in writing and emphasized the didactic and educational functions of literature.

³⁶ Wang Yangming (王陽明, 1472–1528) emphasized the natural self, individual creativity, intense emotion, and direct expression. His ideas influenced Li Zhi (李贄, 1527–1602) and, later, Yuan Hongdao.

³⁷ Tang Shunzhi (唐順之, 1507–1560) was a prose writer of the Ming who was influenced by Wang Yangming.

³⁸ Gui Youguang (歸有光, 1507–1571) was a prose writer of the Ming who advocated the value and style of Tang and Song prose and opposed the archaism of the Seven Masters.

³⁹ The translation of this piece was supported by the Academy of Korean Studies Grant funded by the Korean Government (MEST) (AKS-2011-AAA-2103). Facsimile reproductions of

status, Lady Yi was a great-grandchild of Yi Sanhae (李山海, 1539–1609), who served King Sŏnjo (宣祖, r. 1567–1608) and the wife of Yu Myŏngch'ŏn (柳命天, 1633–1705), an official at the court of King Sukchong (肅宗, r. 1674–1720). By virtue of her husband's position, Lady Yi received official titles: she became *chŏng puin* (貞夫人, junior second rank) in 1676 and, in 1691 the youngest *chŏnggyŏng puin* (貞敬夫人, senior second rank) in Chosŏn history. "The Record" is the only writing attributed to Lady Yi.

Written entirely in the vernacular script on sheets of paper pasted together into a scroll, "The Record" survives today thanks to multigenerational efforts the Chinju Yu family made to treasure this relic of Lady Yi's ruminations and calligraphy. About twenty years after Lady Yi's death, Yu Kyŏngjong (柳慶種, 1714–1784), a nephew of Yu Myŏngch'ŏn, commemorated "The Record" by composing an essay in *hanmun* in 1741. In 1870, one of the daughters-in-law in the Chinju Yu clan known as Madame Cho of Hanyang (漢陽趙氏) copied "The Record" by hand; this edition is not extant. In 1925, Yu Wŏnsŏng (柳遠聲, 1851–1945), an Ansan-based descendant of Yu Myŏngch'ŏn six generations removed and dedicated collator of writings held at the lineage's library, again resuscitated "The Record." His granddaughter Kwŏn T'aeim (1908–1967) took dictation of his recitation of Lady Yi's two-century-old original.

"The Record" pieces together Lady Yi's childhood, wedding, the deaths of her immediate family members (twelve, including her three children), many and chronic illnesses she and her family members endured, the adoption of Yu Mae (柳楳, 1683–1733), and her husband's prolonged exile during the culmination of the power struggle between Namin (南人, Southerners) and Sŏin (西人, Westerners) at the court of King Sukchong.[40] In particular, the adoption of Mae, along with the deaths of Lady Yi's children, merits our attention. When Lady Yi married Yu Myŏngch'ŏn, she was just eighteen and Yu twenty-six years senior to her. Her husband had a daughter from one of his two previous marriages, but no son. The Chinju Yu family's genealogical records reveal that Yu Myŏngch'ŏn and Yu Mae had quite similar lives. The former, fathered by Yu Yŏng (柳潁, dates known), was adopted by his uncle Yu Sŏk (柳碩, 1595–1655) to succeed the clan's ritual heirship. The latter, like his adoptive father, had to marry three times to secure a ritual heir. Lady Yi's unambiguous disappointment when she gave birth to a girl the

---

"The Record of My Hardships," Yu Kyŏngjong's 1741 essay, Yu Wŏnsŏng's 1925 essay, and Kwŏn T'aeim's vernacular rendition are found in the following: Kim Yŏngbae et al., eds., *Hansan Yi-ssi Kohaengnok ŭi ŏmunhakchŏk yŏn'gu* (Seoul: T'aehaksa, 1999); Han'guk Chŏngsin Munhwa Yŏn'guwŏn, ed., *Komunsŏ chipsŏng 58: Ansan Chinju Yu-ssi p'yŏn* (Sŏngnam: Chŏngsin munhwa yŏn'guwŏn, 2002); and Han'guk Chŏngsin Munhwa Yŏn'guwŏn P'yŏnjippu, ed., *Kohaengnok: 17 segi Sŏul sadaebuga yŏin ŭi konan'gi* (Sŏngnam: Han'gukhak chungang yŏn'guwŏn, 2014).

[40]The factionalism during the time of King Sukchong most famously involved the king's favoritism toward Consort Chang (禧嬪張氏, 1659–1701), supported by the Namin, and the dethronement and eventual reinstatement of Queen Inhyŏn (仁顯王后, 1667–1701), supported by the Sŏin.

second time and the details she painstakingly records about Mae's adoption, bridal selections, weddings, and her strong wishes for a grandson through Mae can be beneficially read against the sociocultural context of seventeenth-century Korea, where agnatic adoption (or adoption of a son of the husband's brother) became increasingly common among Chosŏn elite families faced with the absence of a legitimate son.

I deplore, lament, resent—Lady Yi closes "The Record" as if to reassure us that her life was one of pain, but can one draw a neat equation of the narrative's overt dissatisfaction? All in all, "The Record" is a complex text of gushing lamentation chronicling an individual's life journey and the survival of a *yangban* family. Peppered with implicit and explicit references to factional politics, family rituals, and illnesses and diseases, "The Record" enriches our understanding of family, society, and women's literary practice during the Chosŏn.[41]

SP

TRANSLATION

I was born in the third month of the *kihae* year [1659] in Tonghak-tong of Ch'ungch'ŏng province.[42] I lived there until I was six.

Maternal Grandfather Yi Pu's [李阜, b. 1482] knowledge of letters surpassed that of other illustrious men. I hear that he wrote a petition to the throne. After he turned twenty, he passed the preliminary examination, but saying that he should follow the principles of propriety and keeping his moral rectitude as sterling as gold and stone, he spent the rest of his life in Han'ga-dong in Yesan, where Great-Grandfather Agye's[43] grave is located . . . [text illegible]. My family went there to serve him in the spring of the *kapchin* year [1664]. He died in the twelfth month of that year. Having mourned his death for three years, my family moved to Uch'ŏn of Kyŏnggi province in the *chŏngmi* year [1667] and then back to Tonghak-tong in the *kiyu* year [1669].

Then, Father fell ill and spent the summer and autumn that year in pain. No amount of medicine could cure him. So there I was, at the age of eleven, faced with the torment of losing a parent. The pain was excruciating. Father never had the fortune of passing the civil service examination and departed this life at forty-seven. Oh, the difficulty of fully describing the extreme sorrows of mine as a child! The entire family and all our relatives grieved deeply. My three elder

---

[41] Mark A. Peterson, *Korean Adoption and Inheritance: Case Studies in the Creation of a Classic Confucian Society* (Ithaca, N.Y.: East Asia Program, Cornell University, 1996).

[42] All place-names are indicated with their present-day provincial jurisdiction.

[43] Agye is Yi Sanhae's sobriquet.

sisters were the first daughters-in-law of the head families of their husbands' families, so after the funeral they returned to their homes. I, the youngest among my sisters, stayed on to comfort Mother.

Early in the ninth month in the *pyŏngjin* year [1676], I went through the steps of my wedding ceremony—a three-day-long *killye* [吉禮] celebration followed by the rite of the new bride on the fifth day. For your whole life you are in your parents' bosom, and one day you leave it. I was anxious.

But as soon as I married, I was in charge of managing the household. O, I didn't know a thing back then. Not a thing went smoothly.

In the tenth month of that same year, my husband's daughter from his second marriage got engaged, and her wedding was carried out on the twenty-fourth day of the third month in the *chŏngsa* year [1677].

In the fifth month of that year, my body began showing signs of pregnancy. On the twenty-sixth day in the second month of the *muo* year [1678], I gave birth to a girl. Soon after delivery I started burning with fever. On the third day my condition worsened to the point that I even had visions of my own funeral and burial. In the *yu* hour [酉時, 5:00–7:00 p.m.] that afternoon, I started choking, but I regained control of my breath in the *chuk* hour [丑時, 1:00–3:00 a.m.], a couple of hours past midnight. For the next few months, I hovered between life and death. To make matters worse, my left leg swelled and developed an abscess. I grew increasingly emaciated. Even after I had the abscess slashed off, lying down comfortably was difficult. My servants took care of my urination and feces. In the midst of it all, on the tenth day of the fourth month, I came down with smallpox. Nothing was improving and my skin grew rough, like the inside of chestnut shells. As marvelous luck would have it, I survived, but my appearance had completely changed to make me look like a different person.

In the meantime, a wet nurse looked after my baby girl. Then, the baby started showing signs of smallpox herself. After suffering at the *t'obang*,[44] she breathed her last. In no less than five wretched months, my baby girl and I parted without having learned each other's faces. O, how awful things were in those days of disease! Her body was immediately taken to Ansan, where my husband's family's main house and grave site are located, and we buried her there.[45]

---

[44] The exact meaning of *t'obang* is unclear. *T'obang* presumably refers to a "clay-floored room" (土房). Traditional architecture suggests that *t'obang* is a clay-floored area between the main hall (大廳 *taech'ŏng*) and the margin of the courtyard (庭際 *chŏngje*).

[45] The Chinju Yu lineage branch established its third home base in Ansan during the reign of King Sŏnjo. The other two homes are in the capital outside the South Gate and in Koesan. The Ansan home was created when King Sŏnjo granted a large plot of land to the lineage upon the wedding between Yu Chŏk (柳頔, 1595–1619) and Princess Chŏngjŏng (貞正翁主, 1595–1666; the king's ninth daughter).

In the seventh month of that year, my husband was appointed magistrate [牧使 *moksa*] of Ch'ungju. He left for his new office and took along Mother-in-Law. I joined the two in the eighth month.

Early in the ninth month, he was promoted to become a third minister [參議 *ch'am'ŭi*] in the Board of Personnel [吏曹 Ijo], so that we ended up returning to Ansan.

Despite the residual symptoms I had from my past illnesses, I became pregnant again. In the seventh month of the *kimi* year [1679] I gave birth to a girl; what utter disappointment!

However, reminding myself of the fever I developed when I gave birth the first time, I mustered up an appetite to recuperate quickly. A girl was not what I had wished for, but I enjoyed watching her grow up beautifully as she talked, crawled about, and finally toddled.

But I must have accumulated immeasurable sins.[46] My baby girl had a severe fit [驚風 *kyŏng'pung*] in the fifth month of the *kyŏngsin year* [1680]. No medicine proved effective, and I lost her forever. Her pitiful last moves continued to haunt me for a long while. But the onerous nature of managing a household kept me busy, and my obligations toward Mother-in-Law prevented me from expressing agony. I was also too young to dwell on my pain. So, the pain of losing my second child eventually faded away.

In the *kyŏngsin* year the Sŏin faction [西人, Westerners] took over the court. In the tenth month my husband was exiled to Chirye. I took Mother-in-Law to our family's house in Ŏhyŏn [present-day Chungnim-dong] near the South Gate in the capital, and I stayed there with her. That winter Mother-in-Law suffered from terrible hives [風丹 *p'ungdan*]. Recording just how frustrated I was at that time would be impossible. But heaven took pity on us and she quickly recovered. The joy in the house knew no bounds.

Distraught at the thought of her son in exile, Mother-in-Law was overcome with constant worries. I, too, felt dreadful about staying away from my husband. So, on the twentieth day of the third month, I took Mother-in-Law to Chirye. We took our time with the journey. We arrived at our destination in twelve days, even though the trip is commonly six days long, because we rested at each and every post station. Mother-in-Law was astonishingly resilient during our laborious journey. On the contrary, I had a difficult time of it. My delivery day was coming up soon, and on top of that I had been a victim of many grave illnesses. I was barely alive during the trip.

---

[46] There is certainly a Buddhist understanding of the karma from one's past lives in Lady Yi's expression here.

On the sixth day in the fourth month [1681], we stayed at an inn. Mother-in-Law's health had not deteriorated a bit. We thought it was a gift from heaven that the family members could gather together despite my husband's exile.

Around the fifteenth day of the fourth month, Mother-in-Law suddenly showed symptoms of malaria [瘧疾 hakchil]. The robust health that she had retained began withering away.

While this tragedy took hold of us day and night, I delivered a baby boy early in the fifth month. Heaven had stretched out a helping hand to us! My joy was indescribable to the point that I felt like I was in a dream. Day in, day out a boy was what everyone had been hoping for.

Worries over Mother-in-Law's illness made celebration scarce in the house. Mother-in-Law lauded the birth and wished to see the baby. But I could not bring myself to let the newborn near her, so to this day I regret not having shown her the baby. She sent me some fabric for the newborn's clothing, but I did not make use of it.

Fourteen days after his birth, my son suffered from an acute convulsion [驚風 kyŏngp'ung]. For the following month, he choked [窒塞 chilsaek] every single day. But strangely enough, he began putting on weight, promising favorable prospects, so I made every attempt to help him pull through. Then, one night in the sixth month, I lost him forever.

I sent his body to Koesan, another family burial site. Grief and pain pulverized my insides. Every night I caressed the mat he once slept on and squeezed milk out of my breasts that he once suckled. My intestines disintegrated bit by bit. But with Mother-in-Law bedridden because of her illness, I reined in my sorrow.

While Mother-in-Law's condition was growing ever so serious, the state had reduced my husband's sentence and had him relocated to Ŭmsŏng, Ch'ungch'ŏng province. There was no way we could take Mother-in-Law all the way there. The relocation official from the capital came and stayed on for some ten days, urging my husband to depart immediately. My husband, however, had the hardest time forcing himself to leave his mother behind. No sooner would he depart than he would return to bid her farewell again; he repeated this four, five times. To this day my heart throbs recalling that scene. Little did we know that day turned out to be the final farewell between the two.

Around the middle of the seventh month, my husband arrived in Ŭmsŏng, while I stayed behind taking care of Mother-in-Law. Her condition became increasingly critical with each passing day. O, what tragedy it was. Master Yi, my nephew on my husband's side, was living in Sangju, Kyŏngsang province, so I took Mother-in-Law to Yi's house, and we nursed her there.

On the twelfth day in the eighth month, Mother-in-Law left this world. In the middle of this unbearable sadness, I thought of how hard it might be for my husband to hear this sad news in Ŭmsŏng. All things were wretched in every possible way. It was good that I had prepared all the necessary funeral paraphernalia and procured during summer the delivery of materials for making her coffin.

At the time of her funeral, the local magistrate of Sangju, though a Westerner, treated us with the utmost cordiality. The kindness of Kyŏngsang people was exceptional to the point that even the commoners served us as if they had been our own slaves.

On the twenty-sixth day in the eighth month, Mother-in-Law's coffin was transferred to Ŭmsŏng, but my husband, the chief mourner, could not be present for the funeral march. A funeral march without the chief mourner—it's an unthinkably wretched situation. We were pitiful beyond description. I escorted her coffin following closely behind. Have you ever heard of such a sad affair as this? As the march approached our destination, my husband was somewhere an hour's distance on foot from Ŭmsŏng. I went ahead and made a temporary stop at his dwelling while he, in deep sadness, briefly took over the transference of Mother-in-Law's coffin. As the family's ancestral mound was in Ansan, the coffin had to travel all the way there. My husband, the chief mourner, could not accompany us. No other families had to go through sad affairs as this. How could I relate to you the pain I felt then?

On the twelfth day of the eighth month of the *sinyu* year [1682], my husband, although his health was in a frail state, performed the ritual honoring of the first anniversary of her death.

On the twenty-second day of that month, the court issued an order summoning my husband to the capital. The whole thing was triggered by the monstrous words of a sinister man surnamed No.[47] Late that night an official dispatched by the State Tribunal [禁府都事 Kŭmbu Tosa][48] stormed into our house under royal order, and my husband followed him at once. O, what an atrocity! I managed to gather the slaves and horses. With the entire family I rushed out of the house at the crack of dawn. We made haste and arrived at the capital in just two days; getting there usually takes three days.

Once my husband was incarcerated, we had no means to find out news of him. Day and night I pounded my chest, overcome with frustration. I was falling into the deepest abyss and felt stabbed by ten thousand knives. Everything I saw was bleak. But heaven watched over us, and the charge against my husband was proven to be the worthless words of a lunatic. Not even a petition for his pardon was necessary; he was fully exonerated. For the past two weeks, my nerves

---

[47] No Kyesŏn (盧繼善, dates unknown).
[48] The original reads "Tosa," not "Kŭmbu Tosa."

had kept me from taking even a sip of water. But that day of my husband's release gave me joy I had never known in my life of twenty-three years. My body soared up high above the sky. Inky dark clouds couldn't catch me.

My husband first returned to Ŭmsŏng, his original place of exile. In the second month of the year after, his release became final, and so we all returned to our family home in Ansan.

Many were the illnesses I suffered and many were the difficulties that burned my intestines. But what with the due mourning period for Mother-in-Law's death, where could my doleful feelings find vent?

Did I lose so brutally all my children because I had accumulated sins? Anxiety conquered me in such a way that I saw blood in my feces [血便 *hyŏlbyŏn*] and subsequently was no longer able to conceive another child [懷胎頓然 *hoet'ae tonyŏn*]. That would mean that my husband's family would be stripped of its tax-exemption privileges [復 *pokho*]. Because no one among our immediate relatives had multiple sons, my husband and I didn't even have the option of adopting a nephew to carry on with his family name [繼 *kyehu*]. Worries over this matter deprived me of comfort in bed or at table.

However, in the *chŏngmyo* year [1687], the young minister [判書 *p'ansŏ*], my husband's younger brother, had a baby boy. A second son in his family—just marvelous. Immediately after the birth of the new boy, I entertained the thought of adopting him. Sending clothes and toys, I treated the baby boy as a sure son of mine. However, three days later, the collective opinion of the Yu clan decided that because my family was the main branch of the lineage [宗家 *chongga*], the adoption of their first son, Yu Mae, rather than the new baby, was more appropriate. Plus, given that my husband was already quite aged, the firstborn was a better choice. Thus, the adoption of a five-year-old Mae was carried out.

Mae had an outstanding aura about him. He possessed signs of good fortune and virtue. I reveled in how heaven had lent me a womb. He came and went between our house and his parents' house, but he really preferred spending time at our house. I often forgot he was my adopted child. Once his transition had been completed, the family figured that a bride was what he needed for the continuation of the family line. All eagerly looked forward to the day of his fifteenth birthday—the day of his rite-of-passage capping ceremony—and the delight of celebrating his wedding ceremony.

But then the Kapsul Power Shift [甲戌換局 Kapsul Hwan'guk, 1694] happened, and this yet again resulted in my husband's banishment.[49] He departed

---

[49] Yu Myŏngch'ŏn was banished to the island of Hŭksando, Chŏlla province. Exile to islands, also known as *chŏlto anch'i* (絶島安置), was one of the harshest forms of banishment and placed a criminal on an island far away from the mainland to subject him to the suffering of being isolated from family, friends, and, to certain extent, local residents.

for his place of exile in the fourth month of that year, and a few months later I followed him, taking Mae with me. Mae showed no hint of sorrow even as he parted with his birth parents. After Mae bid farewell to his birth mother by prostrating himself before her, Mae and I went on our journey. The poor boy was so extraordinarily mature. Recording every detail about the five years of our lives in exile would make my writing tedious, so I will stop here.

On the second day in the twelfth month of the *ŭrhae* year [1695], my husband became embroiled in a catastrophic incident.[50] As we survived this calamity, Mae turned fifteen.

In the ninth month of the *chŏngch'uk* year [1697], Mae walked through his capping ceremony. He shone in his brilliant constitution. Every aspect of the ceremony filled my heart with joy. Mae's birth parents could not witness the scene, so it goes without saying how deplorable the ceremony must have been for Mae.

Next, the selection of Mae's bride began. Our life in exile had placed us far removed from the capital, and this meant that his bridal selection was not going to be easy. I applied greatest discernment to make the decision.

Sending Mae off to the capital [for his wedding], my husband and I were full of curiosity about the bride's brightness. Surely we were saying good-bye to him for a very happy occasion, but the prospect of certain loneliness we'd feel after separating from him meant our cheer was blended with melancholy. When my husband and I returned home after seeing Mae off, we comforted each other by acknowledging how deep the affection was between him and us.

After his departure, all we cared about day and night was the news of his wedding. At last our family slave who had accompanied Mae to the capital returned. The letters he brought back circulated among the family members, and every reader praised the brilliance of the bride. Her impeccable calligraphy surely made her deservedly Mae's bride. But despite all the joy, it had been almost ten months since we saw Mae last, so that a single day felt as long as three years. I desperately wanted to bring the young couple over from their faraway dwelling but was frustrated because we had no clue when my husband could be pardoned and return to our family home.

In the tenth month of the *muin* year [1698], my husband and I invited Mae and Daughter-in-Law to the place of exile. Daughter-in-Law was a fetching and cheerful girl, as stunning as the autumn moon. She was robust and full of alacrity. I could not have asked for a more befitting bride for him. I began anticipating the prospect of a grandson. It was such a shame my husband and I had no

---

[50]Yu Myŏngch'ŏn was relocated to Yŏngil, Kyŏngsang province, for allegedly making secret connections with Chang Hŭijae (張希載, d. 1701).

one to boast to about what a wonderful a daughter-in-law we had. We simply congratulated each other.

In the second month of the *kimyo* year [1699], my husband was able to leave his place of banishment, and the family went to Koesan to stay, where our family home was.

In the final month of that year, I heard that my mother in Uch'ŏn had fallen gravely ill. The news put me in a state of perpetual anxiety. I finally visited her on the fourth day in the second month of the *kyŏngjin* year [1700]. Mother's illness temporarily took a favorable turn when she greeted me, but the following day her condition quickly turned for the worse. Four days later, Mother departed this world. Despite all my longing and worries, all I was given was serving her for less than a single week before our eternal farewell to each other.

After conducting the due funeral procedures, I, in mourning attire, returned to Koesan. O I cannot recount how tremendous my sorrow was. In the *sinsa* year [1701], my husband came to Ch'ogido to stay.[51] As our lives continued in despondency, my husband was yet again banished, this time to the island of Chido, in Naju, Chŏlla province. He left for his place of exile on an achingly cold day amid a snowstorm in the twelfth month. O, the shock and sadness!

Around the final week of the following year's second month, I set off with Mae and Daughter-in-Law. We stopped at a charcoal maker's hut in Ŭnjin, Ch'ŭngch'ŏng province, for lunch. There, all of sudden, Mae began having great difficulty breathing normally. This turn of affairs was completely unexpected. Luckily, a physician named Anch'an happened to be traveling by and he treated Mae with some acupuncture. Mae calmed down for a while, but there was no way he could continue the journey on horseback. So I decided that Daughter-in-Law and I would share a palanquin while Mae, inside another, traveled ahead of us. We managed to arrive in Yesan, Ch'ungch'ŏng province, and stayed in the central area for six days. Each meal Mae had, however, gave him a bluish cast on his face as he tended to choke on food. We could not resume our journey like this.

On the other hand, we could not stay on the road for too long since our family's ancestral tablet was with us. So, I had my slaves Toson and Kamdŏkpi escort the tablet and proceed with the journey to Chido ahead of us. In the meantime, I took Mae and Daughter-in-Law to Chŏnju, Chŏlla province, and stayed there for a couple of months. I left the two of them behind and headed for Chido on the sixth day in the fourth month. Mae's father-in-law, Master Yi,[52] joined the couple and arrived at Chido about ten days later. I could not possibly record

---

[51] Not locatable, Ch'ogido is probably a place-name.
[52] Yi Hyŏnsu (李玄綏, dates unknown).

how worried my husband was in Chido upon hearing the news of Mae's illness. During and after my five-day journey from Chŏnju to Chido, I was busy making sure that our family slaves constantly reported to me and my husband on every little detail about Mae's illness, my own journey to Chido, and my husband's concerns.

Mae continued to suffer from illness in Chido. We tried every possible medicine, and for days and months we lived in constant worry.

In the sixth month of the *kyemi* year [1703], news reached us that my husband's brother and Mae's birth father, who had been exiled in Namhae, Chŏlla province, fell critically ill. Although Mae himself was ill, I sent him to Namhae in the midst of a spell of extreme sultry summer days despite my anxiety that he himself could be on the brink of life and death because of this trip. Can you imagine that? The news of illness in Namhae was soon replaced by the news of a death in the family; Brother-in-Law died. O, the frustration and sorrow that welled up inside me to hear that news.

His body had to be moved by water from Namhae to Sunch'ŏn, Chŏlla province, first, and then transferred by land all the way to the family burial mound in Ansan. I conducted his burial with the help of pallbearers. Heaven kept Mae's health strong throughout.

In the final month of that year, I suffered a stroke [動風症 *tongp'ŭngjŭng*], which kept me practically immobile until the first month of the following year. I took a great deal of medicine and survived yet again.

In the fourth month of that year, Mae and Daughter-in-Law went to Ansan for the first anniversary of Brother-in-Law's death, the death of Mae's birth father. Their trip to Ansan left no one but the two of us, my husband and me, in this place of his exile. Our slave Toson and Yu Myŏngsŏn[53] were with us, but Toson had to return home to take care of his ill father, and Yu Myŏngsŏn, too, left on the same day. Several other slaves also took off. My husband felt quite melancholy about all this, so I offered him some words of consolation.

But before our conversation was over, those that had left came back along with others. These other people were on their way to my husband with the news of his pardon! It turned out that my slaves chanced upon bearers of the news about an hour into their journey. O the relief! O the great fortune! Words would be insufficient if I were to record how I felt.

Soon we packed for a journey and set off to our family home in Koesan. In the midst of the dog days of summer, we arrived in Koesan on the third day in

---

[53] Note here that Lady Yi calls Yu Myŏngsŏn, Lady Yi's husband's half-brother and the illegitimate son (庶子 *sŏja*) of the family, by his name and surname only, while she addresses Yu Myŏnghyŏn using metonymic expressions like "the *p'ansŏ* family," with reference to his office, or "Namhae," his place of exile.

the sixth month. The house was empty, of course; none of our family members were there to welcome us back. Our slaves excitedly welcomed our return home, but I felt rather strange aching at the sight of no family members.

A couple of months later, Mae and Daughter-in-Law moved to where we were after their visit to Ansan.

That winter my husband began to develop dizziness and fatigue accompanied by occasional violent chills. I sensed ultimate misery was nigh.

In the middle of the following year, my husband all of a sudden began having diarrhea, and from that point on his condition approached the risk of death. Night and day I supplicated to the deities, praying that perhaps heaven would succor us and grant him the vigor of the young.

At long last, however, the sky fell and the earth sank. Everything around me turned ashen. O I should have ended my life then and there. That was the right thing to do. But reminded of the toil and trouble my parents went through raising me, I could not muster determination enough to do so. O how cowardice took hold of me and kept me alive. I thought to myself, "A three-year mourning will exhaust my naturally weak constitution and my body with its long history of illnesses!" To my utter disappointment, my life, though frail like a rough thread, carried on. I harbored regrets at my failure to end my life.

Bad karma I accumulated in my previous life must have done its deeds; in the third month of the *kyŏngsin* year [1710], my ever-robust daughter-in-law died suddenly like a moth consumed by a lamp's flames. Alas! Why didn't I end myself on the very day the sky collapsed and avoid this dismal affair? She died at such a tender age without leaving a trace of the union between man and woman. O I was overwhelmed with sadness.

Human life is filled with calamities. In the sixth month of that year, my stepdaughter—she was the youngest daughter born of my husband and his second wife and was married to Master Mok[54]—died immediately after she delivered a baby. When I married my husband and came to live with his family, she was just a five-year-old girl. I raised her till the day she married. Soon after her wedding, she gave birth to children one by one. Her husband, Master Mok, was so favorably talked of by people that I often thought that he would become a man of great achievements. The two also had a prodigy of a son, and their children, now all grown up, had been married already. Everything about Stepdaughter and her husband had brought nothing but joy to me. But the same year she departed this world, her son, while in mourning for his mother, also died. Could anyone possibly describe the brutality of it all?

---

[54] Mok Ch'ŏnim (睦天任, 1673–1730).

Stepdaughter gave birth to her youngest child on the fifteenth day of the sixth month and died only six days later. I heard that after my stepdaughter's death, her family placed her baby in the house's slaves' quarters. However, no one among the slaves was lactating. But how was I supposed to take the baby in and raise it? I feared that my ill fate would affect the baby adversely. But the situation over at my in-laws seemed just as desperate. And I thought to myself, "What difference would there be even if the baby dies?" After deliberating on the matter, I finally made up my mind and sent off a slave to bring the girl to our house, thinking to myself, "How on earth could this little thing continue its existence anyway?"

But as good fortune would have it, a slave who accompanied me as a maid at the time of my own wedding had just given birth to a baby of her own, so I had her nurse my step-grandchild. However, this slave fell ill and left for her hometown. With no means to nurse the baby, by day I stood by the main entrance of our house and begged strangers on the street to feed her; this went on for a month or so. By night I had her lie next to me, and when the poor thing cried, I put her in my bosom to calm her down. Only heaven knows how the baby survived. She is now seven years old, sturdy and bright; I feel so sorry for her fate. I hope she continues to live and enjoy a comfortable future so that all her childhood's misery is compensated. She has a number of relatives on her father's side, but they did not develop a particular affinity for her or do much with her. She, too, considered our house her home and did not seem to even realize the existence of her paternal relatives. What kind of a sad plight is that? O how I resent my ill fate that laid all possible wretchedness in my life's path.

Time flew like running water. When the ritual for the first anniversary for my deceased daughter-in-law was completed, I gathered myself from the woe and sorrow of sending her off and managed to select another bride for Mae.

A brief yet providential bond was to be made between the Yun family and ours.[55] We set a date for a wedding, and thus their daughter joined our family. Her disposition was like clear water, meek and peaceful, and she was graceful and flawless in her behavior while exceptional in her filial piety. She had a beautiful and small constitution. An impeccable lady she was. My heart was full of joy, thinking that this new joy would help me forget about the sad affairs of the past. I awaited the day I would revel in her filial piety.

But what wishful thinking all of that was! Bad karma I accumulated in my previous life overtook my life through and through. In just three years, Daughter-in-Law was reduced to terrible emaciation and departed this world. Before I

---

[55] A daughter of Yun Hwigye (尹彙啓, dates unknown).

knew it another three years had elapsed as we went through due mourning. My memory of her grew stronger as days went by.

Mae is now married for the third time.[56] He and his wife are praying for a son. I am delighted for them, but given my ill fate, I shouldn't build high hopes and should treat her like a stranger so as to keep her from growing on me. I hope Mae and Daughter-in-Law are blessed with the gift of sons and daughters and longevity—this is my only wish.

When I look back, all the things I went through seem like drifting clouds and the setting sun over the western hills. How many days are left for me in this world? I continue to immerse myself in tedious housework during the day, and when all the slaves have retreated to their residences in the evening, I become stricken with ever-growing and incessant melancholy. Yes, I have had parents, older and younger siblings, but who would have a clue where their spirits are now? O what crimes and punishments were I condemned to that my life has dragged on for sixty years? I deplore, lament, and resent.[57]

SP

---

[56] Yu Mae's third wife was a daughter of Sŏng Man'gyŏm (成萬謙, dates unknown).

[57] In the eighth month of this year (1754), Yu Mae and his wife gave birth to a son, Yu Kyŏngyong (柳慶容).

7. Palace Literature

7.1 ANONYMOUS, *DIARY OF THE KYECH'UK YEAR* (계축일기 *KYECH'UK ILGI*)

There are few more compelling periods in the royal court of the Chosŏn dynasty than the time of the reign of King Kwanghae (光海, r. 1608–1623). *Diary of the Kyech'uk Year*[1] is a fact-based firsthand account of the events surrounding Kwanghae's ascension to the throne in 1608 and systematic elimination of those who posed a threat to his somewhat tenuous status as a monarch. Told from the perspective of most likely a palace woman close to the queen of the late King Sŏnjo (宣祖, r. 1567–1608), this work paints a picture of a tyrannical monarch who seizes power and then sets about eradicating those nearest to the throne: in time Kwanghae murders both his elder brother and half-brother and deposes Sŏnjo's queen. The deposing of Queen Inmok (仁穆大妃, 1584–1632) by Kwanghae is one of the most fascinating episodes of the Chosŏn royal court, and this fact-based novel brings the characters, events, and turmoil to life. Making this Korean-script narrative even more noteworthy is that it is undoubtedly written by a woman, most likely a

---

[1] The *kyech'uk* (癸丑) year was 1613.

palace woman of this period who was at the side of Queen Inmok and witnessed the turmoil and tragic events of this time.

King Sŏnjo had thirteen sons—all born of concubines except for the youngest, Grand Prince Yŏngch'ang (永昌大君, 1606–1614). Kwanghae had been selected as crown prince as a result of his efforts during the Japanese invasions of 1592–1598, but with the birth of a legitimate son—that is, Yŏngch'ang—in 1606, Sŏnjo began to have a change of heart toward Kwanghae, for whom he had developed a distaste. However, before Sŏnjo could change his heir, he died, and Kwanghae immediately took power.

Once on the throne, Kwanghae was ruthless in securing his position. First, he had his elder brother, Prince Imhae (臨海君), murdered, and then deposed his stepmother, Queen Inmok, to exile in the Western Palace and had her father executed. Finally, he exiled his twelve-year-old half-brother, Yŏngch'ang, to Kanghwa Island (江華島) and subsequently had him also executed.

The *Diary* unfolds in 1602 with the pregnancy of Queen Inmok and the machinations of Yu Chasin (柳自新, 1533–1612), the father-in-law of Kwanghae, aimed at causing her to miscarry through various underhanded schemes. The novel continues to detail the subsequent actions of Kwanghae's faction and their manipulations to secure the throne. The narrative ends with the deposing of Kwanghae and the reinstatement of Inmok as queen grandmother in 1623. The writer of this work reveals the hardships experienced by Inmok and Yŏngch'ang, along with a close inspection of Kwanghae's character and his actions. Such details permit a general understanding that this work was written by a palace woman close to Inmok and with great insight into this riveting series of events.

In terms of literary value, the *Diary* is the first in the genre of court narratives written by women in the Chosŏn dynasty. Other works in this genre include *Record of Sorrowful Days* (閑中錄 *Hanjung-rok*) and *Tale of Queen Inhyŏn* (仁顯王后傳 *Inhyŏn wanghu-jŏn*), both written much later.[2] The *Diary* provides an excellent window into the workings of the royal court in the years directly after the catastrophic Japanese invasions, when factional politics dominated a country in dire need of rehabilitation. The language and style of this work are outstanding. This work also provides the modern reader insight into the culture of the palace that only women could truly experience—that is, statuses officially subordinate to males yet nonetheless both influential and tenuous. Thus we can expect the *Diary* to reveal a much different "history" of Kwanghae's reign than the official records of the period.[3]

---

[2]*Inhyŏn wanghu-jŏn* concerns the deposition of Queen Inhyŏn in 1689 and was probably written shortly after her death in 1701. *Hanjung-rok* is a record written by Lady Hong in four installments in 1795, 1801, 1802, and 1805.

[3]The official record is best represented by the dynastic record of Kwanghae's reign, *Kwanghae-gun ilgi* [光海君日記 Records of Prince Kwanghae]. Of course, this record was compiled by those who assisted in taking the throne from Kwanghae, so it is necessarily biased against

The *Diary* also brings to life the palace women of the Chosŏn period. Given the presumed authorship, the work carries much detail about the relationships of these women with each other and the royals that they served. While the lives of these women have sometimes been glamorized in television dramas, the *Diary* demonstrates that competition among these women could be quite fierce since their own fates were closely tied to particular members of the royal family. Exile or dethronement, then, was certainly not an individual matter but affected the lives of many.

We should also note that the work is a rich source for examining the daily customs of the royal palace in early seventeenth-century Korea and for understanding how people at the palace really lived. Rather than an idealized picture of life at the palace, the *Diary* reveals fine details such as the types of foods eaten and living arrangements for both royals and palace women. Such records of Chosŏn-period palace life are indeed few, and the *Diary* facilitates greater understanding of this historical aspect.

The following translated excerpt[4] covers the beginnings of the novel through 1611.

KC and MP

TRANSLATION

In the winter of the *imin* year [1602], Yu[5] heard that the queen[6] was showing signs of pregnancy and schemed to cause her to have a miscarriage. To scare her, he had someone throw stones into the palace, befriended those serving at the palace and had them bore a hole in the women attendants' privy to poke a stick through it, and started a rumor that brigands were attacking and burning houses here and there outside the palace. By this point, even the royal court was suspicious of Yu.

In the *kyemyo* year [1603] a princess was born.[7] The person who brought this special dispatch[8] delivered the message incorrectly, so Yu thought that a

---

Kwanghae. Moreover, it centers on Kwanghae's actions as a monarch, whereas the *Diary* cites flaws more closely related to his character and dislike of his stepmother and her relations. It is also tinged with the indignation of one who witnessed the deposing of the queen mother and the humiliations associated with such an official act.

[4]The primary text used for this translation is Chŏng Unim, ed., *Kyech'uk ilgi* (Seoul: Ihwa, 2005), occasionally supplemented with *Sŏgung ilgi* [서궁일기, The diary of the Western Palace] (Seoul: Minsog'wŏn, 1986), 1–18.

[5]This refers to Yu Chasin (柳自新, 1533–1612), the father-in-law of Prince Kwanghae.

[6]This is Queen Inmok.

[7]This was Princess Chŏngmyŏng (貞明公主, 1603–1685).

[8]The dispatch is the *kibyŏl* (奇別) that was compiled every morning by the Royal Secretariat (承政院 Sŭngjŏngwŏn) for the royal court with the important news of the day.

prince had been born and did not say a word. However, later on, when he heard that it was a princess and not a prince, he summoned the messenger and gave him a reward. One could see how Yu greatly detested the birth of a royal prince and also the queen.

In the *pyŏngo* year [1606] Yu heard that a prince had been born.[9] At his home and thinking that "as a legitimate son has been born, the position of crown prince is at stake," with a spiteful heart he wrapped his head. He cultivated a close relationship with the influential vassals at the palace of the crown price [i.e., Kwanghae] and with Chŏng Inhong[10] and said, "Without fail hold a *kut* and divine for the crown prince."[11]

They further started a rumor of, "Since the first son, Prince Imhae,[12] does not have a son, the king intends to make Imhae crown prince and abdicate the throne to Prince Yŏngch'ang through him."

They also fabricated a scandalous children's song to spread the rumor far and wide[13] and urged the king to petition the royal court of Ming China to approve the appointment of Kwanghae as crown prince.

Already in the *kapchin* year [1604] the king[14] had earnestly prepared a document to formally request that Kwanghae be designated crown prince and presented this to the Ming court. At that time, however, the Ming court was free of bribery, the government righteous, and the emperor strict, and the royal will of the emperor was boundlessly strict and rigorous as well. The Ming emperor[15] resolutely denied the petition: "As established by royal decorum, naming the second son as crown prince would cause the ruin of both family and country.[16] Since the laws of the royal Ming court extend to the four seas, we would not approve an exception for a single royal court."

---

[9] This is Prince Yŏngch'ang.

[10] Chŏng Inhong (鄭仁弘, 1535–1623) was a minister during the reign of Kwanghae and eventually served as chief state councillor (領議政 *yŏngŭijŏng*), the highest civilian post in the Chosŏn government.

[11] A *kut* is a shamanic ritual that can, among other functions, be used to supplicate the gods for good fortune for an individual.

[12] Prince Imhae was the eldest son of King Sŏnjo but is said to have had a violent temper and was thus passed over as crown prince in favor of Kwanghae. After Kwanghae took the throne, Imhae was exiled and forced to drink poison.

[13] The text informs that the song was titled "Sŏn-mokche Man-mokche" and concerned the succession to the throne. The content of the song is unknown.

[14] The king here is Sŏnjo.

[15] The Ming emperor referred to is Shenzong (神宗, r. 1572–1619).

[16] Succession to the throne followed very strict rules based upon primogeniture and legal status. The eldest son of the legal wife was first; in the case of there not being a son by the legal wife, then the eldest son of a secondary wife would take the throne. Kwanghae, being the second son of a secondary wife, would therefore not have been expected to ascend the throne.

After this, any proposal related to investing the crown prince presented to the Ming court was rebuked. Then, the government of Chosŏn feared that any petition to establish Kwanghae as crown prince might be disallowed in the future. Thus, the petitions ceased, and they waited for the minister of the Board of Rites and the prime minister [of Ming] to be changed.

However, Yu and his cronies said, "They do not propose to invest the crown prince because a legitimate son has been born," and eventually when[17] King Sŏnjo was ill, five ministers, including Chŏng Inhong and Yi Ich'ŏm,[18] presented memorials to the king, stating, "Please give us the head of Chief State Councilor [領議政 Yŏngŭijŏng] Yu Yŏnggyŏng[19] since he has not petitioned to name Kwanghae crown prince and rather supports Imhae."

They presented memorials to the king employing words of excessive abuse against his intent. He read the memorials in a state of great weakness because of his not eating or sleeping well after being ill for over a year.

"How could they do such things and repeatedly threaten the king?" asked a vexed and resentful Sŏnjo, and he did away with eating and sleeping altogether.

The king passed away only after issuing a royal command of, "Exile Inhong and the others." Not waiting a moment, the queen mother had the crown prince and his queen come into the king's sleeping chamber, gave them such important items as the *kyeja* seal, the royal seal, and the royal pass,[20] and sent them off right away. One royal concubine presented the will left to the crown prince and assembled courtiers and said, "Please present the last wishes of the king concerning the royal prince now."

The queen mother, while out of her senses with sadness, barely uttered, "It is improper to bring forth that now."

---

[17]The *Diary of the Western Palace* text offers more explanation here: "At that time, they knew there was the stipulation preventing the investiture of the crown prince because of Chief State Councillor Yu Yŏnggyŏng [柳永慶, 1550–1608]. After spreading word that Yu Yŏnggyŏng must have a different intention after he did not appeal to or entreat the king [on behalf of Kwanghae] when the king was feeling poorly in 1607, Yu Hŭibun enticed some six ministers, including Chŏng Inhong and Yi Ich'ŏm, to present memorials to the king [to execute Yu Yŏnggyŏng]."

[18]Yi Ich'ŏm (李爾瞻, 1560–1623) was an official during the reign of Kwanghae, eventually rising to minister (*p'ansŏ*) of the Board of Rites.

[19]At the end of Sŏnjo's reign, Yu Yŏnggyŏng advocated the designation of Prince Yŏngch'ang as crown prince instead of Kwanghae. Because of this position, when Kwanghae took the throne in 1608, Yu was forced to drink poison.

[20]*Kyeja* (啓字) refers to the king's seal of approval used on official documents and petitions. The royal seal (璽寶 *saebo*) was the king's official seal, and the royal pass (馬牌 *map'ae*) was the pass given to officials when they traveled to outlying areas that allowed them both safe passage and fresh horses at post stations throughout the country.

However, they insisted, citing a majority opinion, and showed it to the assembled courtiers first and darted off to the royal court.

In spite of all these circumstances, they found the queen mother at great fault for conveying the last orders [concerning Yŏngch'ang]. If the queen mother truly intended to designate the grand prince as crown prince, she could have done that while she held royal power in her hands—why, then, instead would she have immediately sent all the royal seals to the palace of the crown prince? Also in this last injunction [of Sŏnjo], it stated, "Do not believe or listen to those who would try to entrap the royal prince but, rather, adore him." What possibility was there to designate Yŏngch'ang [as crown prince or king], although she followed the king's last injunction?

In the tenth month of the *chŏngmi* year [1607],[21] when the king was on his sickbed, the queen mother immediately summoned the crown prince and crown princess and had them attend the king and serve him medicines. At that time, even if there was something offensive to the king because of their [the crown prince and his wife] dull-witted behaviors, since the queen covered it up and managed everything well, the crown prince and crown princess were pleased, saying, "The virtue of the queen is lofty and weighty!"

However, gradually in and out [of the court] there were those who tried to alienate them and schemed to eliminate Prince Imhae as a start. They were wicked and atrocious in this unrighteous work and at last incited memorials to lead a great disturbance; where else could such deceitful people exist?

In general, King Sŏnjo considered Kwanghae to be dull witted from when young but had abruptly decided upon him to be crown prince during the Imjin invasions.[22] Although the king often gave royal orders to admonish him and expected him to be penitent, he disobeyed these commands entirely and instead considered every detail of the royal orders to be the subject of a grudge. The king, considering him unrighteous, said, "How could the moral sense of a child toward his own parents be like this?"

Once, Kwanghae intended to take a niece of a royal concubine and make her his concubine before the mourning period for Queen Ŭiin[23] was over. However, the king would not allow this, saying, "You shall not do that; why are you trying to do something so unrighteous?"

---

[21] All dates in premodern Korea were based upon the lunar calendar. Thus, this is the tenth lunar month. All subsequent references to months of the year are lunar unless otherwise noted.

[22] The Imjin invasions (壬辰倭亂) are the Japanese invasions of Chosŏn from 1592 to 1598 led by Toyotomi Hideyoshi. The first invasion occurred in 1592, the year of *imjin*, and the second in 1597, the year of *chŏngyu*.

[23] Queen Ŭiin (懿仁, 1555–1600) was Sŏnjo's first queen.

Kwanghae held a deep grudge concerning this matter in his heart, and one day in the *pyŏngo* year [1606], when he brought about a great disaster to gain power and fulfill his great greed, he threatened the royal concubine in order to secretly take her niece, saying, "If you tell the king of this or do not give your niece to me, you and your family will be exterminated on a later day!"

He threatened her as such and eventually took her niece by force by sending a palace woman to take her; the king heard of this and became greatly angered, saying, "Long ago in our country when King T'aejong tried to depose the legitimate wife of his son, Sejong, because of her father's involvement in a conspiracy, Sejong said [unhesitatingly] that he would do as his father ordered.[24] Only after he asked the king, 'What about the eight princes?' did T'aejong reverse his order. How is one young woman so precious that he [Kwanghae] would deceive his father and take her? This is extremely heinous."

Since that time, the king considered him to be unsatisfactory.[25]

In general, from 1606 Kwanghae's determination to harm Prince Yŏngch'ang grew stronger, and he considered him as painful as a splinter in his eye or as distasteful as a stepchild. As Prince Yŏngch'ang grew older, every day Kwanghae conspired with Yu to raise a great conflict in order to be rid of him. It should have been pitiable and lamentable to see Prince Yŏngch'ang so ignorant of worldly matters, but without fail, Kwanghae was against him in matters small or great and extreme in his mistreatment of him.

Those who had not yet gone into exile, such as Chŏng Inhong, were summoned to the palace on the day the king passed away, and without any proper procedure, they were appointed to high official posts. Only fourteen days[26] after the king's death, Kwanghae had the offices of the Censor General and Inspector General[27] remonstrate regarding the guilt of Prince Imhae. Showing his own older brother, Prince Imhae, the documents indicating his guilt, Kwanghae told him, "If you leave the palace now, your crimes will be pardoned. However,

---

[24] T'aejong (太宗, r. 1400–1418) was the third king of Chosŏn. Sejong (世宗, r. 1418–1450) was his son and the fourth king of Chosŏn. Sejong's queen was Sohyŏn (昭憲, 1395–1446), the eldest daughter of Sim On (沈溫, 1375–1419). She bore Sejong eight sons and two daughters. Sim was executed for treason in 1419.

[25] *The Diary of the Western Palace* adds here, "But he nonetheless did not intend to depose him. However, there remained many who urged on the crown prince and princess with wicked words and eventually brought about resentment and villainous anger."

[26] The entries in the dynastic record describe these events as having taken place on the *sinmi* (辛未) day, the fourteenth day after Kwanghae had taken the throne. See *Records of Prince Kwanghae* [光海君日記 *Kwanghae-gun ilgi*], 1:22a–b (1608-02-14).

[27] The office of the Censor General (司諫院 Saganwŏn) and that of the Inspector General (司憲府 Sahŏnbu) were two of the most powerful investigative offices in the Chosŏn bureaucracy.

if you stay here, your guilt will be redoubled. Must I tell you even this? Leave the palace as soon as possible"

Yet at this same time he had the palace guard secretly surround his palace. As Prince Imhae was deceived by his brother's cunning and went out right away, the palace guard at once rushed and surrounded him, then tied him up, and subsequently detained him for a time at the Border Defense Council.[28] Ultimately, he was sent to Kyodong on Kanghwa Island and isolated within a thorn hedge.[29]

When Ming envoys came to Chosŏn to investigate the truth of Prince Imhae's illness, Kwanghae sent a cousin of his mother's, Kim Yejik, to Imhae and had him courteously coax Imhae, saying, "You will be allowed to live together with your wife and children only if you pretend to be totally paralytic. You will not escape from death if you do not act as told!"

Prince Imhae took this seriously and did as he was told. Directly after the Ming envoy returned to China, Kwanghae sent his trusted medical doctor and had Imhae poisoned with food.

At the time of Imhae's death, a petition to eliminate Prince Yŏngch'ang was presented as well. Yet the royal court disputed the propriety of this: "He is in swaddling clothes, and it would be difficult to do away with two brothers at once in this new reign."

Thus it is said they could not do away with Prince Yŏngch'ang.

Thrice daily Kwanghae pretended to inquire after the queen mother, but gradually he came to do this only every fifteen days, and even this was skipped when there was an excuse. And when he came to greet her, if the queen mother did not shun speaking of an old story, trends of the world, or family, he did not even try to listen or understand with respect, saying only, "Do as you please."

---

[28] The Border Defense Council (備邊司 Pibyŏnsa) was the agency charged with protecting the country in times of need.

[29] Kyodong is a township located on Kanghwa Island. Exile of political criminals was commonly to remote places such as Kanghwa or other islands since it created an even greater degree of isolation from those who might support them. The thorn hedge referred to in the text was yet another barrier and mark of the exile of a truly dangerous political criminal. The dynastic record, however, informs that Imhae was first exiled to Chindo Island off the southwestern coast of the peninsula. See *Records of Prince Kwanghae*, 1:23b (1608-02-14). Subsequently, after much discussion between Kwanghae and his ministers concerning the wisdom of exiling Imhae so far from the capital, he was transferred to Kyodong. See ibid., 1:39a (1608-02-20). Moreover, the thorn hedge referred to in the text seems a metaphoric usage as the dynastic records reveal that Imhae was to be under the guard of troops and a high stone wall was to be constructed around his place of exile. See ibid., 1:23b (1608-02-14).

When the queen mother brought up matters she wished to discuss with Kwanghae, he waved his hand in disgust and, not listening to her, abruptly got up and left. He visited the queen mother only after long intervals of time and got up to leave at the same time he sat down without staying for a moment. What pleasurable and harmonious words [between these two] could there possibly be?

Twenty-one days after the king passed away, Kwanghae visited the queen mother to pay his respects for the first time. Usually, when offering condolences even to a friend, it is proper to weep at the first meeting. However, hearing the queen mother lamenting and wailing, he ran into the room, waving his hand in disgust, and told those around him, "Have her not cry!"

So far from being sad or wailing, he was there stuttering without showing the slightest sign of sorrow; none of the affection of a son toward his parents could be seen. How could anyone be so indifferent to the grieving of relatives? He was indeed greatly inhumane.

When composing the posthumous title[30] for the late king, the queen mother [speaking on behalf of Sŏnjo] told Kwanghae, "Not even mentioning the merit of restoring the country after the Imjin invasions but also to vanquish the embarrassment of past kings by correcting the mistaken record concerning the founder, T'aejo—how could his merit be any less than that of the founder [of the dynasty]?[31] Please do not consider this ordinary and reflect on this before selecting his posthumous title."

After thinking about this for a long time, Kwanghae replied, "Even if he was meritorious, the royal ancestors were not comfortable during the Imjin invasions; so how can we say there was merit? This is not something worthy of discussion again."

---

[30] Commonly the new king would bestow upon his predecessor a posthumous temple name (廟號 myoho).

[31] After the founding of Chosŏn various documents were sent to the Ming court to obtain approval for the new dynasty. In one document the name of Yi Sŏnggye's father was written incorrectly as Yi Inim (李仁任, d. 1388) rather than the correct Yi Chach'un (李子春). This mistake, first discovered by the Chosŏn court in 1394, had long been something that the monarchs of Chosŏn had tried to rectify but were unable to do so. The problem, known as *chonggye pyŏnmu* (宗系辨誣, rectifying errors in the royal genealogy), was exacerbated by the Ming refusal to alter its dynastic records. However, in Sŏnjo's reign an envoy, Hwang Chŏng'uk (黃廷彧, 1532–1607), was able to convince the Ming to change its records in the fifth month of 1587; finally in 1588 a corrected version of the *Collected Legal Codes of the Ming* [大明會典 *Daming huidian*] was brought back to the Chosŏn capital. See *The Veritable Records of King Sŏnjo* [宣祖實錄 *Sŏnjo sillok*], 18:8a (1589-11-01).

The queen mother tried to consult with him many times in order to have him realize the importance of this matter. However, he did not listen to her and said, "Using the suffix *chong* is not lowly [as it was used for most kings]."[32]

Here, his lack of filial piety can be known.

From ancient times, decorum dictated that the wife of a deceased king would visit the royal tomb to pay respects during the mourning period.[33] When the queen mother said to him, "I want to go there," Kwanghae replied, "It is not allowed to go there; if you wish to go there so badly, do so on the first anniversary of the death."[34]

After waiting for a year with difficulty, she again said, "I want to go there."

Kwanghae, again finding fault, retorted, "Since the entire court opposes that, it is not proper for you to go; why don't you go perhaps on the second anniversary of the death?"[35]

On the second anniversary of Sŏnjo's death, he said, "Since it [i.e., the mourning period] has all passed, what benefit would be gained by going now? It was not that decorous for the queen mothers of the past to go there either. It would only be troublesome, so I adamantly refuse to allow you to go."

For three years, she earnestly pleaded but could not go. She devotedly coaxed the king but could not go; there could be nothing more pitiful than this.

By this time the queen mother said, "I at least wish to go to the shrine where his ancestral tablet is enshrined."

However, even that was stopped many times; finally the queen mother pleaded from her heart deeply and asked the queen [the wife of Kwanghae]. The queen replied, "Originally, the king lacks flexibility in his nature. I will do my utmost and try to gain permission for you to go."

The permission was finally issued only after the queen so ordered.

---

[32] Kings in the Chosŏn dynasty were given various posthumous names, including the aforementioned *myoho*. The *myoho* was of two syllables, the second of which was generally *chong* (also transliterated as *jong*, 宗), which meant "king of virtue." This could be elevated to *cho* (also written *jo*, 祖) for kings who had performed great feats, had not come peacefully to the throne, or had lived through great wars. See Keith Pratt and Richard Rutt, *Korea: A Historical and Cultural Dictionary* (Richmond, Surrey, U.K.: Curzon, 1999), 307–8. The gist of the exchange between Kwanghae and the queen mother was that he did not feel that his father was worthy of the higher title.

[33] Mourning periods varied depending upon both who had died and the relationship of the mourner to the deceased. The mourning period for a king was three years.

[34] *Sosang* (小祥) is the first anniversary of a person's death.

[35] *Taesang* (大祥) is the second anniversary of a person's death.

As a date to visit the shrine was hastily selected, the queen sent a palace woman to Yu Hŭibun[36] and had him postpone the visit. However, already in our palace, all the food for the ritual service had been hurriedly prepared. The queen treated this as ordinary and did not intend to hold the rites. As it suddenly came to her mind and she intended to do it only at last, she did not care that it would cause trouble for others. For any major task people might consider only their own convenience and not that of others, but to this extent? To whom can it even be spoken that this was embarrassing? Because of a postponement of many days after all the food had been prepared, all the preparations were thrown out, and everything was newly prepared again in our palace.

If Kwanghae happened to have a meal together with the prince and princess at the inner palace, he treated the princess well but shunned the prince.[37] He also said things like, "I dislike hearing the voice of the prince when I go to inquire after the queen mother."

One day, as the prince pleaded, "I wish to see my elder brother at the royal palace," the queen mother had the prince and princess shown in and seated when Kwanghae came to pay his respects to her. Kwanghae told the princess to come near and patted her, saying, "She is very sagacious and lovely."

But to the prince he did not say a word and pretended not to have seen him. As the prince felt ill at ease, the queen mother said, "Why don't you too go forward to him?"

The prince got up to go forward and stood in front of Kwanghae. However, since Kwanghae pretended as if he did not see him, the prince went out, crying, "My big brother the king was loving to my sister but pretended not to even see me; why wasn't I born a girl like my sister, why am I a boy?"

He cried and cried all day, which was pitiful to even gaze upon.

Kwanghae always said, "When I am here, I am not afraid of anything even if there were ten royal princes. However, the grand prince is a nephew to the crown prince, and even in the royal court of past times there was a king who took the throne after harming his nephew.[38] I worry this might happen. I will certainly

---

[36]Yu Hŭibun (柳希奮, 1564–1623) was the eldest son of Yu Chasin and brother of Kwanghae's queen.

[37]The prince and princess here are Yŏngch'ang and Chŏngmyŏng, Kwanghae's half-siblings.

[38]The grand prince (大君 taegun) is Yŏngch'ang, and the crown prince refers to Kwanghae's son. The most famous incident in which a nephew was deposed by an uncle is that of Sejo (世祖, r. 1455–1468) usurping his nephew Tanjong (端宗, r. 1452–1455) in 1455.

get rid of the Grand Prince [Yŏngch'ang] and allow the crown prince [Kwanghae's son] to live peacefully."

He said this, and as the crown prince heard this, he hated Yŏngch'ang as if he were something terrifying to even look upon.

Three months after King Sŏnjo passed away, Kwanghae could not eat his meals well. When the queen mother presented a meat dish to him, he ate it only after she offered it twice. When she brought beef porridge, he ate some of it and put the rest away, requesting of the palace woman, "This porridge is best. Put it away cold, and then give it to me later."

The palace woman sneered at this, saying, "Originally he does not have even one meal a day without meat dishes. However [since Sŏnjo's death] he has been eating meals only with vegetable dishes for three or four months in the summer season, which is quite an effort for him. As the queen mother offered [a meat dish], he was so grateful that he ate it. Yet even then, since the queen mother was present, he ordered it to be kept and served to him later."

People who heard this considered him pitiful and laughed.

In the tenth month of 1607, as King Sŏnjo was sick in bed, Crown Prince Kwanghae went to the king's residence to attend to him. However, he could not solemnly stay put, and instead went to the administrative palace and sat on a metal chair.

On a later day after Sŏnjo had passed away, he complained, "How can I forget that winter day when I was sitting in that cold place even if I die?"

Not even once a month did he pay respects at the royal mortuary [where Sonjo's corpse was kept].[39] He had no grief in his heart at all, so laughter could be heard during the mourning period like any other day. He merely pretended as if he reduced the number of dishes in his meals and also pretended to suppress his laughter by covering his mouth. However, he could not control himself and laughed so hard, it was said to be quite embarrassing for those looking on.

When the queen mother visited the royal mortuary, her wailing did not cease. Kwanghae asked, "Where is that wailing sound coming from?"

A eunuch replied, "The queen mother is crying."

"Why is she crying like that? He was old and lived his life. It is funny for her to be so sorrowful. Do people live forever? I dislike hearing it."

---

[39]The royal mortuary was where the body of the king was kept until burial.

Hearing his words, those to the left and right found him absurd, and some quietly laughed.

Kwanghae was so poor at managing government affairs that he could not even decide upon one page of work alone. He had his queen stay in a detached hall nearby the court and decided government affairs only after consulting with her day and night.[40] If ever the queen went to the royal tomb or out of the detached hall, he could not manage his duties of governance to such an extent that he would sit alone, unable to keep his hands off the scrolls, papers, or even a knife. He would cut paper into small pieces before again putting them back together. He also held an unsheathed knife beside him, muttering to himself at times. Since he yelled at and scolded any of his eunuchs if they spoke to him, they could not stay near him and just worried outside the court, only looking up at the sky. Once, an old eunuch [who had served the court] since the time of King Myŏngjong[41] boldly went in and asked him, "With what matter are you so upset? You have already gotten rid of your elder brother through listening to others. The work you have now is not that difficult either. It has been long since you learned to read and write, and wisdom stems from writings.[42] Your Majesty is a son of the late king, the house you are in now is also that of the late king, and even the papers, brushes, and ink are all the possessions of the late king. Not being able to manage this much work yourself and sitting quietly without anyone around you—what are you doing with that paper and knife?"

Hearing this, Kwanghae might have been ashamed and did not say a word. As these words continued to spread, Kwanghae began to hate this eunuch and eventually had him killed in 1614 during the turmoil surrounding Prince Yŏngch'ang's death.

Kwanghae modified his orders ten times for a single task when ordering his eunuchs and changed his words ten times for one errand. He did not know when to give reward for good work or to punish bad. Many times his father-in-law was embarrassed and constantly tried to teach him saying, "Now, Minister So-and-so is about to present a memorial, so answer this way, and Minister So-and-so is going to present a report to you, so please give him an answer in this way then."

---

[40] The text refers to the *ingnang-bang* (翼廊房), detached halls to either side of the royal court.
[41] Myŏngjong (明宗) was the thirteenth king of Chosŏn and reigned from 1545 to 1567.
[42] While the eunuch states that it had been long since the king had learned letters (글 *kŭl*), he seems to be indicating that the king had not studied for long.

Oftentimes baskets were carried in and out [of Kwanghae's chamber] with notes written in Literary Chinese or even the vulgar script,[43] and for times when the palace gate was closed, a hole was made in the palace wall near a toilet shed—which was so huge that it was covered from the inside to prevent people from openly seeing it from outside—for a messenger to go in and out by the back mountain. This was such a frequent happening that a hut was built for a servant to secretly live just outside the palace wall, and at night Kwanghae could get answers by contacting Yu via that servant.

Baskets tied with strings and others wrapped with cloth rattled around Kwanghae's sleeping chamber. There was a palace woman charged with going to Yu's house to get answers for court matters. As Kwanghae so often dispatched her with notes concerning every issue, she did not even have time to take her meals. Distressed and annoyed and kicking the baskets on the floor, she grumbled to herself in her grief, "Some man! He cannot even manage this much work and always must ask another. This chamber is just full of baskets!"

Kwanghae heard this and banished her, claiming that she was sent off because she never stayed put near the sleeping chamber.

His personality was inherently cruel. He behaved in ways that had never been seen or heard of before. He beat people with fat sticks,[44] whips, or even with heated irons, and thus cries of pain could be heard from afar as could cries of, "Your Highness the Queen, please save me!"

From early on, the queen mother used daily necessities[45] only as needed. One day Kwanghae ordered, "Give only a portion of honey to the queen mother."[46]

The supervising eunuch,[47] one Yi Pongjŏng, retorted, "Shall I set a price on my own accord and then give it to her? I will give it to her when she needs it."

Kwanghae could not respond to his words. Another time Kwanghae ordered, "First inform me what the queen mother requests before you provide it to her."

Since that time, it became regular to report to Kwanghae before anything was provided to the queen mother.

---

[43] That is, the Korean script *han'gŭl*. The writer is perhaps implying that Kwanghae was not even intelligent enough to communicate in the written language of the royal court (Literary Chinese) but had to resort instead to *han'gŭl*, generally the domain of the uneducated and women.

[44] The text reads that he beat people with a *kidung*, or "a pillar." However, the term can also indicate a stout piece of wood.

[45] Such necessities would include rice, cloth, and other items of daily use.

[46] *Amumanŭl* (아무만을) indicates a certain portion, but the amount is not ascertainable.

[47] This is the *ch'aji naegwan* (次知內官), the eunuch charged with overseeing a particular area of the palace.

As all materials and goods were moved from the administrative palace to elsewhere, one servant said, "This is being done to prevent the queen mother from using these things."

Another said, "If ever any sort of disaster arose, he [i.e., Kwanghae] would later go there to live."

Kwanghae named this Ihyŏn Palace [48] and moved and accumulated all sorts of goods there.

Early in the *musin* year [1608],[49] Kwanghae feigned that he respected the queen mother to the utmost, saying, "What I deem dear is you, Queen Mother, so please let me know whatever you want."

Hearing this, the queen mother was touched and appreciative. She treated the crown prince like her own son and daily taught him how Sŏnjo managed the administration of the country, all the while wishing that he would be a benevolent king as well.[50]

The crown prince was clever, so the queen mother adored him all the more, giving him things useful for a young boy every time he went to inquire after her. The crown prince's nanny,[51] Okhwan, greatly appreciated the virtue of the queen mother, rubbing her hands together while saying, "What would we possibly have if not for the queen mother? With her virtue as lofty as the heavens, she grants something every time the crown prince visits."

She also said such things as, "Who does his father take after, never giving him even a piece of scrap paper?[52] He is so stubborn that he never listens to his servants. Would an ox pulling a carriage be that rigid? Although he is a son of the late king, does he even resemble the crap the late king defecated? When he craps, he sits there from the morning until the seventh watch on winter days,[53]

---

[48] The Ihyŏn-gung (梨峴宮) was built per Kwanghae's orders and renamed several times in subsequent reigns. Today's appellation for the palace is Kyŏnghŭi-gung (慶熙宮), given in 1760 during the reign of Yŏngjo (英祖, r. 1724–1776).

[49] The *musin* year but after the death of Sŏnjo.

[50] The *Diary* is not particularly clear here, and so we have conflated the text with that from *The Diary of the Western Palace*.

[51] This is a palace woman who held the position of *pomo sanggung* (保姆尙宮). Such palace women were charged with the rearing of the royal children, with one palace woman assigned to each of the royal children. See Kim Yongsuk, *Chosŏnjo kungjung p'ungsok yŏn'gu* [A study of the palace customs in the Chosŏn dynasty] (Seoul: Iljisa, 1987), 21.

[52] Here the text refers to *sukpaeji*, which seems to be paper upon which morning and evening inquiries were written. Not being a formal document, the paper on which these notes were written was probably subsequently washed and reused.

[53] Time was reckoned in twelve watches in premodern Korea. *Osi* (午時) is the seventh watch, spanning 11:00 a.m. to 1:00 p.m.

and when he has to go on an inquiry visit, he goes to the privy two or three times additionally and thus does not make the inquiry visit until after the tenth watch.[54] Where else could such a deplorable situation exist?"

She also said, "When he does something, he assumes he gave us orders, yet he does not, and he frequently and easily deceives us. He never listens to anything again that he has heard once. He is no more than that carriage-pulling ox."

Upon hearing this, everyone responded, "How could you speak such words?"

The palace woman replied, "He is like an ox, why wouldn't I say he is like an ox?"

In the beginning, Kwanghae seemed to have listened to others without much trouble and also appeared wise, but gradually his abuses became severe. Between 1610 and 1611 his rudeness and disrespectfulness became all the worse.

Gradually he had a palace woman by the name of Kahi[55] stay close with him and paid no attention to his queen. However, when he had to decide something for the court, he summoned the queen and bade her to do it. When the queen became very displeased and angry and would not go there, Kwanghae went to her in person to bring her, or he went to her quarters to ask. One day the queen said, "Can you not manage this much work alone? From now on, do not ask me."

As Kwanghae suspected Grand Prince Yŏngch'ang in every possible way, he made himself seem fearsome: He ate a lot of raw meat after only touching the meat with a bit of flame and thin rice porridge. He enjoyed eating raw meat to such an extent that his eyes became increasingly red. He refused to eat mountain vegetables, claiming they were dirty, and ate only meat, steamed flounder, and thin taffy.[56]

His behavior was odd and different from that of others. He did not do what others told him to do and did do what others told him not to do. Since he was extremely wicked of mind and not sincere in his words, his manner followed the models of King Jie and King Zhou, and his behavior was worse than that of Yangdi.[57]

---

[54] The text reads *yuksŏk*, which seems to be a combination of *yusi* (酉時, tenth watch, 5:00 p.m.–7:00 p.m.) and *sŏk* (夕, evening). Thus, it is appropriate to read this as the tenth watch. See Chŏng Ŭnim, *Kyech'uk ilgi* [Diary of the *kyech'uk* year] (Seoul: Ihoe, 2005), 46.

[55] Her rank is given as *sanggung* (尚宮) in the text. This was a senior fifth-rank official position (正五品 *chŏng o p'um*), the highest post a palace woman could achieve.

[56] "Thin taffy" refers to *mulgŭn yŏt*, a confection made from wheat gluten and flavored with various other ingredients.

[57] King Jie (桀王) was a king of the Chinese Xia kingdom (夏, ca. 2000–1500 B.C.E.), and King Zhou (紂王) was king during the Yin kingdom (殷); from ancient times these two monarchs have

The queen mother feared him day and night and worried that he might forsake the preceding kings in later days. Surely he brought about a calamity.

Early in 1608 Kwanghae pretended as if he were most generous and asked the palace women for the royal bedroom to attend and to take care of the queen mother well and comfortably, saying, "The queen mother lives comfortably thanks to you people. How could she be in peace without your caring attendance?"

He praised and rewarded the head palace woman of the queen mother's bedchamber[58] every time she visited him, but beginning in 1611 he gradually paid no attention and, even worse, feigned not to see her. When she came to see him, he had her stand outside until the day turned dark; even after that he did not receive her but said, "I cannot see her because of other work, so tell her to leave."

One aged palace woman informed him that when a palace woman of the late queen mother visited the late king, he would let the palace woman come into his bedroom even when he was combing and holding his hair, or when he was washing his face, and ask her about the queen mother. Rebuking the aged palace woman, Kwanghae said, "I cannot stand doing it. I go to inquire after the queen mother twice a month in person—for what reason should I see her attendants additionally? I will do as I want to; shall I model myself after the late king even in that sort of thing? I will act by my own principles, so do not utter a word about that again."

Hearing this, the people around him were speechless.

When Kwanghae went to pay his respects at the royal graves for the first time, the old ministers wanted to wail from the village entrance but withheld their cries with difficulty thinking that they could cry to their hearts' content when Kwanghae began to cry. Thus, they anxiously waited for the moment of his cries. However, he went up to the royal graves and was slowly coming down without any crying. During that time, someone must have instructed him about this, so Kwanghae asked the [minister of] the Board of Rites only after he came down, "Shall I cry or not?"

---

been considered representative of ruthless and evil monarchs. Yangdi (煬帝, 604–617) was the second emperor of the Sui dynasty (隋, 581–617 C.E.) and is known for his licentious lifestyle and also for the failed invasions of the Koguryŏ kingdom (高句麗, 37 B.C.E.–668 C.E.). He further caused the death of millions of workers in constructing the Grand Canal and reconstructing the Great Wall. His misgovernance is cited by many as the reason for the short span of the Sui dynasty.

[58] This is the *ch'imsil sanggung*, the palace woman charged with personally overseeing all matters of a given royal.

The minister answered, "It is proper to cry."

Thus, Kwanghae cried only on the way back. Yu heard the sounds and said, "Since I wept loudly as if to lose my senses, he might think wrong of me for crying excessively."

Like this, Kwanghae did not have filialness in his innate character and was extremely stubborn and dull witted; how could anyone expect him to be an exemplar [in his piety] toward us [i.e., the palace of the queen mother]?

The queen never went to inquire after the queen mother during the mourning period; the queen mother assumed that she would come after the first anniversary of the late king's death. However, even a year after the funeral, she did not even show her face and instead created all sorts of internal disturbances.

In 1611 while the queen mother was at the new palace[59] and sightseeing in the rear garden, the queen said, "I can never stand behind the queen mother since I am older and she is younger. While I stay for a moment with an excuse, attend the queen mother and lead her out first."

Closely observing her many times, sure enough, she never attended the queen mother from behind.[60]

On that day when the queen mother was returning, one of her palanquin bearers fell down and the palanquin tilted sharply to the side. Although the queen mother nearly fell out of the palanquin, the queen, who heard of this, did not even ask after her and instead went to her palace directly. Elderly palace women who had seen how Queen Ŭiin attended Queen Insun saw this and were dumbfounded.[61] The queen heard of this and looked for a chance on a later day to get even with them for this grudge.

KC and MP

---

[59] The new palace is Ch'angdŏk-kung (昌德宮). It was built in 1405 but destroyed during the Japanese invasions of 1592. It was subsequently rebuilt under the order of Kwanghae in 1611.

[60] The conflict here is one of social position. Since the queen mother was the queen of Sŏnjo, the queen of Kwanghae would have been expected to treat her as a parent, notwithstanding the queen mother's being younger than the queen. So the conflict was one of the queen's not wanting to humble herself or give deference to a younger woman despite her higher social position.

[61] Queen Ŭiin was the aforementioned first queen of Sŏnjo, and Queen Insun (仁順王后, 1532–1575) was the queen of King Myŏngjong (r. 1545–1567) and mother of Sŏnjo.

PART III

Oral Tradition

A kite is hanging, a kite is hanging,
caught in a juniper tree.
Gentlemen of Samch'ŏngdong, would you free it?
            (Anonymous)

My love is fair as the flower, firm as the fruit,
many as the branches, deep as the roots.
Alas, I miss him but can't see him,
What could be the matter?
            (Anonymous)

My heart is the blue hill, your heart the green river.
The river flows, but would the hill move?
Perhaps the river, too, is still aching
as it wraps itself around the hill in parting.
            (Lyric credited to Hwang Chini)[1]

---

[1] These verses, including the one credited to Hwang Chini (黃眞伊, 1506?–1567?), have been sung in different tempos in the southwestern oral lyrical repertoire called *yukchabaegi* (slow six

What national or ethnic ethos does an oral tradition reveal, and in what form or style? How much of the indigenous narrative or lyrical consciousness could be communicated or lost in translation? In the entire premodern Korean poetic canon, female authorships are few and far between outside the iconic Hwang Chini, and their poetic prowess has been delivered to modern times as "songs." Are the verses, largely excluded in Korea's literary mainstream for their association with professional female singers formerly known as *kisaeng*, less poetic than "poetry"? This chapter on oral tradition builds on the conviction that the orally transmitted materials hold invaluable textual merits for appreciating premodern Korean literary and performative sensibilities.

By "oral tradition," we mean works that were created and transmitted through word of mouth and presented verbally. In premodern Korea, where literacy, especially in *hanmun*, or "Chinese writing," was a hallmark of social privilege, oral tradition, along with the lesser writing, *han'gŭl*, voiced broader bases of folk literary sentiments. As we can imagine, the domains of writing and orality at times merged to allow the exchange of knowledge and art to take place. Still, under the conventional definition of literature built around written or published text, orally transmitted materials continued to be categorically marginalized. An attempt to rise above the center versus margin and written versus spoken or sung division, this section on the Korean oral tradition presents three translated excerpts from the P'ansori Obat'ang, the canonical "Five Narratives": *Song of Hŭngbo, Song of Sim Ch'ŏng*, and *Song of Ch'unhyang*. In his *Korean Singer of Tales* (University of Hawai`i Press, 1994), Marshall R. Pihl includes a translation of the Wanp'an[2] text of *Song of Sim Ch'ŏng* in its entirety, along with a list and description of the extant texts of the narrative of Sim Ch'ŏng. The Wanp'an texts are "not only the lengthiest written sources but also are stylistically the closest to the oral tradition"[3] of Kangsanje,[4] or "River and Mountain" style. The current translation supplements his textual research with a sung version of the River

---

syllable). The triple-measure six-beat rhythmic pattern in *yukchabaegi* and the six-beat *chinyang* rhythmic pattern in *p'ansori* singing are of the same origin.

[2] Woodblock prints are mostly of novels produced in the area of Chŏnju of North Chŏlla during the later Chosŏn dynasty.

[3] Marshall R. Pihl, *The Korean Singer of Tales* (Honolulu: University of Hawai`i Press, 1994), 116.

[4] According to the past and present heirs of the school, Kangsanje is a metaphoric name given by the regent Taewŏn'gun (大院君, 1820–1898) to his cherished singer Pak Yujŏn (1835–1906) for his exceptional vocal prowess, because "you [Pak] are the true river and mountain!" In Posŏng, South Chŏlla, Pak later transmitted his narrative style to Chŏng Chaegŭn, Chaegŭn to his nephew Ŭngmin, and Ŭngmin to his son Kwŏnjin. The lineage came to be known as the Kangsanje Posŏng school. Cho Sanghyŏn, Sŏng Ch'angsun, and Chŏng Hoesŏk are three of the most renowned singers who have inherited the style and are active today. I studied under Chŏng

and Mountain style, as learned word for word by this translator from the late Chŏng Kwŏnjin, heir of the River and Mountain style. So where does the sung text differ from the various editions? The sung text is artistically mediated by the singer's moment-by-moment cognitive consciousness in handling the rhythm, melodic contours, and interpretation of the text. The ultimate goal of translating a sung text is to impress within the inner consciousness of Korean literature a performative dimension of Korean narrativity involving musical storytelling. Abundant with conventional grooves and material and immaterial referentialities of the times the characters lived, every song in *p'ansori* is a treasure trove of narrative, dramatic, and poetic specimens defining premodern Korean literary culture. *P'ansori* is an oral tradition musically enhanced.

A congenitally interdisciplinary subject, *p'ansori* narrative offers a rich generational accumulation of the poetic and narrative imaginations of Koreans of the past. Until a century ago, the long-held Confucian social hierarchy as a rule blocked sharing of what they considered "literacy" beyond the elite families of the *sadaebu* (士大夫) social status. Insulated within a neo-Confucian sociopolitical system, only the legitimate male heirs of aristocratic households were allowed access to literary scholarship requiring fluency in Literary Chinese. No human system is impermeable, and the rigorous control of scholarship suffered its share of leakages. In the course of several hundred years, many, including women, came to partake in literacy in varying degrees. Still, literature as an artistic exercise was being guarded and exploited as an esoteric means to ensure inaccessibility of privilege. Limiting access translates to limiting vision. The philologist-king Sejong's fifteenth-century promulgation of phonetic *han'gŭl* allowed wider exposure to literary communication, but Korean intellectuals resisted democratization of access until the turn of the twentieth century, when their privileged seat of power collapsed along with the loss of independence. As the Korean saying goes, "If you don't have teeth, you live with your gums"; outside the exclusive chronology and organization of privilege, oral tradition rhizomatically and nomadically sustained folk literary life.[5]

Here, we ask another theoretical question: what is folk literature and its relationship with social change, and how does *p'ansori* fare in this regard? Referred to also as folklore or oral tradition and constructed on the knowledge and

---

Kwŏnjin from 1976 until his passing in 1986. The selected texts given here in translation are taken from Chŏng Kwŏnjin's versions.

[5] In describing the emergence and transmission of the oral tradition, I borrow the philosophical conceptualization of the nomadic pattern of growth of the botanical rhizome from Gilles Deleuze and Félix Guattari, A *Thousand Plateaus: Capitalism and Schizophrenia*, trans. Brian Massumi (London: Continuum, 2004). Unlike the monolithic centricity of written literature by a privileged few, oral tradition can be viewed as a rhizomatic multiple emergence.

beliefs accumulated over generations ("lore"), folk literature is often characterized by its nature of text and transmission: it is handed down orally, and its text is a flexible combination of prose, verse, songs, drama, and storytelling, and its storytelling freely crosses human and mystical realms. *P'ansori* fits the definition, except its identity seemingly shifted from a village marketplace serendipity three centuries ago to today's celebrated national and world oral heritage, thus creating a double vision. Literature, regardless of its being oral or written, cannot be frozen in a finished time zone but absorbs and survives the pressures of changing realities, with its roots and genetic traits largely intact. Generations of creative minds and talents accumulated not only poems and stories but also conventions of their artistic deliverance of *p'ansori*, tastefully garnished with regional indigenous folk consciousness and grassroots worldviews. Tied to no written or published text open to scrutiny or censorship for most of its formative years, this oral tradition perpetuated by the singing of the *kwangdae* of the lowest social strata came to harbor a treasure house of cultural signifiers and literary expressions of high, low, center, and margin.

In the labor and leisure of preindustrial Korea, singing developed as a poetic outlet. Songs accompanied fishermen at sea, farmers in the field, workers at building sites, and vendors in marketplaces. Women, whose lives were a series of never-ending domestic labor and prayers for familial well-being, were particularly passionate singers. Throughout the twentieth century, these songs rapidly lost their existential rationales, as postwar Korea headed toward heavy industrialization that required machinery, not the human voice, to amplify productivity. Leisure, too, once a largely communal activity participated in by community members themselves, turned "professional," packaged for capitalist consumption. The songs were thus erased from the Korean consciousness, to be partially reclaimed and reinvented through the practitioners of *kugak*, or "national music."

As oral communication became sidelined by advancing modernity, singers, in emulating the voices of their predecessors, resorted to writing as visual and recording technology as hearing aids. Acquisition of the deeper artistry of singing continues to be left to the traditional oral style of transmission and acquisition. The persistent adherence to orality in its transmission in singing continues: while the narrative is written down by the practitioners in acquisition, when it comes to learning how to sing the songs, practitioners, even the ones fluent in the sheet music notational system, set it aside to give their ears full authority of hearing and registering.

Folk songs and ritual music had served as key inspiration for many of the salient genres and repertoires of the Korean performative tradition currently preserved as Korea's intangible cultural asset. From the beginning of twentieth century, Korean performative culture encountered a powerful influx of Western forms and concepts. They effected major transformations in native practices, including the Korean oral tradition. Labor-related performances from work sites, outdoor plays, and in *kisaeng* houses were reframed for the modern stage mise-en-scène and into "genres." Inheriting the liberating expressiveness of the folk and ritual narrative singing of the southwestern regions, *p'ansori* narratives developed as an intriguing chanted epic-novel amalgam. Starting in the early 1960s, prominent styles and singers of *p'ansori* gained the designation of Korean intangible cultural assets. In the field of Korean literature, the narratives of *p'ansori* came to occupy a central position in Korean oral literature (口碑文學 *kubi munhak*). In 2003, *p'ansori* singing was recognized by UNESCO as a Masterpiece of the Oral and Intangible World Heritage of Humanity. The questions singers, preservationists, and researchers of *p'ansori* today ask should include how this artistic heritage can be a meaningful practice for Korea and the world.

P'ansori performance was discovered in the mid-eighteenth century in a southwestern provincial marketplace. The oldest written text about the art is *The Two Hundred Lines of the Song of Ch'unhyang* (가사 춘향가 이백구 *Kasa Ch'unhyang-ga ibaekku*), included in the *Literary Collection of Manhwa* (晚華集 *Manhwajip*, 1754), written by Yu Chinhan (柳振漢, 1711–1791).[6] "In *Record of Family Experiences* [*Kajŏng mun'gyŏn nok*], Yu's son relates how his father experienced the regional culture and arts while stationed in the Chŏlla provinces and then returned home to reconstruct in writing, in 1754, 'The Song of Ch'unhyang' with mature plot development and detailed action. For recording a literary version of an oral narrative so 'prurient,' his son continues, Yu 'became the target of slander among his scholarly contemporaries.'"[7]

If the twenty-eight-hundred-character poem capturing the plot and highlights of the love, separation, and reunion of one of the most famous females in Korean fiction ushered *p'ansori* narrative into the domain of print, the art of its deliverance has persisted in the culture of orality as the primary medium. Every learner today has access to writing, printing, and recording technology. They write lines given orally by their teacher in a notebook, use printed texts for learning, and recording for the actual lessons. Nonetheless, the heart of *sori* stoically stays within the parameters of *kusim-jŏnsu*, or "pass down from mouth to mouth." Sin Wi (1769–1847), in *Kwan'gŭk chŏlgu sibi-su* (Twelve seven-character quatrains on viewing a play, 1826), extols four great singers of his time: Mo Hŭnggap (b. ca. 1800), Yŏm Kyedal (b. ca. 1800), Song Hŭngnok (b. ca. 1790), and Ko Sugwan (b. ca. 1800). Many more, including Kwŏn Samdŭk (1772–1841), Kim

---

[6] Customarily referred to as *Manhwabon Ch'unhyang-ga*.

[7] Chan E. Park, *Voices from the Straw Mat: Toward an Ethnography of Korean Story Singing* (Honolulu: University of Hawai'i Press, 2003), 56.

Sŏngok, Song Hŭngnok (1801–1863), Sin Manyŏp, and Chu Tŏkki helped make the nineteenth century a heyday of *p'ansori*. Prominent singers of the late nineteenth century include Pak Yujŏn (1835–1906), Chŏng Ch'unp'ung, Pak Mansun, Yi Nalch'i (1820–1892), Kim Ch'anŏp, and Kim Sejong.[8] A set of obscure names in history including those with no known date of birth or death, they made innovations in songs and styles that are still being transmitted today.

Till the end of Chosŏn, the mainstream Confucian elitists staunchly opposed the "likes of actors, puppeteers, performers of shamanic music, masked dancers, acrobats, and anyone selling wicked words and skills."[9] The shrillness of the tone aimed at, for example, Yu Chinhan's introducing for the first time the Ch'unhyang narrative in writing may have been a reflection of their fear that the cultural foundation sustaining them was being challenged by the growing interest in the culture of the folk: the wall believed to have separated the two domains was permeable. The singers were also seeking venues for enhanced financial and artistic reward. Elevated visibility and patronage catalyzed gentrification of the art. A petty bureaucrat with a literary background, Sin Chaehyo (1812–1884) of Koch'ang county of South Chŏlla, is known to have rendered many talented singers his editorial savvy. From the existing pool of twelve or more, five narratives were selected to form a canon of P'ansori Obat'ang, or "Five Narratives." On the surface, they are in perfect sync with the five Confucian cardinal virtues, the protocol of the elite ruling class during Chosŏn when these narratives were finalized: *Song of Ch'unhyang* (춘향가 *Ch'unhyang-ga*), *Song of Sim Ch'ŏng* (심청가 *Sim Ch'ŏng-ga*), *Song of Hŭngbo* (흥보가 *Hŭngbo-ga*), which teaches sibling order, *Song of the Underwater Palace* (수궁가 *Sugung-ga*), promoting loyalty to higher-ups, and *Song of the Red Cliff* (적벽가 *Chŏkpyŏk-ka*), an adaptation from the Chinese *Romance of the Three Kingdoms* (三國志 *Sanguo zhi*), promoting the code of gentlemanly behavior. "Hereditarily outcast from the Confucian social orbit, the singers took pride in their position as copropagators of Confucian moral paradigms. With utmost devotion they strove to vocalize loyalty and filial piety (*ch'ung-hyo*) as the two-part truth for all."[10] Blanketed under Confucian mores, however, the narratives manifest the Korean indigenous spiritual belief in a compassionate heaven: you do your utmost and justly

---

[8] The anecdotes of the lives and art of some of these singers are included in Chan E. Park, "Singers and Patrons: The Nineteenth-Century Hall of Fame," in Park, *Voices from the Straw Mat*, 60–76.

[9] Kim Hŭnggyu, "P'ansori ŭi sahoejŏk sŏngkyŏk kwa kŭ pyŏnmo" [*P'ansori*'s social characteristics and change], in *P'ansori ŭi pat'ang kwa arŭmdaum* [The characteristics and beauty of *p'ansori*], ed. Chŏng Yang and Ch'oe Tonghyŏn, 102–36 (Seoul: Indong, 1986); also cited in Park, *Voices from the Straw Mat*, 58.

[10] Park, *Voices from the Straw Mat*, 72.

and let heaven intervene; that human existence is part of a larger spirited reality. The nineteenth century also saw the entrance of females into *p'ansori* singing. The first was Chin Ch'aesŏn, Sin Chaehyo's beloved protégé. "At the July 1867 inauguration banquet for the reconstruction of Kyŏnghoeru pavilion at Kyŏngbok Palace, Chin made her debut as the first female *kwangdae* ever . . . He [Sin Chaehyo] was offering two of his greatest innovations: the colorful eulogy and his cherished protégée, Ch'aesŏn."[11]

ELEMENTS OF *P'ANSORI* PERFORMANCE

Etymologically, the term *p'ansori* is a compound of *p'an*, "performative occasion or venue," and *sori*, "the singing voice." Accompanied by a drummer (*kosu*) on a barrel-shaped drum (*puk*), the *p'ansori* singer weaves between spoken passages (*aniri*) and sung passages (*sori*). Between the two distinct styles of deliverance exists a half-sung and half-spoken style, a kind of recitative or crooning sans drum accompaniment. The "timekeeper through all the singer's transformation,"[12] the drummer adds his own by "sympathizing, encouraging, rebutting, countering, coaxing, consoling, conjuring, provoking, grappling, and sparring . . . the two arts merge into a single flow,"[13] hence the saying, "Il-gosu i-myŏngch'ang" (First the drummer, second the singer). In singing, the poetic aspect of storytelling waxes. In *p'ansori*, music and language intimately describe one another: they descriptively resemble one another. *Imyŏn*, or "picture within," is an emic term for a truthful union of language and music toward revelation of a deeper poetics of the songs sung: the singer should not settle with a flawless execution of the music but be able to deliver in his voice the semantic interiority. *Sŏng'ŭm*, or "music of the voice," refers to a vocal prowess capable of painting the inside pictures of the songs sung. The voice is not autonomous but weighted by what moves the heart, and the goal of a *p'ansori* singer is essentially no different from that of an actor striving for a truthful deliverance of his lines. *P'ansori* singing employs several distinct rhythmic cycles (*changdan*) that respond to the changing mood or context of storytelling: the slow six-beat *chinyang*, medium twelve-beat *chungmori*, faster twelve-beat *chungjungmori*, syncopated four-beat *chajinmori*, urgent duple *hwimori*, and the ten-beat *ŏnmori* exuding the feeling of asymmetry in its two-three two-three sequence. *Changdan*, like heartbeats, elicits a psychic energy that unifies singer, drummer, and

---

[11] Ibid., 71.
[12] Ibid., 3.
[13] Ibid.

listener. Melodically, *p'ansori* is sung in several distinct modalities (*cho*): the magnanimous *ujo*, the peaceful and calming *p'yŏngjo*, and the sad *kyemyŏnjo*. The basic qualifications for a singer, according to Sin Chaehyo in his *Kwangdaega* (Song of the *kwangdae*), are *inmul* (appearance, person, or presence), *sasŏl* (narrative composition), *tŭgŭm* (vocal attainment), and *nŏrŭmsae* (accompanying gesture).[14] Translating as "appearance" undercuts the centrality of the art of *p'ansori*, while "person" or "presence" better captures the primary importance of the artist's personality. As exemplified in the cases of Tongp'yŏnje, Sŏp'yŏnje, or Chunggoje, prominent schools of singing formed around exceptional singers and their vocal styles (*je*) and continue to be sustained by succeeding singers and their students.

Prior to a main *p'ansori*, singers customarily do a warm-up with a *tan'ga*, or "short song." "The singer tests his or her voice, the folding and unfolding of the fan, and the set of gestures; the drummer checks the deftness of his hands and fingers, the drum's tautness and suppleness, and his *ch'uimsae* (*ch'wimsae*), stylistic cries of encouragement."[15] Anchored to the twin towers of the Confucian virtues of *ch'ung* (忠, loyalty to the king) and *hyo* (孝, filial piety to parents), the theme of *tan'ga* loosely fluctuates: the beauty in nature, impermanence of the season, inevitability of death, or lessons from history:

> White pines on Namsan, its forest dense and luxuriant,
> the Han River leisurely flows, boundless and triumphant.
> May His Majesty, like these mountains and that river,
> live forever and ever,
> till these hills flatten and that water dries.
> For eternity,
> enjoy peace and prosperity!
>
> . . .
>
> When you reach your midlife,
> abandon the lures of wealth and fame.
> Give them to those who want them.
> Take a trip, anywhere,
> and when you find an auspicious site
> by a great mountain and water,
> build a tiny shack there.

---

[14] More on this, generally referred to as "a tetrad of principles, the golden rules of *p'ansori* theory," is included in Park, *Voices from the Straw Mat*, 72.

[15] Ibid., 2.

Gather your soul friends,
together enjoy music and poetry!

                    (from "Chin'guk myŏngsan")[16]

My dear youths!
Waste not your days,
do what you have to do.
The root of all human conduct is
none but love for your country and parents, is it not?

. . .

Another ancient named Kwakkŏ [Guo Ju],
whenever he had a special dish prepared for his parents, his own child
    would eat it,
so to bury this child away,
(he, Kwakkŏ) dug a grave where he found a pot of gold,
all to better serve his parents.

. . .

Foolish Chinsihwang,[17]
who had the Great Wall built
and sat high on the Abanggung [Epang] palace,
seeking to live forever.
But he, too, became the ghost of Yŏsan.[18]
The rich and dainty food given to us in death
is not nearly as tasty as a cup of crude wine we drink while living.
Enjoy life while living.

                    (from "Hyodo-ga," "Song of Filial Piety")[19]

---

[16]Translatable as, "The auspicious mountains bring peace to our nation": patriotic tone, Daoist in nature, eulogizing the *p'ungsu* (C. *fengsui*) of the surrounding mountains of Seoul; transmitted from Chŏng Kwŏnjin.

[17]The reference is to Qin Shi Huang (260–210 B.C.E.), emperor of Qin, who conquered all the Warring States and unified China in 221 B.C.E. Later in life, he became famously obsessed with power and immortality, to be cited in literature as an example of the impermanence of life and the eventuality of death.

[18]The reference is to Lishan Mountain, located thirty *li* (a *li* is approximately 393 meters) from Xi'an.

[19]Transmitted by Chŏng Kwŏnjin.

P'ANSORI IN TRANSLATION

In translating poetry, ideally the translator's consciousness seamlessly aligns with that of the poet. Translating *p'ansori* narrative involves unraveling and repackaging the syntax and the semantics of an archaic, musico-linguistic performativity that has fallen into almost complete disuse in the popular sphere. Alienated in the vortex of modernization, its narratives often contain words, phrases, and cadences impenetrable for interpretation. Nevertheless, the labor of this translation focuses on making the narrative and performative reality of *p'ansori* relevant to that of our contemporary existence. The challenge in question is how to rekindle for contemporary readers what ignited the imaginations of Korean audiences of the past. An emic metaphor for the art of *sori* is "weaving" (소리짜기), as of a tapestry. Every stitch of the musical and literary sensibility zealously emulated from generation to generation uninhibitedly reveals every bit of the singer's person. And the late *p'ansori* elders, including Chŏng Kwŏnjin, stressed that "if you want to be a good singer, you must first be a human being."

The most difficult aspect to translate between languages, according to Nietzsche, is the tempo of its style.[20] If previous translations have focused on the narrative or storytelling aspect of *p'ansori*, this effort will build on oral elements primarily. It seeks to reveal the fundamental unity of voice and beat, singing and drumming, in *p'ansori*. The goal is to engage the reader to assume the role of audience when reading. In these translations the spoken narrative of *aniri* is presented in a spoken format, and the sung narrative of *sori* is given in a matching verse form. I have added my own summary narrations in italics in order to better help contextualize the translated excerpts. To help with readers' visual identification of the rhythm within the narrative, as much as possible I have entered each translated line into the duration of one *changdan*, a single rhythmic cycle. However, exceptions were generously made whenever a smoother flow in English was deemed weightier. As colorful markers of Korean orality, the onomatopoetic expressions are preserved in romanization as much as possible. In light of the fact that many ancient Chinese names of places and persons had become native in Korean literary and historical references for thousands of years, I opted to romanize these names

---

[20] Friedrich Nietzsche, "On the Problem of Translation," in *Theories of Translation: An Anthology of Essays from Dryden to Derrida*, ed. John Biguenet and Rainer Schulte (Chicago: University of Chicago Press, 1992), 68–70.

primarily according to Korean pronunciation, supplemented with the matching Chinese pronunciation whenever available. The sociolinguistics of social and gender hierarchy, deeply ensconced in premodern Korean dialogue, will continue to be an interesting challenge in our work of translating premodern Korean literature.

CP

8. P'ansori, Narratives in Song

INTRODUCED AND TRANSLATED BY CHAN E. PARK

8.1 SONG OF HŬNGBO (흥보가 HŬNGBO-GA)

Narrative lineage: Song Hŭngnok—Song Kwangnok—Song Uryong—Song Man'gap (1865–1939)—Kim Chŏngmun (1887–1935)—Pak Nokchu (1905–1979)—Han Nongsŏn (1934–2002)

Summary
   Long ago in a valley where the provinces of Kyŏngsang, Chŏlla, and Ch'ungch'ŏng meet, there lived two brothers, Nolbo and Hŭngbo. The younger brother, Hŭngbo, was good, but the elder brother, Nolbo, was obnoxious and greedy. As the Confucian law of inheritance dictated, Nolbo would inherit the family assets with which he would fulfill his basic responsibilities of caring for his family. Instead, he chased Hŭngbo and his family out into the cold. After much wandering,

>   ANIRI: They settle in a district known as the Worthy Luck Village located in Sage Township. Life is harsh, and the starving children—could they be anything but clueless?!

Day and night they badger their mother with never-ending songs of food.

"I want rice cakes!"

"I wish I could eat some rice!"

"Why can't you buy me a piece of taffy?!"

Everyone has different appetites. The eldest son gruntingly expostulates,

"Alas, Mother!"

"What now . . . don't talk to me like a young bull about to have his nose pierced!"

"Mother, I can't sleep. Night and day, I suffer from insomnia, I'm sad."

"What is the nature of your sorrow? Mine is that we all must go hungry."

"Mother, please persuade Father to get me a bride. It's not that I want to be married. It's just about time you and Father should have some grandchildren."

Hŭngbo's wife is speechless at this request.

CHINYANG: Stupid boy, listen to me.
  If only I could afford it,
  would I be postponing your marriage all this time?
  Would I be starving our precious head of the family[1]
  and stripping my little children bare?
  Failing to feed and clothe my own offspring,
    this mother has a heart that rots away."

ANIRI: Hŭngbo enters.

"Dearest wife, life is already hard on us, and you sit and squeeze out tears day after day, so how could luck ever come our way? I plan to make a trip to town today."

"A trip to town, what good is there?"

"I'll talk to the granary officer about borrowing grains on interest . . .[2] what else could be done to resuscitate our children hovering on the verge of death by starvation?"

"If I were the officer in charge, I wouldn't give you a loan, so don't go."

"It's a 'die nine times to live once' situation—not that I have the conviction I'll succeed anyway. Bring me my horsehair hat."

---

[1] Indicating her husband.

[2] A kind of grain banking and mortgaging: during the Chosŏn, each township exercised an administrative system of loaning grains to farmers in spring, then collecting them with interest following harvest.

"Where did you put it?"
"In the chimney."
"Why in the chimney?"
"Let me explain. You've seen the *paengnip*[3] I wore at the national mourning for Queen Mother Cho back during the *sinmyo* year?[4] They say its rim lasts forever, so I am blackening it with chimney soot. Please bring me my official coat."
"Where did you put it?"
"In the closet."
"Darling, we have no closet!"
"*Huh-huh*, isn't a hen closet a closet also?"[5]

Dressed for the occasion, Hŭngbo goes to the township office:

CHAJINMORI: Hŭngbo enters.
Look at the way he's dressed.
A hat that has seen better days,
wire broken and popping out from the brim,
crisscrossed with millet-stem strings.
The tattered headband patched and pasted
with a lump of old rice,
missing its decorative rings,
fixed tightly in place with paper strings
with no chance of coming apart.
His threadbare outer gown tied in the middle
with a thin threadlike belt to quiet his hunger.
In one hand he carries a talc pipe,
in the other a ripped fan.
Ah, but he's still a nobleman!
In a splay-footed walk befitting his distinction,
quite convincingly Hŭngbo enters.

---

[3] Wide-brimmed hat woven with white hemp, worn by the chief mourner at a funeral, also worn by citizens during a national mourning. Queen Mother Cho (1808–1890), following the death of her husband, Ikchong (d. 1830), and enthronement of her son Hŏnjong (憲宗, r. 1834–1849), was raised to the position of queen mother in 1834. Following the death of the next king, Ch'ŏlchong (哲宗, r. 1849–1863) in 1863, she helped enthrone Kojong (高宗, r. 1863–1907) but was soon retired by Kojong's father, the ambitious regent Taewŏn'gun. From the mention of her funeral in the story, it can be inferred that the narrative of Hŭngbo may still have been in the process of completion at the end of the eighteenth century.

[4] Rabbit Year of the Eighth Heavenly Stem in the sexagenary calendrical cycle.

[5] Hŭngbo is making a pun on the rhyming words *otchang* (clothes closet) and *tarkchang* (a small storage loft).

ANIRI: Hŭngbo is suddenly worried. "I may be impoverished, but I'm still a *yangban* of the Pannam Pak[6] clan. Do I address the granary officer in honorific form or not?[7] Perhaps it'd be best to simply blur the endings of my sentences. I'll finish with laughs instead." When Hŭngbo enters the gate, a door opens, and the granary officer looks out.

"Mr. Pak, what brings you here?"

"I happen to be short on grains, and if you'll loan me a bag of rice, I can pay you back in autumn, so what do you sa— uhahaha-ahaha!"

"Mr. Pak, you've come all the way here, so how about some work?"

"If it pays money, why, sure!"

"Let me explain. The chief officer of our village has been incarcerated pending punishment.[8] And if you will, in his place, receive ten cudgel lashings, you'll earn thirty *nyang*[9] guaranteed, plus five *nyang* for hiring a horse.[10] The job is yours if you want it." "I sure will take whatever brings money, yeah! But a horse for ground transportation is a luxury for someone about to be beaten for pay. I'll return on my two galloping feet, so why don't you just give me the five *nyang* instead?"

CHUNGMORI: Look what the granary officer is doing.

Ch'ŏlkkŏng! Unlocking the money chest,
he counts five *nyang* and hands it over,
and Hŭngbo takes it. "I'll be back."
"Fare you well, and see you again."
Bursting with joy,
Pak Hŭngbo dashes out of the building:
"*Ŏlssiguna!* Wonderful!
Look at the money! Look at the money,
money, money, money!
Bring them close to your eyes
and see the cardinal virtues of Samgang Oryun!"[11]
And a little while later,

---

[6] A prominent lineage among the *yangban* aristocracy during the Chosŏn era.

[7] Korean is a sociolinguistically sensitive language in that there are multiple levels of speech to differentiate social status and age. One of the structural differentiations occurs at sentence endings. Hŭngbo in this scene needs to be polite to the granary officer if he wants to get help, but his aristocratic standing is too high to bestow honorific endings on a petty officer.

[8] The nature of the crime or offense is not specified in the text.

[9] In the premodern Korean currency scale, ten *p'un* (푼) equaled one *ton* (돈), and ten *ton* equaled one *nyang* (냥).

[10] Most likely for the return journey home for the beaten.

[11] The Three Bonds and Five Relations (三綱五倫, K. Samgang Oryun) were the foundation of Confucian ethnics: the Three Bonds were those between king and subject, husband and

when I squeeze the cash in my hand,
will I give a damn about the virtues?
It is all money's doing.
Money, money, ah money!"
He enters the soup house,
orders a bowl of *ttŏkkuk*[12] for a penny [*p'un*].
He enters a tavern,
downs two farthings' worth of *makkŏlli*.[13]
Straightening his shoulders, readjusting his bamboo tube,[14]
a real man of men worth thirty-five *nyang*
swaggers home.
"*Ŏlssiguna*, look at the money!"
Entering his house,
"W-i-f-e! Where is my wa—i——fe?
Isn't a proper housewife expected to *ururururu* . . . [15]
dash out and greet the man of the house
with due respect when he returns?
Instead, you just sit, without even getting up!
Why, woman?
You are my own very bad woman!"

CHUNGJUNGMORI: Hŭngbo's wife darts out,
Hŭngbo's wife bolts out.
"Show me the money, the money,
let me see the money, come on!"
"Let go, woman.
Do you really know what money is?
Money breaks a person,
money makes a person,
money is round, money goes round,
like the wheels under the flying chariot carrying Maengsanggun.[16]

---

wife, and parent and child. The Five Relations are loyalty to the king, filial love for one's parent, a woman's chastity to one man, sibling order, and fidelity among friends.

[12] Korean rice-cake soup, prepared on the lunar new year and birthdays: *ttŏk* (rice cake) plus *kuk* (soup).

[13] Rice wine for ordinary Koreans.

[14] Long bamboo tube used in the former times to carry wine, soy sauce, or cooking oil.

[15] Onomatopoeic description of the rushing movement Hŭngbo demands to see from his wife upon his return.

[16] Referring to Lord Mengchang (孟嘗君, d. 279 B.C.E.), a statesman of Qi (齊) from the Chinese Warring States era. His historic escape from Qin to his homeland of Qi left many episodic as well as metaphoric legacies in East Asian literature, including Korean. In his admiration for

Money is the power to let you live or die,
it brings you wealth and fame.
You naughty money!
You heartless money!
Where have you been all this time?!
Ŏlssiguna! Chŏlssigu!
Money, money, money, money!
Money, money, money, look at money at last!"

ANIRI: "Look, wife, take this money and go buy some rice and meat. Prepare eleven buckets of porridge. Make it so it is not too thick and not too thin, just right."

The children and adults evenhandedly finish one bucket each. Unable to fight the after-meal drowsiness, the children one by one succumb to a *kojabaegi* snooze,[17] and *drip-drop*! Snot slobbers from the tips of their noses like clear drops of liquor falling off a *soju*[18] brewing spout. Hŭngbo and his wife seize the opportunity to make their youngest child.[19]

"Husband, darling, where did you get the money? I want to know."

"If you only knew, you'd be amazed. The chief officer of our village is in jail, and his punishment is ten lashings. If I take them in his stead, he'll pay me three *nyang* per lashing. I agreed, and that was the prepayment. Please do not breathe a word of this to anyone. If Kkwesae-*aebi*[20] next door hears of this, he'll surely steal the gig from me."

At these words, Hŭngbo's wife weeps.

"Aigo, my dear husband, selling out the precious head of a household to be beaten for pay—wherever in this world has anyone heard of such a thing?"

CHINYANG: "Please don't go, please don't go.
My poor husband, please don't go.
'There is no one born of heaven that does not know someone,

---

the talented Mengchang, the king of Qin offered him a position as chancellor. Warned by his ministers that Mengchang was a loyal minister of Qi and not to be trusted, the king put him under house arrest instead. It was the king's beloved consort who decided to help Mengchang escape. With a forged document, Mengchang raced his chariot to the border. There, the guards, unaware he was being pursued, opened the barrier for Mengchang and his men to cross into Qi.

[17] One of the meanings of *kojabaegi* is "castrated man." The metaphor may be directed to their limpness caused by sudden satiation after prolonged hunger.

[18] *Soju* is a traditional Korean liquor brewed from rice, millet, or corn.

[19] Humorous observation that Hŭngbo and his wife are coupling again!

[20] The suffix *aebi* is used in reference to a person's "father."

there is nothing growing from the earth that does not have a name.'[21]
The sky may tumble,
but there is always a way out.
Do you really think we will simply perish?
Please listen to me and don't go.
One lashing at the courthouse
would maim you for good, I hear.
Husband, my poor husband,
please don't go."

ANIRI: Hearing their mother's sobs, the children stir, craning their necks like a flock of geese compelled by the gushing of water.

"Father, are you going to the courthouse?"

"I am indeed."

"Father, on your way home, would you please buy me a pair of spectacles?" "Spectacles?! What do you need them for?"

"If I wear them when gathering firewood on the mountain, I can protect my eyes from all the dust."

Hŭngbo's eldest son slinks up to him.

"*Aigo*, Father!"

"Dimwit, you again?!"[22]

"Father, on your way back from the courthouse, please buy me a whore."

"What will you do with a whore?"

"You and Mother are too poor to wed me, so with her I'll run a tavern."[23]

CHUNGMORI: After breakfast early,
Hŭngbo's on the road in the direction of the courthouse.
Hurrying down the lane,
he weeps over his pitiful choice.
"Alas, my rotten life!
How is it that some people so effortlessly
enjoy fame and wealth in their lifetimes,
while the lot of this unfortunate human is this hard?"
Hŭngbo arrives at the courthouse.

---

[21] That there is help on the way for every life is what Hŭngbo's wife tells him.

[22] In the several dialogues between the eldest son and his parents in the narrative, he appears incapable of comprehending the dire situation his family is in: his character may have been set up as mentally challenged.

[23] The eldest son thinks he can first get a whore to help him make money, because the lack of money prevents him from being wed.

Above, the colorful flags flutter furiously,
below, the warnings, "Quiet," "Respect,"[24] inscribed all over the walls.
With faces scary as tigers' deep in the mountains,
the soldiers march around this way and that.
The clueless Pak Hŭngbo stands there trembling.

ANIRI: *Ttŏllŏng!* The bell tolls. "Yei-i-i-i!" The soldiers chant in unison. Peeking through a crack in the Three Gates,[25] Hŭngbo views the scene of the morning flogging punishment of the criminals. Assuming they are also there with the same enterprise as his own—a beating for profit—Hŭngbo convinces himself of it.

"Those guys came here before me and must have made several hundred *nyang* already. I should bear my buttocks and wait."

Hŭngbo lays himself down on his stomach and waits. A pair of officers approach.

"*Huh-huh,* another beating for pay volunteer is here!. . . Oh wait! Are you Sir Pak?"

"You've guessed right."

"Have you cracked up?"

"Cracked up?! What am I, an egg?"

"Earlier someone came saying he had come in your place, took thirty *nyang* for ten lashings, and left."

Hŭngbo is dumbfounded.

"What did he look like?"

"Really tall, bulging eyes, muscular, strong."

Hŭngbo despairs.

RECITATIVE WITHOUT DRUM: "Last night my wife cried all night long, and it was that Kkwesae-*aebi* next door that tripped me!"

CHUNGMORI: "Officers, is that so?
I quit, I'm going home,
I have no more business here with you.
Enjoy your guarding.
Now what do I do when I return home?
I had promised to buy rice cakes for those who begged for taffy,
and steaming rice for those who cried for rice cakes,
now with what money could we even begin to talk?"
Weeping and lamenting, he returns home.

---

[24] Reminder to be quiet carved or written on wooden panels placed around the traditional courthouse, forbidding visitors from making noise while executions are in session.

[25] Main gate with smaller gate to the east and another to the west.

ANIRI: With her newborn in her arms, Hŭngbo's wife waits for her husband.
"Baby, don't cry. Your father will soon return with a ton of money."
Hŭngbo approaches.
"My darling husband, show me your wounds! Let me see!"
"Don't touch me, you wicked woman! You whined all night long and it backfired on me! If I ever made a penny by receiving even one lashing, you could call me a senseless son of a cow!"[26]

CHUNGJUNGMORI: Hŭngbo's wife is relieved,
Hŭngbo's wife is overjoyed.
Ŏlssiguna chŏlssigu!
Chŏlssiguna ŏlssigu!
Days ago when you left for the courthouse,
I prayed and prayed to heaven
to bring you back home unhurt,
now you return without a scratch!
Isn't this a joyous occasion?
Ŏlssiguna chŏlssigu!
We could be naked, no matter.
We could be starving, I don't care.
Ŏlssiguna chŏlssigu!
Miraculous, wonderful, fabulous!
Ŏlssigu chŏlssigu, oh happy days!"

Summary

 Trouble was deepening, they were about to give up, when one day a Daoist monk came to their shack to beg for alms. Taking pity on them, the monk took Hŭngbo deep into the valley and found for him a home site. There, Hŭngbo built a mud hut and moved his family in. Life seemed a bit more bearable, and all of them survived the harsh winter. One day, a pair of swallows flew in and built a nest under the eaves. Soon two chicks were hatched. During their first flight one of them fell and broke its leg. Kind Hŭngbo and his wife treated it with utmost care and put it back in the nest. Autumn came. All the birds began preparing for the journey to their winter lands in the south. Hŭngbo's swallow took his leave.

---

[26]There is a semantic disconnect in Hŭngbo's speech in translation. He likely means that if he actually made any money but is lying to her, he would deserve to be called less than human.

It was homecoming in the Great Hall of the Swallow Kingdom as millions of swallows from all over the world flocked in to report their arrivals. Hŭngbo's swallow limped in and recounted to the swallow king his birth, broken leg, and resuscitation thanks to the man named Hŭngbo. Greatly moved, the swallow king presented a magic gourd seed for Hŭngbo's swallow to deliver back home. Next spring, Hŭngbo's swallow returned home with the gourd seed. With a thankful heart, Hŭngbo planted the seed behind his house. The plant grew and grew, yielding three enormous gourds. Ch'usŏk, Korean Thanksgiving, was approaching, but Hŭngbo and his family had nothing to celebrate the holiday with. One day, Hŭngbo's wife, seated at her empty loom, laments.

CHUNGMORI: Poverty! Poverty!
    This wench's wretched poverty!
    How do you get what is known as luck?
    Do the Seven Stars of the North arrange that?
    Is it the Three Gods that decide life and luck
    when we fall into this world?
    My wretched lot!
    Why is my lot so damned?
    Why have I fallen so low?
    She sits and wails unrestrainedly.
ANIRI: Hŭngbo enters.
    "Come on, wife, stop crying. See those beautiful gourds sitting atop the roof? Let's get them down, saw them open, eat the fruit, and dry the shells and sell them to a wealthy household and with that feed our children. How about it?"
    "Darling, let's do that." They saw the first gourd.
CHINYANG: *Siririri-rŏng silgŭn,*
    Saw it!
    Eh-yŏru, pull it, saw it!
    "When this gourd opens,
    may a pot of rice come out,
    and nothing else!
    It is our lifetime dream!"
    Eh-yŏru, pull it, saw it!
    "Look, my dear wife,
    you sing us a verse, too."
    "Even if I wanted to sing,
    I'm too hungry to."
    "If you're that hungry,
    make your belt tighter."

E-yŏru, pull it, saw it!
"Younger son, go to your mama,
elder son, come to me.
When we saw this gourd,
we'll cook and eat the fruit inside,
and dry the shells and sell them to a rich neighbor,
we'll manage so."
Pull it!
The ship floating down the river
boasts of its cargo a thousand sacks of grain full.
But it does not compare with even just one of our gourds!
Siririri-rŏng silgŏn,
sirirŏng sirirŏ—ng.
Pull it, saw it!
Sirirŏng, sirirŏng sirirŏng sirirŏng
Sirirŏng, sirirŏng, siksak t'okkwaek!

ANIRI: The first gourd opens, and it is empty! They say that if you are unlucky, you crack an egg only to see it is full of bones. A thief must have stolen the fruit inside, leaving it empty. But then, Hŭngbo peers in closely and sees two chests! He lifts one lid—it is full of rice! He lifts the other—it is full of money!

HWIMORI: Hŭngbo is ecstatic! Hŭngbo is ecstatic!
He empties the chests,
t'ok t'ok, bottoms up!
Turn around, turn back, they've filled up again!
Empty them, turn around, turn back,
see rice and money fill up!
Turn around, turn back, they fill up,
turn around, turn back, fill up again.
Aigu, I'm so happy!
May rice and money spring out endlessly, *kkuyŏk kkuyŏk*!
Every day out of three hundred sixty-five days!
. . .

ANIRI: Nolbo, hearing the rumor his younger brother, Hŭngbo, had become rich, one day goes over to see for himself.
"What, is this really his house?! Here, come out, Hŭngbo-*ya* . . . !"
Hearing the voice of his older brother, Hŭngbo dashes out to greet him.
"Is this really your house?"
"Yes, Elder Brother, it happens so."
"It's a very nice place . . . let's swap houses."

"As you wish, Elder Brother."

"I have heard tell lately that you've been sighted here and there drenched in morning dew."[27]

"Dear Elder Brother, what can you mean? There can be no such possibility!"

"Then why are there so many police officers after you? I tell you what you should do—leave me the keys to your barns and storerooms, with all the chests and lockers inside untouched. Flee this place and go as far as you can, to Manchuria, for five years at the least. I'll take good care of your homestead."

"Elder Brother, that's not it."

"Then how did you become so rich?"

"This is what happened. One of our baby swallows fell and broke its leg, so we got some pollock skin and a bit of Chinese silken thread, dressed its wound, and put it back in the nest—and it lived! The next spring, it came back with a gourd seed, so I planted it, and it yielded three gourds. From inside them, all the gold, silver, and treasures came out."

"Ho, it's so easy to get rich, hm . . . so you broke one swallow leg and became this rich. Then I'll break many swallow legs and will be many times richer!"

Hŭngbo escorts Nolbo to his study, then enters the inner quarter and calls, "Look, wife, your brother-in-law has graciously granted a visit to us, so please make your appearance to welcome him."

Reflecting on all the mistreatment and abuses she had endured in the past under her brother-in-law, her heart pounds, *pŏllŏng, pŏllŏng!*[28] She trembles in all four limbs. Still, unable to disobey her husband's order, she comes out:

CHUNGJUNGMORI: Hŭngbo's wife appears.

Think back on the times when she was starved, ragged, and famished.

Now does she ever lack money, rice, silver,

gold, treasures, *insam,* and *nogyong?*[29]

Reverentially escorted by her luxuriously adorned daughters-in-law,

---

[27] In making this remark, Nolbo tries to provoke Hŭngbo by suggesting that Hŭngbo has been burglarizing houses at night.

[28] Onomatopoeic description of the trembling sensation caused by blood coursing through one's veins.

[29] *Insam* is Korean ginseng, and *nogyong* is deer antler. Used as energy-boosting components in Korean traditional medicine, they are costly.

Hŭngbo's wife is stunningly dressed in a full, beautiful azure skirt,
densely pleated and generously banded at the waist.
Look how tall and ladylike she walks!

ANIRI: Hŭngbo's wife offers a formal greeting to her elder brother-in-law. Too upset to simply reciprocate her in kind, Nolbo sneers, "Hey Hŭngbo, it's been a long while since I last saw this sister-in-law of mine—that was when I drove her out, yes? Really, 'yesterday's mudfish is today's dragon!'

Ignoring this, Hŭngbo's wife proceeds to the kitchen and prepares special dishes for the occasion.

CHAJINMORI: Look at the items she is preparing!
Brassware from Ansŏng, a T'ongyŏng pan-grill,
pure-silver spoons and chopsticks,
and a copper gridiron,
churururu . . . , laid like a line of subordinates in attendance.
The serving table carved from black bamboo with floral inlays,
China porcelain with bamboo designs.
Heaps of half-moon cakes,
white-rice cake and red-bean cake cut in squares.
Apples, honey, raw honey,
kebabs in bird-egg batch dipping.
Cow rumen sashimi,
liver, omasum, raw kidney slices set in two rows.
Rice-ball cakes soaked in diluted honey and *Maximowiczia* extract,
pine-nut crackers, shredded *insam*[30] and balloon-flower roots,
sliced and dried octopus meat
    dressed in bean oil and garnished with numerous fancy condiments.
Boiled mountain vegetables,
ferns, water parsley, watercress,
steamed mung-bean sprouts
drenched in tasty broth, *churururu*, poured over them.[31]
Bronze brazier heated with fine charcoals and,
hwal-hwal, energetically fanned.
When you crack the eggs,
pick up the top of the shell,

---

[30] Korean term for ginseng.

[31] It seems Hŭngbo's wife is preparing here a kind of *chŏn'gol*, a special stew elaborately prepared with fresh meats and vegetables dipped in boiling beef broth.

>   pour it upside down, long enough to get it all out.
>   *Kkokkyo!* pullet soup crows.
>   *Ottok p'ottok!* quail soup clatters.[32]
>   Watch out! The metal poker is scalding hot!
>   Use a pair of wooden chopsticks instead.
>   Pick up a slice of meat and,
>   *p'uungdŏng!*, dip it in sesame oil first,
>   next in the soy stew, *p'isssssiiiiii!*[33]

ANIRI: Hŭngbo's wife pours into an exquisite flower cup delicious berry and flower wine. "Brother-in-Law, please accept this humble drink."

Instead of just taking the cup from his sister-in-law, Nolbo snickers.

"Look here, Hŭngbo, you're my brother, so you know more than anyone that, even at a funeral, I do not drink unless accompanied with a drinking song. Your wife is dressed to kill, so why not make her sing a song while I drink?"

Hŭngbo's wife is repulsed:

CHINYANG: "Look here, Brother-in-Law,
>   Listen up, my brother-in-law,
>   telling your sister-in-law to sing a drinking song for you,
>   wherever in this world past and present
>   have you heard such blasphemy?
>   'Sincerity moves heaven,' and so it was,
>   today I have so much money and rice.
>   Stop acting high and mighty
>   just because you have a little too.
>   On that snowy and icy winter day,
>   driven out of home with my poor children in front,
>   humiliated and mistreated,
>   even in my grave I'll never forget!
>   I can't bear the sight of you, go away!
>   I truly detest the sight of you!
>   If you were in your right mind, would you have come here in the first place?
>   Go! If you don't, I will!"

Disgusted, she returns to the inner quarter.

ANIRI: Seeing this, Nolbo tells Hŭngbo, "Hey, Hŭngbo, your wife is no good. Throw her out—I'll match you with a better woman."

---

[32] Onomatopoeic insertions of the cries of the birds cooked in the soups.

[33] Searing sound of burning meat touching the liquid of the soy stew.

"I'm obliged, Elder Brother."

Nolbo inquires, "What is that reddish object standing in the corner over there?"

"*Hwach'ojang*, a flower chest, Elder Brother."

"Give it to me, I'll carry it home."

"I already set one aside for you. I'll have one of our servants carry it to your house tomorrow so you can return home lightly today."

"You dirt bag! You just want to empty it out all night long and send me just the empty chest. No, everything in this world must be done in a secure way—I'll carry it myself." Carrying the flower chest on his back, Nolbo recites as he goes so as not to lose sight of its name:

CHUNGJUNGMORI: *"Hwach'ojang, hwach'ojang, hwach'ojang,*
I got me a *hwach'ojang*.
I got me, I got me, I got me a *hwach'ojang*,
hwach'ojang, hwach'ojang, hwach'ojang . . ."
He jumps over a brook and . . .
"Oh heck, I forgot the name!"

Summary

Determined to get wealthier than his brother, Nolbo caught a dozen swallows and, one by one, broke and then bandaged their legs. The next fall, he, too, harvested three beautiful gourds. When they were opened one by one, instead of treasures and rice, demons and goblins rushed out amid oozing feces and shrill curses. Nolbo became destitute overnight. But good Hŭngbo took in his brother and his family to share his wealth and his home, and they lived happily ever after.

CP

8.2. SONG OF SIM CH'ŎNG
(심청가 SIM CH'ŎNG-GA)

Narrative lineage: Pak Yujŏn—Chŏng Chaegŭn—Chŏng Ŭngmin (1896–1964)—Chŏng Kwŏnjin (1927–1986)—Sŏng Uhyang (b. 1935)

Summary

Long, long ago, in Peace Blossom Village in the Hwangju district, there lived a blind man by the name of Sim Hakkyu and his good wife, Kwak-ssi. She was diligent and resourceful and took care of her husband with utmost devotion. Life was good, except they did not have a son to carry on his name, an unpardonable breach of Confucian filial responsibility, so they prayed for a son. At last they begot a child, but to their great disappointment it was a girl. They named her Sim Ch'ŏng. Weakened by the birth, Kwak-ssi fell ill and died, and Blindman Sim was left alone to care for the newborn baby. Thanks to the kind women of the village who took turns nursing her, Sim Ch'ŏng grew to be a beautiful girl with a filial heart, and Blindman Sim found joy and happiness in her tender loving care.

Sim Ch'ŏng turned fifteen. Having heard of her beauty and virtue, Lady Chang, widow of the late Minister Chang, one day sent for Ch'ŏng to come to her mansion in Arcadia Village. While Ch'ŏng was visiting Lady Chang, the sun was setting. Home alone, Blindman Sim was anxiously awaiting her return. Cold, hungry, and worried, he groped his way out into the drifting snow to look for her. He slipped into an icy stream and nearly drowned, but a Buddhist monk passing by pulled him out of the water. Feeling sorry for Blindman Sim, the monk told him that omnipotent Lord Buddha in his temple would help him regain his sight, but he would first have to donate as many as three hundred straw sacks of sacrificial rice for the prayer. Beside himself with hope and excitement, despite his penniless state and against the monk's warning Blindman Sim pledged to donate the proposed sum. Back home, he sorely regretted his thoughtless blunder, but the pledge was final and, according to the monk, he would become crippled for offering false commitment to Lord Buddha.

When Ch'ŏng returned home and heard what had happened, instead of scolding she comforted her father not to despair. From that day forth, she prayed to her guardian spirits to help procure the sacrificial rice.

CHINYANG: In her backyard she raises an altar for the Seven Stars of the North that shine deep into the Hour of the Rat.[34]
    Candlelight burning bright,
    freshly drawn water in a new bowl
    arranged on a small portable meal table.
    On her knees, she joins her two hands:
    "I pray to you, I pray to you,
    Venerable Heaven, I pray to you.
    Bright spirits of heaven, earth, sun, moon, stars,
    join your benevolent hearts for me!
    Heaven created the sun and the moon
    to provide us humans with sights to see.
    If the sun and the moon fell off the sky,
    would we still be able to see?

---

[34] The Hour of the Rat is approximately 11:00 p.m. to 1:00 a.m.

My father, born in the year of the rat of the fifth celestial stem,[35]
went blind after twenty—
he can't see.
Allow me to pay for his imperfections with my life.
Please let him be able to see once again!
We were told he can regain his sight
if we offer three hundred bags of sacrificial rice to Lord Buddha.
O bright heaven, please hear my prayer!
Help me procure three hundred bags of rice!

ANIRI: As if an answer to her fervent prayers,
CHUNGMORI: (In *chunggoche tŏllŏngcho*)[36]
One day, outside, loud cries.
"We are merchant sailors from the Southern Capital![37]
We plan to sacrifice a human offering at the waters of Indangsu.
We seek to buy a virgin girl of fifteen or sixteen!
Anyone interested?
Let us know if you are!
Anybody? Anyone?"
The sound of their cries ring through hills and dales,
across streams far and near.

ANIRI: Convinced this was the grace of heaven she had been praying for,
Sim Ch'ŏng discreetly invited the chief boatman to see her.
"I am of this village. My blind father hopes to regain his sight by the grace of Lord Buddha. He needs three hundred bags of sacrificial rice

---

[35] The Korean traditional calendar is a cycle of sixty years ordered around two axles, ten heavenly stems and twelve earthly branches. Blindman Sim's birth year is *muja*, the crossing of the fifth heavenly stem (*mu*) and the first earthly branch (*ja*), the twenty-fifth of the sixty-year cycle.

[36] Chunggoche, middle-old style," refers to the style developed in Kyŏnggi and Ch'ungch'ŏng provinces, centered around the nineteenth-century virtuosos Yŏm Kyedal, Mo Hŭnggap, and Chŏn Sŏngok and in decline beginning with the passing of Yi Tongbaek (1866–1947). Tongp'yŏnche (eastern school) and *sŏp'yŏnche* (western school) are the two other major schools of singing, developed east and west, respectively, of the Sŏmjin River in the southern Chŏlla provinces. For further reading, see Chan E. Park, *Voices from the Straw Mat: Toward an Ethnography of Korean Story Singing* (Honolulu: University of Hawai`i Press, 2003),178–80. *Tŏllŏngcho*, attributed to Kwŏn Samdŭk (1772–1841), has its origin in the characteristic cries uttered by the attendants escorting the traditional procession of honored personages. Typically accompanying loud, boisterous action, it adds sobering urgency to the plot. Chŏng Kwŏnjin (1927–1986), whose version is translated here, transmitted this particular song as a blend of *chunggoche* and *tŏllŏngche*.

[37] Namgyŏng—most likely Nanjing (南京), China.

for a donation to the temple. But we are extremely poor, so I wish to offer myself for sale. Would you take me?"

Hearing this, the sailors exclaimed.

"A heaven-sent filial devotion! Don't worry about the rice—however, we set sail as early as the next full moon. Will you be able to come with us then?"

"A hefty price you pay to take me—I have no objection, so worry not."

With confirmation, the sailors send the promised sum of rice to Mongŭnsa Temple before the following full moon. Sim Ch'ŏng saw them off and entered her father's room. "Father."

"What is it, child?"

"I had the rice sent to the Lord Buddha's altar. Please don't worry about a thing from now on."

"What? My child, how did you manage to send such a sum of rice?"

"Remember some time ago I paid a visit to the lady of the late Prime Minister Chang, and she wished to take me in as her adoptive daughter, and I didn't know whether to take her offer? Today I went to seek her advice on our situation, and Her Ladyship promised to have three hundred bags of rice sent to Mongŭnsa Temple and to take me in to live with her."

"Great, that's really great! 'A child of *yangban*[38] sold to another household' is not the most comfortable prospect, but becoming a daughter of that esteemed household—who'd ever call me a child seller? On which day will she send for you?"

"The fifteenth of next month, Father."

"The full moon, a very good day! Bright will be the moon, wonderful! By the way, Ch'ŏng, what will Her Ladyship do about me?"

"She will send for you, too, she promised."

"I knew it! It wouldn't make sense for such a virtuous lady to abandon me here all alone! You'll be riding a palanquin to your new mansion, I am sure—and me? Oh, I know! How about riding the black heifer that belongs to Teacher Kim?!"

Sim Ch'ŏng loved her father too much to lie to him, but lying was all her devoted heart could do.

RECITATIVE: Comforting her father so,
    she passes time, a day at a time.
    It is now the eve of her departure.

---

[38] Nobility or aristocrat.

CHINYANG: At the thought of dying,
    leaving her blind old father forever,
    she feels utterly fraught with sorrow.
    Unable to think, unable to act,
    tears spring uncontrollably
    from the deep folds of her heart.
    His four-season change of clothes
    she laundered and folded and neatly shelved.
    She mended his horsehair hat and headband
    and hung them at his convenient reach.
    She visited her mother's grave
    with an offering of a ceremonial tableful
    of wine, fruit, beef jerky, and fermented rice juice.[39]
    Burning incense, making two ceremonial bows, she weeps:
    "My dear mother!
    Your ungrateful daughter, Sim Ch'ŏng,
    to help Father regain his sight,
    sold her life for three hundred bags of rice.
    I am about to depart as a human sacrifice.
    The day of your memorial each year,
    who'd care to remember year after year?
    The grass overgrown on your grave,
    whose hands would cut?
    This is the last of my offering, please accept it!"
    Bidding her final farewell with the four ceremonial bows,
    Ch'ŏng returns home to prepare dinner for her father.
    Night deepens, it is midnight.
    Her father is deep in sleep, not a care in the world.
    Lest he wake, she cannot cry aloud.
    Choked with grief,
    caressing and massaging his hands and feet,
    putting her face against his,
    she weeps noiselessly.
    "My father, how could I leave him?
    Ever since I reached an age of awareness,
    he stopped begging for our sustenance,
    but from tomorrow he'll be a village beggar again,
    how could I leave him?

---

[39] Metonym for the ceremonial offering at memorial services.

If only I could rest the fifth hour[40] at Sunset Lake [41] tonight
and stay the sun at Sunrise Sea [42] tomorrow morning,
I could care for my poor father a bit more,
but isn't that beyond human powers?
Heaven and earth take their own course,
And *kkokkiyo!*, already the crowing of cocks!
Rooster, O rooster, please don't crow.
Alas, I am not
'Maengsanggŭn in the land of Chin in the dead of night.'[43]
If you crow, day breaks.
When day breaks, I die.
My death I grieve not,
leaving my father with none to rely on I grieve."

ANIRI: The eastern sky gradually brightens. Sim Ch'ŏng cooks rice soaked in her tears and carries the breakfast tray into the room. "Father." "Yes, my child." "It's breakfast time." "Yes, my child. It's an early breakfast this morning . . . and quite an impressive spread! Did someone have an ancestral memorial ceremony?"[44] Between father and daughter, a heaven-made bond, how could there not be a premonition? "Listen to me, Ch'ŏng. Last night I had a strange dream. I saw you on a raft going far out toward the endless ocean. I was jumping up and down, throwing myself and rolling on the ground . . . I made such a scene that it woke me. Let me interpret: riding a raft or wagon in a dream is a sign that you'll be riding a palanquin in real life. How I cried and wept—did you know tears in a dream are liquor in reality? It is a foretelling I'll be sumptuously wined and dined at the prime ministerial residence later today, don't you think?" Sim Ch'ŏng intuitively knows it is the dream of her drowning. "Father, you had a fantastic dream." "Fantastic indeed! Child, put away this tray. Let's save our

---

[40] Fifth in the Korean traditional twelve hours equivalent to the Western twenty-four hours in a day; corresponds to 3:00 a.m.–5:00 a.m.

[41] *Hamji* is the legendary western lake where the sun sets.

[42] *Pusang* is the legendary sea whence the sun rises.

[43] 반야진관맹상군 (Panya-jingwan Maengsanggŭn, 半夜秦關孟嘗君): Mengchang of Qi (齊), while escaping from the land of Qin, arrived at a checkpoint where the gate was closed. Someone imitated the crowing of a rooster and tricked the gatekeeper into thinking it was sunrise and thus opening the gate, allowing Mengchang to escape.

[44] *Chesa* (祭祀), a ritual offering of food, wine, and undying respect for the ancestral spirits of each household. Blindman Sim guesses that is where his daughter was given the particularly sumptuous breakfast that day. In reality, Sim Ch'ŏng overreached her means to prepare this last meal for her father.

stomachs for a real meal at the minister's. The whole household must be in an uproar to welcome their new daughter, cooking this and that, and stir-frying *sanjŏk*.[45] Let's save ourselves for later. When it comes to food, one must eat heartily to make his host happy." Sim Ch'ŏng obligingly put away the food tray, lit the tobacco, and put the pipe into her father's mouth. She paid her final visit to the ancestral shrine. The moment of revelation has come. She cannot lie to him anymore.

CHAJINMORI: Look at Sim Ch'ŏng!
She dashes toward her father, *urŭrŭrŭrŭrŭrŭrŭ* . . .
holds her father by the neck and calls,
"Father!—"
Unable to utter another word
she faints and collapses.
Startled, Blindman Sim calls out.
"Alas, what is wrong, my child?
Breakfast was unusually decadent—
could you be suffering from indigestion?
My child, what is it?
Oh no! Did some moron jeer at you
for having a blind father?
Is that what happened?"
"Father!—"
"Yes, yes, my child?"
"Three hundred bags of rice—who'd so freely give them to me?"
"Oh, the sacrificial rice? Don't fret,
we can go to the temple and annul the pledge at once—
you frighten me like this!"
"I've been sold for three hundred bags of rice
to merchant sailors from the Southern Capital.
Today they set sail, this is the last of me for you!
When will I ever see you again?!"
Blindman Sim, hearing this,
doesn't know what to do.
"What? What did you say?
You were sold for three hundred bags of rice?!
Is that what you said?!"

CHUNGJUNGMORI: "*Huh-huh!*—
Can someone explain what this is all about?

---

[45] Korean-style kebab.

What is this all about?
Without first consulting your own father,
you did this all by yourself?!
This shouldn't be.
I sold *you* to open my eyes?
When *I* should be selling my eyes to buy *you*!
To see whom would I open my eyes?
You mustn't do this to me!
My unthinking and reckless child,
listen to the sad story of your father.
Your mother died within a week of giving birth to you.
And I, your blind father, carrying you in my arms,
went door to door begging women to kindly nurse you.
With their help,
I kept you alive and growing.
Look at you now, a big girl.
With you I've been able to forget
my old cares and worries.
What catastrophe has befallen us?!"
Already the sailors appear at the door, calling out,
"Maiden Sim, we're missing the high tide!"
As they nag mercilessly,
Blindman Sim, utterly lost for words . . .
urururururu! . . . dashes out, stumbles, crying,
"You barbaric ignorant bastards!
Doing business is one thing,
but purchasing a human for sacrifice—
wherever have you learned that?
Haven't you heard it said that
during the seven-year drought,
the benevolent Emperor Tang[46]
forbade his people to make human sacrifices?
Instead he did to himself the unthinkable—
he trimmed his fingernails and toenails and cut his hair
and put on a beaded rosary and white belt,[47]

---

[46] Founder of the Shang dynasty (湯), lived around 1600 B.C.E.

[47] The meaning of 신영백모 is difficult to clarify; 영 represents "rosary" and 모 corresponds to "belt." They may be props used in a shamanic prayer ceremony. In many ancient East Asian cultures, trimming nails and cutting hair was considered sacrilegious, since they are given by one's parents. It could be that the emperor took it upon himself to perform the ceremony, and

and he prayed in the mulberry field.
And a great rain fell, covering many thousand *li*,[48]
yielding a great harvest!
If you want to buy a human for sacrifice,
take me!
I don't want money, I don't want rice,
I don't want my vision back!"
Pounding himself on his chest, bobbing his head up and down,
rolling on the ground, he abandons himself to abject despair.

Summary

The sad news reaches Murŭngch'on village. Lady Chang sends for Sim Ch'ŏng with an offer to send the three hundred bags of rice to the temple instead. Sim Ch'ŏng respectfully declines, as "It's too late to turn back, it will inconvenience the sailors." Unable to dissuade her, Lady Chang orders a portrait of Sim Ch'ŏng to be made, then comes a tearful parting.

ANIRI: "The tide is receding quickly, so allow me to take my leave, dear lady." When she returns home, the anxious sailors are restless, and her father jumps up and down wailing. Taking pity, the sailor left extra provisions for Blindman Sim with a trustworthy villager. One hundred bags of rice, a roll of linen and hemp each, and food and clothing to cover the rest of his life.

CHUNGMORI: She follows, she follows,
    the sailors she follows.
    Grabbing fold on fold the train of her skirt
    that drags on the ground,
    tears flowing down her cheeks like rainfall
    staining the collar of her blouse.
    Falling, tripping, she follows as if in abandonment.
    Gazing at the village across, she reminisces:
    "My friend, Sir Lee's younger daughter,
    On May Day last year,
    we were having so much fun picking cherries—
    you can't have forgotten?
    Our plan to enjoy the evening promenade

---

his demonstration of humility, symbolized by cutting and trimming these gifts from his parents, moved heaven, and heaven responded by sending down the rain.

[48] A *li* is equivalent to 393 meters.

on the seventh day of the seventh moon this year—
all to naught.
With whom will you do the backstitching decorations[49] and embroidery?
All of you are fortunate to have both your parents living.
Take good care of them and be well.
Today, I take leave of my father
to travel the road of death."
All the villagers, male, female, old and young,
their eyes are puffy from so much weeping.
Heaven, too, is mournful.
As the sun slips behind the quickly spreading black clouds,
the blue mountain scowls.
Trees and shrubs, as if weeping,
stand languid and pale.
Spring birds mournfully cry, "Good-bye! Good-bye!"
Nightingale,
what heartbreaking separation is your song?[50]
Suddenly, a cuckoo perched on a tree branch cries,
Kwich'okto, kwich'okto, puryŏgwi![51]
How could I, priced and sold, ever return?
As she turns a corner,
a violent gale rises,
and a sweetbrier blossom falls on Sim Ch'ŏng's face.
Holding the flower in her hand, she speaks:
"If the spring breeze did not understand what I'm feeling,
why would it send a flower in my direction?"[52]
Perhaps for the *maehwajang* facial treatment
used by Princess Suyang, daughter of Emperor Muje?[53]

---

[49] *Sangch'imjil* refers to a decorative sort of backstitch.

[50] *Hwanusŏng* is the cry of a bird missing its mate.

[51] This onomatopoeic transcription of the cuckoo's cry has a legendary origin as well. King Mangje of the Shu kingdom once saved a drowning man named Pyŏllyŏng and gave him a home, title, and even a bride. Pyŏllyŏng betrayed the king by usurping the throne. Cast away and harboring a smoldering grudge in his heart, the king cried himself to death. It is said that his soul reincarnated as the cuckoo that cries, "Let me return to Shu, to Shu, but I can't!"

[52] 道春風不解意 [약도춘풍불해의], 何因吹送落花來 [하인취송낙화래] is the final line of "Xiti pan-shi" [戱題盤石, 희제반석, K. "Hŭije-bansŏk" (Writing on a rock for fun)], written by the poet Wang Wei (699–759) of the Tang dynasty.

[53] *Maehwajang*, "plum-flower facial," is a facial-care method popular among women in ancient China. A story goes that one day Princess Suyang, the beautiful daughter of Muje in the

Such can't be for one who goes to die.
I am not dying because I want to die.
Still, I have no one to blame for my death.
Not knowing which way was which,
she arrives at the river landing.
A deckhand lays the foot plate
and guides Sim Ch'ŏng onto the boat.
They seat her on the floor in the middle—
her journey begins.

Summary

After several months onboard, it is now early autumn. Between real and unreal, between sleep and waking, Sim Ch'ŏng is visited by a number of legendary and historical characters. Some spill their heartrending stories of injustices and their tragic deaths, and some comfort or encourage her, even foreshadowing her glorious return to the world.

CHINYANG: How many nights on this ship,
how many days on this water?
It has been four or five moons
of flowing with the waves.
"Chilly autumn winds rise in the evening,
the jade sky shines clear."[54]
"Into the evening glow a lone crested ibis flies,
the clear water of autumn is the color of the sky high above."[55]
The orange glow on the riverbank splatters into a thousand pieces
of gold,
the reed flowers in the rising wind
blow into ten thousand flakes of white snow.
Fresh reed maces and slender willow branches,
falling leaves on the river scattered by the autumn breeze.

---

era of the Northern and Southern dynasties (420–589), was resting in her palace garden. It was the season of plum blossoms, and every time the wind blew, plum petals fell on her forehead as everyone admired the sight.

[54] 금풍삽이석기허고 옥우곽이쟁영이라 (金風颯而夕起, 玉宇廓而崢嶸), a phrase from "Rhyme for the Seventh Day of the Seventh Month" [七夕賦 Ch'ilsŏkpu] written by Kim Inhu (金麟厚, 1510–1560) of the Chosŏn dynasty. Telling of the meeting and parting of Kyŏnu and Chingnyŏ, legendary lovers, the fifty-five-line poem, composed at a writing contest held at Sŏnggyun'gwan, won the first prize. Kim was nineteen.

[55] Line from the poem by the Tang poet Wang Bo (王勃).

Clear dewdrops and chilly winds.
Lonesome fishing boats
light their lamps and
call out to one another with their fisherman's songs,
kindling this sorrowful yearning in me.⁵⁶
Blue peak after peak along the coast
turn to blades upon blades
to pierce my heart.
"The sun goes down on Changsa, the autumn colors deepen,
I know not where to deliver my condolences to the two queens."⁵⁷
Could Song Ok's ballad of the "Sorrowful Autumn"
be sadder than this?⁵⁸
 A virgin embarked—could this be Chinsihwang's quest for the immortal herb?⁵⁹
Is it Chinsihwang's discovery mission vessel without a counsel?
I make attempts to end my life,
but the sailors take turns to stand watch over me.
Even if I could stay alive,
home is too far from here.
Unable to die, unable to live,
what am I to do?

ŎNMORI: At last!
We've arrived at Indangsu!
Thunderbolts crash down
as if all the fish were warring with the dragons!
In the wide ocean's midst
wind howls, waves roar,
fog thickens, the day blackens.
We still have a thousand, no,
ten thousand *li* to cover,

---

⁵⁶ I translate this song as Sim Ch'ŏng's revelation of her own thoughts and feelings.

⁵⁷ 일락장사추색원 [日落長沙秋色遠], 부지하처조상군 [不知何處弔湘君]. The ancient city of Changsha (K. Changsa) is currently the capital of Hunan province. Sanggun refers to the reincarnation of the two faithful queens of the ancient legendary Emperor Shun.

⁵⁸ Disciple of the poet and statesman Quyuan (屈原, 340–278 B.C.E.) of the Chu kingdom (楚, 1030–221 B.C.E.), Song Yu (宋玉) expressed his sorrowful feelings about his teacher's banishment in his poem "Song of the Sorrowful Autumn" [悲秋賦 Beiqiu fu].

⁵⁹ Shihuang Di (始皇帝, 259–210 B.C.E.) is the founder of the Qin, the first dynasty to unify China. Desiring to live forever, he sent boys and girls out to sea in search of the immortal herb. None of them returned.

but the darkness all around blurs the horizon.
Rising and falling, the waves advance,
T'ang! T'ang! Push against the prow!
Wagŭrŭrŭrŭ! Pour out!
Ch'ullŏng, ch'ullong! Sinks and swells.
The captain and the crew rush to action
to prepare for the sacrificial rite.
An entire sack of rice cooked fresh,
live slaughter of a cow and a barrelful of wine,
five-color cakes, soups, three-color fruits,
all placed in observation of the directional rule.
A wild boar butchered, pierced with a large blade,
and propped into a crawling position.
Sim Ch'ŏng is bathed, dressed,
and seated on the prow.
The captain straightens his attire
and picks up drumsticks, one in each hand.

CHAJINMORI: *Duridoong duridoong, doong doong doong duridoong doong doong . . .*

"Hŏnwŏn[60] invented the boat
and made accessible what had been inaccessible.
Those who came after him emulated his virtue
and respectively achieved their own.
Was that not a weighty service to humanity?
Ha U,[61] tasked with managing a nine-year flood,
fulfilled his duty from his ship
while traveling through five tax zones
across nine provinces.
When O Chasŏ was escaping to the O land,
it was a boatman's rowing song that accompanied his crossing.[62]
And what other than a boat
waited to carry the defeated general across the Ogang [River Wu][63]

---

[60] C. Xian Yuan, a legendary emperor who also taught humans the use of spears and shields.

[61] C. Xia Yu, the founder of the ancient kingdom of Xia. For his meritorious handling of the flood, he succeeded the throne to found the Xia.

[62] C. Wu Zixu (d. 485 B.C.E.). A native of the Chu kingdom, he had a tumultuous political life. Having his father and brother murdered by the king, he fled to the state of Wu. A boatman, singing a rowing song, helped him cross safely to Wu.

[63] The defeated general refers to Xiang Yu. In 202 B.C.E., he fell to the forces of Liu Bang, the founder of the Han dynasty, at the battle of Gaixia Fortress (垓下之戰).

from the battlefield of Haehwasŏng?
And Kongmyŏng, with his preternatural elusiveness,
stirred up the southeasterly wind
and put Chu Yu to the task of burning
Cho Cho's million troops with fire.
Could he have succeeded without his ships?[64]
Duridoong duridoong, doong doong doong . . . !
"Gently rocking, the boat forward advances,"
a line from "Kwigŏrae," a poem by To Yŏnmyŏng.[65]
"Wide is the ocean, a lonely sailboat leisurely floats.
And Chang Han departs to the river's east."[66]
"Autumn, the seventh moon of the *imsul* year,"
croons So Dongp'a.[67]
Chigukch'ong, chigukch'ong, ŏsawa![68]
Rest the oar and simply ride the wave—
is this not a fisherman's pleasure?
Cinnamon oars and orchid poles in the Hwajŏng River,
navigating the lotus-picking boats for the women of O and Wŏl.[69]
This vessel carrying us is a merchant ship indeed—
this is the lifelong career of us the twenty-four sailors
that wander west and south year after year.
Today at the waters of Indangsu,
we offer you a human sacrifice.
O Guardian Spirit of the East Sea,
Spirit of the West Sea,
Black Dragon Spirit of the North Sea,
Blue Dragon Spirit of the South Sea,

---

[64] C. Gongming, courtesy name of Zhuge Liang (181–234), a strategist for Liu Bei (161–223), founder of the Shu kingdom (蜀, 221–263). His brilliant achievements are chronicled in the historical novel *Romance of the Three Kingdoms* [三國演義 *Sanguo yanyi*] by Luo Guanzhong.

[65] "Homecoming" [歸去來辭 Guiqu laici], a prose poem about resigning from an official position and returning home by Tao Yuanming (陶淵明, 365–427).

[66] First line of a poem, 送張舍人之江東 [송장사인지강동], by Li Bai (李白, 701–762).

[67] First line of the poem "Chibifu" [赤壁賦] by Su Dongpo (蘇東坡, 1037–1101). *Imsul*, the fifty-ninth year in the sexagenary cycle, is the Year of the Black Dog.

[68] Onomatopoeic representation of the creaking sound of oaring and weighing anchor, also likening to the more acoustically familiar sound of lapping waves, *ch'ulsŏk ch'ulsŏk sswaaa*.

[69] Line from "Lotus-Picking Song" [采蓮曲 Cailian qu] by the Tang poet Wang Bo (王勃, fl. 649–676). Hwajŏng is a place in Jiangsu (江蘇省). O (吳, C. Wu) and Wŏl (越, C. Yue) were rival states during the Spring and Autumn period, and their women shared the style of the lotus-picking boat described.

General of the Large Rivers,
Lord of the Streams, Lakes, and Ponds,
watch over us!
Let the Spirit of the Wind rise
to guide us toward harmony and joy,
help us dispel worries and disasters
and make tons of profits!
Hoist the phoenix flag on the mast,
receive the lotus blossom on it,
help us,
Kosire!"[70]
Concluding the ceremony,
"Maiden Sim, enter the water!"
Hearing their command for her death, Sim Ch'ŏng speaks:
"Sailors, which way is Peach Blossom Village?"[71]
The captain steps forward
and points in the direction of her home.
"Over there,
shrouded in fog and clouds,
is your Peach Blossom Village."
Stricken with grief,
Sim Ch'ŏng makes four ceremonial bows in that direction and collapses.
"My father!
Please don't think of your ungrateful daughter, Sim Ch'ŏng,
even for a moment.
Hurry and open your eyes to see the bright, open world again,
find a good woman to wed,
and, even at seventy, experience the joy of begetting a son!
Dear sailors,
after you make tons of money and return home,
please comfort my father."
"Don't you fear.
Now hurry up and enter the water!"
Faster CHAJINMORI: Look at Sim Ch'ŏng!
Closing her starlike eyes,
covering her face with her outer skirt, *ururururu* ... ,

---

[70] Utterance of wishing done at Korean traditional well-wishing rites.
[71] Name of her village.

>   she dashes to the gunwale and,
>   like a seagull flying over the waves of the boundless sea,
>   takes off into the water,
>   *poong!* splash!
> CHINYANG: The smoke from burning incense chases the storm,
>   the bright moon sinks below the horizon.
>   The captain weeps, the boatmen weep,
>   the oarsmen and the cook all weep.
>   "Doing business is fine and good,
>   and every year we buy someone to drown in this water.
>   But how could we hope for the positive well-being of our descendants?[72]
>   Heave-ho, *ŏgiya, ŏgiya, ŏgiya, ŏgiya.*
>   "After the rain, on the surface of the water a scenic expansion."
>   White seagull up above, let me ask you,
>   you who spend your days by the drizzly river,
>   how is it that you are so free?"
>   Bobbing over the big blue waves,
>   the ship floats away.[73]

Summary

Virtuous deeds do not pass unnoticed by omniscient heaven. Sim Ch'ŏng was sent back to float on the surface of the sea in a magical lotus bud. The sailors, on their way home from a profitable season, in passing Indangsu, were reminiscing about Sim Ch'ŏng's tragically ended life. To console her spirit, they offered a ritual ceremony. Drums and chants invoked her from the other world, and, lo and behold, they spotted a mysterious lotus bud floating afar. The sailors hoisted it onto the deck and returned home.

Meanwhile, the empress had passed away, and the emperor, instead of remarrying, tried his hand at horticulture by collecting in his garden all sorts of plants from all over the world. He was delighted when the captain of a merchant ship presented him with a mysterious lotus bud from the open sea. One night, the emperor, unable to fall asleep, was strolling through his flower garden. As he was drawn to the fragrance of the lotus bud, it suddenly bloomed. And from within emerged a most magnificent beauty, Sim Ch'ŏng. The emperor fell in love at once and made het his empress.

---

[72] The speaker is alluding to the law of karma, expressing his fear their murderous act may have negative effects on their descendants.

[73] It is unclear whether the poet is referring to the seagull or the ship that floats or flies away.

Though Empress Sim had the whole world at her disposal, she longed to see her father. To help find him, the emperor decreed that all blind men of the country attend a royal banquet for the blind to be held at the palace for one hundred days. Back in the village, Blindman Sim had been living in grief and remorse until a woman by the name of Ppaengdŏgine appeared and married him. When the royal decree arrived at the village, Blindman Sim set out for the capital with his new wife, but at a roadside inn, she took all the valuables and eloped with a younger blind man. After numerous hardships, Blindman Sim arrived on the very last day of the banquet. Commotion erupted as his name was announced. Several officers rushed out to escort him to the inner palace, where Empress Sim was anxiously awaiting the good news of her father's arrival. Seeing that it was indeed her father, forgoing her shoes, the empress rushed down the aisle to embrace her father in only her stockings. In the intensity and shock of the surprise, Blindman Sim regained his sight. The wonders did not cease there! Blessed by Empress Sim's heavenly piety, all the blind people of the country one by one regained their vision. The story ends with great jubilation and celebration.

CP

8.3. SONG OF CH'UNHYANG (춘향가 CH'UNHYANG-GA)

Narrative Lineage: Kim Sejong—Kim Ch'anŏp—Chŏng Ŭngmin—Chŏng Kwŏnjin, Sŏng Uhyang

Summary

Early in the reign of King Sukchong the Great [肅宗, r. 1674–1720], a young gentleman was staying in Namwŏn—Yi Mongnyong, the handsome, intelligent, and gallant son of the new magistrate from Seoul. One brilliant spring day, Mongnyong had an urge to take a stroll. He closed his book and rode out to the scenic Kwanghallu Pavilion escorted by the servant Pangja. There he saw in the hazy distance amid dancing willow branches and flitting butterflies the beautiful maiden Ch'unhyang on a swing. It was love at first sight. That evening, Mongnyong visited Ch'unhyang's house and persuaded her mother, Wŏlmae, a retired kisaeng, to let him have her. The two exchanged nuptial vows. Love deepened and time flew.

Meanwhile, the magistrate was promoted back to the central government in Seoul and, as a good filial son, Mongnyong had to accompany his parents. In a Confucian society, it was unthinkable for a son of a nobleman to take a concubine prior to passing the state examination and being properly wedded to a girl from a noble family. Exchanging their tokens of everlasting love, Ch'unhyang's jade ring to Mongnyong, and Mongnyong's stone mirror to Ch'unhyang, sadly they parted.

An official by the name of Pyŏn Hakto, having heard of the beautiful Ch'unhyang, petitioned to be stationed in the township of Namwŏn as the new magistrate. Immediately following his inauguration, Pyŏn relentlessly harassed Ch'unhyang to serve him. She refused, saying she was already wedded, and Pyŏn ordered her torture and imprisonment. She was to be beheaded on the magistrate's birthday as the highlight of the banquet.

Meanwhile, Mongnyong applied himself wholeheartedly to his scholarship and won the first-place honor in the state examination. He was awarded with royal insignia to serve the state as inspector incognito. He led his secret police forces to Namwŏn, righting wrongs along the way.

CHINYANG: "Looking around atop Paksŏk Hill,
    It is the same mountain I knew,
    the same water I remember!
    And this is the land of Taebangguk [74] where I used to tarry,
    fairer with the surging energy of spring.
    'The once departed Yurang now returns,
    it is the Hyŏndogwan for sure.'[75]
    The peaches and pears abloom in the village far away are picture-perfect
    as in the poetic world of Panak.[76]
    How have you been, Kwanghallu Pavilion?[77]
    And you, Ojakkyo Bridge?
    That tall veranda of Kwanghallu is where I used to compose poetry.
    Across, amid the flowery forest,
    where are all the beauties who flew through the air on a swing?
    She wouldn't let go of the sleeve of my summer silken jacket—

---

[74] Refers to the township of Namwŏn in the first line of the *Song of Ch'unhyang*: 호남좌도 남원부는 옛날 대방국이라, meaning, "Namwŏn township in the Left Province of Honam [Chŏlla provinces] long ago used to be the state of Taebang."

[75] Phrase from a poem by Liu Yuxi (劉禹錫, 772–842) of Tang.

[76] C. Pan Yue (潘岳, 247–300), a poet of the Western Qin (西晉).

[77] Built in 1414, Kwanghallu Pavilion (광한루, 廣寒樓) is South Korea's National Scenic Treasure No. 33. A spacious pond, completed in 1582, to the front was fashioned after the bridge spanning the Milky Way as told of in the legend of the Cowherd Boy and Weaving Girl (牽牛織女 Kyŏnu Chingnyŏ). There are three islands in the pond named after three auspicious mountains and dedicated to the indigenous Three Gods. Yŏngju is one of the minor hills around Halla Mountain on Cheju Island.

how many years has it been since our tearful good-bye?
Where the Yŏngjugak[78] stands, 'the clear shade has not changed.'[79]
Butterflies dance as if savoring the last of the passing spring breeze.
An oriole's call for its mate makes me nostalgic.
At sunset, I arrive at Ch'unhyang's house.
The paint on the main building is chipping off,
the servants' quarter adjacent to the main gate is collapsing.
Wasn't it I who wrote and pasted on the gate
'Welcome spring' [立春, K. *Ipch'un*] and 'Loyal heart' [忠, K. *Ch'ung*]?
The 'middle' [中, K. *chung*] is gone in the wind,
leaving just the 'heart' [心, K. *sim*] to barely hang on."

ANIRI: Hiding behind the gate, the royal inspector peeps in.

SEMACH'I: At this time Ch'unhyang's mother,
in her backyard at a raised altar,
prepares a midnight offering to the Seven Stars of the North
with candlelight and a bowl of freshly drawn water:
"I pray, I pray, to heaven I pray.
Please help Sir Yi Mongnyong, son of the departed magistrate,
to be assigned to either Chŏlla governor or royal inspector.
Help him achieve one or the other.
Please bestow upon him the power to save my daughter, Ch'unhyang!
What sin has she ever committed?
She is a loving daughter to her mother and an exemplary wife to her husband.
Heaven should surely help loving children, loyal ministers, and faithful wives.
Hyangdan![80]
Change the water on the table.
It is our last day of praying, the end of our offerings."
Hyangdan, heartbroken, replaces the holy water
with some freshly drawn and collapses on the ground, crying,
"Aigo! Heaven, what sin has my young lady committed?
Please, may the bright spirit of heaven be moved to save my young lady in prison!"
Grief-stricken, Ch'unhyang's mother comforts her.

---

[78] Pavilion built on one of the manmade islands in Kwanghallu Pond.
[79] From a line in a poem by the Tang poet Jian Qi (錢起, 710–782).
[80] Female servant in Ch'unhyang's household.

"Don't cry, Hyangdan, don't cry.
If you shed tears from your eyes, I shed tears of blood from mine."
Embracing each other, Hyangdan and her old lady weep,
comforting each other to not cry.
What a pitiful sight!

ANIRI: Seeing this, the royal inspector observes, "*Huh-huh*, I've been thinking all along that it was the spirits of my ancestors who helped me rise to royal inspector. I see now it was the prayers of my mother-in-law and Hyangdan that contributed more than half. But if I appear in this state, I'll have myself yanked by the topknot by that petulant old woman. A bit of slapstick is called for here."

"Hello, there! Is no one here? Hello, there!"

Taken off guard, Ch'unhyang's mother exclaims, "Oh my, Hyangdan! The spirits of this house run amok at the horrible injustice of your young lady's imminent death! Why else the disagreeable sound of a clay wall collapsing under a summer monsoon rain! Go and find out what it is."

Hyangdan returns to report.

"Madam, a beggar man asks you to come out for a minute."

"I have no mind to go out to meet this person. Go and tell him I'm not home."

"Sir, my lady's not home."

"*Huh-huh*, I heard her tell you to tell me she's not home. It's futile to try to fool me. Ask her again to come out."

"My Lady, the gentleman says he already heard you tell me to get rid of him. He asks you to stop trying and come out instead."

"Pox on you! You told him that I had told you to get rid of him—no wonder he's not leaving!"

Irked by the hecklings Ch'unhyang's mother had been enduring even from beggars, she dashes out to shoo him away.

CHUNGJUNGMORI: "*Huh-huh*, that beggar!—
    insensitive beggar,
    stupid beggar,
    you haven't heard the rumor about me
    spread across the entire township of Namwŏn?
    It's my rotten luck
    that I let my one and only child
    whom I raised like pure gold and precious jade
    be locked up in jail.
    Her life is at death's door,
    and you ask me for alms?!

No alms, just go, go, now!"
"*Huh-huh*, the old woman is senile,
huh-huh, my old woman has lost her head.
If you can't give me alms,
you shouldn't bust my beggar's bowl
before driving me out the door!
How many years have passed
since I saw you last?
Time flies, turning your hair gray.
Your hair is so white,
my poor woman.
I have come, I have come,
huh-huh, you don't know me?"
"Who is 'me'?
The sun has set,
I know neither your surname nor first name—
how would I know who you are?
Don't you have a surname or first name?"
"If I say my surname is Yi,
would you still say you don't know me?"
"Yi? Yi of which clan?
This township is flooded with Yis—
how could I know which Yi you are?
Aha, now I know.
You, aren't you that playboy Yi
that can croon a song or two
and has some classy taste,
the one living inside the East Gate?"
"No, no, no, not that Yi."
"Then who are you?"
"*Huh-huh*, my mother-in-law has really turned senile.
My dear mother-in-law has lost her mind."
"Mother-in-law? Mother-in-law?
How am I your mother-in-law?
All you playboys of Namwŏn are nauseating.
You detest
my youthful daughter, Ch'unhyang,
for getting herself a *yangban* husband.
When you pass my gate,
instead of saying hello,
you tease me with your greasy smile:

'Here look, Mother-in-Law.'
You think I'd be so thankful to be called that.
I hate the sight of you—go, go, now!"
"*Huh-huh*, my old lady is really senile.
My mother-in-law is truly senile.
Since you insist you don't know who I am,
I'll tell you where I live and who I am.
I reside in Samch'ŏngdong of Seoul,
and I am Yi Mongnyong, husband of Ch'unhyang.
You still don't know me, yes?"
Hearing this,
Ch'unhyang's mother bolts out
to hold her son-in-law by the neck.
"*Aigo*, who is this?!
Aigo, it is you!
Why have you come so late?!"

Slower CHUNGJUNGMORI: He has come! My son-in-law has come at last!
Oh happy! Oh welcome!
Like a spring breeze blowing away the snow at last!
Since you left, you forgot all about us,
not a single letter from you!
'A man of cold heart,' I said.
And now you've come back! Where have you been all this time?
Did you fall from the sky with a thud?
Boing! Did you shoot up from the earth?
Summer clouds hung over many shapes of hills—
did you return wrapped in those clouds?
A great storm was rising—
did you come blown in by the wind?
Spring water fills all the lakes—
did you wait for the water to rise?
At whose house would you hem and haw and not enter?
Before whose room do you dillydally and not enter?
Let's go in, let's go in.
Let's go into my room.

ANIRI: Hyangdan! Our master from Hanyang[81] has returned. Quickly come out and greet him!

CHUNGMORI: Her feet hurriedly tapping the floor,

---

[81] 漢陽, an old name for Seoul.

Hyangdan dashes in.
"This is the unworthy[82] Hyangdan greeting you.
Since his departure,
has His Excellency, your father, been in favorable health?
During your lengthy journey back,
have you not suffered from road fatigue?[83]
Please, sir! Please, sir!
Please help save my lady in prison!"
"I hear you, Hyangdan, do not cry.
I may have fallen this low,
still, would I endure seeing your lady die?
I say, do not cry."

ANIRI: "Look, Hyangdan, I'm hungry. Give me a spoonful of rice[84] if there's any."

Ch'unhyang's mother instructs Hyangdan, "Hurry up and prepare some *panch'an*,[85] and also some fresh, hot rice. More urgently, I need a candle."

"Mother-in-law, what would you need a candle for?"

"All these years I have missed the face of my son-in-law, I must see it now!"

"View it tomorrow morning in daylight."

RECITATIVE: "You're a great man of bountiful patience, but not me. I've been waiting impatiently day and night—I have to see your face now!"

ANIRI: Hyangdan fetches a candle. Ch'unhyang's mother holds it up to examine her son-in-law and blurts, "*Huh-huh*, look at the husband of the filial wife, Ch'unhyang!"

Faster CHUNGMORI: Slamming down the candle in her hand,
"How wonderful! Fabulous!
O happy day for the virtuous wife, Ch'unhyang!
When he was here and in his study, he was so beautiful,
you could hardly take your eyes off his noble face—
now how is it that he returns as a beggar?
Here I've been praying night and day for his return
either as governor-general of Chŏlla or a royal inspector.
But now he's back as the most beggarly of beggars!"

---

[82] *Sonyŏ* (小女)—literally, "small female"—is an expression of self-deprecation women used largely before men or those of higher rank or position in past times.

[83] In Korean, *nodok*.

[84] "A spoonful of rice" is a deferential request for rice.

[85] Side dishes.

Dashing to the backyard,
she grabs the ceremonial water bowl
and—bang! Crrrash!
The ground is flooded like the riverbank of Namwŏn!
In utter despair,
Ch'unhyang's mother flops down,
"Dead! Dead!
My daughter, Ch'unhyang, is really dead!
Aigo! What am I to do?
What am I supposed to do?"
She wails to her heart's content.

ANIRI: "Look, Mother-in-Law, please calm down for my sake. I'm hungry—give me a spoonful of rice if you have any."

Ch'unhyang's mother is utterly speechless.

"If I had rice to give you, I'd rather use it to starch the clothes I'm wearing!"

Hyangdan feels sorry for him.

Faster CHUNGMORI: "My dear lady, please don't be so unkind.
You can't be doing this to our dear master
who has returned a thousand *li*
for his dear love, for our young lady."
Entering the kitchen,
she assembles on a tray a half-eaten bowl of rice,[86]
sliced turnip kimchi,
and a bowl of cold water.
"Here, Master, here, Master,
with this please satisfy your hunger
while I prepare hot rice."

ANIRI: The royal inspector's eating is accompanied with a *hwimori*,[87] a playful protesting of angry outbursts from Ch'unhyang's mother.

HWIMORI: Like a tiger from a faraway hill
that jumps over Chiri Mountain,
like a toad snatching a fly in flight,
like a Buddhist monk rhythmically playing his wooden gong,
like a crab, in a flash, that hides its eyes in the southerly wind,
like that drummer[88] exuberantly beating his drum, *hudak ttukttak!*

---

[86] Mongnyong is given one someone has already started eating.
[87] Upbeat duple beat used to accompany playfully exaggerated hurriedness in this context.
[88] Imaginatively, the singer is pointing to his accompanying drummer.

"Huh-huh, that was good!"

ANIRI: Glaring at the royal inspector working at the food, Ch'unhyang's mother exclaims, "What a churl! You've been mooching for quite a while, I see . . . That's not 'eating' rice, that's 'shooting' rice into your mouth."[89]

"When I was here as a student, I never had an appetite, not even for a bowl of dragon tail and phoenix soup[90] with pine-nut porridge. A man's appetite works alongside the state of his affairs. A while ago, I was so starved I couldn't think of anything else. Now that the matters of my innards are satisfied, I miss Ch'unhyang. Where is Ch'unhyang?"

"Excuse me?! Ch'unhyang's dead!"

"It was only a while ago, over there in the backyard you were praying to save her—was that a different Ch'unhyang?"

Hyangdan intervenes, "Master, please wait until the curfew has been lifted,[91] then we'll go."

"I see—the bell should toll first? How cumbersome!"

CHINYANG: The first watch[92] passes,
followed by the second, third, fourth, and fifth watches.
Teng-teng! the bell tolls, lifting curfew.
The jade water clock, emptied of fluid, quiets.[93]
Hyangdan holds the lantern,
Ch'unhyang's mother carries a bowl of rice porridge
while her down-and-out son-in-law follows behind,
down the path toward the prison.
The night, dreary and desolate, deepens.
No trace of human traffic.
Pu-uk pu-uk! the night birds cry.
Hwi-i hwi-i! the hobgoblins swirl,

---

[89] Ch'unhyang's mother ridicules the speed with which Mongnyong eats.

[90] A bowl of soup containing such legendary creatures indicates metaphorically a rare and carefully prepared dish.

[91] Korea of the time imposed curfews in cities and towns: twenty-eight tolls were rung at around 10:00 p.m. to prohibit traffic, and thirty-three were sounded at around 4:00 a.m. to signal the lifting of curfew.

[92] In the Korean traditional time system, the night hours are divided into five watches (*kyŏng*), each corresponding approximately to two hours in the Western system. *Ch'ogyŏng*, 7:00 p.m.–9:00 p.m., is the first; *yigyŏng*, the second, is 9:00 p.m.–11:00 p.m.; *samgyŏng*, the third, is 11:00 p.m.–1:00 a.m.; *sagyŏng*, the fourth, is 1:00 a.m.–3:00 a.m.; and *ogyŏng*, the fifth, is 3:00 a.m.–5:00 a.m.

[93] The *onglu* was invented by Chang Yŏngsil in 1438 during the reign of King Sejong. The night has passed to the fifth watch, and the water clock has emptied.

ururururu! the wind blows,
blows as if to upset the earth,
as the rain tediously pours.
From all directions rise the wailings of ghosts.
I-i-i-ii . . . iii . . . ii, i-hee-hee . . . eee . . . e . . . eee!
Ch'unhyang's mother, stricken with more grief, weeps.
"*Aigo*, my unfortunate lot!
It is you, my daughter, who should mourn for me when I'm gone,
but I mourn for you instead.
So who then will cry for me when I'm gone?
And it is you who should hold my funeral,
but woefully, I'll be holding yours.
And who will bury me when I'm gone?"
Arriving at the prison gate,
gingerly she whispers,
"Guard! Guard!" There is no answer.
"Warden! Prison warden!" Still no answer.
"Wretches—they must be gambling somewhere deep.
Darling, your mother is here, can you hear me?"
At this time, Ch'unhyang,
thinking of her death scheduled for the following day,
head resting on her cangue,
momentarily drops into sleep.
Half-dreaming, half-awake,
a white tiger from South Mountain jumps over the prison wall
and dashes into her cell,
opening its bright red mouth wide, and roars, *Urŭrŭrŭrŭ . . . ŏhŏng!*
Startled awake,
Ch'unhyang is fearful,
beads of sweat roll down her neck,
her heart pounds loudly.
Now and again she hears someone calling her.
Unaware it is her mother,
she thinks it the voices of ghosts.
"You vile ghosts!
If you wish to take me away,
simply do so—don't haggle!
What sin have I committed?
If I don't get out of this prison
but die here in this cell,
all you creatures will be my companions.

Ah, my legs are sore, ah, my waist is hurting!"
ANIRI: "My baby, your mother's here, please pull yourself together."
"Who's there?"
"It's me, your mama."
"Mother? What brings you here in the middle of the night?"
"He's come. He's here."
RECITATIVE: Come? Who? Is it a letter from Hanyang? Or a sedan to fetch me to Seoul?"
ANIRI: "If it were a letter or sedan, how wonderful it would be! Instead, it's the one you crave for even in your dying moments. Yi-sŏbang[94] or Yi-nambang[95] from Hanyang has returned as a pauper."
RECITATIVE: Sŏbangnim's here! If he's really here, let me hold his hand! Sŏbangnim!
CHUNGMORI: "Last night in my dream, I saw him—
now I see him in real life—how unreal!
Hyangdan, bring the lantern closer.
He who appeared so anguished in my dream,
I must see him in reality."
Raising and moving the long end of her cangue out of the way,
she lifts her harrowed legs with both hands,
struggling to endure the pain:
"*Aigo! Aigo!* My legs! My waist!"
Crawling, sidling, and inching forward,
she grabs the column of her cell door
and raises herself with great difficulty.
"My darling, why have you come so late?
Were you in the clear waters of the Yŏngch'ŏnsu River
bathing with Sobu and Hŏyu?[96]
Or were you playing *paduk* with the four old white-haired and white-browed hermits
of Sangsan Mountain?
'Spring water fills up the lakes everywhere,'[97] goes the saying.

---

[94] *Sŏbang* is an archaic term for "sir," "master," or "husband," Yi-*sŏbang* thus meaning "Mr. Yi." Ch'unhyang's mother mocks him with a double entendre, juxtaposing *sŏbang*, which also means "westerly," and *nambang*, "southerly."

[95] Ch'unhyang's mother is again making fun of Mongnyong's name and title; see n. 94.

[96] Two legendary scholars during the reign of Emperor Yao, rejecting worldly power, entered the mountains in an effort to remain untainted.

[97] Phrase from "Song of the Yellow Rooster" [黃鷄詞 Hwanggyesa], one of the twelve *kasa* poems of the late Chosŏn anonymously composed and anthologized in the collection *Enduring*

Did you have to wait for the water level to rise?
'No one bedridden with illness could fulfill his duty,' they say.
Then were you ill all this time?
When you were here studying, you were such a beautiful youth—
now you're the handsomest of men!"
Seeing this, Ch'unhyang's mother laments,
"Alas, he returns in such a state,
and she instantly falls under his spell—look at her."
"Mother, just what are you saying?
He's mine in good fortune, and still mine in failure.
I covet neither a husband as high official nor his fat salary.
You approved him as my spouse, Mother,
so how can you dispute that?"
The royal inspector thrusts his hand between the slats of the prison door
to hold Ch'unhyang's hand.
"Ch'unhyang, I'm here.
Your hand once soft and tender is now all skin and bone.
What has happened to you?!"
"I'm in this situation of my own fault,
but, dearest sir, what misfortune has befallen you?"
"I, too, have earned my lot."
"Tomorrow at the end of the magistrate's birthday banquet,
when the order for my execution is handed down,
could you walk me by holding up the top end of my pillory?
When you hear that I have expired,
swiftly retrieve my remains while posing as a hired hand.
Bring me to the Lotus Flower Room where we first made love.
Lay me down and take my undershirt off me, and with it,
shout out my name three times to wish me a good journey.
Have Hyangdan let her hair down and mourn loudly for me,
then you, my lord, take off the coat you're wearing
and drape it over me as a funeral shroud.[98]
As for the burial, find a clean and unobstructed spot
and dig deep to lay me in.
On my tombstone have the following eight characters carved:

Poetry of the Green Hills [青丘永言 *Ch'ŏnggu yŏngŏn*], compiled by Kim Ch'ŏnt'aek (金天澤) in 1728.

[98] Ch'unhyang's instructions for her death and funeral are personal and intimate and follow Korean traditional funerary conventions.

*The Grave of Chaste Ch'unhyang Who Died Unjustly.*⁹⁹
I will then rest without regret."
The royal inspector is stricken with sorrow.
"Yes, my Ch'unhyang, do not cry.
Tomorrow at daybreak,
whether you'll ride a funeral bier or a luxury sedan, no one knows.
Surely 'the sky may tumble, but there's a way out.'
There should be a way out.
Don't cry, I say; don't cry."

ANIRI: Letting go of Ch'unhyang's hand, the royal inspector turns to go. Ch'unhyang adds,

RECITATIVE: "Hyangdan, escort our master home and make sure he rests comfortably."

ANIRI: The royal inspector, at a loss for words, reassures.
"Ch'unhyang, bear with this one night, and I will see you tomorrow."
"Huh-huh, this is much worse than I thought."
Standing next to him, Ch'unhyang's mother retorts, "Ch'unhyang, did you hear that? He said from Hanyang he managed to come, *uh-duh mŏkko.*"¹⁰⁰
On the way home, Ch'unhyang's mother's attitude toward him sours further as fermented rice juice in the summer sun would.
"Hey you, where do you plan to go for the night?"
"Why, your house of course."
"My house? I have no house for you!"
"Really, then in whose house did I find you earlier?"
"That belongs to Widow Oh."
"A widow's house—hm . . . I like it even better!"
"Hyangdan, escort your lady safely home. My lodging for the night is at the spacious open hall of the Great Eastern Inn."¹⁰¹
The royal inspector takes leave of Hyangdan and Ch'unhyang's mother.

CHAJINMORI: The following morning early,
the birthday banquet for the magistrate unfolds
at Kwanghallu Pavilion—oh, what a sight!
The colorfully adorned columns pierce the azure sky,

---

⁹⁹ *Su-jŏl-wŏn-sa-Ch'un-hyang-ji-myŏ* (수절원사춘향지묘, 守節冤死春香之墓).

¹⁰⁰ The phrase means "begging for food." Ch'unhyang's mother is apparently going deaf.

¹⁰¹ It is not clear what he means by this, but it could be witty talk—that he plans to be homeless for the night by the East Gate.

and all around are white awnings as numerous as the clouds above.
Mats woven with the finest slender flat sedge from Ullŭngdo Island,
decorated with a pair of phoenixes
with inscriptions of "longevity" and "fortune"[102] woven in the middle,
edges framed with multicolored swastíkas[103]
finely tinted with ink extracted from the *hongsu* tree,[104]
are laid proportionate to the dimension of the expansive main parlor.
Tiger-skin cushions, elegant mattresses with embroidered flowers.
Red silk, white silk, every other color of silk mats
sparsely positioned here and there with
beautiful blue silk drapes drawn all around.
Lanterns with red-and-blue silk shades glowing with beeswax candles
hang at every corner of the boulevards.
Yongal-pukch'um[105] and *paettaragi* dancing,[106]
and various instruments for a celebratory occasion.
Kisaeng and *kwangdae*[107] singers and musicians
readied on the right and on the left.
And here arrive the town leaders!

HWIMORI: The lord of Unbong and the chief of the Army of the Left,
the lofty Sŭngji recently promoted to governor of Sunch'ŏn-bu,[108]
the elderly magistrate of Koksŏng-hyŏn,
the handsome governor of Sunch'ang-gun,
the *kisaeng*-loving governor of Tamyang-bu,
the most favorably positioned magistrate of Okkwa-hyŏn,
the governor of Namp'yŏng-hyŏn flourishing the fanciest fan,
the happy-go-lucky governor of Kwangju,
the magistrate of Ch'angp'yŏng-hyŏn

---

[102] Known as *pong-hwang*, male and female, respectively, and typically translated as "phoenixes," these legendary birds are auspicious symbols in Korean culture, frequently combined with the characters for "longevity" (壽 *su*) and "fortune" (福 *pok*).

[103] Sanskrit and Buddhist symbol of well-being.

[104] A tree of coastal Korea, its bark produces a red dye.

[105] A drum dance originating in Tang China and practiced in Koryŏ.

[106] Dance choreographed to impersonate a foreign envoy returning home on a ship.

[107] Mostly male performing artists.

[108] From the Three Kingdoms down to the Chosŏn (1392–1910), governance was effected according to the four divisions of *chu*, *pu*, *kun*, and *hyŏn* (州府郡縣), *chu* (province) being the largest and *hyŏn* the smallest.

always fearful of deficient production of grain and cloth—
all arrive one by one.
The high-pitched cries announcing the arrivals of their luxurious palanquins,
Pop! Pop! Like the popping of green onion buds
the fireworks blast.
The escort servants race through the crowd, bumping shoulders,[109]
in search of their masters
to deliver private messages.
Seated in rows on the veranda of Kwanghallu,
the distinguished guests
one by one offer the birthday host
a drink for his longevity and accolades.
The orchestra begins,
and the nymphlike *kisaeng* dancers
showcase all their talent.
The blinding candle flames
dance in the fragrant breeze.
The singers seamlessly shift from major scales to minor modes,
their enchanting voices
ringing clear and high in the air.

ANIRI: The entrée course is complete, next follow tea and cookies for dessert. The disguised inspector general appears in the parlor of Kwanghallu. *Ururururu!* ... ,[110] he darts in, and, "Shwiiiiii!"[111] the officers pounce on him.

HWIMORI: "Announce, announce,
announce me, attendant!
I am a passerby who happened to
encounter this marvelous banquet.
I request a share of your wine and eatables!"

ANIRI: The officers push him from behind and both sides.
"Do not touch me! Though poor, I am a *yangban*! You're ripping the tail of a *yangban*'s coat! This *yangban*, too, has the right to be here!"
Unbong notices that this cheeky guest, though humbly dressed, has an unmistakable air of distinction about him.
"Where is my servant? Escort the gentleman in."

---

[109] There are so many of them they cannot form one straight line.
[110] Onomatopoeic description of a darting or running movement.
[111] Comparable to the police order, "Hold It!" or "Stop!"

At last seated, the royal inspector casually remarks, "Huh-huh, I almost got struck out first.[112] How about a proper introduction? You, sir, seated at the head, must be the host—are you not?"

A major calamity is about to fall on this magistrate, and would his less-than-cordial reply help the situation? No way!

"That young punk! If he hopes to get anything, he'd better disappear quietly into a corner and accept what may come his way. Instead, he asks for a proper introduction? What introduction? Ha!"

"Sir, this is a birthday celebration for you, I hear. You picked a perfect day for your birth, and I simply wanted to congratulate you on that. Sir Unbong, please get me a drinking table also."

A table is laid before the royal inspector, and it is crummy. The royal inspector grumbles.

"They say, 'If the wine is tasteless, at least the food should make up for it, and a latecomer must be treated equally well.' I see what I have here and what he has over there, and it makes my blood boil!"

Unbong intervenes.

"We came earlier, and you came later. I guess the servers were in a rush to put together a table for you and may have omitted a few items. Please come and help yourself to mine, we'll share."

"Unbong, you, too, are here as a guest, and you're not responsible for this. I think it will be best if our host trades tables with me."

How utterly infuriating this must have been for the magistrate! The orchestra strikes a long, drawn-out tune signaling the clearing of tables. The beautiful *kisaeng* girls take this as a cue to wedge between the guests, cravingly serenading them with such flirtatious wine-offering songs as "Kwŏnjuga"[113] and "Changjinju."[114] As no *kisaeng* comes to entertain him at his side, the royal inspector demands, "Unbong, would you please summon one of those *kisaeng* to sing a song or two for me?"

One of the *kisaeng*, not daring to disobey Unbong, insipidly approaches and sings,

RECITATION IN *SIJO* STYLE:[115] "Verily, drink from this cup!
May you scrounge a living
for ten thousand years!"

---

[112] The royal inspector hints jokingly of the imminent attack on the magistrate he is planning.

[113] One of the twelve *kasa* songs of the Chosŏn.

[114] Song adapted from the poem "Let's Drink and Drink" [將進酒辭 Changjinjusa] by the scholar-poet Chŏng Ch'ŏl (鄭澈, 1536–1594).

[115] Three-line lyrical chant in fixed style.

ANIRI: "Confound it, saucy bitch! More blameworthy than she is the director of the town's Department of Art Education."[116]

The royal inspector bolts up.

"All right, the witch curses me with this cup to ten-thousand-year beggary. There is no possible way I could drink it alone to handle even ten generations of the curse. Therefore, it is my decision to share it with all of you so none of us will have to panhandle beyond this generation."

Saying thus, the royal inspector splashes the wine upon the guests. It is no longer a celebration for the magistrate but a show for this unwelcome passer-by. Unable to tolerate it any longer, the magistrate ponders a way to get rid of him. Assuming the young gadfly is poorly educated and ignorant, the magistrate proposes, "Everyone, I have a proposal for all of us. Let us each take this opportunity to compose a poem for our future legacy. Whoever fails to do so will be flogged and thrown out."

"Great, let's do that!"

The magistrate gives out the rhyme words:

RECITATIVE: Oil *ko* and high *ko*![117]

ANIRI: Each guest takes turn to compose a poem. At his turn, the royal inspector dashes one off in a single brushstroke, and hands it to Unbong.

"Mine is not much to look at, but feel free to correct or edit as you see fit."

Upon reading it, Unbong's hands as he holds the roll of paper visibly shake.

Koksŏng's face turns a pale yellow as he reads out,

RECITATIVE: "*Kŭmjunmiju-nŭn ch'ŏninhyŏl-iyo,*

The delicious wine in the golden jar is the blood of a thousand people,

okpan'gahyo mansŏnggo-ra,

the tasty hors d'oeuvres on the jade plate are the oil squeezed from ten thousand people,

ch'ongnunaksi millunak-iyo,

when the drops of melted wax flow, so do the tears of the people,

kasŏnggoch'o wŏnsŏnggo-ra.

---

[116] One of the six regional governmental departments overseeing performances, memorial ceremonies, and educational facilities. Training of *kisaeng* for proper manners and performance skills was the responsibility of this department.

[117] *Ko* (膏), "oil," and *ko* (高), "high," are homonyms. The guests, including the royal inspector, are being challenged to compose a poem using them.

when the banquet singing rises high, so do the angry voices of the people."[118]

ANIRI: "A massive catastrophe in this poem! Let's get out before the first frost."

Commotion erupts.

CHAJINMORI: All of a sudden a court servant
flies into the office complex and affixes the sign,
"The Royal Inspector General Has Been Dispatched."
All six departments whirl into action.
The magistrate's birthday banquet—
does anybody still care about that now?
The officers waste no time preparing
for the coming of the royal inspector.
Has the housing chief arranged lodging for the inspector?
Lay a silken mattress over a bamboo mat,
surround the mat with white cotton drapes.
Have the manager of housekeeping line up the palanquin bearers,
inspect the ropes for the sedan, place a tiger skin on the seat.
Deacon, prepare a new set of official attire for the inspector.
Traffic officer, bring out the flags!
Chief officer, line up the soldiers!
Make sure the crier has the message and when![119]
Warn the messenger to watch for the time of his appearance.
Instruct the butcher to start on a plump cow,
also to make several supersize candles with the beef tallow.
Granary officer, bring out the tables for his soldiers.
Staff assistant, add several more tables
to be ready to feed extra numbers.
Let's not forget the post horses and drivers.
Have the tax collector thoroughly review the land-use files.
Military supply officer, where is the list of the infantry?
Did the infantrymen duly receive cotton for pay?
Prison warden, any disturbances or disputes?
Weaponry Manufacture Department, is the welding up to standards?
Bring all documents,

---

[118] The original poem is transcribed and paired with the translated lines. Notice the rhyming of the two homonyms mentioned in n. 117.

[119] The *kŭpch'ang* had the responsibility of crying out public messages in a timely fashion.

and set up an executive review committee of three or four members.
Chief of performance and ceremony,
discreetly instruct the head *kisaeng*
that, judging from his demeanor, the royal inspector is from Seoul
and doubtless takes the affairs of *kisaeng* seriously.
Prepare them in courtesy and performance to minimize mishaps!
As all this is going on,
the lord of Koksŏng rises from his seat with an excuse:
"I have the shakes—
maybe I'm coming down with malaria,
and it happens to be my malarial day.[120]
I really should go home."
The royal inspector responds,
"I have spent a lot of time in the countryside,
and I'm familiar with remedies for malaria.
Kiss a cow on the mouth, and you'll get over it in a flash."
"That is not a very common prescription, but I'll try it."
"I'll come by your home soon—
may I expect your hospitality for doctoring you?"
The lord of Unbong rises with an excuse.
"I, too, have matters to oversee in my jurisdiction.
I barely made it here—I must return without delay."
The royal inspector quips,
"It must be a pain to go only to be back soon."
"Wh— why would I come back here??
I may, only if I am to be the master of ceremonies
for the Kwanwang Shrine Memorial of the tenth month."[121]
"Are you so sure of the affairs of personnel?
Are you quite sure you won't be here again tomorrow?"

The inspector was foreshadowing that there would be the official prosecution of the magistrate of Namwŏn the next day.

The magistrate himself is still clueless.
The governor of Sunch'ŏn gets up.
"My wife is really sick—I shouldn't have come,
I need to get back to her without delay."

---

[120] *Chingnal*, in traditional Korean medicine, is "the day when one has an attack of malaria," where the symptoms worsen.

[121] Shrine for the Late Han warrior Guan Yu (關羽, 162?–219), a major character in the historical Chinese novel *Romance of the Three Kingdoms*. In time, Guan Yu came to be worshipped throughout East Asia as a godly hero of warfare.

Without giving the magistrate the opportunity,
the royal inspector plays host.
"Sir, you must adore your mistress to death."
"Who would not love his concubine?"
"Wouldn't there be at least one among us?
I'll visit you soon if you promise to give me a tour
of the famous Hwansŏnjŏng Pavilion."[122]
The Sunch'ŏn governor is worried
he may indeed be visited by this inspector general suspect,
so responds in his best and most amicable manner.
"Once I served as inspector general east of the Kangwŏn provinces,
I saw many gorgeous pavilions of the Eight Famous Scenic Sites,[123]
but there were none like Hwansŏnjŏng!
Please pay us a visit—
it'll be my immense pleasure to accompany you there."
The inspector general checks the hour.
"*Huh-huh*, at this pace we may lose them all
before we start the main show."
Stepping forth on the wooden floor,
the inspector general spreads his fan and claps his hands.
The secret police officers,
earlier dispersed among the spectators,
gather like a swarm of bees.
With their six-sided cudgels slung over their shoulders,
they shout in a chorus of booming voices,
"The inspector general incognito is here!
The inspector general is here!
The inspector general incognito is here!"
The sky tumbles, the earth sinks,
the crowd of several hundred disperses
like a stone wall collapsing,
like ocean waves dissipating.
Would the commanding voice of Chang Pi[124]
have been more frightening than this?

---

[122] A famous pavilion in Sunch'ŏn.

[123] They are Ch'ongsŏkchŏng in T'ongch'ŏn (currently in North Korea), Ch'ŏngganjŏng in Kansŏng, Naksansa in Yangyang, Samilp'o in Kosŏng, Kyŏngp'odae in Kangreung, Chuksŏru in Samch'ŏk, Mangyangjŏng in Ulchin, and Wŏlsongjŏng in P'yŏnghae.

[124] Zhang Fei (165–221), one of the three heroes—the other two being Liu Bei and Guan Yu—from the Chinese *Romance of the Three Kingdoms*.

When a summer wind sweeps in frost,
who wouldn't tremble?
All the guests frantically run for cover,
and where are their servants?
Several, covering their heads with their master's tall hats,
are looking for their masters!
The court servant, unable to locate the encased seal of governance,
is carrying a watermelon in his arms!
The chef, instead of his master's spoon and chopsticks holder,
is carrying a flute case!
The footman packs the dish-washing tub
in place of his master's wash basin!
Another picks up a *yanggŭm*,[125]
thinking it is his master's extra clothing box!
The foot soldiers are lifting a wicker dessert tray
in place of their master's sunshade,
and the horseman is loading a chaff sack
instead of a rice sack!
Seeing the sedan carriers bring the ropes but no chair,
the magistrate loudly berates them.
"Worthless sons of bitches, you bring only the ropes—
what am I supposed to ride?"
"Sir, can you really lay down the law at this hour?
Spread your legs and rest them on the two ropes
like a tightrope walker—
I'll carry you on my back, hurry!"
"Stupid jackasses! I'm not a cripple!"
The food dishes are trampled and trashed under scurrying feet,
Taaang! Dunk! Puk[126] and *changgo*[127] cracking and smashing!
The hoops of the *changgo* drums snap at the waist
and roll into the rolling barrel drums, *tŏng-ttak!*
Altogether making wonderful music.
The fiddle strings snap, the bamboo flute cracks
under the soles of the running feet!

---

[125] Trapezoidal-shaped zither with fourteen steel strings, originated from the Arabian dulcimer or santir from the Caucasus. According to a Chosŏn document, it was transmitted to Ming China by Mateo Ricci and introduced to Korea during the early reign of King Yŏngjo (英祖, r. 1724–1776).

[126] Barrel-shaped drum.

[127] Hourglass-shaped drum.

With her hairpin nowhere to be found,
a *kisaeng* fixes her bun with a poker.
The trumpeter without his trumpet
sings through his two fists, *honga-e-ng, hongae-ng!*
Not remembering where the cannonry is,
the artillery man shouts at the top of his lungs, *Kkuuung!*
Heads butting, foreheads colliding,
noses bleeding, feet dragged into the traffic,
people collapsing to the floor, weeping, *Aigo, aigo!*
Even those who have nothing to fear
simply run back and forth for no particular reason.
"*Huh-huh*, what's happening to our town?!"
. . .

The secret agents and police officers are lined up.
"Where is the chief of housing?"
Scared out of his wits,
the chief of housing crawls forward
with a quilted winter jacket and dog skin covering his back
and a rolled-up quilted winter comforter under his arm.[128]
Hudakttak! An officer lashes him.
"*Aigo*, I'm the only son through five generations,
let me live!"
"Damn you! That doesn't matter!"
The officers ruthlessly render punishment.
Everywhere, the screams of *Aigu! Aigu!*

ANIRI: The royal inspector general is benevolent and forgiving. After all, he remembers that these officials previously served his father, the former magistrate. The beating stops, it is quiet now. The inspector general changes into official attire at Kwanghallu Pavilion and is now seated at the Eastern Wing[129] and looks out. The place is exactly as he remembered! The court secretary details for him the magistrate's corruption and abuse of power. Having reviewed the names of prisoners and their charges, the inspector demands, "Free all the prisoners except Ch'unhyang. Bring her to me."

CHUNGMORI: The prison warden briskly exits
with a bundle of cell keys jingling.

---

[128] It is unclear why the chief of housing is carrying these items. He could be either disoriented or trying to hide in them.

[129] Office building.

Noisily unlocking and opening the prison door,
"Ch'unhyang, come on out, come on out!
The new magistrate in an embroidered gown[130]
has freed all the prisoners,
but he wants you."
Ch'unhyang, dumbfounded, asks,
"Warden?"
"Yes? I'm here."
"Outside the prison gate or outside the Three Gates,
did you not see a beggar standing around?"
"A beggar? None.
All hell broke loose, and you couldn't tell even if you did see one.
Hurry up and come out."
"Ah, what am I to do?
Where have the seagulls gone, not realizing the tide is in,
where is the boatman, not knowing his boat is drifting out,
where did my husband go, unaware that I am dying?"
Led by the prison warden, she enters the East Wing.
"Your Excellency, Ch'unhyang is retrieved here!"

ANIRI: "Remove the cangue!"
"Aye, Your Excellency, Ch'unhyang is now released!"
The royal inspector hands down an order.
"Ch'unhyang, listen carefully. As a daughter of a lowly *kisaeng*, you insulted the magistrate by refusing to serve him. That is a serious crime punishable by ten thousand executions. Still, would you not serve this magistrate, tarrying here only a short while?"

RECITATIVE: Her four limbs shaking uncontrollably, Ch'unhyang replies.
"You who are dressed in an embroidered gown, pardon my words, but I'll soon be dead from beatings, so there isn't anything I can't say. A royal inspector should be the pillar and cornerstone of this country, investigating wanderers and righting wrongs. Sadly, you're just another one here to arrest a woman for being faithful to her husband. You are no different from this magistrate!

CHUNGMORI: "You are as 'exemplary' as this magistrate.[131]
Kill me, just kill me.

---

[130] Refers to the inspector general. "Embroidered gown" seems to be being used as a metaphor for his administrative rank.
[131] Meant as sarcasm.

Burn me if you will with the fire flaming red in the brazier!
Be my guest, without delay!
Better still, do me the favor of a quick end
with a sharp seven-*ch'ŏk*[132] sword—
my soul will soar through the air to my husband.
The one who'll claim my remains is standing outside the gate waiting,
so hurry up and kill me!"

ANIRI: The royal inspector is pleased.

"A truly virtuous woman . . . Attendant! Bring the head *kisaeng*!"

The head *kisaeng* enters, and the royal inspector takes out from his golden embroidered pouch a ring and hands it to her with an instruction.

"Show this to Ch'unhyang and have her look at my face."

The head *kisaeng* takes the ring and steps down to the courtyard.

"Ch'unhyang, His Excellency orders you to take a good look at this, then rise, and look at the noble face of His Excellency."

RECITATIVE: Ch'unhyang takes the ring, looks at it, and it is none other than the jade ring she had given to her own Mongnyong.

"My ring! Where have you been all this time?!"

ANIRI: Ch'unhyang raises her head to face the royal inspector, and there he is, her beggar husband who had visited her prison cell the night before!

Summary

Ch'unhyang, overwhelmed and overjoyed at the sight of her long-lost love, could only chide him for not having given her even a tiny hint of his plot the night before so she might have slept easier. The royal inspector and Ch'unhyang are then joined together. Though not his first and legitimate wife under the strict class hierarchic society, they are still man and wife. His Majesty, hearing of Ch'unhyang's devotion, bestowed upon her the honorable title of virtuous and exemplary wife. They lived happily ever after, enjoying wealth, happiness, and lots of love.

CP

---

[132] One *cha* is equivalent to 30.3 centimeters.

CONTRIBUTORS

KIL CHA is a lecturer in Korean at Binghamton University (SUNY). Among her current projects are full translations of the *Kyech'ul ilgi* (Diary of the *kyech'uk* year) and the *Kyuhap ch'ongsŏ* (Encyclopedia of women's daily life).

KSENIA CHIZHOVA is an assistant professor of Korean studies at Princeton University. Her research interests include vernacular Korean calligraphy, women's culture, and the history of emotions in premodern and early modern Korea.

SOOKJA CHO is an assistant professor in the School of International Letters and Cultures at Arizona State University. Her research and teaching focus on premodern Korean and Chinese literature and culture, Sino-Korean exchange, and East Asian comparative literature.

GREGORY N. EVON is a senior lecturer in the School of Humanities and Languages at the University of New South Wales. His research focuses on premodern and early modern Korean intellectual and religious history in its broader East Asian context.

CONTRIBUTORS

YOUNGMIN KIM is a professor in the Department of Political Science and International Relations at Seoul National University.

YOUNGYEON KIM is a graduate student in the Department of Korean Language and Literature at Seoul National University.

CHARLES LA SHURE is an assistant professor of Korean literature at Seoul National University. His primary field of research is Korean folklore, and his interests in this field include Korean trickster figures, the relationship between orality and literacy, ethnographical examinations of Korean gaming culture, and folklore in a multicultural society.

PETER LEE is an assistant professor in the School of English at Kookmin University in Korea. He teaches translation and interpreting, and his research interests include literary translation, narrative studies, and translation theory.

CHAN E. PARK is a professor of Korean language, literature, and performance and director of the Sungkyu Chris Lee Korean Performance Research Program at the Ohio State University. Park does research on and performance of Korean musical and narrative traditions.

SI NAE PARK is an assistant professor of East Asian languages and civilizations at Harvard University. Her research and teaching focus on literature, literary culture, and inscriptional practices of Korea before and around the twentieth century.

MICHAEL J. PETTID is a professor of premodern Korean studies at Binghamton University (SUNY). His research and teaching focus on premodern Korea's history, literature, religion, and culture.

MARSHALL R. PIHL was a professor of Korean literature at the University of Hawai`i at Mānoa. He passed away in 1995.

JEONGSOO SHIN is an assistant professor of Korean classics at the Academy of Korean Studies in Korea. His research interest is Sino-Korean literature in the East Asian and global contexts.

SEM VERMEERSCH is an associate professor in the Department of Religious Studies, Seoul National University. He concurrently serves as director of the International Center for Korean Studies at the Kyujanggak Institute for Korean Studies. His main field of interest is the history of Korean Buddhism in its East Asian context, on which he has published numerous articles and book chapters.

HYANGSOON YI is a professor of comparative literature at the University of Georgia. Her main research areas are Buddhist aesthetics in literature and film, Korean Buddhist nuns, and spirituality and the visual arts.

JAMIE JUNGMIN YOO is a research fellow at the Kyujanggak Institute at Seoul National University as well as a postdoctoral fellow at the Chinese Academy of Social Sciences in Beijing. Jamie is currently working on how book culture and censorship in eighteenth-century East Asia influenced the making of early modern Korean literature.